CROSS DOWN

A list of titles by James Patterson appears
at the back of this book

JAMES PATTERSON

& BRENDAN DuBOIS

CROSS DOWN

1 3 5 7 9 10 8 6 4 2

Century
20 Vauxhall Bridge Road
London SW1V 2SA

Century is part of the Penguin Random House group of companies
whose addresses can be found at global.penguinrandomhouse.com.

First published in the UK by Century in 2023

www.penguin.co.uk

A CIP catalogue record for this book is available from the British Library.

ISBN: 978–1–529–13669–2
ISBN: 978–1–529–13670–8 (trade paperback edition)

Printed and bound in Great Britain by Clays Ltd, Elcograf S.p.A.

The authorised representative in the EEA is Penguin Random House Ireland,
Morrison Chambers, 32 Nassau Street, Dublin D02 YH68

www.greenpenguin.co.uk

Prologue

ONE

IN FRONT OF President Kent and the historic Resolute Desk, General Wayne Grissom, chairman of the Joint Chiefs of Staff, sits with his uniform hat in his lap and says, "Thank you for seeing me on such short notice, Mr. President."

President Lucas Kent nods. The former Maine governor and senator is sixty, in good shape, with thick brown hair and half-frame reading glasses that he never allows the public to see him in. He's dressed casually in gray slacks, a blue oxford button-down shirt, a red necktie.

He's an old Yankee spirit, and he brought to the White House an insistence on saving money, which is why the Oval Office is only dimly lit, as if for a funeral, this mid-September afternoon. The heavy glass windows—bulletproof, of course—don't allow much outside light in.

President Kent is the third president Grissom has served under since he rose to the rank of general. Grissom finds this one as smart and dedicated as the previous two. Kent pays attention to detail and has a strong bullshit detector; his personality, a mix of flattery and hardness, is typical for a political animal. This president also has the same weakness as his two predecessors: he wants to be liked by all the people he serves.

Which, Grissom thinks wryly, is a good attribute for a car salesman but not for the leader of the free world.

Earlier, when Grissom arrived at the White House—by himself, with no aides or staff—he'd noticed the change in the Secret Service detail. Outside, they were in full tactical gear, with Kevlar vests, jumpsuits, helmets, and automatic weapons, and even inside, agents in tactical gear roamed the corridors. Grissom has never seen this before.

At Grissom's request, neither the president's chief of staff, Helen Taft, nor any other presidential aides are at this Oval Office meeting. Grissom is sure Helen will raise hell about this with the president later, but that's not his concern.

Preventing leaks is his concern.

It is just the two of them. A highly unusual step, but these are dangerous and unusual times.

"Go ahead, General, please tell me what you've got," the president says.

Grissom says, "Ever since the attack on Fort Leavenworth, Army Intelligence has been aggressively working with other domestic intelligence and law enforcement agencies. We've operated within the bounds of the Posse Comitatus Act—the law barring the military from participating in civilian law—but I'll admit we've pushed those bounds. I'm sure you've received complaints about how hard we've pushed, but we didn't have much choice."

The president makes a dismissive gesture. "I've heard the complaints and I don't care. You've been doing a good job under difficult circumstances. Go on."

"Sir, since April, more than three hundred Americans have been killed and thousands more injured in these attacks."

The president sighs. "With not one demand, not one reliable or verifiable claim of responsibility. Nothing! One week it's a shooting in a Seattle office building, the next week, a pipe bomb at a supermarket in Omaha, and the week after that, poisoned bottled water given away on the streets of Manhattan."

Grissom nods. "Yes, sir, and those are just the attacks that we have concluded are originating from a terrorist organization."

The president pauses, then says, "You mean we may be undercounting the casualties?"

Grissom says, "I think we are. That school-bus shooting in Compton earlier this month, the one where the bus was caught in the cross fire between two rival gangs? The LAPD's counterterrorism division now believes that wasn't what happened. They think it was a coordinated attack, that there were no local gangs involved."

The president closes his eyes. "Children in a school bus stopped at a red light. Automatic gunfire swept back and forth...at least ten dead, am I right?"

Grissom says, "Two more later died. Official death toll from that attack now stands at twelve, sir."

There is silence in the Oval Office. President Kent opens his eyes, clenches his right hand into a fist. "General, what the hell is going on? Who are these people?"

Grissom speaks without notes or a PowerPoint presentation, nothing that can be subpoenaed or leaked. "Sir, the random terrorist attacks aren't random. It's taken a lot of interagency work, but Army Intelligence and other agencies believe there's one common thread connecting these terrorists. They're all working to disrupt our economy and our sense of security. That's why we've received no demands. They're looking for disruption. That's all."

"Who's behind the attacks?" the president asks. "Foreign terrorists or domestic?"

Grissom shakes his head. "Looks like both, sir. You've heard the saying 'The enemy of my enemy is my friend'?"

"Of course."

"That's the situation we're facing. Disparate nations around the world who are our sworn enemies—like China and Russia—are finding it convenient to support and fund these terror groups. We don't have solid evidence because each attack comes from a separate cell that communicates with its paymasters via encrypted e-mail using the farthest corners of the dark web."

"What can we do about it?"

Grissom stands up and points to the French doors leading out of the Oval Office. "Sir, we need to talk outside."

TWO

GENERAL GRISSOM LETS the president lead the way.

A female Secret Service agent wearing a black pantsuit with a white blouse opens the French doors; she's backed up by another agent wearing tactical gear and holding an automatic weapon. On the Oval Office patio, a closed-off area terraced with small trees and bushes, the president takes one wrought-iron chair and Grissom takes the other.

"This is what we've learned," Grissom says, leaning forward, hands clasped in front of him. A weathered pink scar runs across the top of his right hand, courtesy of militants in Somalia. "It's like a swarm of wasps flying in random directions, seeking out targets, attacking, disappearing, then attacking again. Car bombs, one attempt at a dirty bomb, poisonings, shootings, attacks at malls and shopping centers. At first it was the randomness that confused law enforcement and intelligence agencies. What was the point? And the terrorists who were captured, they were a mix: Teenage boys. Honorably discharged veterans. Even a few goddamn grandmothers. Angry wasps out there, each attacking for a separate reason. They're anti-government or anti-liberal or anti-conservative. No real thread connecting them."

The president says, "So where's the wasps' nest? The source?"

"Good question, sir, and we've narrowed it down. We have located a few lines of financing and other support from Iran, China, Russia, and some Mexican cartels. Nothing that would stand up in a court of law. But this support is deep and widespread. The previous attacks, they were practice. Domestic terrorist cells are planning assaults, and, sir, they're coming here. To the District."

The president sags in his chair. "When?"

"Possibly within a week. The chatter—some open communications and some partially deciphered e-mails—is pointing to the attack coming soon."

"Any chance it's just random chatter? False flags?"

Grissom shakes his head. "With two or three threats, that's possible. But no, these threats are too deep, too specific. There is a lot of anger and bitterness out there among Americans, sir, and someone is expertly tapping into that resentment, firing people up and pointing them at us. During the January sixth riots, most of the protesters were initially peaceful, crazed though they might have been. It took only a small number of hard men goading the demonstrators to turn that crowd into a violent mob that threatened our institutions."

Grissom looks the president in the eye. "The American people are normally a peaceful lot. But in these troubled times...they can be molded, shaped, encouraged to commit violence. That's what we're up against, sir."

The president says, "What do we do, then?"

"Sir, I'd like to have a principals' meeting as soon as possible. Perhaps this evening, with you in attendance, and representatives from the NSA, the FBI, the CIA, Homeland Security, and the DC Metro Police. A task force to take the lead and try to prevent future attacks."

"And you?"

"I'd be there, of course."

The president smiles. "This task force will need a leader."

"The head of the FBI or Homeland Security should take that role, sir. I'd be on hand with the military to supply any resources they need."

The president shakes his head. "I'm thinking of someone else, General. Someone I can rely on and who won't bullshit me."

"The secretary of defense?"

The president says, "You."

Grissom is startled into silence. He hasn't been this surprised since that hot morning in Mogadishu when a brother-and-sister team who sold sweet tea outside the main gate delivered Russian-made F-1 hand grenades in the battered cups.

"Mr. President, the civilian leadership won't like it," he says. "Pushback and resistance won't work in our favor."

"The civilian leadership will do as I say or they'll be replaced. But if I put you in charge, what has to be done?"

Grissom thinks for a moment. "We'll need a presidential finding. And a confidential executive order temporarily suspending Posse Comitatus."

"Remind me, how many military bases do we have domestically?"

"Nearly five hundred," Grissom says.

With more confidence in his voice, the president says, "That's an incredible resource that would allow the military—working with civilian law enforcement—to respond quickly to emerging threats if we find out that these attacks are coming from within our borders. Which you believe they are, based on the traffic analysis of the encrypted messages."

Grissom hears sirens racing by beyond the grounds of the White House. "That's a good point, sir," he says.

"Then you'll take the lead?"

He rubs his hands together for a moment. "I will, but reluctantly, sir. Mr. President, you have tough decisions ahead. Restriction of civilian movement, control and oversight of the internet to prevent the spread of misinformation and fake news. Your administration may have to consider a temporary declaration of martial law. I don't envy you, Mr. President."

The president says with a wry look on his face, "You ever see the side-by-side photos of presidents on the day they're inaugurated and the day they leave office? It's all there, all the burdens, all the decisions, in the lines on their faces and their white hair." A faint smile. "That's why we get the big bucks, right?"

Grissom says, "With your permission, sir."

The president nods.

Grissom stands up and retrieves his uniform hat; the president remains seated. "But why did you ask to come out to this terrace?" he asks. "The Secret Service sweeps the Oval Office for listening devices at least three times a day."

Grissom puts his hat on his head. "Sir, these are difficult times."

"Meaning?"

"I don't know if you can trust your Secret Service detail anymore."

Part One

CHAPTER 1

THE DISTRICT OF COLUMBIA is a place of contradictions and secrets. Pockets of extreme poverty where troubled folks shoot up on street corners are only a brisk walk away from gourmet restaurants where the price of an evening meal would cover the cost of a month's groceries for my daughter and me. And the residents of the District, the hub of American representative government, have no real congressional representation.

Those are the contradictions. But it's the secrets—written and geographical—that are the coin of the realm here in DC, and I'm entering one of these secret places along with my best friend, a man I consider my brother, Dr. Alex Cross.

We're near Arlington, Virginia, at a Homewood Suites by Hilton, a nice-looking small hotel in the midst of a score of other nice-looking small hotels in one of a score of anonymous strip malls in the area, but this place is different.

In the small lobby, there's a coffee service and an unmanned check-in counter with a little bell. I say, "We got time for coffee?"

"Won't make a very good impression if you walk in carrying a go-cup," Alex says.

"It's been a rough day and I could use a pick-me-up," I say. "And when did I ever care about making a good impression?"

That causes Alex to smile. We go down a short hallway, passing a sign reading EMPLOYEES ONLY, to a metal door with a keypad lock. Alex punches in the combination, then holds the door open for me, and we walk three flights down to a subbasement. There, Alex punches in another series of numbers on a second keypad lock, and after the *click,* I open the heavy metal door and hold it for Alex. He goes in and I follow, and we both stop at a checkpoint.

Three unsmiling men wearing green tactical fatigues, body armor, and black knit caps stare at us. Two of them are holding automatic weapons; the third is standing behind a plain wooden lectern stacked with papers and folders. He consults a list, and a smile appears on his fierce face.

"Dr. Cross," he says to my old friend. "My daughter is reading your latest book in her criminal justice course at Georgetown. Something about dark minds, dark desires. Is that it?"

Alex nods. "That's right. *Dark Minds, Dark Desires: Case Histories of the Criminally Insane.* What does she think of it?"

"She says it's informative and well written, but twice it has given her nightmares. You go ahead, Dr. Cross."

I'm next and the man's frown returns. "Name?"

"Detective John Sampson," I say. "Metro Police."

He makes a check mark on the list. "ID, please, and place your hand on this biometric pad. And I'll need you to sign this pad over here too, for signature comparison."

All of this means I'm a couple of minutes behind Alex when I enter a low-ceilinged room in the center of which is a large polished wood conference table surrounded by comfortable chairs, each one filled by Someone Important. True to the way of DC, if a meeting is set for eight p.m.—like this one—certain folks will arrive at seven p.m. to ensure they get good places at the table.

Alex and I make do with two of the less comfortable chairs along the near wall. We both get looks from the important people as we settle in, Alex because he's Alex, and me because I'm a Black man who stands six feet nine inches. That has its advantages when I'm working the streets of DC as a homicide detective, but it's a royal pain in the ass on other occasions, like when I'm trying to get comfortable and keep a low profile in a crowded conference room.

This room is equipped with computers operated by uniformed army and air force personnel and three large, ceiling-mounted screens, each one displaying the seal of the president of the United States.

I've learned from my contacts in the Metro Police and from people I've worked with in my army and reserve service over the years that there are multiple White House situation rooms scattered around the Beltway. If all the top officials of the U.S. government are huddled together in a room under the White House, well-armed enemies can drop a single bunker-buster bomb or tactical nuke, and that's it, the United States is leaderless.

A side door opens and we all stand up when President Lucas Kent enters and takes a seat at the table. He's followed by General Wayne Grissom, chairman of the Joint Chiefs of Staff, and a female army colonel. A couple of seconds later, the president's chief of staff, Helen Taft, follows and takes a chair next to the president. Seeing the president isn't all that exciting for me—I learned a long time ago that presidents are like most men and women, and as politicians, they will always break your heart—but I'm pleased to see General Grissom take a seat on the other side of the president.

Grissom and I served in the army at the same time, probably breathed the same air and dust while stationed in Afghanistan and Iraq, and he still carries himself with the bearing of a working-class guy who fought his way up through the ranks and who saw his first duty as protecting his troops in all branches. If there is a service ribbon for kissing political asses, it's notably absent on General Grissom's dress uniform. It's good to see him here, especially considering what's going on in the United States three stories above us.

The president says, "Folks, let's get right to it. Random terrorist attacks against this country began this past April and continued throughout the summer. A while back, I directed General Grissom to start gathering and collating information from the agencies represented here." The president glances at General Grissom, then continues. "To cut to the proverbial chase, ladies and gentlemen, these attacks are just the beginning. We have a week to stop them or our nation and its people will be crippled and might never recover."

CHAPTER 2

I WATCH THE general's face. One of these terrorist attacks occurred this morning on F Street, right outside the General Services Administration Building. A red Toyota RAV4 stuffed with C-4 and roofing nails exploded, killing eight and injuring thirty-four. The bomb wasn't designed to take down the building, although a number of its windows were blown out by the force of the explosion. No, it was designed to scythe down government workers streaming into the building's lobby, none of whom knew that those would be the last steps they would ever take.

Like it had in two other recent car bombings in DC, the FBI bigfooted its way into the MPD's investigation and took over. When the FBI arrives, that's it. Protocol allows them to be the lead agency in terrorist attacks. As a homicide detective for the Metro Police, I should still be there at the car-bombing crime scene, but an urgent text took me away from F Street to this hidden bunker.

I fold my arms. There's a slight murmur from the principals sitting close to the president, among them the secretaries of state, defense, and homeland security. Also at the table are representatives from the FBI, the NSA, and the CIA as well as assorted handlers and assistants. I'm pleased to see a familiar face among the bunch: FBI supervising special agent Ned Mahoney. Alex and I have gotten to know him well over the years.

The president says, "This is not a time for turf battles, withholding information, or nursing old grudges. General Grissom has my full support to take command of the situation, and I expect everyone in this room to give him his or her complete cooperation. If you feel you cannot work with General Grissom, I want your resignation within the hour. General?"

"Thank you, Mr. President," he says. "First, I'd like to thank the intelligence and law enforcement agencies who have cooperated with me over these past few months. And as for those who haven't returned my phone calls yet, an hour after this meeting will work just fine." He turns to a female officer. "Colonel?"

The colonel's name tag says KENDRICKS. From a soft black leather briefcase, she pulls out a sheaf of papers. She splits them into two stacks and sends a stack down each side of the table. Each person takes one, and there are none left for those of us sitting in the cheap seats.

Grissom says, "This is a single-sheet briefing on the terrorist attacks—the details, locations, and resulting casualties. You'll see that each page is numbered. When this meeting is over, Colonel Kendricks will ensure that each sheet is returned."

The two men in front of us are leaning into each other, talking in low tones, and I get up and put my hands on their shoulders and say, "I bet you fellows won't mind sharing, right?" Before they can answer, I pluck the sheet from one man's hands and return to sit next to Alex.

He whispers, "And that's why we love having Big John around."

I say, "You love having Big John around because when we go out, I pay your bar tab." I hold the sheet of heavy white stock, which has only the insignia of the chairman of the Joint Chiefs of Staff, no TOP SECRET or NOFORN or CLASSIFIED stamps or stickers. Just a list.

It starts this past April 15—Columbus, Georgia, a sniper attack downtown; six killed, fourteen wounded.

Alex and I look at the list of familiar and less familiar city names: San Francisco; Los Angeles; Leavenworth; Tulsa; Arapahoe, Nebraska; Manchester, Vermont; and on and on.

A woman's voice cuts through the chatter. "Excuse me, General, a moment?"

The room falls silent as Secretary of Homeland Security Doris Landsdale speaks. "I'm curious why you're keeping this briefing sheet so closely guarded. These attacks have been in the news all spring and summer."

Grissom says, "Madam Secretary, agreed, but this is the first time we've identified all of these attacks as coming from a single source."

Landsdale says, "You really think the terrorists are unaware that we know this?"

Next to the president, his chief of staff smiles slightly, like she's in agreement with Secretary Landsdale.

The general's voice is ice-cold calm when he says, "Some of these attacks are still considered one-offs by the public, industrial accidents or random crimes. Like the school-bus shooting in Los Angeles. The initial investigation and news reports said the school bus got caught in the cross fire between two feuding street gangs. We now know that is not true."

Alex takes a breath and I know exactly what he's envisioning: his younger son, Ali, in a similar school bus in the midst of gunfire.

And I know that's on Alex's mind because I'm thinking almost the same thing: My sweet seven-year-old, Willow, in a school-bus seat, feet not quite touching the floor, excitedly talking to a friend; a vehicle pulls up, its windows roll down, and black barrels of automatic weapons emerge…

Focus, I think, *stop with the nightmares.*

One man nattily dressed in an expensive-looking gray suit and a Harvard tie says, "General, at the beginning of your presentation, you said we have a week. What does that mean?"

Grissom says, "A massive attack on Washington will occur in approximately one week. And from what we've learned so far, it's going to make the January sixth attacks look like a junior-high dance."

CHAPTER

3

WHILE THAT NEWS sinks in, Grissom says, "General Martinez, tell us the latest from the NSA and how you've determined the deadline we're facing."

A slim Hispanic woman in a dark blue suit answers. "We were called in after the third terrorist attack, the dual car bombs in Kansas City and St. Louis. In those cities, we worked with the respective FBI offices and their terrorism task forces. We did a data sweep within a certain radius of the bombing—e-mails, texts, cell phone data, internet traffic patterns, and GPS locations. We found an increase in encrypted data from the cell phone towers nearest to the bombing locations about an hour before the attack. We went back to the previous two terrorist attacks, Columbus and then DC, and found the same pattern."

Grissom says, "But nothing useful was determined."

Martinez shakes her head. "No. The attackers used onetime cipher pads and burner phones. But in the minutes before every attack, there was an uptick in encrypted data using disposable phones. It appears that those setting up the attacks were waiting for final orders to proceed."

A well-dressed woman sitting across from Martinez asks, "What does that tell us, General?"

"The attackers are sophisticated, well financed, and have deep resources. They also have allies that communicate on chat sites on the dark web. On six separate occasions, the same time frame has popped up in messages we've decrypted, and what it tells us is we have approximately seven days before the attack."

Grissom says, "Tony, what does the CIA have?"

A heavyset man with thick glasses and thin black hair combed carefully over a bald spot says, "Thanks, Wayne. I'll be brief. The information we've developed from various HUMINT and technical sources is that there are at least three entities funding these organizations. The funding is in cryptocurrency and travels the dark web through a number of cutouts. Nothing we can take to a court of law, but we believe the sources are in Russia, China, and Iran, with some assistance from Mexican drug cartels."

There's another fifteen minutes or so reviewing investigative methodology, and then—

"Very good," Grissom says, glancing at his watch. "We'll reconvene at nine a.m. tomorrow and I expect your recommendations for plans of action. You'll be informed later of the meeting's location. Mr. President?"

I stand up and Alex's hand brushes my wrist like he wants me to stay seated, but I won't have it. I've made a lot of near-career-ending moves over the years facing off against my higher-ups, but if it's important enough, I don't care.

"Sorry to interrupt, General Grissom, Mr. President," I say, "but before this meeting adjourns, we need to address a major point of concern."

As if controlled by some hidden puppeteer, every head in the room swivels toward me. Alex whispers, "John..."

I go on. "With all due respect, all of you have done your best to work out who's behind these attacks and why they're happening, but there's one huge issue you're all missing."

Grissom says, "And who are you, sir?"

"Detective John Sampson, Metro Police," I say. "Representing the department here tonight."

The president says, "Is that Dr. Alex Cross sitting next to you?"

"Yes, Mr. President," Alex says. "I'm also representing Metro Police."

Grissom says, "For real? Where is the chief?"

I think, *The chief is busy meeting with the mayor, desperate to keep his job after he promised that DC crime rates would come down, but the latest crime stats show the exact opposite happened.* I say, "He's not available due to sensitive circumstances, General. Dr. Cross and I were sent here as trusted personnel to represent DC Metro. To speak plainly, General Grissom, Mr. President, you've not sought our opinion and input, but you're going to get it now."

The president is quiet. General Grissom is looking straight at me. Some of the older DC hands around the table are smiling slightly, enjoying seeing somebody immolate his own career.

The president says, "Go on, Detective."

"Dr. Cross and I are representing more than our police department," I say, keeping my voice firm and my words to the point. "We're also representing the nearly seven hundred thousand people who live in the District, scores of whom have been killed by these terrorists, and you folks are ignoring them and their safety."

CHAPTER

4

VOICES SPEAK OUT and there's cross talk, and I remain standing, looking defiant. Doris Landsdale, secretary of homeland security, breaks through the chatter.

"Detective Sampson, you are way, way out of line," she says, leaning over the conference table so I can see the anger on her flushed face. "For the past hour, all of our activities here have been directed to stopping this upcoming attack—whatever it is—and in doing so, we're protecting your people."

I shoot back at her, "My people happen to be American citizens, and all I've heard here is cold-blooded analyses of data packets, cryptocurrency, electronic surveillance, and so forth. No one's talking about the steps that should be taken right now."

"Like what?" a male attendee demands. "Should we issue a general warning and spread panic? Scare the crap out of people?"

"That might be a start," I tell him. "No one here can say for certain what kind of attack is coming, only that it is coming. Right? Could be a dirty bomb, anthrax, a series of car bombs—hell, even paramilitary guys raiding the Capitol or another federal building. And what have you done?"

Secretary Landsdale says with a sneer, "Have you been sleeping the past hour or so, Detective?"

I feel a flash of the old anger, buried way deep but still there, at being thought lazy and shiftless because of what I look like. I say, "Certainly not, ma'am. I took note of everything, the discussion of all this gadgetry, the analyses, and the dark web searches. But I didn't hear word one about protecting our people. About alerting the hospitals. Preparing shelters. Activating the National Guard. Seeing if we can get resources from the state police in Virginia and Maryland. Being proactive for once."

"Is that all?" Landsdale says. "How about erecting barbed-wire fences around the entire District? Setting up armed checkpoints? Closing down the schools? Telling people to huddle and be scared?"

"I'm not talking about being scared," I say. "I'm talking about the poor kids, moms, and dads out there, from Anacostia to Woodley Park, none of them knowing there are targets on their backs."

She starts to reply and other members of the task force join in, but the president raises a hand.

"Detective Sampson makes a number of good points," he says. "General, the DC National Guard can be activated only on my orders, right?"

"That is correct, sir," the general replies. "The National Guard in other states and territories can also be activated only by their respective governors."

"Then I'll make it happen when it's necessary," he says. "Got that, Helen?"

His chief of staff says, "Gotten, sir."

He says, "As to the other suggestions, Doris, make those happen as well."

The secretary of homeland security gives me a look with

flamethrower eyes; if she could, she'd cut me down right now and leave a pile of ash. "Absolutely, Mr. President," she says reluctantly.

He stands up, meaning the meeting is over. "General, tomorrow at nine a.m.?"

"Yes, sir," he says. "I'll let the participants know the location."

"Very well," the president says, and suddenly he looks tired and overwhelmed. "Bless you all."

Once the president leaves, the briefing papers get passed up to the front of the room, where they are carefully collected by Colonel Kendricks. Alex, at my side, says in a low voice, "Guess that's what they mean about speaking truth to power, eh?"

"Somebody had to do it, Alex."

He gently slaps me on the back. "Good job. You beat me by about sixty seconds. Let's brief the chief and then go home and grab some dinner. It's a little late, but everyone's been waiting for us."

I smile, though now I feel as tired as the president looks. "Nana Mama cooking?"

"Doesn't she always?"

CHAPTER 5

ALEX CROSS'S HOME on Fifth Street in Southeast DC is its usual rolling chaos of laughing, good-natured insults, and more laughter. When we finish dinner, we crowd into the kitchen to help clean up after another one of Nana Mama's memorable meals. Tonight's roast pork loin was so tender it melted off the bone; it was served with potatoes and green beans and a dish of homemade applesauce at each table setting.

Alex, me, my daughter, Willow, and Alex's two youngest kids—Ali and Jannie—wash and dry the dishes. Nana Mama slaps Ali's hand as he tries to clean her big black cast-iron skillet.

"You leave that skillet alone, young man."

"But it's dirty and heavy," he says. "I was just trying to help."

She smiles and rubs his head. "That's being a good boy, and thank you, but nobody cleans that skillet 'cept me. It took me months to season it right so it cooks perfect, and one good scrubbing with soap and a sponge will ruin it."

After we wash the dishes, dry them, and put them all away, it's time for dessert. I eat my homemade brownies with vanilla ice cream standing by the counter, remembering many, many years back when Nana Mama brought me to stay here after my mother went to prison the first time. My father had abandoned us long before that.

This old house with the well-kept rooms has always been my shelter, even with my home not far away. The Cross family is one that I proudly call my own.

When some form of calm returns to the kitchen, Ali goes upstairs to his room, allegedly to do homework, while Nana Mama, Willow, and Jannie move to the living room. The girls keep their eyes on the screens of their individual game consoles, and Nana Mama watches a reality-TV show about rich and pampered women who call themselves housewives. "If I had their money and jewels," she once said, "no network would want to film me, 'cause I'd be so damn boring and happy."

Alex and I slip out to the front porch, sit on old wicker chairs, and sip from the tumblers of bourbon in our hands. It's reasonably quiet out here tonight, with only a few cars driving by and the occasional blare of a horn or a siren. I ask, "How's Bree?"

"Working late," he says. "Nana Mama saved a plate for her."

"How's she doing?"

"Busy," Alex says.

I take another sip from my bourbon. "Busy with what? Government work?"

"She doesn't say and I don't ask."

Alex's wife, Bree, used to be with me at DC Metro, where she was the chief of detectives, and a good one at that. But politics and idiot bosses caused her to leave and now she's working as an investigator at the Bluestone Group, an international private security firm.

"You okay with that?"

"No," Alex says. "But we're doing the best we can. She's got a car service that takes her to and from work. I don't have to worry about her safety."

"What do you worry about, sugar?" I ask.

He ponders that for a moment. "Everything. How can I not?"

"What did you think about our high-level meeting earlier?"

"Impressive and detailed, except for that major absence that you pointed out. And it went about as well as our briefing with the chief. But something about that meeting bothered me."

That's my Alex. Always able to look ahead, peer around, and see patterns that others miss. "Go on."

He shrugs. "It looks to be random, but to me it's not. Why it's not, I can't see clearly right now, but I know the pattern's there."

"The general said someone or a group of people are orchestrating all the attacks. You don't think they're tossing the dice and saying, 'Okay, we came up with eleven, it's Kansas City's turn'—you think the sequence is more deliberate?"

Alex says, "I do. The attacks seem random, unusual—everything from a shooting at a mall to car bombs here and in other major cities—but I think they're driving toward a goal."

"You think there'll be a major strike here in DC in a week, like they said?"

He takes a sip of his bourbon. "Maybe." He sighs. "I won't be sleeping tonight. I'm trying to figure this out."

"Think you'll have something for the nine a.m. meeting?"

"That's the goal, my friend."

We sit in silence, each with our own thoughts, until I say, "I should get going. Let's meet at Metro headquarters tomorrow morning before we head off to our next secret and secure location. Say, eight thirty?"

He clinks his tumbler against mine. "Works for me."

The door opens and Nana Mama comes onto the porch. "What are you two wildcats up to?"

Alex says, "Just shop talk."

I say, "We're trying to save the world."

"Huh," she says. "You two fools 'bout twenty years too late for that."

I laugh, put my tumbler down, pick her up, and give her a kiss on her wrinkled cheek. "Nana Mama, if we had ten more of you, we could take over the world, never mind save it."

She struggles but not too much. "John Sampson, you put me down. And the world couldn't handle ten more of me."

Alex laughs. "Sure would love to find out, Nana Mama."

CHAPTER

6

IN UNIT 14 AT the Planet Storage facility in Chevy Chase, Maryland, four men work slowly and methodically to get ready for tomorrow's mission. Taking up most of the interior storage room is what appears to be a dark blue Amazon delivery van emblazoned with the company's swooping insignia. A police check of the license plate on the Mercedes-Benz Sprinter, the typical vehicle for the behemoth corporation, would show that the van was registered to Amazon.

On one side of the van is a workbench with tools and paint, and on the opposite side there's another workbench holding the items to be used and delivered tomorrow, including bullet-resistant vests and two HK MP5 submachine guns.

Tucked away in the rear of the storage room, in a blue plastic tarp tightly wrapped with gray duct tape, is the still cooling body of the facility's night manager. He had heard the sounds of power tools and used a master key to enter through the side door.

A man named Franklin sips at a Red Bull and considers the situation. Except for the night manager's interruption, things seem to be mostly on track.

"Hey, Pope," he calls out to a squat man sitting in the front seat of the van.

"Yeah, what's up?"

"I want another test of the sliding door."

"Whatever you say, boss."

Pope gets out of the van, and the two others, Clyde and Leon, walk around to join him. All the men are hard-looking with short hair, and they're all wearing black jumpsuits.

Franklin says, "Another dry run."

Clyde says, "That's the fourth one tonight."

"You have a problem?" Franklin asks. "Go file a complaint with HR. Get into positions, run it through, but first make sure your weapons are unloaded."

Pope goes to the weapons counter and picks up a Glock 17 pistol. He empties and checks the magazine, works the action.

Clear.

He replaces the magazine and goes back to the front seat of the van. Clyde and Leon, having ensured their MP5s are unloaded and safe, take up positions behind the driver's seat. The van's door slides shut.

Pope looks at Franklin, and Franklin nods. He checks his digital watch.

A short beep of the van's horn.

The sliding door rolls open, revealing Clyde and Leon, each on one knee, their MP5s up to their shoulders. Seven seconds pass according to Franklin's watch before the sliding door is closed by Leon.

Pope yells, "Mark."

"All right, come on out, guys," Franklin says. The sliding door opens once more. Franklin shakes his head.

Clyde says, "The problem?"

"The problem is that it took three seconds longer to open the door than it did the last two times," Franklin says. "Fix it."

"Fix it how?" Clyde asks.

"Use your fucking imagination and training," Franklin says. "Make sure the mechanism is working properly, isn't fouled, make sure Leon's hand doesn't slip when he grabs the handle. Hell, spray WD-40 everywhere to give it a good lube."

The driver, Pope, laughs. Franklin turns to him and says, "Nice to see you have a sense of humor."

"I try."

"Okay, jokester, how long from here to the target site?"

"Thirty to forty minutes, depending on the traffic."

"Time to be on-site?"

"Eight thirty a.m. tomorrow."

Franklin says, "Address of target site?"

Pope replies, "Three hundred Indiana Avenue Northwest, Washington, DC."

From the van, Clyde says, "All right, genius, what's waiting for us at Indiana Avenue Northwest?"

Pope grins. "Metro Police headquarters."

CHAPTER

7

IT'S A SUNNY September morning and there's a hint of fall in the air. After parking my black Jeep Grand Cherokee, I walk my daughter, Willow, the few blocks to her school. Other students are walking along as well, and I see more parents than usual taking their children into the old one-story brick-and-concrete building.

I'm so tall that Willow has to reach up to take my hand, but she doesn't seem to mind and I certainly don't. I'm already dreading that future time when Willow won't want to hold her daddy's hand. For now, I relish every precious moment with my little girl, even the weird way she insists on eating her two eggs cooked sunny-side up—out of a bowl and with a spoon.

A Metro Police cruiser rolls by, followed by a National Guard Humvee, and I feel a bit less worried, knowing that at least some preparations are under way for the coming attack.

We stop at a corner, look both ways, and cross when it's clear. We're less than a block from school when Willow says, "Daddy?"

"Right here, sweetie."

"Daddy, are we safe?"

I squeeze her hand. "Of course we are. Why are you asking?"

In a concerned voice, she says, "Mrs. Brewer looks scared, and so does Mrs. Lucianne. They talk a lot in whispers, and the teachers seem scared too." Mrs. Brewer is the school principal, and Mrs. Lucianne is the assistant principal. Willow says, "We usually have a safety drill every month, but now we have them every few days. Like they're scared. Like we're not safe."

The safety drill covers everything from a fire in the school to a gas leak, but its real purpose is to prepare for an active shooter in the building. *The way of our troubled lives,* I think.

We get to the school entrance. Usually when I walk Willow to school, I drop her off at the front door with a quick hug and kiss. But not today. Today I take her inside.

We pass through the doors, and there are four school security officers, double the usual complement. Willow drops her knapsack and it goes through the X-ray machine, and she goes through a metal detector. I display my detective shield and walk around the detectors, and some aides and teachers call out hello to Willow and me.

I feel better with Willow inside her school.

She picks up her knapsack from the X-ray machine and shrugs it over her tiny shoulders. "You're getting a ride home from Mrs. Doolittle, remember?" I say.

Mrs. Doolittle is a reliable, helpful neighbor who works from home as an IT consultant and has a son, Tomas, a year younger than Willow.

Willow nods and says, "I know. But Daddy?"

"Yes?"

"I don't like this new knapsack you got me. It feels heavy and stiff."

"But I like the way it looks on you," I say.

"I want something different," she says. "Can we do that?"

I lean down and kiss the top of her head. "Give it a couple of weeks, all right? Maybe you just need some time to get used to it."

Willow smiles, and although I always love that smile, there's a sad ghost there, the spirit of her dead mother, Billie.

"Have a good day, Willow. Love you lots."

"Bye, Daddy," she says. "Love you lots too."

With her safely in school, I walk outside and head to my Grand Cherokee. I'm ready to get back to work, confident in my ability to protect this city and its people, confident that I can protect my family.

Like that heavy and stiff knapsack Willow is carrying, a special gift to her that contains a secret only I know: the backpack has bullet-resistant panels sewn into the stiff fabric to give her protection if and when the shooting starts.

CHAPTER

POPE, WEARING AN Amazon driver's uniform, quickly and efficiently navigates the van through the streets of the District of Columbia; they're heading southeast along Connecticut Avenue NW, moving toward their target site, Motorola radios on their belts, earbuds in their ears, and small microphones attached to their shirt collars. Clyde and Leon, hidden behind a rigid pile of cardboard, are prepped.

Ever since they left the storage facility in Maryland, all have kept radio silence.

So far, so good.

At the intersection with Davenport SW, the traffic light turns yellow, and Pope slows and brings the van to a complete halt.

This is not the time to draw a cop's attention.

He waits.

Waits.

A shadow appears to the left, and he swivels in his seat, right hand on his Glock 17. There's a man out there in some sort of uniform.

He raps on the window and says, "Open up, please. Now."

CHAPTER 9

I'M DRIVING TO Metro Police headquarters when my iPhone chimes with an incoming text.

I break the local regulation that prohibits driving while using an electronic device and check the screen. What I see makes me gasp in surprise.

A good guy from my complicated past, reaching out.

Big John, Mel Carr. Still at Ft. Bragg. Desperate to talk to you. Plz?

I look ahead at the heavy traffic. The only open space to pull over and park in is under a large NO PARKING sign. But if there ever comes a time when a traffic sign—or anything else—prevents me from returning a call from a fellow grunt, just find a way to put me out of my misery, because I'll be too far gone to care.

I pull my black Jeep Grand Cherokee over and scroll through my contact list as the morning rush-hour traffic grinds by on the eastbound lane of Pennsylvania Avenue.

There. I push the button to call and put the iPhone up to my ear.

It rings and rings and eventually goes to voice mail: "This is Mel Carr," the familiar voice says. "You know what to do."

I say, "Hey, sport, got an urgent text from you about a minute ago. You drop your phone in a storm drain or something? Call me back."

I hang up and I'm about to get back into traffic when my phone rings. The screen reads Unknown Caller.

Which usually means someone wanting to talk to me about my car's extended warranty, but a call coming in so soon after I tried to reach Mel? I answer the phone with "Sampson," and the voice I hear is filled with relief.

"John, thank God you picked up."

"What's up, Mel? What's with the blocked number?"

He says, "I'm using a burner phone. Glad you still answered."

"A burner? What's up? You transfer over to Army Intelligence?"

"I wish," he says. "That'd mean I could stop jumping out of perfectly good airplanes. No, I'm still with the Eighty-Second, but something big is going on. The base is on lockdown, and certain soldiers are being called up and sent out on secret TDYs. I didn't know who to trust, so I went with you."

"Thanks for the vote of confidence," I say, seeing a female parking enforcement officer coming down the sidewalk toward me. "What's going on, Mel?"

"Remember when you got called back on active duty? And you and me and the others, we did that little classified visit into the 'Stan two years back, right after Kabul fell?"

"Still classified, far as I know," I say, remembering how the Army Reserve had called up me and a couple of others with "special talents" to be part of a highly classified CIA operation. "Be careful here, Mel."

"I will," he says. "But I need to talk to you about it, John. Face to face. Not over the phone, not via e-mail. It's very important."

The parking enforcement officer gets closer, nods in my direction, takes out the handheld device for issuing tickets.

"Mel," I say, "I'll do my best, but I'm balls to the wall here. It might be a week or so before I'm free."

"It can't wait that long, John. Trust me."

The officer is at the front of my Grand Cherokee, noting my license plate. I give the horn a quick beep to get her attention. It works but she doesn't look happy. "It's got to wait, Mel, because—"

"Because you and the Metro Police and every other agency in DC are up to their necks in these terrorist attacks, right?"

"A good guess," I say, "but you know I can't talk about that." I reach into my jacket pocket, pull out a slim leather wallet, unfold it, and display my detective shield to the parking officer. She leans in to look, sticks her tongue out at me, and gets back up on the sidewalk.

"That's why I've got to see you," he says. "I don't know who might be listening in on my phone calls. But you figure out a way to see me as quick as you can."

I try to keep my voice light. "You're beginning to sound paranoid, Mel," I say.

Mel says, "You should be paranoid. All of us who went on that cross-border expedition into Afghanistan should be paranoid. I think what we did and saw there is connected to all these bombings and shootings."

Then he ends the call.

CHAPTER 10

IN THE COUNTERFEIT Amazon delivery van, Pope looks at the uniformed man knocking on the window.

He could floor the accelerator or lower the window and put a round through the man's forehead, but the point of this mission is to stay quiet and under the radar until the real shooting begins.

Pope powers the window down. "What's wrong?"

The man passes over a sheet of paper and says, "What's wrong is how you, me, and thousands of others are being oppressed by this mega-rich corporation that doesn't pay any taxes and works us to the bone with minimum pay and benefits."

Pope looks at the orange leaflet, sees that it's about some sort of meeting for Amazon workers. He looks again at the man and realizes with embarrassment that the guy is just wearing a private security firm uniform.

The man says, "Besides being a security guard, I also work over at Amazon Logistics in Springfield, and I know that's where you get dispatched from. There's a meeting coming up about filing the proper paperwork to get unionized. Come join us, brother."

Pope drops the leaflet on the seat next to him. “I don’t think so.” The light ahead turns green.

“We’re trying to change the world!”

Pope takes his foot off the brake, steps on the gas, and says, “Aren’t we all.”

He drives a few yards and then Leon’s voice comes through his earpiece. “Everything all right up there? We thought we heard you talking to someone.”

Pope says, “Just a concerned citizen, that’s all. Looking to spread the joys of unionization.”

“I don’t think there’s a union for what we do,” Leon says, laughing.

“Me either,” Pope says.

CHAPTER

11

I PARK MY Grand Cherokee in a rare empty spot across the street from Metro Police headquarters, an old and depressing-looking stone and marble building. If you put a barbed-wire fence around it, it could pass for a state penitentiary.

I look at the self-important DC residents strolling by—Smithsonian museums don't open until ten, so tourists aren't out in full force yet—and wait for Alex to show up. Last night we agreed to meet outside of headquarters at eight thirty so we could make it to the next task force meeting by nine. This one is being held in a secret subbasement of the original Smithsonian building, so we won't have far to travel.

At eight thirty, I see my old friend coming up the sidewalk holding two Starbucks coffee containers. I smile as I get out of my Grand Cherokee and stretch my long legs.

Alex hands over one of the coffee cups and says, "Get Willow to school okay?"

"Just fine," I say. "Today I walked her right into the building. They've doubled the security personnel, which is good. I also saw a National Guard Humvee patrol drive by."

Alex leads me to the crosswalk opposite the entrance, adjacent to a row of Jersey barriers, and says, "News this morning said a few local National Guard units were being deployed as part of a training drill."

I stand next to him, waiting for the traffic to ease up. There are the usual cars, trucks, and other vehicles coming our way, and among them I spot the familiar dark blue of an Amazon delivery van. There's a stop sign on each side of the crosswalk, but several of the drivers barrel past.

I say, "As long as the attackers are out there, I don't care if the news says National Guard members are delivering flowers to nursing homes."

Alex smiles at that and says, "Hey, it's clear. Let's hustle across. I got something to tell you."

CHAPTER 12

IN THE AMAZON van, Pope says into the Motorola microphone pinned to his shirt collar, “Target in sight, guys.”

“Copy,” Leon says.

“Copy,” Clyde says.

Pope eases up on the accelerator and says, “He’s on a crosswalk, heading to police headquarters. I’ll pull a U-turn right on the crosswalk and hit the brakes and the horn. That’s your signal.”

Both men say, “Copy,” and Pope grips the steering wheel tighter, looks at the tall Black man holding a Starbucks coffee container, whispers, “Nothing personal, pal,” and makes a sudden U-turn.

There’s a few horn blasts and he gets to the widely spaced crosswalk, hits the brakes, and taps his own horn.

From behind him, he hears the rattle of the sliding door opening up, then the first sweet sounds of gunfire from Leon’s and Clyde’s MP5s.

CHAPTER

13

WHEN WE GET to the other side of Indiana Avenue, I say, “What’s going on, Alex?”

He stops and looks at me, smiling and with his eyes alight, and I know my very intelligent friend has come up with something.

Alex says, “Remember what I said yesterday, about the patterns in the terrorist attacks?”

“Of course. Did you figure something out?”

A quick, satisfied nod. “I did. Spent half the night in my office examining and reexamining the evidence, and Bree got angry at me for not coming to bed at a reasonable hour after she got home. But what I found out…John, the task force is looking at this the wrong way. The patterns are too random, like they’ve been carefully planned to look random and unconnected, which is why I’m going to tell the president and Grissom that we need to—”

There’s a blare of horns and I turn my head, see the Amazon van slow down and make a U-turn in front of us on the crosswalk—*What the hell is that driver doing,* I think, *hanging an illegal U-turn in front of police headquarters?*—then brake to a halt. The side door quickly slides open—*Damn, I know they have to hustle to make deliveries on time, but this is ridiculous*—and something black and familiar emerges from the van.

"Gun!" I yell, dropping my coffee cup. With one hand, I reach for my police-issue Glock, and with the other, I grab Alex's shoulder and push him to the ground just as the first stammer of automatic rifle fire roars out.

CHAPTER 14

LEON IS THE first to get out of the van and put his booted feet on the pavement, and Clyde is right behind him, and they both open up, and Leon thinks this will be a straight and easy drive-by, but damn it all to hell, the target ducks, and now return gunfire is coming back at them.

He fires off another burst, but damn it again, the target is behind a Jersey barrier and out of sight, and Leon knows better than to leave this job undone. People are running, screaming, falling to the ground, but Clyde's own fire keeps him focused.

Clyde walks up to the Jersey barrier, firing in disciplined three-round bursts, and Leon moves up on the left in a flanking maneuver. In a few seconds, he will get to the nearest barrier, lean over, and hose the area, taking out the target and whoever else might be seeking refuge there. *Sorry,* Leon thinks as he echoes Clyde's three-round bursts. If there's going to be collateral damage, better it's these guys than him or Clyde. DC Metro HQ is shit-infested with cops, and in a very few seconds, there's going to be a heavy response, and he and Clyde need to get the job done.

He leans over the Jersey barrier and sees a fearsome sight on the pavement below. A determined and angry man is looking up at him with his arms extended and a pistol in his large hands.

In his last seconds of consciousness, Leon knows he's looking into the dark and unyielding eyes of Death.

CHAPTER

15

WHEN I JOINED the army, the evaluators said I had the ability to go into tunnel-vision mode when a threat emerged, focusing solely on the threat and how to neutralize it, and that familiar feeling drops right into me now, like a heavy bolt into a metal hole.

Threat.

A moment ago, when I saw the weapon, I grabbed my Glock and pushed Alex to the ground. Two men holding MP5s jumped out of the van and started firing.

Response.

Now I return fire, spoiling their aim, hopefully wounding or killing at least one of the attackers.

Secondary response.

Alex grabs his own pistol and starts shooting as well.

Tertiary response.

Get cover.

We are next to a U-shaped row of Jersey barriers, and the near two have a gap between them. I duck down and push through the gap, dragging Alex with me, and he grunts, and the gunfire returns from the two attackers, rounds snapping overhead, the noise getting louder as the two assailants get closer.

Counterattack.

I roll to my side and hold up my pistol, my eyes flitting from one set of barriers to the other.

I won't wait long.

Through the gap between the Jersey barriers, I see a parked Volvo, and one of the gunmen is reflected in the Volvo's side mirror.

Come to Papa, I think.

In the mirror, I see the man coming over to the concrete barrier, and I quickly calculate where he's going to appear. I struggled with math and algebra in school, but in combat situations, I'm golden when it comes to pinpointing the location of a threat.

Like now.

I see the MP5 and his arms emerge over the concrete, then his torso, then his face, which has an expression of surprise when I drill a bullet through his forehead.

Secondary threat.

I crawl over to the gap between the Jersey barriers. In the distance, I hear my fellow Metro Police officers yelling, "Put the weapon down, hands up, put the weapon down!"

Waste of breath with professional gunmen.

I poke my head through the Jersey barrier gap, see the second gunman approaching, and fire off two rounds. One misses but the other strikes his right arm, and he spins around and falls to the ground.

The action of my Glock has snapped back and remains in position.

Out of ammo.

I duck down behind the barrier as gunfire erupts from MPD headquarters; I pop out the empty magazine, grab a spare magazine from my mag pouch, insert it, and release the action as it snaps shut.

Reloaded.

With all the gunfire from my fellow officers whistling overhead, I crawl to the street side of the Jersey barriers, and through a smaller gap I spot the van's driver dragging the second shooter into the van through the side door. After he dumps the guy in, he opens the front door, and I snap off another half a dozen rounds. But the driver's protected by the open door; my rounds sink into the door and thud against its window.

Bullet-resistant.

Serious professionals.

The driver gets into the Amazon van, and the vehicle screeches out.

I see cops run to a couple of parked cruisers.

Good.

Let them do the chase.

I turn around, and there are more shouts, sounds of car engines starting up, sirens being tripped on, and I realize it's too quiet in my little Jersey barrier fort.

"Alex!" I yell.

I holster my pistol and run over to Alex, who's lying on his back, mouth open, gasping. A puddle of blood is slowly oozing across the dirty concrete.

I kneel down, open up his dark blue suit coat, spot the bullet wound. Mid-left chest area, blood spreading across his white shirt.

His eyes are open. He whispers, "Oh, John..."

I pull out an oversize handkerchief, press it against the bloody wound, and turn and yell, "Officer down! Officer down! We need help over here!" I turn back, say, "Alex, hold on, hold on, we got an ambulance coming."

His lips move again:

"Oh, Bree..."

CHAPTER

16

THIRTY SECONDS EARLIER, DC firefighter/paramedic Rachel Gonzalez was complaining to her partner, DC firefighter/paramedic Trudy Waxman, that her twelve-year-old son was still phoning her at the station house with homework questions—"I keep telling him, 'Your father's equally capable of answering the damn phone at work' "—when the call came in for a shooting outside Metro Police Headquarters, one man seriously wounded and an officer down.

Now she's racing south on Fifth Street NW, lights flashing and siren wailing, in the department's International DuraStar 4300 diesel ambulance—also known as an advanced life system—only two blocks away from the shooting scene, disposable gloves on her hands. Her partner, Trudy, is working the communications system and watching for idiots not stopping at the cross streets, and she says, "Another terrorist attack, I'll bet."

Rachel says, "About time somebody did something to stop this shit."

She makes a tight left turn onto Indiana Avenue NW, and unlike nighttime shooting scenes, when bystanders run away and you have to use a spotlight to find the crumpled victim on the sidewalk, the cops frantically waving her in show her exactly where to go.

The cops move aside and keep waving her in, and Rachel brakes the ALS unit to a halt. Trudy gets on the radio mic and says, "Medic Two arrived."

Trudy opens her door, and Rachel switches off the siren and makes sure they have a clear path out of here once they have the vic secured for transport. She gets out and meets Trudy at the rear to gear up with a first-responder bag, a backboard, a cardiac monitor, and a portable oxygen tank.

Lights flashing, Engine Company 2's fire truck and a heavy rescue vehicle, the EMS 6 supervisor's, stop in the middle of the street. Cops are lined up and shouting and waving the two paramedics up onto the sidewalk and then to a U-shaped Jersey barrier structure patrolled by officers wearing tactical gear and helmets and carrying automatic rifles. There's a well-dressed man on his back, legs and arms spread out. Crouched over him is a large man pressing a cloth to the victim's chest, blood soaking through.

Rachel and Trudy drop their gear and get to work. Firefighters from Engine Company 2 follow them in, rolling the ambulance's collapsible gurney.

Rachel says, "What do we have? What's his name?"

The kneeling man, who's wearing a detective shield on a chain around his thick neck, says, "Alex. Alex Cross. He got shot a few minutes ago, chest wound, middle left side. I saw the shooting. Gunmen used MP5s, which carry nine-mil rounds."

There's blood on the ground, and Trudy quickly puts a nasal cannula under the man's nose, cranks up the dial on the small green oxygen tank, and checks his pulse and blood pressure. Two firefighters help Trudy fasten a C-collar around his neck, and then they slide the backboard under Alex and strap him on. Rachel puts gauze on top of the soaked cloth that the detective has been pressing down with his large hands.

She holds Alex's hand and says, "Alex? Can you hear me? My name is Rachel. We're taking you to the hospital. Can you squeeze my hand or blink your eyes?"

His hand doesn't move.

His eyes, closed, don't blink.

She stands up. "Let's get him on the gurney."

Trudy gathers up their response bag, and Rachel, accompanied by the other firefighters and the detective—Jesus, look how tall he is!—gets Alex onto the stretcher. More straps are secured, and they go back to the open door of their ALS unit. Curtis Young, a firefighter/EMT assigned to Engine Company 2 who's dressed in dull yellow turnout gear, yells, "I'll drive, Rachel. To GW?"

"Right," she says. "Level-one trauma center and less than ten minutes away."

A police captain yells, "You're getting an escort—we'll make sure the streets are clear."

The collapsible gurney is pushed into the rear of the unit and secured. Trudy goes left and Rachel goes right and they're ready to really get to work when the huge detective climbs in.

"Sir," Rachel snaps, "you can't be here."

"He's my best friend," he says, and she notes tears in his eyes. "Please, I've got to be here."

Rachel thinks, *It'll be crowded, but there's no time to argue,* and she says, "Stay where you are and keep quiet."

The doors are slammed shut and there's a hard slap of a hand on the rear panel, and up front, Curtis flips on the siren and they're on their way.

CHAPTER 17

I HUNCH OVER in the rear of the ambulance, trying to keep my balance as it roars its way to George Washington University Hospital. The two female paramedics get to work on Alex. The nasal oxygen tube is removed and replaced by a high-flow oxygen mask. His shirt is torn open, and round adhesive leads from a cardiac monitor are slapped on his chest. They slice off his suit jacket and dress shirt with a pair of shears. The interior of the ambulance has a familiar, metallic smell.

The smell of blood.

Alex's blood.

The paramedic who'd told Alex her name was Rachel and who yelled at me earlier says, "Trudy, give me an IV kit."

"Sixteen- or fourteen-gauge?"

"Fourteen."

Trudy tears open a package and hands Rachel the contents. A tourniquet is tied just above Alex's left elbow, the skin is scrubbed with an alcohol wipe, and then Rachel slides the needle into a vein. Blood flashes, and Rachel removes the needle, leaving the catheter in place. She attaches the catheter to a hanging IV bag and releases the tourniquet. Another bandage is placed on top of the bullet wound. The paramedic turns a dial on her waist radio and into the mic on her lapel says, "GW, GW, this is Medic Two, transporting priority trauma."

A quick and clear reply from the radio. "Medic Two, this is GW. Go."

"GW, we are about eight minutes out with a male gunshot victim, wound on left middle side of chest," she says. "Patient unresponsive. Respirations thirty-five and shallow. Heart rate is one twenty, BP is one ten over seventy, and we are pushing fluids."

Hold on, Alex, I pray, *hold on.*

I glance out the small rear windows and see something that chokes me up. At each cross street, blue-and-white cruisers are blocking traffic, giving us a clear path to George Washington University Hospital, and I know there must be at least three or four other cruisers up ahead clearing traffic away.

"Hey," Rachel says. "I don't like this!"

Trudy says, "Shit, I see it. His BP is falling. Now at ninety over sixty, and his heart rate is increasing. He's pretty tachy."

Rachel puts her stethoscope to his chest and says, "Decreased breath sounds on the left."

I bite my tongue.

They know what they're doing. They're good at what they do. Many times I've watched paramedics work desperately on DC sidewalks to save the life of some poor wounded boy or girl who's struggling to stay alive.

But this is different.

This is Alex.

Rachel says, "I think he's got a tension pneumothorax—shit, this isn't good."

A memory comes back of a similar circumstance, a young male riding home on his bicycle, shot by mistake by a gang member who thought he was somebody else. Like Alex, the boy had been shot in the chest. One lung had collapsed, and air entered the chest cavity from the wound outside and from a leak in the damaged lung inside. There was nowhere for that air to go, and it built up in the chest cavity and compressed the heart until it could no longer pump.

Trudy says, "BP is crashing, heart rate is up... we're losing him."

I get to my knees in prayer. "Alex," I choke out. "Hang in there, hang in there." Whatever happens in the next few seconds, I want him to know I'm here.

The monitor screams out a long flat tone.

"He's coding," Trudy says.

CHAPTER

18

MAYNARD, WEARING BOOTS, khaki slacks, a blue shirt, a lime-green safety vest, and a baseball cap bearing the logo of Dominion Energy, calmly walks behind a three-story home in McLean, Virginia, to the door leading into a two-car garage.

Inside, there's a black GMC van. There's also Franklin, the man who ran that morning's op, and one of the shooters, a man called Pope. A third man, Clyde, is lying on a pile of blankets and sheets in a corner of the garage, moaning.

Maynard asks, "Leon?"

"Dead at the scene," Franklin says, arms crossed, looking both pissed off and ashamed, which was appropriate, considering how much they had fucked up this morning.

"The target?"

"Still alive," Pope says. "The fucker is good. Took out Leon, hit Clyde in his arm, and nearly took off my head."

"The Amazon van?"

"In Chesapeake Bay."

Maynard is about to ask another question when his burner phone vibrates. "Hold on, you idiots. Incoming call."

He goes back outside and is pleased to see tall fencing around the rear yard; it'll keep nosy neighbors away from this temporary safe house. He answers the phone with "Maynard," and the click and burst of static tells him that the Boss is on the line.

The Boss says, "I'm seeing the news reports. But there's confusion as to who got serviced. What happened?"

Although Maynard has been working on this project for months, he's still not used to the Boss's voice. He's using some sort of high-tech voice synthesizer, disguising his real voice, sounding almost like that Brit physicist, the guy crumpled up in a wheelchair who could only talk via computer.

Maynard says, "It was a fuckup. Our crew took out the wrong guy. The target got free."

"Do you know who got shot?"

Maynard says, "A consultant to the FBI and Metro Police, a guy named Alex Cross."

A pause, and then the mechanical-sounding voice erupts in fury: "You goddamn fool! Alex Cross? The man who's solved more serial-killer cases than anyone else in the FBI? The guy who works with the FBI, Secret Service, and Homeland Security and who's written books on crime and psychology?"

Maynard feels the flush of embarrassment come over him. "I thought the name sounded familiar."

"Is that all the thinking you did this morning? Can you imagine the heat that'll be coming down on us in the hours ahead? Killing a DC police detective—that won't even make the New York newspapers. But killing Alex Cross? You idiot. Why didn't you kill the mayor or the president while you were at it?"

Maynard waits. Apologies are worthless at this time.

When the Boss speaks again, his voice is under control. "What else?"

"We lost one of our team at the scene. The other is wounded, and he's with me and the other team member."

"Your plan?"

"Clean up and clear out," Maynard says. "Wait to hear back from you."

"At last you've said something that makes sense. I'll contact you again this afternoon. And when you clean the place, I want it spotless. Understand?"

"Yes, sir."

"You sure I don't need to explain it?"

"No, sir," Maynard says, voice tight.

"Good," the Boss says in his funny mechanical voice. He hangs up and Maynard goes back into the garage. Pope has packed everything away in the black unmarked van. Clyde is still on his back, moaning.

Maynard notes with approval that Pope had the foresight to put a thick plastic tarpaulin underneath the blankets the wounded Clyde is lying on. He gestures for Pope to join him in front of the van. "His condition?"

"Took a round to the upper arm," Pope says quietly. "Looks like it nicked a major artery. He bled a lot before I got a tourniquet secured. The only way he'll make it is if he gets to an ER in the next few minutes."

Maynard nods, reaches into his waist holster, takes out his SIG Sauer nine-millimeter pistol. "All right," he says, "let's get this done."

Maynard, followed by Pope, goes over to Clyde. Maynard recalls that Clyde is from Arizona, served with the Tenth Mountain Division in Afghanistan back in the day, and was a good scrounger when you needed something quick.

He goes down on one knee next to Clyde, hiding the pistol behind his back. "How's it going, Clyde?"

Clyde's face is the color of old paper. "Not good...it hurts like shit. Can you do something for the pain?"

"Can't take you to a hospital. Too many questions. But you knew that when you signed up, right?"

Maynard brings forth the SIG Sauer and Clyde whispers, "Take care of my parents, will you?"

"Of course," Maynard says, and he puts the muzzle against Clyde's forehead and pulls the trigger once.

About fifteen minutes later, Maynard, Franklin, and Pope are ready to leave. The body of Clyde, wrapped in the tarpaulin and secured with duct tape, is in the rear of the van. The garage smells of bleach.

Pope says to Maynard, "I can help you."

"What?"

Pope says, "I heard what Clyde said, about taking care of his parents. I know their names and where they live. I can give that to you so you can keep your promise."

Maynard opens up the front passenger door of the van. "You believed that shit?"

CHAPTER 19

STILL ON MY knees, I hear the paramedic named Rachel say, "Not today, bitch. Trudy, chest dart."

Trudy fumbles in a drawer for a moment, tears open a sterile plastic wrapper, pulls out a large needle, hands it to Rachel. From the front of the ambulance, the driver yells, "ER in sight! Thirty seconds!"

Alex's eyes are wide open, and the raspy breathing has stopped. From experience, I know that for paramedics, *bitch* is another word for *death*.

Rachel smears some sort of antiseptic just below the middle of Alex's clavicle, on the same side as the gunshot wound, and shoves the needle in at a ninety-degree angle. I wince. There's a hiss of air. She pulls out the needle, leaving the catheter around it in place, and says, "Jesus, I'm good."

I feel the ambulance turn, and the interior darkens as it goes through the bay for the GWU Hospital emergency room.

"Rachel."

"Hold on, Trudy."

Rachel and Trudy both look at the monitor as the ambulance comes to a halt.

"Good God, we've got a heartbeat, Trudy."

Trudy grins and goes past me to open the rear doors.

Rachel says, "I'm not God, but at times like this, I am *a* god. Let's go."

I jump out first to give them room, and the two paramedics take Alex out on the gurney and move him briskly through the automatic sliding doors of the emergency department.

Trudy and Rachel know where they're going, and we pass a nurses' station and go through another set of automatic sliding doors into a two-bed trauma bay filled with medical equipment and about eight or nine emergency personnel, all dressed in gowns and masks.

One gowned nurse notes my detective shield and says, "Jack, get the detective here dressed."

Rachel says in a loud and clear voice, "Male gunshot victim, entry wound left middle side of chest. No apparent exit wound. Blood pressure eighty over forty, heart rate one forty, and respirations twenty-six. Inbound, the victim was in distress and showed signs of a tension pneumo. The victim went asystolic approximately ninety seconds ago, and we did a needle decompression. He's now back in sinus rhythm."

As Rachel talks, the ER personnel move through their tasks smoothly, like a troupe performing a well-rehearsed dance. Alex is taken off the firefighter's gurney and placed on the trauma-bay bed, his shoes are pulled off and put away, and two ER techs with large shears cut away his remaining clothing. Sensors attached to electrical leads are slapped on his chest, and other equipment is moved in close around him.

The gowned man named Jack steps up to me, rips open a plastic package, takes out a surgical gown. I extend my arms and Jack does his best to fit me, but I'm so large he can't even fasten the ties at the rear. I put on my mask, swing my attention back to Alex, and listen to the quick, professional conversations.

I realize the two paramedics—Rachel and Trudy—are gone.

I didn't even have the chance to thank them.

CHAPTER 20

AS I STAND there, only able to see Alex's feet, I remember the times I've spent in this same trauma bay with countless other gunshot victims. I've forgotten most of them, but this one I'll never forget.

Alex.

I want to go hold his hand, but there's no room. An ED resident once gave me a tour of the trauma bay, and I remember what he taught me about the algorithm for advanced trauma life support. The mnemonic is *ABC,* and the protocol is always followed.

A is for airway—you have to make sure the patient's airway is clear. One ED physician at Alex's head says now, "Airway is patent."

B is for breathing—assessing whether the patient is moving air. Another physician, stethoscope in hand, says, "Right lung is clear, but there are no breath sounds on the left. Definitely a pneumothorax. Let's get a chest tube in, and type and cross him. Tell the blood bank we're going to need a lot of units, ASAP."

A phone call is made and one of the gowned nurses rolls up a slim piece of medical equipment with empty hooks on the top, and within seconds, someone races into the trauma bay with a hand cooler that's filled with IV bags containing blood.

Rapid blood infuser, I remember from a previous visit. To replace massive amounts of blood and—

A physician inserts a chest tube into the left side of Alex's chest. The tube is attached to suction to remove the air in the chest cavity and allow the collapsed lung to reinflate, but a flood of blood exits the chest cavity as well.

"Okay, okay," someone murmurs. "Let's get the blood going."

C is for circulation, and given how much blood he's lost, more has to be pushed in. The nurse hangs a unit of blood on the infuser, starts another IV in Alex's right arm, and the new blood starts to flow.

"X-ray?" someone says.

A portable X-ray machine is brought in; there's a click and hum, and then the X-ray machine is pulled back. It has a display screen, and two of the doctors look at it.

"There's the bullet, right there. Looks to be in an okay place, but shit, that lung is torn up. How's his belly look?"

On the other side, a tech is doing an ultrasound. With a thick wand pressed against Alex's abdomen, the tech says, "All clear, no blood pooling."

I stand still and watch them work.

Tears in my eyes.

So many memories of Alex and me growing up together and raising hell as Nana Mama tried to keep us safe and away from the deadly temptations of the streets. School saved Alex, and the army did the same for me, and our paths came back together at the Metro Police.

I feel useless in this corner of the trauma bay. I remember seeing my wife, Billie, in a similar situation, on the edge, fighting for her life, until her heart finally gave out.

I blink away the tears.

"Good," an ED physician says. "Molly, call the OR, prep them. Trauma team will be up there in ten minutes."

"On it," a gowned nurse says.

The attending trauma surgeon says, "Good job, people. Let's prep him for transport, all right?"

Empty bags and other debris are swept aside, and the monitors are unplugged, and in my overwhelmed mind, it's like a very slow-moving parade. I catch a glimpse of Alex, oxygen mask over his face, his eyes closed, and I reach out to squeeze his hand but I can't make it through the crush of people slowly moving him, holding the portable medical gear and monitors as they roll along with the bed.

I try to follow the procession, but the male nurse who gowned me—Jack—holds me back. "Sorry, Detective, they're going to the OR. You can't go in there with them."

"I've got to go somewhere."

"There's a room on that floor for family and friends to wait. I'll show you where it is."

Jack strips off his gown, mask, and gloves and tosses them into a heavy blue plastic bin. I follow him and do the same, then wipe at my face. Jack looks like he's in his early twenties.

"How..." I start. "I mean..."

Jack says, "The patient you brought in is stable for now, stable enough for surgery. That bullet tore him up pretty good and damaged his left lung. But he's a lucky guy. The trauma department here is the best in the world. Your patient is critical, but he's got a chance."

I say, "He's not my patient."

"Oh?"

"He..." I choke up. "He's my best friend," I manage to get out. "He's my brother."

CHAPTER 21

MAYNARD HAS A status meeting with the whole team after the morning's unsuccessful mission; he spends some time reviewing their upcoming operation, then says, "Everyone out except for Lisa."

The eight other men and women file out, and he says, "Lisa, have a seat."

"Sure," she says. She takes a folding metal chair and sits in front of his battered wooden desk. They are in the large basement of a McMansion that's owned by a mortgage company in Cincinnati and that has been on the market and empty for three years. The basement has been crudely divided into an office and sleeping, kitchen, and dining areas; all the windows are carefully blocked with black cloth.

Lisa is a short but tough-looking woman, and today she's wearing jeans and a black jersey tank top that shows off some serious ink, mostly American flags, eagles, explosions, and bullets. Her black hair is thick, luxurious, and carefully styled.

"What's up?" she asks.

Maynard says, "How goes the training?"

"It's going good. I'm impressed by how well the team has come together. Except for McCaffery."

"What's McCaffery's problem?"

A slight shrug. "He doesn't like taking orders from a woman."

"Do you want me to handle it?"

Lisa smiles. "I already took care of it. Broke his index finger. He listens to me now."

Maynard says, "We're going to need him. He's on the breach crew."

"He'll be fine," she says. "I broke the finger on his right hand. He's left-handed."

Maynard smiles. "Smart. Two more things. I might need you to make a hospital visit to take care of a problem. You all right with that?"

"Is it a part of the operation?"

"In your wheelhouse, Lisa. Operational security."

"Okay."

"Speaking of operational security, what's the situation with Stuart?"

She pauses for a second before answering, and that tells Maynard all he needs to know. "Twice I've followed him into our training area out in the rear. Both times, he was calling someone on a cell phone."

"Were you close enough to hear what he was saying?"

"No."

Maynard sighs. "All right. Go find him, bring him in."

Lisa gets up. "You want me to help when I get him here?"

"You up for it?"

"Is he threatening the op?"

"I intend to find out."

"Then I'll give you a hand."

"Thanks," Maynard says.

Lisa leaves, and Maynard sighs again and looks around the room. On the walls are topo maps of DC and a whiteboard with a list of teams, names, target areas, and responsibilities.

He opens the left desk drawer and takes out a number of items: Two sets of handcuffs. Plastic flex ties. Ice pick. Two pairs of pliers. One set of tinner's snips. Ball gag with leather strap. A small butane torch.

"The burden of command," he whispers as he hears Lisa's and Stuart's voices.

CHAPTER

22

I GO UP to the waiting area that's on the same floor as the operating room where Alex is having surgery, but I can't sit on the comfortable chairs. I find the remote and turn off the television, then pace back and forth, back and forth.

Nana Mama comes in, her face creased with worry; Alex's daughter, Jannie, and his son Ali are each holding one of her hands. We come together in a group hug and Nana Mama says, "Why? Why?"

I sit them down on the chairs and quickly tell them what happened: the brief gunfight, how Alex was treated at the scene and brought here.

I hold Jannie's and Nana Mama's hands. Ali leans back in his chair, arms folded, quietly sobbing.

Nana Mama's face looks like carved granite. "Where's my boy now?"

"He's in the operating room, Nana Mama. He—"

Bree storms in, tears rolling down her cheeks, and I grab her and hold her tight.

"John, John—"

I say, "He's in surgery. He's being treated by the best."

Bree sobs and says, "What happened? Why? Who did it?"

I tell the story again, still holding Bree tight, and at the end of the story, I realize I don't know the why or the who. "I don't know, Bree," I whisper in her ear. "But I promise I'll find out. And kill every last one of them."

Bree steps back, wipes at her eyes, then goes over and hugs Ali and Jannie. Their soft sobs cut right through me. Bree says, "Damon's coming back from Davidson, catching a flight from Charlotte. He should be at Dulles in just over two hours. One of the people from Bluestone will pick him up and bring him here." She wipes at her eyes again, face haunted, and I know what she's thinking: Will Damon's father still be alive when he gets here?

Nana Mama stands up, face set, her eyes blazing like an Old Testament prophetess, like Miriam, and she says, "Enough of this sobbing and crying. The only thing that makes sense now is to send prayers to guide the hands of those doctors and nurses workin' to save Alex's life." She holds out her wrinkled and strong hands. "Prayer circle, now. I'll lead."

We stand in a circle. I hold Bree's and Ali's hands, and Nana Mama closes her eyes, dips her head, and starts reciting the old familiar prayer.

"Our Father, who art in Heaven, hallowed be Thy name..."

I think, *I need to contact Mrs. Doolittle, have her take Willow to her house after school.*

"Thy kingdom come, Thy will be done, on earth as it is in heaven..."

I'm missing the morning principals' meeting regarding the terrorist attacks, and I don't really give a shit.

"Give us this day our daily bread..."

I should go back to headquarters, make a statement, get involved in the investigation, but there's no force on earth that's taking me away from Alex and this family.

"And forgive us our trespasses, as we forgive those who trespass against us..."

When I get a free minute, I need to write down what I saw, what happened, and what I did when the gunfire erupted.

"And lead us not into temptation, but deliver us from evil..."

Evil. That was evil right in front of me, riding up in a blue Amazon van, gunmen jumping out, firing without hesitation. No doubt the FBI will try to take the lead on this one, and I'll pretend to stand back and let them do it, but by God, those who planned and took part in this attack are dead men walking.

Nana Mama's once strong and firm voice starts to waver. "For Thine is the kingdom, and the power, and the glory, for ever and ever. Amen."

"Amen," we all repeat, and without anyone saying anything else, we move in for another group hug, and we stand there holding one another, some praying under their breath, others sobbing, until we hear someone coming in, and we turn toward the doorway.

A tall, tired-looking man wearing scrubs and a scrub cap stands there. He says, "I'm Dr. Sarani Babak. I'm Alex Cross's surgeon. Is there a family member here I can speak with in private?"

Bree straightens up, tall and proud. "I'm his wife. Anything you have to say, you can say to all of us."

CHAPTER 23

IT'S LATE IN the afternoon, and Maynard is not a happy insurrectionist. His bandaged left thumb throbs from a burn he received earlier while interrogating Stuart. Now his crew is down a man and that means reshuffling the remaining crew or bringing a new recruit up to speed—challenging indeed, considering how little time remains before strike day.

He's standing in a remote and nearly inaccessible stretch of Virginia woods looking at top-quality training resources: tents, parked vans, and pickup trucks; long folding metal tables where meals are eaten, weapons cleaned, and training modules examined again and again. Overhead are stretched government-issue tarpaulins that hide the assembly from eyes-in-the-skies such as satellites and drones and that mask radio emissions and heat signatures.

Still, as he watches his highly trained team come back from their latest drill, Maynard feels they are falling short. They move in two lines—eight in one and seven in the other—and somebody laughs, and then there's another burst of laughter, and that really pisses off Maynard.

One more burst of laughter.

Enough is enough. "All right," Maynard says. "Huddle up, let's go over a few things."

Even though there is anger in his voice, there is also admiration for these men and women. They are not resting on their laurels, bitching to their neighbors about the state of the world, or spending evenings on the internet arguing with strangers around the globe. No, they are men and women of action, people he carefully evaluated and selected. Wearing various types of uniforms and tactical gear, they form a half-circle in front of him, their faces expectant and tired.

"That was a shitty run-through, and you know it," Maynard says in a clipped voice. "Only three checkpoints were reached on time, the second squad left a way out for hostages, and you guys were laughing and joking as you came back here like the only thing facing you was the loss of weekend privileges."

No one replies; nobody moves.

Maynard says, "This is a serious operation with serious consequences. I shouldn't have to remind you just how vital this part of the action is to the success of our goal, but due to your sloppy behavior, I guess I have to. Ruffner!"

"Sir." A short, wide-shouldered woman wearing the uniform of the Virginia State Police and carrying an M4 automatic rifle steps forward.

Maynard says, "You enjoy being the armorer?"

"Sir, it's what I'm trained for."

"Good," he says. "Our next drill is in thirty minutes. Between now and then, I want all magazines emptied and placed on the weapons table. We've been using blanks in our training modules. That changes now. Each magazine contains fifteen rounds. I want two live rounds randomly put into every magazine."

"Sir..." says someone in his assembled team.

Maynard says, "When the next training starts and you're firing off your weapons, you won't know if the one coming at you is a blank or the real thing." He steps away and heads to his own tent. "I expect to see an impressive improvement in the next drill. Any questions?"

Not a one.

Now Maynard is in a better mood.

CHAPTER

24

IN THE LONG seconds after Bree tells the surgeon that he can say whatever he has to say to all of us, I picture those ancient insects stuck in amber, frozen forever in time. I feel exactly like that.

I'm remembering meeting Alex when we were just kids, the hell-raising we did as children when Nana Mama brought me into her house, and the work I did with Alex over the years after we reconnected at Metro PD. I saved his life numerous times, saw him marry and grieve and then marry again, and I've been present when he's solved the most heinous crimes known to man.

And, most important, I've watched him raise a family any man would be lucky to call his own.

Dr. Babak says, "He's alive and—"

His next words are drowned out by sobs, handclaps, and a murmured "Thank God" from Jannie. Bree hugs the surgeon, and he smiles, gently pats her on the back, and steps away.

"My assistants are finishing up now, and soon he'll be on his way to recovery, and after that, he'll go up to the trauma ICU on the sixth floor," Dr. Babak says. "When Alex arrived, he was in critical condition, with a bullet wound here." The trauma surgeon taps the left side of his chest. "He has two broken ribs, and his left lung collapsed. Air got into the chest cavity and couldn't get out, and the pressure built up until it was crushing his heart. For a brief moment in the ambulance, his heart stopped, but the paramedics with him were able to insert a needle and relieve some of the pressure so his heart could beat again."

He pauses as if he's expecting lots of questions to be tossed at him, but for once in the history of the world, the Cross family and I are at a loss for words.

The trauma surgeon goes on. "In the operating room, we repaired some of the damage and did a thorough examination. The bleeding has stopped, but he's on a ventilator and in critical condition."

We stand there, quiet, and I find that we're all holding hands again.

"The next few days will be important," he says. "His oxygen level is quite low, possibly because of the damage to the lung, and the ventilator is breathing for him. If we see an improvement, we'll try to get him off the vent."

Voice trembling, Bree says, "And if the oxygen levels don't improve? What then?"

Dr. Babak gives her a patient but understanding smile. "We have other options available to us, but let's wait and see what happens."

I ask, "Where's the bullet?"

"Still in him," the doctor says.

"What?" Bree asks. "Why?"

"About ninety percent of the time, it makes medical sense to leave the bullet in a patient," he explains. "If it's not near the skin or close to a vulnerable part of the body, it's safer to leave it in than to try and dig it out. The more surgery you do, the higher the chances of complications."

Bree nods, biting her lower lip. "I understand."

Ali says, "Can we see him?"

Dr. Babak says, "Absolutely, but only two people at a time. Fifteen minutes per visit. Don't be surprised at how he looks. His face is swollen and there's a ventilator tube down his throat. And another thing—be careful what you say."

Alex's daughter, Jannie, says, "What do you mean?"

Another smile from Dr. Babak. "Even when a patient is unconscious or unresponsive, sometimes he or she can still hear. When you're in there, be upbeat, hold his hand, kiss his head, tell him all sorts of good things. Trust me, it'll make a difference."

Nana Mama says, "Fine. I'm gonna tell him that he'd better heal up and get his butt out of here soon or he'll have to answer to me." And we all laugh through our tears.

CHAPTER

25

ANY OTHER DAY, seeing Ali leave half a cheeseburger and plenty of French fries on his plate would have had me concerned about his health, but not today. Bree told me to get some food into him, so we're in the hospital's cafeteria, but Alex's youngest child obviously doesn't feel like eating.

Truth be told, I don't have much of an appetite myself.

An hour ago, a fellow detective, Javier Sanchez, came by for my statement. After I gave it to him, he said, "Word to the wise, Big John: Everyone knows how you feel about Alex, but you not returning to HQ after the shooting is gonna come back to bite you bad."

I replied with a creative obscenity I had learned in Iraq, and that was that.

Now to Ali I say, "How are you holding up, big guy?"

"Okay, I guess," he says, looking down, slumped in the chair, eyes red-rimmed from all the earlier crying.

"Good," I say. "Bree and your sister and even Nana Mama are going to need your help over the next few days."

Around us, hospital staffers are eating their meals, chatting away like it's just another day. But here and there in the cafeteria, there are family members worrying about loved ones who are being cared for somewhere in this huge complex.

In a trembling voice, Ali says, "Can I ask you a question?"

"Absolutely."

"Is Dad going to make it?"

I look into his dark, serious eyes. The boy, as young as he is, doesn't deserve any bullshit. "He should make it," I say. "This is one of the best hospitals in the city, he's getting top-notch care, and he should make it, Ali."

"But there's a chance he might die."

I sigh. "Always that chance, Ali."

He crosses his arms and holds them tight against his skinny chest. "When you and Dad went on that camping trip to Montana, Dad said I was too young to go. He said maybe next time. Do...do you think if he gets better, he'll take me this year?"

"Absolutely," I say. "And I'll be there too. Maybe with Willow, if she's up for it."

Tears are trickling down his cheeks. "If Dad's...not around...will you take me?"

I stand up. "He'll be around," I say. "And he'll be going with us. Come on, let's go up to his room."

CHAPTER 26

OUTSIDE OF ALEX'S ROOM in the trauma ICU there's a visitor: FBI supervising special agent Ned Mahoney. I go up to him and give him a big bear hug. "Damn, it's good to see you."

He slaps me a couple of times on the back and grunts, then says, "Hey, how about leaving my spine and ribs intact?"

I pull free and look at him. There's exhaustion on his face, along with a few bits of stubble he missed shaving this morning. His tie is askew, and there are coffee stains on his normally crisp white shirt. "You look like crap, Ned," I say.

"Right back at ya," he replies, glancing around the busy ICU. "Look, we need to talk."

"I'll find an empty room."

He shakes his head. "Not going to work. Come with me."

I go with him to a door that leads to a stairwell. Ned makes a point of gently closing the door behind us, and we walk down two flights. He stops at a landing, peers over the banister, then looks up. Apparently satisfied, he says, "Okay, this should work."

"A touch suspicious?" I ask.

He leans against the wall. "You should be suspicious too, John, after this morning."

"Because it wasn't a random terrorist attack but a straight hit?" I ask.

He says, "What makes you think that?"

"Alex and I had planned to meet each other outside of headquarters this morning at eight thirty. That's when the dummy Amazon delivery van pulled up and started blasting."

"Could be—"

"A coincidence? No, not a chance. It wasn't a random spray-and-run-away. They were coming straight at us. I guess you guys have taken the lead on this one?"

He sighs. "We have, but we're running out of resources pretty quick, given all the previous attacks. But this one is personal for me, and for the Bureau."

"Well, same here, Ned. And I took it personally when I dropped one of the assholes. What have you been able to find out about him?"

"Nothing. Blank slate. Fingerprints didn't come back with anything. We're running DNA analyses and facial recognition on the guy. Nothing from his clothes or body armor."

"His weapon?"

"Blank, just like the shooter."

"But even with the serial number removed by acid or grinding, there's still a way to recover the info, right?"

Ned shakes his head. "You don't get it, John. There was never any serial number on the weapon. You know who has weapons like that?"

A chill tickled the back of my neck. "Special-ops forces from around the world who have secret contracts with Heckler and Koch because they need weapons that are untraceable."

"Yeah," Ned says. "And you know that Amazon van?"

"Stolen plates?"

Another shake of the head. "No. Which is even scarier. From surveillance video and witness accounts, we got that license plate number. Ran it through the DMV in Virginia, and the plates came back belonging to Amazon and its logistics center in Springfield. We contacted Amazon. They said it wasn't theirs. We sent an agent to the DMV and got a report an hour ago."

I think for a moment. "The plate was salted into the Virginia DMV's database. If a cop had pulled the van over on the way to the hit, its plates would have checked out."

Ned steps forward and again looks up and down the stairwell. "That takes a high level of sophistication, John. Plus we heard from witnesses that the van had been up-armored. No return fire was going to hit the driver or engine or take out the tires."

"I saw that as well," I say. "High level indeed. How did the principals' meeting go?"

"A cluster you-know-what. Lots of finger-pointing, blame game going full force, and a couple of shouting matches. General Grissom did his best to rein them in, but Secretary Landsdale from Homeland Security kept needling him. Big disagreement as to the breadth and depth of the attack coming our way. President Kent just sat there looking depressed. Congress is still sitting on its hands regarding his legislative program. Poor guy."

I rub the back of my head. "Who represented Metro PD?"

"Some captain I didn't know."

"Figures," I say. I look around—paranoia can spread easily—and say, "Alex told me something just before he was shot, something he'd figured out and planned to bring up at the meeting. He said we were looking at the terrorist attacks in the wrong way. The patterns are too random, like they've been carefully planned out to look random and unconnected."

"Interesting. Then what?"

"Then the bullets started flying."

"Shit."

"Yeah, would've loved to know more about what he was thinking."

Ned steps up to me and motions me closer. "Things are worse than we'd imagined, John."

CHAPTER

27

I'VE KNOWN NED for many years, have worked with him on a number of hard cases, but there's something in his eyes now I've never seen before.

Pure despair.

"There's a…rot or something going on within all areas of the government, civilian and military. Different philosophies—anti-government, anti-progressive, anti-conservative. Just a series of hate groups that have members everywhere. Shit, John, last week, half the members of the FBI field office in Des Moines were arrested for giving support to extremist groups."

"Didn't see that on the news."

"And you won't. Things just seem to be…slipping away."

My phone vibrates. I check the incoming call, see it's from Metro PD. I let it go to voice mail to join its brethren. "I've got something to pass along," I say. "Got a text and phone call from an army buddy of mine, Mel Carr. We served together, did a classified mission two years back in Afghanistan."

"Whoa, wait a sec. I thought you've been out of the army for years."

"But I stayed in the Army Reserve. And I got called up."

"What was the mission?"

"Classified."

"John..."

I say, "I was part of a small group of highly skilled soldiers—both active duty and reserve—escorting a CIA officer into Afghanistan. In and out, but dangerous. Mel is stationed at Fort Bragg with the Eighty-Second Airborne. He said that the base is on lockdown, and certain soldiers are being called up and sent out on secret TDYs. He also said something that just didn't make sense."

"Go on."

"Mel was using a burner phone, and he said that what we did and saw in Afghanistan two years back is connected to the terrorist attacks."

"Crap, John, what did you guys do over there?"

"A typical mission, Ned, nothing that really stands out when I think about it."

Ned says, "You need to go see your guy Mel."

"But Alex—"

Ned's face changes from sympathy to something else. "Alex has his family around him. He's getting the best care. If you want to do what's right for him, for his family, and, damn it, for all of us, you need to go to Fort Bragg."

I loudly exhale. "You're right. I just hate leaving everyone, especially Willow. She's scared. She's scared of going to school. She sees how the teachers are acting."

"You don't think Bree or Nana Mama will take care of her?"

"No, it's just—"

Ned softly slaps my shoulder. "I know. It's hard leaving her behind and letting others protect her, no matter how much you trust them. You know you'd do a better job. But John, it has to be done."

I hear a phone chime; this time, it's Ned's. He looks at it and says to me, "You can reach me anytime, anyplace. But John, I'm going to say something to you I've never said before."

"Be careful?" I ask.

"No," he says, bringing his phone to his ear. "Don't trust anyone."

Part Two

CHAPTER

28

MY MIND IS racing as I try to figure out who I should call, what I should pack, and when to talk to Willow, but all these urgent thoughts stop when I go see Alex in the ICU. I enter his glassed-in room in front of the nurses' station and find myself unexpectedly alone. There's humming, clicking, and hissing from the complicated equipment in here that's keeping Alex alive.

I go to the side of his bed, pick up his hand, give it a squeeze. "I know you can hear me, Alex, no matter how wired up you are."

His eyes are closed; there's a tube in his mouth; his face is swollen, and his skin has an unhealthy pallor. IVs are in both arms, and hanging from the bed's lower frame is a clear plastic bag holding his urine.

I give his hand another squeeze. "You and I…we've been in tough scrapes before. Beat up, cut, wounded, trapped in places where we had to fight hard to make it out. But this time…I failed you, Alex. I should have protected you better. That's always been my job, right from the start. You had the brains, I had the brawn, and I was supposed to keep you safe."

My voice breaks, and I have to swallow a few times to continue.

"I could use your brains now, Alex. It seems like a lot of bad stuff is happening. It's like that Irish poet wrote in that poem you quoted to me a long time back: 'The center cannot hold.' Right? We're scrambling to keep the center together, me and a lot of others. But Alex...we're missing you. We surely could use you." I lean in closer. "Whatever happens, I'll be back to protect you and your family. You can count on that."

I kiss his dry forehead.

"I love you, Alex."

A few hours later, everything is packed, everything is arranged, and I'm at Alex's home with Jannie and Willow. His son Damon has arrived and is at the hospital with Nana Mama and Bree. Jannie is in the kitchen fixing a meal for herself and Willow and preparing additional food to bring back to the rest of the family keeping vigil by Alex's bed in the trauma ICU.

I sit across the dining-room table from my daughter. Willow's pretty face is scrunched up in sadness and fear. She looks like she's been cast forward decades to deal with the problems of an adult woman. "Is Uncle Alex going to be all right?" she asks, her voice quavering just a bit.

I reach across the shiny dining-room table and take her hands in mine. "He's in the best hospital we've got being treated by the best doctors and nurses." I don't want to lie to my little girl, and she lets my nonanswer pass.

A solemn nod. "We're all praying for him."

"We are."

"Then he'll be safe, I know it."

And the deep, dark cynical part of me thinks, *Prayers to God didn't help your mom in the end, did they,* but I shut that down. I say, "I've got to go away for a while. I'll try to call you every day and I want you to listen to Jannie and Bree and Damon and Nana Mama."

Willow wrinkles her nose. "Do I have to listen to Ali?"

I nearly laugh. "No, you don't have to listen to Ali."

"Are you going after the bad men who hurt Uncle Alex?"

Good question. "I'm going after some bad men for sure, honey. But don't worry, I'll be fine."

Another nod. "I know you'll catch them."

"Thanks," I say. "Will you do me one favor while I'm away?"

"Sure, Daddy."

I say, "I know it's heavy and uncomfortable, but please wear your new knapsack to school every day. Please?"

"It feels stiff. I don't like it."

"But wear it for me. Please. When I get back, I'll get you a new one that feels better."

"Okay."

I stand up, go around the table, and give her a big smothering hug that I want to last forever, knowing that at this moment, at least, she is safe.

But I have to go.

I kneel down, give her kisses on her cheeks—now slick with tears—and say, "Love you, Willow."

"Love you too, Daddy."

I get up and walk quickly out of the house, going after the bad men.

Alone.

CHAPTER

29

AT A GAS station with a convenience store off the highway just outside of Raleigh, North Carolina, I decide it's time to take a break from a night of driving. I'm about an hour away from Fort Bragg, but my body is weary and my eyelids are heavy, and me nodding off and wrapping my Grand Cherokee around a tall pine tree won't do anybody any good.

I go into the store. There's a *ding-ding* as the door opens.

An older man sits on a stool, and a younger man who looks like him—probably his son—stands at a corner rack restocking cigarettes and cigars. The older man slides off the stool and I note the pistol riding high on a waist holster. "Help you?" he asks. His son glares at me, and I spot a pump-action shotgun leaning against the wall next to him.

"I'd like to fill up my car, please," I say.

The older man says, "All of our pumps have credit card readers."

I slowly and deliberately take my wallet out. "I'd rather pay cash."

He nods. "Gonna need a deposit—you can come back in and get

your change. Sorry, that's the way it is. Can't trust no one, even your neighbors or the government. Bad times."

Bad times indeed, I think. I open my wallet, slip out three twenty-dollar bills. "This enough of a deposit?"

"Guess so."

I go out into the late evening—or early morning—and top off my Cherokee, then go back into the store and pick up some bottled water, beef jerky, crackers, a few other snacks. I go to the counter and he rings up my purchases and says, "With what you bought in gas and the money you left, that's five bucks even."

I take out my wallet again. "Ask you a question?"

He starts putting my purchases into a white plastic bag. "Questions are free, son. Not sure about the answers."

I put down a twenty-dollar bill. "I'm looking for a motel nearby. Quiet. Out of the way. Managers who aren't too nosy and will take cash."

"Well..."

I place another twenty on the counter. "I'm not looking for any trouble, you understand. Just a clean place to sleep for a few hours."

He smiles, scoops up the money, hands me the bulging white plastic bag. "The Pine Grove Motel. You leave here, take a right, go down the road a piece, maybe two miles. Take a right onto Youngstown Road. You'll come to an intersection. It'll be right there."

"Thanks," I say, picking up the bag.

The old man adds, "Fella, from the height and size of you, maybe you're not looking for trouble, but I got a feeling trouble is looking for you."

"If it comes here," I say, "will you send it in the other direction?"

The son in the corner by the shotgun laughs, and I leave.

Not much of a drive to the Pine Grove Motel, but I flip through the stations on the Cherokee's radio, looking to hear what's going on out there in talk-show land this early morning in America. In my travels south from DC, I played various jazz stations on satellite radio, but after a while I realized I wasn't doing my job. I needed to know what was being said out there, from coast to coast. I had to gather intelligence.

It wasn't pretty.

In my hours of driving, I heard the terrorist attacks—although not officially linked together—blamed on the Jews, the Muslims, gun-owner nuts, gun-control nuts, feminazis, incels (involuntary celibates), vegans, anti-vaxxers, pro-vaxxers, and about a half a dozen other groups.

Every caller, every talk-show host, was sure that he or she was the only one who knew the real truth and had the real solutions. It was always "the others" who should be arrested.

In the darkness of the night and my own thoughts, I think of my rough upbringing, how I'd practically lived by myself as a preteen with my father long gone and my mother gone most of the time, both sucked into the world of drugs and crime. If it weren't for one determined older woman—Nana Mama—I would have ended up in prison or dead within the decade. I could have been one of those nameless forgotten "others." But she had saved me, and so had the army and the DC Metro Police.

I have large debts there, debts I'm honor bound to repay.

I pull into the lot of the Pine Grove Motel. Two red lights flickering—OPEN and VACANCY—tell me what I need to know.

Behind a low counter in the office sits a yawning young blond woman wearing black leggings and a UNC Tar Heels football T-shirt. She looks to be six or seven months pregnant. In the corner is a small crib where a toddler is sleeping. Low sounds come from a TV playing what looks like an old Hallmark Channel movie.

I pay cash for my room and I'm pleased the clerk doesn't ask for my identification or license plate number. From the office in the center of the one-story building, I walk to the end room. It has two beds, a moldy bathroom, and not much else.

I drop a black duffel bag on the far bed and suddenly I'm tired from hunting bad guys.

I whisper, "Sure wish I was back home with you, Willow."

Then I get to work.

CHAPTER

30

I TWIST AND turn; it's always a struggle to get my six-foot-nine-inch frame comfortable. Billie used to tease me that she wasn't sure which half of my body she was going to cuddle up against.

I shift again.

It's been a long while since I've thought of those funny, loving moments.

Don't think about that. Don't get distracted with memories of your Billie. Think about what's ahead. The talk with Mel Carr.

I try to decipher what he said to me yesterday about our mission to Afghanistan, about the current state of affairs at Fort Bragg.

You should be paranoid. All of us who went on that cross-border expedition into Afghanistan should be paranoid. I think what we did and saw there is connected to all these bombings and shootings.

The trip to Afghanistan.

Sheep-dipped so we were no longer with the army but attached to the CIA. The CIA provided transportation and a woman field officer to supervise us.

We didn't land in Afghanistan but in a cold, windswept airfield in neighboring Tajikistan.

What did we see there?

What did we see in Afghanistan?

What—

There's a noise.

CHAPTER 31

THE THREE ATTACKERS move silently across the motel's parking lot to John Sampson's room, and the lead armed man places small detonation charges on the door's knob and three hinges.

The charges flare into life, and the lead man flips down his NVGs and kicks down the door, which falls with a satisfying *bang*.

They do a quick sweep of the room's two beds, and the near one holds a huddled shape, blankets pulled up, boots lined up on the floor; a duffel bag is on the other bed. All three open up with bursts from their silencer-equipped MP5s, tearing up the bedding and sheets and the shape underneath. Spent brass thuds on the floor, and the room smells of gunpowder.

They advance slowly and carefully—they wouldn't put it past their highly trained target to sleep with a Kevlar blanket—and the lead man reaches down with a gloved hand and tugs the sheet and blankets away.

Revealing a row of shot-up pillows.

Time to get the hell out and regroup.

The lead man looks around, wonders why the room is so crowded. The four of them are nearly elbow to elbow.

Wait.

Four?

He brings up his MP5, but he's not quick enough.

CHAPTER

32

BEFORE I SET up my bedding in the rear seat of the Cherokee, I placed a small motion-detection night-vision camera in the grille, pointed right at the door of my motel room. A cable threaded through the Cherokee led to a small laptop that would chime if something stopped in front of my motel-room door.

There.

When the chime sounds, I roll over, look at the laptop's screen.

Three armed men, ready to break into my room.

I watch their well-planned action, and when the door to my room drops, I put on my night-vision goggles and push open the rear door of the Cherokee. I slip out of my car, Glock 17 in my right hand, my bare feet on the cold pavement. Even shoes designed for my huge feet squeak as I walk because of my weight and size, which is why I'm shoeless now.

I hear the *thud-thud-thud* of suppressed gunfire and see the flicker-flicker-flicker of the muzzle flashes, and I move into the room right behind the three attackers. If we were in DC and these three were standard street thugs, I'd have to follow a host of procedures and regulations. But not in this place.

The only rule now is they go down and I stay standing.

I go into the room, dodging the fallen door, see the three clustered around my so-called bed. The one to the left seems to notice me and moves and—

Two shots to him.

He falls.

Whip-quick, I put two shots in his companion and two more into the third one.

They fall in a jumble.

All of them are wearing body armor. But that won't keep them safe. Shots to the head for all three of them.

Not much time now. With the night-vision goggles on, I collect their weapons and toss them into the bathroom, my breathing heavy but measured, my heart racing.

I go back to the three dead attackers. Like the ones who went after Alex and me yesterday, they're well armed. I have no doubt they carry no identification and that their MP5s have no serial numbers.

There's a cough.

I freeze, then look at the first man I shot. I reach down, tug away the night-vision goggles on his bloody head.

My first shot went a bit too high, hitting his goggles, grazing his forehead, and it looks like my second shot took out a chunk of his neck.

His right hand is pressed tight against the bloody wound. His eyes roll and then focus on me. "Good shooting," he murmurs. "Well done."

"Hang on," I say. "Keep holding pressure on that."

I get towels from the bathroom and come back. I think, *If I can save this guy, I can contact Ned Mahoney, have the FBI take over. At last we'll have a live connection to the terror attacks.* I kneel down next to him. "Give me a sec, guy. Keep that pressure on."

"Sorry, not going to happen." He smiles and takes his hand off his neck wound; arterial blood sprays out, keeps on spraying. I do my best to hold pressure on the wound but the thin towels are quickly soaked through, and my first-aid kit is back in my Cherokee.

Damn it.

When the man is dead, I pick up my spent shell casings, go back to the bathroom, and wash my hands.

CHAPTER

33

I GET INTO my Cherokee, start it up with the lights off, and back out onto the state road. The poor woman holding down the desk overnight is probably calling the cops.

I feel sorry for the responding units in this small town. They're going to come across a crime scene with more gunfire and killing than they've ever encountered; it'll be like some upstate New York two-man police department investigating a Mafia-style hit at a local restaurant.

About fifty feet down the dark road, I turn the headlights on and keep driving.

A while later, I'm on the busy interstate, joining the early-morning commuters, most of them heading southwest to Fort Bragg and the city of Fayetteville, now just a few minutes away.

I play and replay in my mind the ambush back there at that small motel out in the proverbial middle of nowhere.

First things first: I was tracked. No question about that.

Question: Was I followed from DC or were the attackers somewhere local, ready to respond when I stopped to rest?

Answer: It doesn't matter. Either way, it means a real depth and breadth of organizational skills.

And how was I tracked?

I pull off the road and take a black box about the size of a small brick out of my duffel bag. It was a gift from Ned Mahoney and the FBI a couple of years back, a sensing device that tells you if there's a tracking device or wiretap nearby.

I switch it on. Five red lights come on and remain red. My Cherokee and everything within twenty feet of it is clear.

I shut the unit off and get back on the road.

I consider the briefly surviving gunman. He didn't want first aid, didn't want to live, didn't want to face an interrogation. Sheer dedication and a willingness to die for his mission. Not many people like that still around, and it chills me, knowing what we're up against.

I should be tired with so little sleep, but I'm wired tight, the smell of burned gunpowder in my nose. I grab my cell to call Alex, and—

Damn.

What a fool.

What about Ned Mahoney of the FBI?

Tempting, but it's still early in the morning. The poor guy is surviving on coffee and Red Bulls, trying to make sense of what's going on.

The same applies to me. I pick up speed, heading to Fort Bragg, working my cell phone with my free hand.

CHAPTER

34

I'M IN THE city of Fayetteville, Fort Bragg's neighbor and, some would say, its largest parasite. The numerous pawnshops, bars, stores, strip clubs, and other similar businesses that ring the fort are designed to suck as much money as possible from the army personnel stationed there.

On the All American Freeway, I spot a lane of backed-up traffic leading into the access control point of Fort Bragg, where a brown sign announces in white lettering:

FT. BRAGG ACP
PREPARE TO STOP

By the grass medians, soldiers in full battle rattle are patrolling alongside two armored Humvees with roof-mounted machine guns.

As traffic crawls, I exchange a series of texts with Mel Carr and set a meeting point at the Drop Zone Café.

I finally get there, and we sit at the rear, close to the swinging doors of the kitchen.

Mel is a couple of years younger than me; he has a narrow face, dark eyes, and black hair cut in a high-and-tight. Today he's wearing civvy clothes: jeans and a dungaree jacket. He sees me remove my Glock 17 and put it on the seat next to me, then shift my position so it's hidden by my right buttock.

"Glad to see you're taking my warnings seriously," he says.

"Nothing to do with your warnings," I say. "In the past twenty-four hours, I've been shot at twice by men intent on killing me. I want to be ready if they try again. I like to keep my perfect survival record."

Mel swears and says, "What the hell happened?"

I tell him about the ambush yesterday morning that nearly killed Alex Cross and go on to describe what happened at the Pine Grove Motel last night.

He shakes his head. "Jesus, John, you took one hell of a risk coming down here."

"We're both at risk," I say. "No getting around that. We need to find out the how and why, and soon. One thing's for certain—these guys are tough and dedicated."

"Dedicated how?"

"In the motel attack, there was one survivor, briefly, wound to the neck. Looked like my bullet tore open a major artery. I tried to help, but he wouldn't cooperate. Just smiled at me, lifted his hand off the towels, and bled out within seconds."

Mel shivered. "That's hard core. Not wanting to get saved so you won't get captured and questioned."

A plump young blond waitress in a black uniform takes our orders, and I take stock of the other customers. A few locals, it looks like, but mostly army personnel sitting and talking low. No laughter, no smiles.

I can feel the tension in the air. It's like being in an FOB in Afghanistan and getting ready to go out on patrol when you know you're going to run into heavily armed and strongly motivated bad guys.

But here, the bad guys aren't outside the wire. They could be sitting right next to me. I say, "What's going on at the fort?"

"Not much since I first talked to you. Lots of guys being shuffled out, lots of rumors. It's hell on morale and unit cohesion."

"I saw one giant traffic backup at the main gate," I say. "Soldiers were patrolling the median, and there were two Humvees there too."

Coffee mugs are placed before us by the waitress, and when she leaves, Mel says, "Yeah, it takes about twice as long to get into base than it used to, but after the attacks on Leavenworth and Fort Irwin, nobody's taking any chances."

"Fort Irwin? In California? I didn't hear about any attacks on the news."

"What, you think all news gets reported? Tell you what, remember Sergeants Ortiz and Powell, they were with us when we went into the 'Stan?"

"Sure, I remember them," I say. "Good guys to have at your back. Always had spare dry socks if you needed them."

Mel leans across the table, lowers his voice: "They both died this past week. Initial reports are that they were suicides and that they died at their off-base housing. But I've got a friend in CID investigating the matter, and she says otherwise."

I sure as hell don't like where this is going, and when Mel speaks again, he confirms what I'm dreading.

"John, they were straight-up murdered, and it's being swept under the rug."

CHAPTER 35

AT GEORGE WASHINGTON University Hospital, a woman carrying a fake ID that identifies her as Mary Mullen, a nurse at the facility, walks in along with the morning stream of people. She has a black leather purse over her shoulder and a Starbucks coffee cup in her right hand. She also has a key card that gives her access to every part of the hospital.

She goes through the main lobby with purpose and direction, having earlier memorized the floor plan for the lobby and the floor where the trauma ICU and her target are located.

She takes the elevator to the sixth floor, gets off, ducks into a restroom, and dumps her purse in a trash bin. On a floor like this one, if you're walking around with a purse, you don't belong. And she is determined to blend in.

She uses her key card to enter the ICU. There is quiet lighting, smooth white floors, and light brown cabinets and wood trim. Voices are low. Nurses and doctors are moving back and forth, and there are plenty of low counters and workstations with black computers.

There. Around the corner and she'll be at Alex Cross's room.

She pats her right pocket, feels the form of the syringe.

Inside the syringe is another bit of equipment supplied to her a few hours ago along with the fake ID and key card. It contains a nontraceable and unique drug cocktail that will stop Alex Cross's heart and won't show up on any drug screen.

She's not sure where the syringe and its contents are from, but she guesses it has something to do with her former employer down in Atlanta, the Centers for Disease Control and Prevention.

She goes around the corner and thinks, *Get in, give the shot, get out.*

But she halts.

There's a uniformed DC Metro cop sitting in a chair right outside the door of Alex Cross's ICU room.

CHAPTER

36

I SAY TO Mel, "Murdered?"

"Yeah," he says.

The homicide detective part of me kicks in. "Any idea how? Methods? Witnesses?"

"No," he says. "My CID contact was reluctant to say more. Not that I'm getting paranoid, John, but what are the chances that two of our cross-border teammates randomly get killed in the same week?"

I nod. "About the same as the chances of two completely different sets of gunmen coming after me. Shit, that shooting yesterday—they weren't going for Alex Cross. They were after me."

As I'm talking to Mel, I'm also watching the interior of the Drop Zone Café. Two women wearing gray business attire, slacks and jackets, come in. They sit two tables away from us. One woman says to her companion, laughing, "And I told the colonel that if he wants those air-intake covers before their next deployment, he'd better light a fire under his general. And then—"

Contractors, I think. *Similar to the pawnshops, jewelry shops, and other stores around here that take advantage of the nearby post and boost their prices: Thank you for your service. All invoices are due within thirty days of receipt.*

I tell Mel, "Alex and I are on a task force in DC that's trying to find the people responsible for these terrorist attacks along with their supporters and financers. Everybody from the FBI to the NSA and CIA are represented on the task force. Lots of whispers and chatter, but no hard evidence."

"Who's running the show?"

"General Wayne Grissom."

For the first time since I sat down with Mel, he looks relieved. "A good choice. He won't put up with any bullshit. But there's something else I need to tell you, John. Maybe something you can bring back to DC with you."

"Go ahead."

"There's a first sergeant in Second Platoon who's a real asshole. Name of Bravura. He was drunk the other night at a roadhouse up the street, and he told me and others that he was heading out on a TDY. Wouldn't say for what or for how long. But two things he said to me stuck out. One was that, quote, 'We screwed up big-time in Afghanistan, but now we're gonna do it right.' Unquote."

"He explain that further?"

"Hell no."

"And what was the other thing?"

"The prick said, 'Hey, Mel, maybe you'll be a suicide victim by the time I get back.'"

"Hell of a threat."

"You got it," Mel says. "Like he knew what happened to Powell and Ortiz."

Before I can respond, our waitress comes through the kitchen's swinging doors and drops the tray she's carrying with a loud bang.

The two women I thought were contractors are up and away from their table, pistols in hand, walking straight toward us.

CHAPTER

37

IN THE TRAUMA ICU, the fake nurse walks past Alex's room, remembering her training back when she worked security for the CDC.

He or she who hesitates is lost. No matter where you are or what you're doing, act like you belong there. The moment you fail to show confidence, you're dead.

She goes to the MPD cop sitting outside Alex's door, a young guy in his mid-twenties. His short legs are spread out, and—to her relief—he seems to be playing solitaire on his cell.

He looks up and she says, "How many more hours stuck here?"

The cop smiles. He has a pleasant, soft face. "Too many."

"Well, I'm working a double, so pray for me, okay?"

He laughs and goes back to his game.

She takes her key card and flashes it against a rectangular black reader. A tiny red light flashes green, and the door slides open.

Here we go.

The door slides closed behind her. The room is empty of other staff, thank God. There's the usual apparatus of monitors and IV stands, and she hears the hiss/hum of the ventilator as it sends air in and out of the target's lungs. Said target is lying in the hospital bed, nearly invisible under the blanket. IVs are in his arms, and there's a tube running out of his mouth.

She steps forward, takes the syringe out of her right pocket, pops off the plastic safety cap, and goes to the nearest IV line. Simplest thing in the world: Just slide the needle into the plastic tubing, depress the plunger, and, by the time she hits the parking lot, so long, Alex Cross.

She grabs the IV tubing with her left hand and brings up the syringe with her right just as a tired and angry-looking woman rises up from the other side of the bed and says, "Who the hell are you and what are you doing?"

Ignore her and do your job, she thinks, but now the woman is pointing a pistol at her, and the simplest thing in the world just got a hell of a lot more complicated.

CHAPTER 38

MY HAND DROPS to the Glock 17 at my side, and both women now have open wallets in their non-gun-holding hands. The one on the right says, "I'm Agent Lily Wagner, Army CID, and this is my partner, Agent Camille DeGrasse. I'll ask you both to show me your hands. Now, Sergeant Carr. Now, Detective Sampson."

When you have weapons pointed at you like this, your options drastically narrow. I could kick up the table and cause a distraction, but the place is full of civilians.

Mel eyes me warily and gives me a look that says: *Please, John. Don't.*

I've been known to take good advice occasionally. My hands go up and so do Mel's, and I say, "Always happy to work with the CID."

"Nice lie, Detective Sampson," Agent Wagner says, pistol covering both of us as her partner comes toward us with handcuffs in her hands. "But if and when charges are drawn up, I'll be a nice cop and not mention it."

Mel and I are separated, and I'm placed in the rear seat of an old black Chevrolet Impala, although it takes a lot of maneuvering and cursing before I can get my six-foot-nine-inch frame into the unmarked CID cruiser.

Mel goes into another Impala, and I keep my mouth shut as Agent Wagner drives out on Route 24 and, in another surprise of the day, away from Fort Bragg. Several minutes pass and she turns into an office park and drives to the rear of one of the two-story brick buildings. She parks next to a green dumpster, helps me out of the Impala, and brings me into the building.

About sixty seconds later, we are in an austere, windowless office with bare walls and a metal desk. No phone, no computer. Only a yellow legal pad and a pen.

There's a chair for her and a chair for me. The cuffs come off and Agent Wagner says, "Thanks for not putting up any resistance, Detective Sampson."

"No problem," I say. "I left my service weapon back at the diner. Where is it?"

"In my briefcase under this desk." She picks up the pen, fiddles with it for a moment.

I say, "Pretty spartan office."

"It serves its purpose."

"Like helping you avoid going onto the post and having my visit officially recorded?"

A pursed smile. "You have a vivid imagination."

"It's worked for me so far," I say. "Care to disagree? Or is this just the start of having me Gitmo'ed to Cuba or some other black site?"

"That depends," she says, "on how cooperative you are."

"Thanks for giving me a goal," I say. "But one-way cooperation has always been something I stay away from."

CHAPTER

39

IN ALEX CROSS'S room, his would-be killer freezes. The armed woman steps toward her, revealing a couple of couch cushions on the floor where she's apparently been napping.

Always be on offense. "Hey, hey, hey," she says. "Tell me who you are first! And put that damn gun down!"

The woman says, "I'm Brianna Stone, Alex Cross's wife, and I want to know who you are and what you're doing."

Shit. "I'm doing my job, ma'am," she says. "My name is Mary Mullen, I'm an RN on this floor. And please put that gun down or I'll get security."

The gun is unwavering, still pointed at her.

"I know every nurse and doctor who comes here," Cross's wife says, motioning to a whiteboard on the wall. "And you're not on that list."

"Something's come up and—"

Brianna starts walking around the bed. "Security? Sure. Go get security. I'll stay right here and wait for you to come back."

Shit, she thinks again. "All right, fine, right after I administer this medication." She pulls the IV tubing closer to her and brings up the syringe, and the armed woman says, "You put that syringe away. You get it any closer, I'll shoot you."

"No, you won't," she says.

The sound of the gunshot is deafening in the ICU room. The pain erupting from her right shoulder causes her to cry out, and as she falls to the floor, the syringe flying from her hand, she thinks, *Damn, the bitch wasn't joking.*

CHAPTER 40

AGENT WAGNER SAYS, "Why are you here, Detective Sampson?"

"Meeting up with an old buddy of mine," I say. "Sergeant Mel Carr. Eighty-Second Airborne Division, Third Brigade, First Battalion. But I imagine you already know that."

"Why did you come from DC to see Sergeant Carr?"

"I heard the Drop Zone Café serves a great breakfast," I say. "But now I'll never know, since you and your partner interrupted us before we were served."

"Sorry about that," she said.

"Thanks," I say. "Maybe CID will comp us."

"Trust me, Detective Sampson, you've got a lot more to worry about than missing some eggs and bacon."

"It was French toast and sausage," I say. "So, do tell, Agent Wagner, why the big production in taking us out of the restaurant? Why are you so interested in my travels? You two could have joined us for breakfast without all the official doom and gloom. I would even have picked up the check. Or were you just interested in making a show for your superior officers?"

A long pause. "I'm never interested in making a show for my superiors. I'm interested in your travels because we believe you might be involved in an ongoing investigation."

"What kind of investigation?" I ask.

"The confidential kind," she says. "Detective, why are you really here, right outside of a sensitive military installation? And what did the two of you talk about?"

"Your ongoing investigation, of course," I say. "And Army Intelligence's too, I'm sure."

That gets her attention. "What are you saying?"

"The series of terrorist attacks that began last April and include assaults on Fort Leavenworth and Fort Irwin."

"There was no attack on Fort Irwin."

"I've heard otherwise," I say. "As to your earlier question, we caught up on old business and talked about old times."

Agent Wagner says, "Like your trip to Afghanistan?"

An interesting development. "I'm afraid I'm not in a position to comment on any operations conducted in Afghanistan or even if any such operations occurred," I say.

"You went to Afghanistan as part of a CIA-sponsored operation," she says. "I would like to know more about that mission, its participants, and its goals."

"Give the CIA a call," I say. "In the spirit of interagency cooperation, I'm sure they'll tell you everything." She looks hard at me and I add, "That is, if anything did happen over there."

I let a few seconds slide by before going on. "Why are you so interested in what may or may not have happened in Afghanistan?"

She continues the hard stare.

"Part of your confidential investigation, I imagine," I say.

Agent Wagner says, "Please answer the question."

And something odd happens. I see it in her eyes.

Army CID investigators have a tough reputation; they have the duty and responsibility to investigate any and all malfeasance conducted by any soldier, from a private to a five-star general. Yet Agent Wagner seems unsettled.

I give her my best smile. "I'm afraid I'm not in a position to assist you in any aspects of your investigation, Agent Wagner."

"Try."

There's a tone of pleading in that word. What the hell is going on here? Maybe I should stay, spar with her a bit, try to squeeze more helpful information out of her.

Or maybe I should get back to work.

I say, "In the words of the immortal Bartleby the scrivener, 'I would prefer not to.' It's been a delight to make your acquaintance, Agent Wagner, but I must be leaving."

I stand up and she says, "Sit down!"

"Not happening."

"Detective Sampson—Sergeant Sampson—I'm ordering you to stay and answer my questions."

"Agent Wagner, you have no authority over me," I say. "I'm a member of the Individual Ready Reserve. If I am activated, I have to follow your orders. But since I'm not, I'm leaving."

Her eyes narrow. "I could get you activated, force you to answer my questions."

"I doubt you can do that in the next five minutes," I say. "But in those few minutes, you can return my service weapon. Please."

"No."

"You have no authority to hold my weapon. Please return it."

"I have a feeling you're violating the laws of pistol ownership in the state of North Carolina." She sounds like she's trying everything she can think of to keep me here.

"As you're not a peace officer in the state of North Carolina, and since the law requires following the law, not one's feelings, please return my weapon."

We stare at each other for a few seconds, then she ducks down and retrieves my Glock 17 from her soft leather briefcase. She pops out the magazine, expertly works the action to eject the cartridge contained in the pistol, catches it, and hands over all three items to me.

"Please don't reassemble your weapon in my presence," she says. "If you do, I will take it as a threat and put a round through your large head."

"No worries, Agent Wagner," I say, holding the magazine, round, and unloaded pistol in one hand. "Any chance you could give me a ride back to the Drop Zone Café? That's where I'm parked."

She drops her pen on the metal desk. "Don't push your luck."

"Sorry, ma'am, that's part of my job description."

CHAPTER 41

SHE OPENS HER eyes, feeling woozy as hell. She takes in her surroundings. A hospital room, curtains drawn around the bed, monitors tracking her respiration, blood pressure, heart rate. IV in her left hand, and in her right hand—

Something jingle-jangles.

She's handcuffed to the bed railing.

Well, shit, then.

She tries to move her left shoulder and it feels like that entire part of her body has been replaced with stiff Styrofoam.

The curtain zips open, and a woman in blue scrubs who identifies herself as an anesthesiologist comes in holding a thick binder in her hands. After some blah-blah-blah, she leaves, and she's followed a few minutes later by a male OR nurse in scrubs who gives her an additional blah-blah-blah about her upcoming surgery.

"Any questions?" the nurse asks.

Yeah, she thinks, *got any ideas what I should tell my boss about how I screwed up?* "No," she says. "This isn't my first rodeo. I'll be fine."

He leaves; a tall, thin woman enters and identifies herself as the surgeon. More blah-blah-blah about how hopefully she'll be out of the OR and in recovery in two hours, blah-blah-blah.

The doctor says, "You're lucky to be alive and lucky that the bullet didn't do more damage. But this isn't like television or the movies. You're facing months of rehab before you're fully recovered."

"Thanks for the cheerful message," she responds. "But now I feel like taking a nap. Why don't you get the hell out and leave me alone?"

The surgeon's face reddens and she leaves, but, damn it, only about a minute later, another figure enters, a woman wearing blue scrubs, and, damn it some more, the woman in the bed recognizes that angry face.

The angry woman takes a chair next to the bed, pulls out a pistol, points it at her, and says, "I'm Brianna Stone. You tried to kill my husband a half hour ago. Let's chat."

CHAPTER

42

THROUGH LUCK AND the services of Uber, I get back to the Drop Zone Café, where I find a pleasant surprise. Mel Carr is standing in the parking lot, leaning up against my Grand Cherokee's front left fender and sipping coffee from a cardboard cup.

He smiles as I approach. "Big John," he says.

"M' man Mel," I say.

"Good to see you out and about," he says. "I figured you'd be coming back here to fetch your wheels. How did you get bounced out?"

I say, "Agent Wagner was prepared, aggressive, and knew what she wanted. Unfortunately for her, she lacked jurisdiction over my ass. How about you?"

He lifts his cup in a salute. "I told you I have a friend in CID, the one who told me that those two suicides were really homicides," he says. "I asked Agent DeGrasse to contact my friend, who happens to be her superior, and here I am. Free as a bird for the foreseeable future."

I remember the parting words of Agent Ned Mahoney as I say, "Feel like a drive? We need to get some stuff squared away."

He takes a final swig of his coffee, drops the cup into an overflowing orange and white trash bin, and gets into the passenger seat.

I get in and return to Route 210; the highway is fairly busy. "What did Agent DeGrasse say to you?"

"Not much," he says. "She started chatting and I slipped in my friend's name and that was that."

"What was she chatting about?"

"This and that," Mel says. "You know."

"Working in DC homicide, you get familiar with chitchat. Hold on, I need to take a leak."

I turn into a large lot containing a Waffle House, a Piggly Wiggly, and a plumbing-supply store. I drive to the far end of the lot, where there's nothing but a guardrail and low brush and trees. I pull up and take a look around, making sure we're not being watched or followed.

Mel says, "Looks pretty isolated."

"Exactly."

With my left hand I open the door; with my right, I grab my Glock 17, whirl it around, jam it into Mel's left ear. I let go of the door, grab his shirt collar, and give it a sharp twist.

"Hey, hey, hey, what the hell—"

I twist the muzzle of the Glock harder into his ear. "What the hell is that your story is bullshit, and you know it," I say. "You're active-duty army, you're pulled in for an interrogation from a CID special agent, and now you're out because of a supposed friend in CID? You don't think that story is hard to believe?"

I stop talking, remembering FBI agent Ned Mahoney's parting words: *Don't trust anyone.*

CHAPTER

43

IN HER HOSPITAL bed, the handcuffed woman smiles, even though she feels like she's tripping something awful; the light green curtains over there look like they're melting.

"Lady, I hate to disappoint you, but as you know, this isn't the first time I've had a pistol pointed in my direction," she says, smiling wider. "And this isn't the first time I've been wounded either."

"I don't doubt that at all," Brianna says. "Let's start by finding out who you are. Your ID was fake. There's no Mary Mullen employed in this hospital. But your identification looked just like the real thing, and you even had key-card access."

"Wow," she says.

"Your fingerprints aren't in any database," Brianna says. "And I expect DNA analysis and facial-recognition software will have the same results. So who are you?"

She says, "Just a hardworking gal trying to make her way in this crazy, mixed-up world."

"By committing murder?"

"That's the way of the entire world, isn't it? Survival of the fittest."

"And killing an unarmed man in a hospital bed, that's survival of the fittest?"

"It had to be done for the greater good."

"Says who?"

She's fighting sleepiness but she likes giving this member of the deep state the runaround. "I've said too much already."

"Not a word, then?" Brianna asks.

"Not a word..."

The curtain slides open and there are two men and one woman in scrubs, and the woman says, "Sorry, we need to take this patient to surgery."

She whispers, "See, cop? Not...one...word..."

Brianna is frozen with anger and frustration, and then she spots something on the woman's left arm, and the woman thinks, *Oh no, not that.*

But Brianna moves quickly to her side.

The woman knows what's exposed.

And so does Brianna.

"Well, well," Brianna says, her voice triumphant. "What do we have here? I'll tell you. A tattoo. And not just any old tattoo. It's a red numeral one on a green background. The emblem of the U.S. Army's famed First Infantry Division, the Big Red One."

The three medical workers come in and start moving her hospital bed.

The last thing the woman hears is "I'll see you when you wake up, and we'll talk again. By then, I'll know who you are."

CHAPTER

44

IN A STRAINED voice, Mel says, "John, what the hell are you doing?"

I twist his collar again. "Watching my six, pal. Forget our friendship and what we've done together. All I know is that I come down here to talk about Afghanistan, we both get picked up by CID, and you—active-duty army!—get cut loose before I do."

"But my friend—"

"Yeah, your mysterious friend who has the power to get you set free. He must have one set of brass ones to get that done."

Mel says, "It's not a he. It's a she. Captain Andrea Sharkey."

"Go on."

"Come on, John..."

"Go on."

"Or what? You going to splatter my brains and bones over your car's interior?"

I say, "I can afford to dump this car and get a new one. Can you get a new head?"

Mel mutters something profoundly obscene, then says, "We're seeing each other. Met eight months ago when she came to my platoon looking into the theft of some ammo. We hit it off and…you know how it is."

"How come you never told me this?"

"Because I wanted to keep it a secret. Colonel Michael Sharkey wouldn't be happy to find out what I'm doing with his wife."

I pull my pistol back a few inches. "You got your girlfriend to spring you?"

"Sort of," he says. "I burned a pretty sweet bridge back there, John. I told her that unless she got me cleared and off post, I'd tell her hubby about our relationship."

I pull back the pistol just a little bit more. "Crap, Mel, that was a hell of a thing to do."

He says, "Well, damn, it wasn't going to last forever, right? Her husband is in CID but rumor has it he served in Delta Force before going into law. But if he ever found out…shit, John, I didn't want to spend my last hours on earth having my legs fed to a wood chipper."

I stare at him and he stares back and I put my weapon down. "Sorry." I feel ashamed, pulling a weapon on an old friend. One of the rules that's hammered into you at basic training the first day on the range: Never, ever, point a weapon at someone unless you intend to shoot.

But I'd had to do it in this new world.

Mel says, "Yeah, we're all jumpy. What now?"

I holster my pistol. "Time to kick it up a notch. We need to reach out to the CIA officer who was our tour guide into the 'Stan, see if she can shed some light on what went on over there and how it's connected to these terror attacks."

"Deacon, right?"

"That's right, Elizabeth Deacon."

"You just gonna call up Langley and ask them to put you through?"

I put the Cherokee in reverse, make a turn, and head back to Route 210. "No, I'm going to call someone who has sources all around the globe," I say. "I bet we'll have her home address in less than an hour."

"She your girlfriend?"

I don't answer right away. "I should be so lucky."

I want to put some miles behind us in case a concerned citizen saw me putting a gun to Mel's head, and once we're north of Fayetteville, Mel says, "How did your CID interview go? More than just chitchat?"

"She took me off post so she could interview me without any official records. She asked me why I was here and what you and I talked about, and after a while, I got bored and left."

Mel says, "I bet she was pissed. How did you manage to slip out without all sorts of bad things happening to you?"

"I reminded her that I was in the Individual Ready Reserve, that unless I was called up, she had no authority over me. Then I left."

Mel shakes his head. "Why didn't you do that back at the café's parking lot? Why wait until you were taken away?"

I say, "I wanted to find out what they know. Mel, she pressed me on Afghanistan. That means the army also knows something about our trip being linked to the terrorist attacks, and they're doing their very best to find out why. I also noticed something else."

"What's that?"

"The CID special agent looked spooked, like she sensed something big was coming and she and her investigators couldn't do a damn thing about it."

CHAPTER

45

MAYNARD IS IN McLean, Virginia, sitting on a picnic bench near a McDonald's playground, doing his best to ignore the cheerful sounds of the kids playing as he updates the Boss on the past twenty-four hours.

When he's done, the Boss says, "We've an emerging situation and I want you to take care of it. Personally. Especially since the hit on Sampson was a failure."

"Absolutely, sir," Maynard replies, feeling good that the Boss isn't blaming him for that mess, three unidentified dead men found in a small motel in rural North Carolina. Even made goddamn CNN.

The Boss says, "Sampson has met up with an army buddy of his from Fort Bragg. It looks like they're getting the band back together, the survivors who went to Afghanistan. Their reunion needs to be terminated quickly and efficiently."

"Yes, sir."

"Pick three of your finest. I'll contact you in a few hours with the target situation. I want you on Sampson. When other members of that Afghan unit make themselves known, I'll assign teams to them as well."

"Very good, sir. But what about Alex Cross? Today's mission didn't get the job done."

"His time will come in another day or two. Anything else?"

"No, sir," he says.

The Boss disconnects, and Maynard starts eating his Quarter Pounder with Cheese, in his opinion one of the finest burgers in the land, no matter what the prissy foodies say. All Maynard knows is that a Quarter Pounder in Virginia tastes the same as one in California, and that's a fine achievement indeed.

As he eats his lunch, Maynard thinks, *The Boss's voice is really starting to irritate me.* He's been working for the Boss for more than two years, preparing this operation, doing the planning, sweating, and bleeding to get to this point, and he's had enough. He wants to know who the hell the Boss is and what his credentials are. He thinks of the voice synthesizer the Boss uses. Supposedly it's impossible to clean it up to get to the real voice, but from his years working at the National Security Agency, Maynard knows there are back doors to all sorts of encryption that will allow him to run a recording of the voice through software and hear the real voice.

He looks at his phone. According to the Boss's orders, it should be a low-tech burner phone. But today it's not. It's a government-issue device from where he once worked, and it has astounding abilities.

Time to find out who the hell he's working for.

CHAPTER

46

WE TAKE A break at mile marker 142 on I-95 north at a rest area with a pleasant-looking one-story wooden building with a peaked white roof; it wouldn't look out of place in New England.

Mel is working his phone, trying to reach out to other military personnel who were with us on our secret cross-border mission to Afghanistan, and I get out of the car and call Bree Stone for a variety of reasons.

She picks up after one ring and says, sobbing, "Oh, John, I wish you were here."

My heart feels like a chunk of granite and I feel sweat pop out at the base of my neck. "Tell me what's going on with Alex."

Another muffled sob. "He's okay. He's doing all right. But a few hours ago, somebody tried to kill him in his bed in the ICU."

Happy families and travelers swirl around me while I stand at the entrance to the rest stop. Bree tells me the details of what happened earlier this morning at George Washington University Hospital, how the assassin has only one form of legitimate ID—her Big Red

One tattoo—and how Bree's people at Bluestone Group are trying to track down her real identity.

When she takes a breath, I say, "Where's Alex now? Have they moved him?"

"No, he has to stay in the ICU. There's now a Metro Police checkpoint in the corridor outside the ICU, and there's an officer in his room twenty-four/seven. That idiot officer who let the would-be killer in is going to end up in the traffic bureau, if he's lucky. How are you?"

One hell of a question, and I'm not about to tell her what happened to me at the motel. I say, "I'm coming back north with an army buddy of mine, Sergeant Mel Carr. We're tracking down some information that might help us get to the source of these terror attacks. And the shooting of Alex."

"Good. You be safe now."

"Safe as I can," I say. "How's Willow?"

"Good, though she misses her daddy," Bree says. "And after Alex got shot yesterday, I arranged for my firm to send security personnel to her school."

I choke up for a moment. Willow has been on my mind nearly every minute since I left her at the Cross home, and now I feel better about her safety. I say, "Can you go to the Bluestone Group favor bank one more time for me?"

"Yes, of course," Bree says. "What do you need?"

"I need a current phone number and address for Elizabeth Deacon," I say. "Two years ago she was an officer with the CIA. I don't know where she is now, but it's vital I get in contact with her."

"Got it, John," she says. "Anything else?"

"Not at the moment," I say. "And you be safe as well."

A harsh chuckle. "I nearly killed a woman who was threatening Alex. Don't you worry about me."

CHAPTER 47

JUST AFTER THE SUV crosses the border from Virginia into North Carolina, Maynard hears his driver, Cameron, say, “Ah, shit.”

“What’s up?” he asks.

“Flashing blue lights behind us, that’s what,” Cameron says.

Maynard doesn’t make the rookie mistake of swiveling in his seat and alerting the cop that the front-seat passenger is nervous enough to look back; instead, he glances at the Ford Explorer’s side-view mirror.

A North Carolina highway patrol cruiser is coming right up on their ass.

In the rear seat are Juarez and Roccilli, good men he can trust. Juarez says, “What now, boss?”

“What do you think?” Maynard says. “Cameron, pull over. And how fast were you going when you spotted the blues back there?”

“About eighty-one,” he says.

“Fool,” Roccilli says from the rear seat.

“All right, stay cool,” Maynard says. “Juarez, hand me that blanket.

You and the others get ready. And for Christ's sake, Cameron, look cheerful when the trooper asks for your license and registration."

After pulling her silver and black Dodge Charger over behind the Explorer with Virginia plates, Belinda Gorman calls in the stop to dispatch, then steps out, puts on her dark gray campaign hat, and approaches the vehicle.

As she passes the tail end of the SUV, she gently presses her hand against the smooth black metal, a reminder from her training days that job number one is going home safe and sound after the shift is over, something she's kept close to her heart for the past seven years. She has a lot to go home to: her husband, Raymond—who works from home for Atrium Health's IT department—and their three-year-old twin boys, Peter and Paul. But if the worst happens, at least she's left a handprint on the vehicle to prove she was here, despite what any future defense lawyers might say.

Belinda walks up to the driver's side of the SUV as the window comes down. She's pleased to see the driver has both hands on the steering wheel. Nice way to proceed with a traffic stop. Right hand on her holstered SIG Sauer .357 pistol, she notes that the vehicle has four occupants. "Afternoon, sir," she says. "License and registration, please."

"Certainly, ma'am," the driver says, and in that instant, Belinda notices something odd about the four men in the SUV. All are wearing orange earplugs, like the ones you use on a firing range.

She starts to move back as the front passenger drops a blanket from his lap and raises a sawed-off pump-action shotgun, and the orange-yellow light blossoming from the end of the barrel is the last thing she sees.

A few minutes later, as Cameron is back driving on I-95, Maynard holds out his hand for everyone's orange foam earplugs. Once he has them all, he lowers his window and scatters them to the breeze that clears out the smell of the burned gunpowder.

He rolls up the window and says, “Cameron, take the next exit, let’s find a car wash.”

“I don’t think there’s any blood or brains on us,” he says.

“Don’t care,” Maynard says. “I care about the handprint that cop put on the back of our vehicle. Need to get that cleaned off. And since you’re responsible for this little dustup, you’re going to find new plates to replace the Virginia ones. Got it?”

Cameron’s face flushes but he instantly says, “Yes, sir.”

“And another thing,” Maynard says. “When I say to stick to the speed limit, stick to the fucking speed limit. You got that?”

Cameron says nothing but the two men in the rear laugh.

CHAPTER 48

WE DECIDE TO stop at a fishing camp belonging to a friend of Mel's. It's a fifteen-minute drive from the interstate to a bumpy dirt access road for a few houses and cottages on an isolated lake.

It's starting to get dark, and I keep the Cherokee's headlights on as Mel goes up a set of worn wooden steps, picks up a corner board, and retrieves a key. Once he opens the door of the house, I drive the Cherokee down the dirt road a bit, find a vehicle-size opening in the trees, and back it in. Crickets chirp and a nearly full moon is rising in the east as I walk back to the cottage.

We store our gear and I check the place out. Single story, combination kitchen/living area, two large bedrooms, a bathroom, and an enclosed porch looking out onto the placid lake.

Each of us takes a brisk shower; I'm pleasantly surprised to find clean and fluffy towels, and when I mention that, Mel says, "What, you think we're barbarians out here?" I see Bree has texted me the information about Elizabeth Deacon, our CIA escort when we crossed into Afghanistan two years ago.

I call Deacon, and her initial response is "How in the hell did you get this number?" But eventually I convince her to have a Zoom meeting with us and another member of the Afghanistan team.

Mel and I sit at the kitchen table on metal and plastic chairs likely bought at a yard sale about half a century ago. In front of us is Mel's laptop, which a nephew set up with multiple VPNs and other goodies so it's untraceable.

Our heads share one screen, Elizabeth Deacon joins us from Vermont on another screen, and a former Eighty-Second Airborne sergeant, Paco Ruiz, joins us from rural Pennsylvania on a third screen. Ruiz has a black goatee now and looks to have put on a few pounds since I last saw him. Deacon wears her blond hair in the same short style, and she stares out at us with cold blue eyes that tell you nothing other than that they've seen a lot of bad things.

Deacon wastes no time taking charge. "Just to remind you all, this call is not encrypted, so be careful what you say. And make it quick. I've got an appointment I can't miss."

Ruiz smiles. "Zoom call with the CIA director?"

"No," she says, not smiling. "A town meeting. I chair the budget committee. John, you've called us together, now make your case."

I review the basics, from the months of terrorist attacks that have plagued the country to Mel receiving the odd indication from one of his fellow soldiers that these attacks had something to do with our little trip two years back. Supposedly we witnessed something there that has to do with the current troubles.

Ruiz rubs his goatee and says, "That was a while ago. How about Ortiz and Powell? Have you talked to them?"

Mel says, "Both are dead. Officially suicides, but I've got a good CID source that says they were murdered and for some reason it's being broomed. That leaves us and Bastinelli."

Ruiz looks stunned. Then he says, "Where the hell is Bastinelli?"

There's a pause before Deacon says, "He's turned prepper and lives in New Hampshire, off the grid."

Mel says, "Anybody remember anything we did or saw that might be relevant?"

Two years. Lot of water under the proverbial bridge. Back then I was a married man, and now I'm a widower.

Some of my memories about that classified trip remain a bit fuzzy. But a scene crystallizes in my mind: Canvas tents, men and women in medical garb working hard to save some wounded civilians.

Ruiz says, "I remember hearing a couple of rumors about a village from our local guides, but it had nothing to do with our mission so I didn't pay much attention."

I ask, "What did they say?"

Ruiz says, "That a village had been destroyed a few klicks from near where we crossed the border."

"*Destroyed* as in bombed?" I ask.

"*Destroyed* as in flattened from one end to the other, nothing left but broken stone, timber, dust, and the bodies of the villagers and their animals. Our guides heard about it and thought we had done it."

Mel says, "Bullshit. No strike missions since the pullout, just classified missions like ours."

Deacon says, "I heard the same rumor from the locals and dismissed it just like you. We would have been briefed if an attack package had been delivered in our vicinity. It couldn't have been our forces."

I say, "But suppose that somehow, somewhere, forces under our control mistakenly destroyed that village and killed innocents. Maybe that's the connection to the terrorist attacks. A revenge mission, some sort of jihad."

Ruiz says, "Two years later?"

"C'mon," I say. "Tribes up in those mountains have been bearing grudges and swearing blood oaths since the Brits marched in two centuries ago. What's two years to avenge an injustice?"

Deacon slowly nods, and I think, *She knows something. She knows something.*

Outside, I hear the hooting of owls.

Ruiz says, "John, what about you?"

I say, "I remember coming across an aid camp over the border. Anybody else?"

Mel says, "Hold on, yeah, give me a minute."

Ruiz says, "Don't waste that minute."

CHAPTER

49

MAYNARD AND HIS armed crew are in position, wearing tactical gear, ballistic helmets, and vests that say in loud yellow letters NCSBI SWAT—NCSBI is for North Carolina State Bureau of Investigation. If Maynard were a grateful sort of guy, he'd thank Sampson for bringing his army pal to a location so remote, there's only one streetlight in the area.

Maynard raises a fist and gives a quick pump, and they move quietly and deliberately through the darkness and across the dirt road to the cottage where Sampson and his army friend are staying.

Too bad that in about thirty seconds, Sampson won't be alive to hear any thanks.

CHAPTER 50

THE LOOK ON Deacon's face reminds me of something I saw on the highly classified and remote airfield in Tajikistan where we were stationed in tents on wooden floors. I'd just met Deacon but I'm certain that the expression she wears today is identical to the one she had while talking to a two-star army general not long before we crossed over to Afghanistan.

What was that general's name? Why was he there? I say, "Elizabeth, anything to add? Any intelligence reports or sources indicate that these domestic attacks might be someone trying to get revenge?"

"No, not a word." She says it so quickly and confidently that I'm sure she's lying.

On the Zoom screen, Ruiz's head starts to slide away, and Mel calls out, "Hey, Paco, secure your camera. Looks like you're about to pass out and sink to the floor."

His hand reaches out, and the screen returns to its earlier position. "Considering what we're talking about, getting drunk and hitting the floor might be a good idea. What next, guys?"

I say, "We all meet with General Grissom and his interagency team."

At my side, Mel says, "Sounds good. Elizabeth?"

She shrugs. "Can't hurt, I suppose. When?"

I look at my watch. "Based on what I know about them, they're probably meeting right now, and they'll schedule another session for tomorrow morning. Plenty of time for you and Ruiz to haul your asses to DC." I check out Ruiz but the screen has shifted once more; the camera is pointing at the ceiling.

Mel says, "Jesus, Paco, fix your screen again, will you?"

Something seems off.

Something sounds off.

The owls outside have stopped their hooting.

I hear a creak of a wooden step outside the door.

The screen belonging to Ruiz is shifting again, and his face appears.

His eyes are wide open.

The camera lowers, lowers, until the raw stump of his neck appears, dripping blood in long streams.

CHAPTER

51

IN FRONT OF the cottage, Maynard holds up a hand. He'd thought about NVGs, but with the moonlight, it's bright enough.

He turns and points to Cameron, who hustles up to a window, grabs a flash-bang grenade off his vest, pulls the pin, punches in the window, and tosses the device inside.

"Go!" Maynard says in a sharp whisper, and they move almost as one.

CHAPTER

52

THINGS MOVE QUICKLY.

Mel and I take out our weapons; I slam the computer lid shut and heave aside the kitchen table as I hear the sound of glass smashing.

A small cylindrical object hits the floor. "Flash-bang!" I yell.

The explosion rocks the cottage, and even with my eyes covered and my body turned away, the bright flare of the grenade gets through.

But I'm not blinded.

I turn and drop to one knee, and Mel and I start firing on whoever is opening the door. We saw Ruiz's severed head; this is not a time to ask, *Hey, who's there?*

We know who's there.

Mel and I shoot the door dead center and pump more rounds on either side. The cottage's walls are thin wood and plaster, and a couple of Molotov cocktails would torch this indefensible place. No time to waste.

Mel yells, "Reloading!"

"Covered," I yell back, and we both duck the return fire. I give Mel a heavy smack on his left shoulder and point to the lake side of the house; we flop on our bellies and fire front as we crawl toward the rear porch.

We get to the porch and in the moonlight see the lake and a dock with two moored kayaks. I send one last volley out to the front and another at a shadow moving across the yard. I see the shadow collapse.

Mel sets down suppressing fire too, and I follow, hitting the dirt, and we crawl, then leap across the road in front of the cottage and take cover in the woods.

We catch our breath and I'm tempted to open fire again, but I don't know how many guys we're up against, how well armed they are, or whether they have backup.

Mel says, "Look."

As I burrow into the dirt and leaves around the base of a wide pine tree, I say, "What the hell am I looking at?"

"Lights," Mel says, lifting his head a bit. "My neighbors tend to keep to themselves, but they won't ignore the sound of a flash-bang or gunshots. We keep low, we can keep to the shoreline, and—"

A sharp *snap* and the top of Mel's head is blown off.

CHAPTER 53

IN ONE OF the Pentagon's conference rooms, the dreary status meeting is coming to an end, and General Wayne Grissom is struggling to keep a positive outlook. At least he and his assistant, Colonel Carla Kendricks, a rising star at the Pentagon, will have a short walk back to his office. Nearly two years ago, impressed by the colonel's work ethic, Grissom chose her for a position usually staffed by a lieutenant general.

The short walk back is about all there is to be thankful for this evening. He takes one more look around the shiny table at the meeting's attendees. With each successive meeting, there've been fewer and fewer leaders and more and more followers. Those in positions of power are sensing failure, and by not attending the meetings, they can claim they were out of the loop.

Sitting next to Grissom in a dark blue power suit and white blouse is the president's chief of staff, Helen Taft, who's been uncharacteristically quiet in representing the White House.

One *Post* columnist had referred to Helen Taft—who's red-haired and red-faced, though the shades of red are different—as the most even-tempered person in Washington because she was constantly in a rage. But it's not Taft whom Grissom feels has it in for him; it's another woman.

Now the only person who's made every meeting, the only one who hasn't given up, catches Grissom's eye and speaks. "Is that it, General?" asks Doris Landsdale, secretary of homeland security.

Grissom says, "Unless someone is holding something back, I suppose it is."

She taps the fingers of her right hand on the table. "To repeat, then, our friends at the NSA and the CIA are still listening to the chatter, and so far there's been no increase of encrypted messages at cell towers we're surveilling. Meaning what? They're waiting for further orders? Or they've decided to give up and go back to their moms' basements?"

Grissom thinks with envy of his predecessors, especially the generals of World War II. Marshall, Eisenhower, Patton, Truscott, Bradley, Abrams—they all had one advantage that Grissom does not. Back then, the enemies were clear, well defined, out in the open. They didn't hide in the shadows or at home like the people who've been killing Americans over the past several months.

To Secretary Landsdale, he says, "We don't know what we don't know. The moment we get clearer intelligence—perhaps a target—we'll inform you. In the meantime, Secretary Landsdale, with all due respect, our terrorist opponents aren't basement-dwellers. They show sophisticated planning and technical proficiency. Agent Mahoney? What do you have to say?"

Like most of the others at the table, the FBI man looks exhausted. "We're still chasing down leads. We're even bringing agents home from embassy assignments overseas. But as you noted, General, nothing concrete, nothing solid."

Landsdale shakes her head. "Given the YouTube videos showing how to make IEDs, car bombs, and other types of weapons, I don't think so."

"Meaning what?" Grissom asks.

"I still don't see the evidence of a large-scale operation that'll result in us curbing civil liberties, putting troops and armored vehicles on the street, and trying to control news coverage. That kind of shit happens in Venezuela. Not here."

Grissom says, "Then we'll have to agree to disagree on this issue, Madam Secretary."

She snaps, "Unless we do this the right way, this will be the new normal. Don't you see it? Every time a bunch of knuckle-draggers get together on the dark web and start raising hell, we'll overreact and go after them. More cops and police departments using tactical gear, using armored cars, tear gas, machine guns. It's like using a sledgehammer to kill a mosquito."

"Then what do you suggest, Madam Secretary?"

"Let local and state law enforcement take over," she says. "They know their turf; they probably know the players. Give them support where asked. The federal government should be in an assisting role, General, not taking lead."

The eyes of everyone at the table are going from Grissom to Landsdale and back. Mommy and Daddy are fighting.

Grissom looks for an ally, says, "Ms. Taft, do you have anything to add?"

Just a crisp shake of the head. Grissom thinks, *No, she doesn't want to get in the middle of this.*

Looking back at the homeland secretary, Grissom says, "If we don't do this right, pretty soon we might not have a federal government. And then you'll get what you want—the states will be on their own."

CHAPTER 54

OVERALL, MAYNARD FEELS good about the operation, even with just a 50 percent success rate. He came in with three personnel and he's leaving with three personnel. Cameron and Roccilli are bitching and moaning because they took rounds to their ballistic vests, but they're alive, although they might have broken ribs.

Juarez got the worst of it, with a round taking off most of his left pinkie, but since he's right-handed, a stump wrapped with a bandage won't slow him down much. Juarez endures the pain in silence, and Maynard gives him props.

Maynard sustained a hit to his ballistic helmet. His head is throbbing, a reminder that if the bullet had been a few inches lower, this crew would be wondering what to do with his body.

Cameron comes back from the tree line. "Definitely Carr," he says. "Face is fucked up, but yeah, it's him."

"Any blood trail leading out?" Maynard asks.

"Nope," Cameron says. "Sampson got away. Probably heading down the shoreline."

Maynard rubs his aching head. “Maybe. But the guy is good. The best I’ve ever come up against.”

Juarez asks, “Meaning what?”

“Meaning I wouldn’t be surprised if the slippery bastard is out there in the dark looking at us.”

Roccilli says, “Think we should try to track him?”

“You want to give him another chance to shoot you? When he and his bud were in the cabin, that was a good target. Going after him now won’t have a happy outcome. No, we’ve done what we can. We’re following him. We’ll get him tomorrow or the day after.”

“Why not stake out his vehicle?” Cameron asks.

“Sure, and explain that to the neighbors while we’re stumbling through their property.”

Juarez says, “We should burn this place down, then.”

“Why?” Maynard asks. “You pissed because you got an ouchie on your left finger? Really? Macho man like you? You want to burn down his place for revenge?”

Juarez and the two others are quiet. Maynard says, “You see the lights around the lake? That means neighbors. They hear gunshots, they figure, *What the hell, maybe somebody’s drunk, shooting into the air.* We burn down this cottage, the volunteer fire department will respond and they’ll see the spent brass and the guy in the woods with half a head. Then local law enforcement gets spun up. No, we get going now, regroup, and choose a time to hit him again.”

Nods from his crew and they start moving back to where their truck is hidden. Maynard can’t resist. He pauses, waves to the woods. “Later, John.”

CHAPTER 55

IN MY HIDING spot, I grit my teeth in anger and to control the shivering that threatens to take over my body. I'm focusing on my own survival and getting what intelligence I can on the crew who ambushed us.

Mel is dead.

And it's my fault.

I should have prepped the cottage better, should have set up better routes for bailing out when the shooting broke out, and we should have kept on moving once we got out of the cottage. Instead, we felt a bit safe outside of the kill zone and turned to gauge our enemy, and that's when Mel got clipped.

I keep looking at the crew. There are four of them and they're talking and pointing, and my pistol is firm in my cold hand. But I don't have a good shot. I could get one, maybe two, but then I'd be a target for return fire and in an indefensible position, one Glock pistol against several automatic weapons. This isn't a James Bond movie, where one guy can take out four men armed with high-powered machine guns in a lengthy shooting scene. In the real world, that one guy would be down in fifteen seconds.

I wait.

Continue to shiver.

I hear voices rise up and then they're done. They grab their gear and start walking up the dirt road—luckily away from my vehicle—then the tail-end guy stops. He's partially illuminated by this stretch's lone streetlight. It feels like he's staring right at me.

He raises his arm and calls out, "Later, John."

Then he joins his three companions, and they fade into the darkness.

And with horror I think, *I know that guy.*

CHAPTER

56

LAURIE PIERCE IS waiting outside George Washington University's Aston residence hall—reserved for grad students like herself—looking for the Uber that's bringing her boyfriend down New Hampshire Avenue. He's going to pick her up for a late dinner and—hopefully—a status change for both of them.

Instead of boyfriend and girlfriend, they'll be fiancé and fiancée.

It's a warm pleasant night, lots of traffic zooming by, and she feels slightly embarrassed at what she knows. Because she shouldn't know.

Her boyfriend, Arthur Foss, goes to GWU's Graduate School of Political Management; she's a grad student at GWU's School of Media and Public Affairs. On their second date, Arthur said, "I can see a future when I'm a congressman from Connecticut, and you're a reporter at the *Post* who's coming at me."

She smiled and said, "And if you do anything illegal, I'll burn your ass and put it on the front page."

With mock disappointment, Arthur said, "Even though I'm a fellow GWU grad?"

"*Especially* because you're a fellow GWU grad."

That led to lots more laughs, another bottle of wine, and an overnight in Georgetown at the condo his father owned. Arthur comes from a wealthy family in Greenwich, Connecticut; Laurie is from a small town in a depressed logging county in Oregon. She gets by on scholarships, grants, part-time work at Starbucks, and lots of ramen noodles.

There. That must be him.

A dark blue Honda with an Uber sticker in the window passes the nearby Yours Truly DC, a four-star hotel. He's right on time, and someday soon, Laurie knows there'll be no more ramen noodles for her, because dear Arthur made a mistake last night. He has a habit of e-mailing funny cartoons and memes to their parents and his two sisters, and last night, he sent out an e-mail that mistakenly included Laurie in the address field.

The message said: Tomorrow night I give this! Wish me luck! Attached was a photo of a blue box from Tiffany, open and displaying a diamond ring in a gold setting.

So she knows, and she smiles when the Uber stops and Arthur steps out and holds the door open for her.

She gives him a quick kiss, climbs in, and fastens the seat belt. Arthur, always well dressed and well groomed, looking more like a successful trial attorney than a grad student, sits beside Laurie and grabs her hand as the car starts moving.

"Hon," he says, "tonight…it's going to be special."

"Special how?" she asks as the Uber comes to a halt at the intersection with L Street.

He pauses, smiling, his brown eyes dancing with laughter, then says, "Oh, I can't wait. Hold on."

He reaches into a side pocket of his dark blue suit coat. Laurie hears a noise and looks up, and it seems like the sun is glaring right next to them.

CHAPTER 57

EVEN FROM TWO blocks away, Ned Mahoney can smell what's ahead for him at the latest bombing site: gasoline, burned rubber, charred vehicle upholstery, and the sickly sweet scent of seared flesh from the most recent victims to die on the streets of the nation's capital.

His ID gets him through the police perimeter on L Street, and he parks his FBI-issue black Impala as close as he can to where the car bomb went off. The street is crowded with police cruisers, fire department vehicles, and even trucks from the local utility, Washington Gas, there to switch off gas mains in case something else blows up. High-intensity floodlights shine down from tall metal stands, and the roar of the generators sets his teeth on edge.

He walks up to a stretch of yellow tape, flashes his FBI ID one more time, and makes the latest in a series of sad, tired walks, surveying the scene.

The car exploded at the intersection of L Street and New Hampshire Avenue NW. Windows in the surrounding businesses were shattered. One overhead traffic light is dangling from wires. A fire truck is still hosing down the suspected car bomb, which is now just a twisted frame and four shredded and melted tires.

A DC ambulance roars out, and Mahoney steps closer, notes five shapes under five yellow blankets on the street.

At least five dead, then.

Damn it.

Cars are strewn around as if they were toys grabbed and tossed by some angry child. The most heavily damaged vehicle appears to be a Honda. It's a charred mess, its roof peeled off.

Three yellow blankets are inside, one over the driver's seat, two in the rear.

Okay. At least eight dead, then.

A young man in a dark suit wearing his FBI shield around his neck comes over and says, "Agent Burt Nansen."

Ned identifies himself and says, "What do we have here?"

"Apparent car bomb," Nansen says, notebook and pen in his smooth hands. "Parked in an illegal spot over there. Most of the damage was to storefronts and pedestrians. This Honda over here"—he points to it with his pen—"took the brunt of the explosion. There were three people in there, an Uber driver and two passengers."

Firefighters carrying tools and a large yellow sheet approach the charred Honda.

Agent Nansen says, "Found the ID of one of the two victims in the rear of the Honda. The woman was a student at a place called George Washington. Is that near here?"

Mahoney stares at the young agent in disbelief. "You don't know where George Washington University is?"

"Sorry, sir, I'm from the Augusta, Maine, field office," he says. "I was temporarily transferred to DC to help shore up the staffing. My apologies."

Mahoney shakes his head. "None needed. Sorry."

"Yes, sir," the young agent says, and he spends the next few minutes telling Mahoney the familiar story of how the investigation will proceed: interviewing witnesses, tracking down any surveillance-camera footage along L Street and New Hampshire Avenue, and looking into the origin of the car that held the bomb. Was it stolen? Purchased? Borrowed from some innocent?

All of which will probably turn up nothing of use. It hasn't for the previous car bombings in the District.

Mahoney hands his business card to the young agent as a dark blue stretch van bearing the insignia of the Office of the Chief Medical Examiner and the flag of the District arrives. Men and women, their dark blue windbreakers marked ATF in large yellow letters, are examining the bombed vehicle. "It looks like you've got a good handle on the scene, Agent Nansen. Call me if anything of interest comes up."

"Yes, sir," he says, and Mahoney looks over at the destroyed Honda with the three victims. Two DC firefighters have unfolded the large yellow sheet, blocking bystanders' view of the delicate yet ugly work happening on the other side: removing burned bodies that have partially fused with the burned upholstery of the car.

Mahoney breathes deeply through his mouth, walks a few steps, takes out his phone, and hits a number on speed-dial.

It rings twice and then John Sampson's recorded voice says, "You know the drill."

After a sharp beep, Mahoney says, "John, you okay? Give me a ring ASAP. Things here are…they're getting worse. Hope you and your army buddy have found something out. We…" He pauses, then says, "We have nothing. Not a damn thing. We're depending on you, John."

Mahoney ends the call and walks away from the scene. Now he'll head to the trauma ICU at GWU Hospital to see how Alex is doing.

But his thoughts go back to John.

This is the third time he's tried to call him.

Why isn't he answering? Where is he?

CHAPTER 58

I WAIT UNTIL I can't wait anymore, then I wait a little longer.

The yard is quiet.

Even the smell of gunpowder has dissipated.

Time to move.

I slosh my way out from underneath the boat dock, Glock pistol in my shivering hands. I move as quickly and quietly as I can back into the cottage, strip off my wet clothes, rub myself down with the thick towels in the bathroom, and dress in dry clothes. The inside of the cottage is a mess; it looks like the aftermath of a battle in downtown Baghdad. I don't envy the police detectives who will have to figure out what happened here. I grab my gear bag and leave.

On the dirt road, I quickly walk to my parked Cherokee. Part of me wants to go back to Mel's body and maybe say some words or prayers over him, but the practical side of me is telling me to get the hell out of here before neighbors or cops arrive.

I climb into my Cherokee, switch on the engine, and flip on the heat, and I'm hoping and praying that the spirit of Mel Carr agrees with my decision.

* * *

About an hour later I'm at the Southpark Mall in Colonial Heights, Virginia. I've driven here in silence, not wanting to hear the conspiracy theories and hate being spewed across the satellite-radio bandwidths. Jazz would be a good escape, but I don't want to escape.

I want to think.

I find an empty spot at the south end of the large mall, which has all kinds of stores, from Dick's Sporting Goods to Victoria's Secret and everything in between.

I check my phone and see I have several voice-mail messages from a restricted number, which means it's either someone high up in the Metro Police or Ned Mahoney from the FBI.

I ignore the messages for a moment, take out the surveillance sniffer I used after the attack at the motel, and switch it on. All five lights remain red.

Yet I've been followed, probably since I left DC.

But how? It takes at least five cars to shadow a target vehicle, and that's a lot of work.

Drones?

Maybe, but I've been in some rural areas where the roads are canopied by trees.

How, then?

I get out of my Cherokee, flashlight in hand, and get as much of my large frame under the car as possible, eyeballing every inch of the undercarriage.

It doesn't take long for me to find it: a little black box about the size of a matchbox. I tug it free. It's magnetized. I wiggle my way out along the cold pavement, sit up against the rear wheel, give the little box a close look.

No opening, no seams, no antenna. Just a little black box.

I turn it around in my big hands and I'm reminded of something, a training drill a few years back with the Metro Police and technicians from the Nuclear Emergency Support Team, part of the Department of Energy. Their mission is to respond to any number of nuclear emergencies, including—and most important—threats from terrorists or criminals who claim to have dirty bombs or small nuclear devices. If such a threat is received, a team with a variety of detection equipment is sent to the target area to look for the telltale radioactive signatures. During drills, like the one I participated in, low-level radioactive sources were placed around the city. Nothing dangerous, but radioactive enough to be detected with the right equipment.

I turn the little shape over again. Radioactive sources that looked similar to this one.

That's why I've been followed so well and so closely: overhead drones—hell, even satellites—are tracking this radioactive source firmly attached to my vehicle.

Meaning?

I take a closer look at the radioactive source.

Meaning that the people out there planning and executing these random terrorist attacks and planning for the big one aren't members of an oddball militia group or a bunch of misfits who got their hands on weapons and explosives.

Oh, there are tracking drones that can be purchased on the open market, but nothing you can buy from Amazon has a highly sensitive radiation detector tacked on.

I rub the metal.

The people who are chasing me, who nearly killed Alex Cross, and who have murdered hundreds of innocent Americans over these past months are heavily funded and have government or military-level assets.

People like Harry Maynard. The man who'd said, *Later, John.*

Former New York Police officer. Former Army Special Forces.

Last I heard, he was a Treasury enforcement agent, chasing down financial criminals connected with drug cartels all over the world. Maynard was hard, tough, and smart, and I had gotten to know him over the years at training sessions involving security officers and agents from various federal agencies.

What made him cross over to whatever the hell is going on out there? Is it a foreign-sponsored group hiring former military? A rogue element in the U.S. government? A militia with deep-pocketed fellow travelers?

I don't know, but if it has to do with Afghanistan and our mission, I won't learn anything by sitting on my ass in a Virginia mall parking lot.

I get up and take in the buildings and nearby vehicles. I spot a familiar brown UPS delivery truck parked near the sidewalk, flashers blinking, and I casually stroll over and put the tracker under the bumper. In a few minutes, this tracker will be going places.

I need some supplies, and I need to move quickly, because I'm heading for Vermont and Elizabeth Deacon, the CIA officer who led us into Afghanistan and who has seemingly lit the fuse of one huge explosion.

CHAPTER

59

MY TRIP NORTH is delayed for a few minutes, because when I get to the entrance of the Southpark Mall, there's a line outside, and I quickly spot the metal detectors and the security guards with wands slowly letting shoppers in.

Even with my detective's shield, I don't want to pass through while carrying my pistol; people would remember me. I wander away from the line, find a row of shrubbery planted out front, kneel down as if I'm tying my shoe, and hide my Glock there.

About forty minutes later, I've gotten what I need from the shops in the mall, but I'm not finished.

I need new transportation, because finding one radioactive tracking cube on my vehicle doesn't mean there isn't another one, maybe even more carefully hidden. But one tracker is traveling with UPS, which'll confuse my enemies, and confusing enemies is always a good strategy.

I take a position outside a chain steak-and-seafood restaurant that has a separate entrance from the mall, and I wait, pacing back and forth behind a set of concrete planters, glancing at my watch like I'm waiting for someone.

There are some open parking spaces near the restaurant, and I wait and wait, knowing that the people tracking me might be circling the mall parking lot, looking for a very tall and very large Black man who stands out in crowds.

Since my wife's death, I've not been much of a praying man, but I do offer up prayers and requests to the sweet spirit of my wife: *Billie, I need your help. I need some sort of intercession. Please help me.*

I pace some more.

A silver Lexus comes up and parks in a nearby space. Two young well-dressed women in heels come out, one a blonde, the other a redhead. The redhead is the driver, and as she accompanies her friend to the restaurant, she makes a quick motion with her right hand.

Beep-bleep.

The Lexus is now locked.

But it's not safe.

A few minutes later, I follow the women into the restaurant, still without my Glock, and that turns out to be a wise choice, as the entrance to the joint is guarded by two fellows about my weight but a foot shorter, both wearing tight black T-shirts and black slacks.

They're quick and polite as they wand me, and one apologizes. "Sorry we have to do this, bro. But it's new rules, you know?"

I raise a hand, smile. "No worries. There's some crazy shit out there and we've all got to adjust."

I step into the dark and cool restaurant, the dining area to the right, the large bar up ahead. I spot the red-haired woman at the end of the bar and slowly walk toward her, dodging waiters and waitresses exiting the kitchen. The place has leather booths, white linen tablecloths, and exposed dark wooden beams and brickwork.

I maneuver my way to the bar. The attractive redhead, sitting on a barstool, is deep in conversation with her blond companion, and I stand behind her, hold up my hand, and wave at the overworked bartender at the other end.

A couple of minutes pass, and the redhead notices me and says, "Trying to get a drink?"

I smile down at her. "Trying not to die of thirst."

She smiles back. "I'll get up from my seat and you can take it. Maybe he'll see you better."

"That's fine," I say, my left arm still up. "But I appreciate it."

Her smile gets wider. "I don't mind at all. Besides, I warmed it up for you."

We laugh at the flirtation. I keep trying to get the bartender's attention with my left hand.

While slipping my right hand into her purse and removing her Lexus fob.

Once I'm outside in the fresh air—after lying to the nice redhead and saying I needed to call and check in on my mother (wherever she might be)—I pick up my Glock and head over to the Lexus. I *beep-bleep* the door open, slide in, adjust the seat quickly, and start it up.

I drive around to my Cherokee, transfer my duffel bag and other belongings into the freshly stolen Lexus, then exit the mall and get back on I-95, heading north. The Cherokee is left behind; the radioactive source I pulled free is doing its silent job in the moving UPS truck for my unknown watchers out there.

After about ten minutes, I find what I'm looking for. I say, *Thanks again, Billie,* and pull the car over on a bridge spanning what looks to be a large stream or small river. I rummage through a plastic bag and take out a burner phone I purchased and activated back at the mall.

Over the next few minutes I transfer some important phone

numbers to the new phone, and when I'm finished, I get out of the Lexus and walk to the bridge railing.

It's a beautiful Virginia night, perfectly still, the air warm, and behind me are the rushing red and white lights of good people heading home or going to work. Each set of lights represents a person with a life story to be told, so many tales of love and loss, setbacks and triumphs, all taking place in this wonderful nation.

But I know there are other powerful and far-reaching forces that are also in play this night, rushing to some type of explosive and dangerous end.

I look at my old phone in my right hand. It's a special phone, given to me months ago by Ned Mahoney of the FBI. It's unhackable and untraceable. It's a perfect phone for what I'm facing in the next few days.

I trust Ned Mahoney, and I would trust him with my life and that of my daughter. But I don't know who put this phone together or who gave it to Ned to give to me.

I hold my hand over the bridge and drop the expensive, complicated phone into the river.

It's time to resume driving and not stop until I get to Vermont and Elizabeth Deacon.

As I get back into the stolen Lexus, I again remember the urgent cautionary words of Ned Mahoney:

Don't trust anyone.

CHAPTER

60

BREE STONE IS yawning as she walks down the hospital hall to see Alex in the ICU. Behind her, in the waiting room, both Nana Mama and Ali are fast asleep, Ali stretched out with his head in his great-grandmother's lap.

Damon and Jannie are back at the house, heating up some leftovers to bring with them, since there's only so much hospital food they can stand. Nana Mama even had a suggestion: "You bring a bowl of my chicken gumbo, and we'll sneak it into Alex's room."

"But Nana Mama, you know he can't eat."

Arms folded, chin jutting out, Nana Mama said, "I don't intend to feed him, girl, I'm not stupid. If that good surgeon thinks he's aware of what's going on around him in that damn coma of his, then let's put a bowl of that gumbo under his nose. Maybe the scent will stir him awake."

Bree smiles as she walks to the ICU, recalling that brief moment when everyone laughed over Nana Mama's fine idea.

A nurse recognizes her and opens the sliding door to the ICU, and as Bree walks in, she senses that something is off, something is disturbed.

She turns the corner and sees a cluster of folks around Alex's room, and her hands grow cold. There are DC Metro Police officers there, and two large men from her security firm, the Bluestone Group.

No one is smiling as she approaches.

"What's wrong?" she says to no one in particular.

A DC Metro officer says, "Ma'am, you shouldn't go in there."

"The hell I shouldn't," Bree says, pushing past him.

The room is crowded with nurses and doctors, and their voices are low and urgent as they work on her Alex. Various medical devices are emitting either alarm signals or a constant tone. One doctor is leaning over Alex's hidden head, and a nurse is drawing medication into a syringe, and Bree's mouth instantly goes dry.

A nurse spots her and says, "Ma'am, you shouldn't be in here!"

"The hell I shouldn't, that's my husband," she snaps back, surprised at how cool and even her voice is when her heart is breaking at what she sees. All that's visible of her Alex—the smart, loving, complex, and sometimes infuriating husband and father—is one bare arm with IV tubes in it.

Bree can't even see his face, as swollen and bruised as it is and with the ventilator tube taped to his mouth.

If Alex is about to pass, she needs to be close.

"What's going on?" she demands.

One of the nurses says without looking at her, "We've been weaning him from his sedation, hoping to wake him up so we could remove his breathing tube and get him off the ventilator. But he started crashing. Doctor, his blood pressure is really low, seventy over fifty, and his heart rate is one hundred thirty."

"What's his oxygen saturation?" a doctor asks.

"Eighty-six percent and dropping."

The last time Bree was here, Alex's oxygen saturation was 100 percent.

He's passing. "I'm his wife," she repeats, "and I'm going to be with him." Bree steps forward, and no one stops her, no one tells her to go.

But the frantic work goes on.

"We need that pulse ox up, damn it," one of the physicians says.

Bree gets as close as she can to Alex. "Right here, Alex," she says through tears. "Right here, forever."

CHAPTER 61

IN HIS LARGE yet spartan office at the Pentagon, General Wayne Grissom waits for his next appointment to arrive, and while he's not looking forward to it, he considers it his duty, as old-fashioned as that sounds. American taxpayers foot the bill for the Defense Department's annual $725 billion budget, and as one of those accountable for its spending, he sees it as his responsibility to allow himself to be interviewed by certain members of the fourth estate.

There's a soft knock on the door, and his aide, Colonel Carla Kendricks, steps in. "Sir, are you ready?"

Grissom stands up. "Absolutely. Show him in."

The door opens wider and a familiar man strides in. He's in his mid-thirties, with thin brown hair, and he's wearing black-rimmed glasses, a blue dress shirt with no tie, a navy blue suit jacket, and gray slacks.

Justin Foote, national affairs reporter for the *Washington Post.*

He smiles, nods, reaches over for a quick handshake, and takes a chair in front of Grissom's wide but clear desk.

"Thanks for seeing me on such short notice this evening, General Grissom," Justin says.

Grissom takes his own seat. "Glad I can help, Justin, but I'm afraid I can only give you ten minutes."

Justin takes out an old-fashioned reporter's notebook and a ballpoint pen. "That should be enough, I hope."

"Let's get to it, then. A reminder that from now on, anything I say is to be attributed to a 'senior military official.' Agreed?"

Justin nods. "Agreed." He flips a page on his notebook. "It's just been announced that the president is going to address the nation tonight. Were you aware of this, General?"

Grissom thinks, *Crap, no,* and aloud he says, "What do you think?"

A faint smile. "Any idea what he'll be talking about?"

"The current crisis, I imagine."

Justin says, "The continuing terrorist attacks that began last April and that have continued right up to this morning. At least several hundred Americans dead, thousands injured."

"There's no question there, Justin." He checks his watch. "Seven minutes left."

"Here's a question then, General," he says. "For the past few days, there's been a secret committee working to locate the command, control, and financing of these terrorist attacks. Local agencies, intelligence agencies, Defense Department. I have contacts in most of those agencies. I hear you're running this secret committee."

Grissom pauses. If Justin has this story, others will get it as well. "That's true," he says.

"Any progress made?"

"Some, but not enough."

"Why is that?" Foote asks.

He spends a few minutes explaining the technological challenges of trying to track down a well-organized and well-financed organization that reaches across the United States and uses the latest technology to keep two or three steps ahead of investigators.

"You said you believe it's a large, organized, and well-financed group," Justin says. "Some on your committee disagree. Like Secretary of Homeland Security Landsdale."

"You've talked to her?"

"At length."

"Care to share?"

Justin smiles. "You've been straight with me since becoming chair, General. I'll tell you this. She thinks you and others are overreacting, that you're taking a cannon to go after a mosquito. She thinks the terrorist attacks are being conducted by loosely linked militia groups across the country and that a large, unwieldy organization like the committee you're heading is too clumsy to respond quickly. She also thinks it's setting a terrible precedent and will turn this nation into a security state."

"That's quite an opinion," Grissom says.

"And what's your opinion?"

Grissom feels anger rising up inside of him, and he knows what he's about to say would probably be a career-ender in a normal world.

But the world hasn't been normal for months. He's been given a job to do by the president, and by God, he's going to do it.

The general says, "With all due respect to Secretary Landsdale, she has no idea what she's talking about. She has no tactical or strategic vision of how to deal with these terrorist attacks, and her theory is dead wrong."

Justin's hand moves quickly as he writes this down, then he looks up. "Uh, General, just to make sure I know the rules—this is still all on background, correct?"

Grissom makes another decision. "No. That last part is all on the record. Print it."

CHAPTER

62

BREE WATCHES ALEX'S face as the doctors and nurses crowd around him, trying to keep him from slipping away.

A nurse looks up at the monitors and says, "Doctor, BP is still dropping, heart rate still increasing."

The doctor says, "Quiet, everyone."

Through the crowd standing around her Alex, Bree sees the doctor put a stethoscope on his chest. He shakes his head, removes the earpieces from his ears. "I'm not hearing any breath sounds in his left lung, and his trachea is deviated to the right. Is the chest tube clogged? He's got another tension pneumo."

The doctor looks at the monitors, shakes his head again. "We'll do a needle decompression."

More quick yet steady movement from the personnel around Alex, and Bree is bumped into a few times, but that doesn't matter. She's staying near Alex, where she belongs.

"Okay," the doctor says when the nurse hands him a large needle. "Here we go."

Bree watches, frozen, as the doctor swabs the skin below Alex's left clavicle with an antiseptic solution and then inserts a needle straight into his chest.

There's a hiss of air, and as one, the small group of medical personnel look up at the monitors.

A nurse says, "BP is increasing, heart rate is dropping, and pulse ox is up to ninety."

"A close call, eh?" the physician says. "Now let's get a new chest tube in place." The nurses assemble the needed apparatus to do the job.

Bree closes her eyes and whispers a prayer, then takes Alex's hand and squeezes it. She wants to believe that Alex squeezes her hand back, however slightly.

About fifteen minutes later, Bree is in the waiting room with Nana Mama and Ali. One of the ICU physicians, Dr. Tom Smith, comes in. He's tired but looks pleased.

Bree, Nana Mama, and Ali are sitting in a row holding hands, and Dr. Smith sits in front of them. "What happened is this," he says. "As we were weaning Alex off sedation to see if we could take him off the ventilator, his heart rate went up and his blood pressure began dropping."

Nana Mama asks, "What does that mean?"

Dr. Smith says, "In this case, it meant that air was going into his chest cavity, not his lungs, and there was no way for that air to get out, so the pressure built up around his heart and prevented it from pumping. I did what the paramedics did—I inserted a needle to release that air, and once the pressure on his heart was relieved, it was able to pump normally. He's in stable condition at the moment."

Bree holds Ali's and Nana Mama's hands tight. "Sounds like a setback."

A small nod. "I won't lie to you," he says, "it's a setback, of course. We can't take him off the ventilator at this point. In a day or two, we'll try again. But I have to warn you, if we still have a problem then, we'll have to take him back to the OR to figure out what the issue is."

Bree says in a whisper, "Is he strong enough to go through surgery again?"

The doctor hesitates slightly, which tells Bree volumes. "We'll have to see," he says. "Any other questions?"

Bree looks to Ali and Nana Mama. "I think we're all set for now," Bree says.

"Good," Dr. Smith says, standing up. "Alex is getting the best care in the world, I promise you that. Most likely, this is just a small bump in the road. If other questions come up, just ask one of the nurses to find me."

He gives them a reassuring smile and leaves the room, and Nana Mama lets out a big sigh. "Ali, I have a hankering for a cool treat. Do you think you can show me the way to the cafeteria here so I can see if there's ice cream?"

Ali's face brightens. "Sure, Nana Mama. I know the way."

He gets out of his chair and Nana Mama holds Bree's hand a moment longer. "Can we bring anything back for you?" she asks.

Bree shakes her head. "Thanks, Nana Mama, but right now I can't think of a thing."

Alone now in the waiting room, she allows herself to sob for a few minutes, head in her hands, and then she stops, wipes her eyes with a tissue, and takes a deep breath.

So close. So very, very close.

Alex had been in danger before—he'd been shot at, threatened, nearly killed on a few occasions—but never anything as bad as this. Alex always joked that he was golden, a god ("Not *the* God, but *a* god"), and that none of the enemies he'd collected over the years could hurt him, but Bree knows better.

Gamble again and again, and eventually the house—Death—will win.

Bree whispers, "You come back to me, Alex Cross. I'll take you even if you are a mere mortal."

The door opens, and a man wearing a dark blue business suit, a white shirt, and a light yellow tie comes in. "Ms. Stone? A moment?"

She's confused but then recognizes the man: Jacob Springer, the hospital's director of security. A number of hours ago, the two of them had had a heated but eventually reasonable discussion about how Bree had come to be carrying a weapon on hospital property and why she'd shot the fake nurse who called herself Mary Mullen. Springer knows Alex and is a former DC Metro Police detective himself, which helped defuse the situation.

So far, Bree's security firm hasn't come up with the woman's real identity, even with the clue of the Big Red One tattoo on her upper arm.

"Sure, Mr. Springer," Bree says.

"It's about the woman claiming to be Mary Mullen," he says.

"Right," Bree says. "She should be out of the OR by now. Can I talk to her?"

He shakes his head. "I'm afraid you can't, Ms. Stone."

"Why not?"

"Because she died in surgery."

CHAPTER

63

IN ATLANTA'S WEST End, most of the streetlights are burned out. Waiting in a stolen black Pontiac G6 sedan are Humphrey, a former Atlanta cop who was let go after too many civilian complaints of excessive force, and George, a former Atlanta firefighter who lost his job after stripping the clothes off a rookie and tossing him into a firehouse shower as part of a hazing routine. (The fact that the aforementioned rookie was the nephew of a city councillor didn't help George's case.)

Each has an illegal sawed-off twelve-gauge shotgun in his lap. Inside the row house a few yards from them is a meeting of the local chapter of Black Lives Matter. The two of them plan to break up the meeting, and shotguns are the best weapons to use in close quarters. Pistols and submachine guns, while impressive as hell, can miss, even in a crowded room.

It's not their plan; an anonymous person who seems to know and support their cause provided the money, the weapons, and the strategy.

The radio inside the Pontiac is on, and the president is speaking:

"My fellow citizens, I come to you tonight from this historic Oval Office, where so many of my predecessors have spoken to the American people about important issues facing this great nation..."

Humphrey says, "All right, enough of this fool. Let's get the job done."

"Works for me."

"Since last April, our homeland has been under constant and deadly attack by terrorists unknown, funded by parties unknown, only united in their desire to kill our fellow citizens and wreak havoc in our daily lives..."

It's night at a remote ranch near Coeur d'Alene, Idaho, when three men—Renaldo, Jesus, and Pharrell—take a break after carefully going through the forests surrounding the main farmhouse. All three men are in NVGs and heavily armed with automatic rifles that have flash and sound suppressors.

The building houses the largest neo-Nazi militia group in this part of the state, and these three men—who previously resided in Los Angeles, where many of their friends and family members were killed or wounded by this neo-Nazi militia—are getting ready to seriously cut down the group's size.

It's not their plan; an anonymous person who seems to know and support their cause provided the money, the weapons, and the strategy.

"How much more time, Renaldo?"

"Sixty seconds, *jefe*."

"You sure you did a good job?"

Renaldo says, "Positive, *jefe*."

The seconds slide by. For the past few weeks, Renaldo has frequently gone to this house, posing as a carpenter and gardener. He endured the taunts and insults from the tattooed residents as he prepped the place for what's about to happen.

Pharrell sees blossoms of lights appear in the house. "Boom," he whispers.

Preset explosive and incendiary devices go off, and those who are desperately trying to escape are learning the windows won't open, and two of the home's three doors are jammed shut.

Only the front door can be opened, and the figures tumbling out of it and running for safety are quickly cut down by the three men firing their automatic weapons.

"This nation has faced great challenges before, but this is the first time that we have suffered constant and nearly daily attacks across our homeland. Many of our fellow citizens have been brutally murdered, and many more grievously injured..."

In Boston, Massachusetts, a clinic offering reproductive services to poor women is blown up. In Lansing, Michigan, two leaders of a prominent anti-abortion organization who are sitting in their BMW at a traffic light are shot to death.

"I pledge to you tonight that your government will continue working diligently to prevent these attacks and to track down those responsible. The terrorists who are in our streets should know that they will face the full wrath and fury of the American people once they are identified..."

Random sniper fire breaks out in Seattle, Detroit, Austin, and El Paso. By the time dawn breaks in the continental United States, scores of American citizens are dead and nearly a hundred are wounded.

"Members of law enforcement, the military, and cybersecurity agencies have been working as one across the nation to meet this terrible challenge. Support them where you can, and report anything—anything at all—that seems suspicious..."

* * *

Justin Foote, national affairs reporter for the *Washington Post,* is in his small and overpriced condo in Georgetown, half listening to CNN's broadcast of the president's speech while working on a story that will appear in tomorrow's paper and will blow this town and the nation apart.

His doorbell rings. He checks the time. His source—he hasn't given her a funny name, like Deep Throat—is right on schedule. He gets up from his desk in the small second bedroom he's converted into a home office, goes to the door, quickly looks through the peephole.

Yep, here she is, and apologies to General Wayne Grissom, but this source has been more forthcoming about what's really going on in the shadows, and her leaks are the foundation of tomorrow's story. "Come on in," he says, and she nods and follows him back to his office, keeping her coat on. Justin says, "If you've got a moment, I'd like you to read the two paragraphs about how the funds for these attacks are obtained and laundered."

"Certainly," she says.

He sits down and says, "Here. Start on this paragraph."

His source leans over his shoulder, and after a minute she says, "Justin, this is incredible. A grand story. Talk about a blockbuster."

He can't help himself; he smiles with pleasure at his source signing off on what he's written. His laptop has a large screen, and the pages are sharp and clear.

Then he feels cold metal on the base of his neck, and the last words he hears are "Too bad nobody's going to read it."

There's blood and brain spatter all over Foote's laptop. She turns it off and shuts it. She sees he's made her job easier by piling up his notebooks in one place, and she quickly packs them away.

Job done.

Time to leave.

The TV is still on.

"But tonight I ask you, the American people, to remain calm and keep trusting your friends and neighbors. The goal of terrorism is terror—to make us retreat from our lives, to make us suspicious and fearful of our countrymen. We are better than that. You are better than that. And I trust in the inherent goodness of the American people."

Part Three

CHAPTER 64

AFTER NEARLY TEN hours of very fast driving—breaking only for two short naps and a quick phone call to FBI agent Ned Mahoney—I'm finally in Slocum, Vermont, where Elizabeth Deacon, our CIA tour guide, supposedly lives. I pull over and rub my eyes. I've had plenty to think about these past several hours, but one scene has been playing over and over in my mind.

Later, John.

My call to Ned went to his voice mail, so I left him a message: "Ned, check into the background of Harry Maynard, a Treasury enforcement agent, former Special Forces, former NYPD, contract worker with the NSA. He and three others ambushed me and Mel Carr a few hours ago. Mel got killed."

I turn on a small flashlight—it's still dark—and cup the beam in my hand so it doesn't flare out and expose me. I scan the detailed map of Vermont I picked up at an all-night gas station just over the border from Massachusetts. It gives me a fair overview of the town of Slocum. A small squiggly line denotes Mast Road, where Deacon lives.

If the information I got from Bree is accurate. If someone from the CIA didn't spoof Bree. If Deacon didn't bail after seeing Ruiz's bloody head displayed on our Zoom call.

Too many ifs.

I check the clock. Close to dawn.

I'm tempted to send her a text saying I'm coming, but I want to surprise her so she won't decide to skip town before I arrive.

I remember Deacon was a light sleeper.

Time to see if that's still true.

Mast Road is one lane, twisty and turning, flanked by two farms and a few houses and not much in the way of street numbers. No sidewalks, just stone walls topped by barbed wire or fences holding in cows or horses.

Deacon's address is 9 Mast Road, but through stopping and starting and using my flashlight, I find just two mailboxes: 1 Mast Road and 11 Mast Road. I spend a few minutes puzzling over this and decide a small two-story home built in the Federal style must be hers.

I pull over about a hundred yards down the dirt road and get out of the stolen Lexus, again apologizing to the sweet young lady who's the real owner. I grab my duffel bag in one hand and hold my Glock in the other and start walking.

It's a long heavy walk. I'm thinking of Alex, of Willow, of Bree and the entire Cross family, and of the attacks, bombings, and snipers out there that are tearing this country apart.

I plan to get to the end of her driveway and send her a text saying *Surprise, I'm here! Let's talk.* There's a lightening of the sky to the east that promises the start of a new day and whatever bad news and horror it will bring.

Like what I see now.

About twenty yards from the driveway, I see a narrow line of bright red light come from near the mailbox. It ends with a red dot in the middle of my chest.

I stop. I call out, "Elizabeth, I certainly hope it's you. John Sampson here."

The dot doesn't move.

CHAPTER 65

I'M RELIEVED WHEN I finally hear her familiar voice: "You alone?"

"I am."

"Where's Mel Carr?"

"Dead," I say. "Back in North Carolina. You want to move your targeting laser, Elizabeth? It's making me nervous."

"What happened in North Carolina?"

"We were followed," I say. "During that Zoom meeting, after Ruiz was killed, the fishing cabin we were in was attacked. Mel got shot."

The little red dot remains centered on my chest.

Then moves away.

"You kill any of them?" she asks.

"Don't think so," I say. "We were pretty much outgunned."

"Too bad. Come on up, we'll grab some coffee and get the hell out of here."

She emerges from a shelter of tree branches and camouflage fabric by the driveway. I join her on a walk to a breezeway connecting her garage to the house, and in the dawn light, I see she's wearing a black jumpsuit, boots, kneepads and elbow pads, a bullet-resistant vest, and a ballistic helmet, and she's carrying a cut-down M4 automatic equipped with night vision and a laser scope and a black duffel bag.

"Expecting visitors?" I ask.

"I am," she says. "You're the first."

"You've been waiting all night?"

At the garage, she puts down her duffel, takes out a thermos, and pours coffee into two tall metal travel mugs. "Don't be stupid, John," she says, handing me a mug. "I figured you were near Fort Bragg, and after poor Ruiz got nailed, you had a certain number of hours to get here."

I don't like being called stupid, and in any other time or place, I would make that clearly known to this CIA officer. But I want to get moving. "So here I am. Where do we go next?"

"To see Gary Bastinelli," she says. "Other than the two of us, he's the last survivor of our mission. We need to talk to him before someone else gets there, though I doubt anything bad will happen to Bastinelli."

I do the gentlemanly thing and pick up her duffel bag. "Say again?"

"Bastinelli is a full hard-core prepper," she says. "Anybody trying to get into his compound without permission is going to run into a buzz saw."

I follow her into the neat and tidy garage, black Chevrolet Tahoe parked in the center. We put our coffee in the cupholders and the gear and the M4 in the rear seat. She gets behind the wheel and I take the passenger side and say, "Do we have permission to visit him? And how do you know this?"

She toggles a switch on the Tahoe and the garage door lifts up. "We do have permission, and it's my job to know things."

I say, "What do you know about me?"

We go down the driveway, and she makes a right. "Don't have the time. Sorry, John."

We travel less than fifty yards and we're getting near the parked Lexus, and I'm about to ask Deacon if she learned anything else after our Zoom call when she says, "Shit."

I say the same thing, haul my Glock out of the holster.

Up ahead is the Lexus on four shot-up and flat tires; the rear window is shattered, bullet rounds pockmark the metal, and I see shapes on the side of the road.

Deacon brakes hard, and the Tahoe shudders to a halt; she throws the car into reverse and slams the accelerator. We roar back up the road in reverse, and then, in a series of quick and smooth moves, Deacon puts the gear in neutral and rotates the steering wheel.

I grab the dashboard of the Tahoe as she expertly does an evasive J-turn and then shifts into drive and punches the accelerator. We speed away from the ambushers.

"Impressive," I say.

"And our goddamn coffee is still in the cupholders," she says.

CHAPTER 66

LESS THAN TWO hours later we're in the small town of Healy, New Hampshire, and it's been an interesting drive, although Deacon knocked down all my attempts to talk to her about the people trying to kill us, the terrorist attacks, and the important thing we might have seen or heard in Afghanistan.

"John, why waste time?" she says. "We'll just be repeating ourselves when we meet up with Bastinelli. If you want to do something useful, catch some shut-eye while I drive. I promise I'll wake you if I see anything interesting."

The interior of the Tahoe is warm, and the seat is comfortable, and damn if I don't sleep some as we get deeper and deeper into rural New Hampshire.

I wake up when we stop. We're on a dirt road surrounded by tall trees. I rub my eyes. "Did I miss downtown Healy?"

Deacon checks something on her iPhone. "There is no downtown Healy. Or uptown Healy. This is an unincorporated community in northern New Hampshire."

"Doesn't sound too appealing."

"There's no town government, no police, no zoning laws, and no property taxes. For a person like Bastinelli, this is very attractive indeed. We should be at his place in a couple of minutes."

I shift my feet, try to stretch my long legs, fail in the tight quarters. "You didn't wake me up. I guess you didn't see anything interesting."

"A male moose humping a female moose, but I didn't think that was your style."

"Good guess."

She drives on, checking the odometer and her watch, then stops.

"This is it," she says.

I lean over and see more brush, saplings, and tree trunks. "I'll take your word for it, even if you do work for the mean ol' CIA."

Deacon turns the steering wheel to the left. "It's not that mean anymore, and I don't work there. I'm just a consultant."

I want to point out that we're not turning into any kind of road or lane, but Deacon seems confident and I keep my mouth shut.

Then I see something unusual. The brush and the saplings aren't high enough to block us and I hear the *whip-snap* sound of the Tahoe driving over firmly packed terrain. And we're not sinking into the soft forest soil.

Interesting—we're on an invisible road.

The brush thins out and now we're on a visible gravel road heading up a gentle slope to a one-story brick and concrete house with what looks to be a concrete watchtower or steeple rising from its center. There's a large, well-tended garden with a small pond off to the left, and attached to the opposite side is a garage, its exterior lined with white propane tanks. About twenty yards away, two cows and a number of goats and chickens mill about a freestanding barn.

The windows in the neat and well-maintained house are narrow, and when Deacon stops the Tahoe and we step out, I look at them again and realize why they're narrow.

Firing slits.

The front door opens up and Gary Bastinelli steps onto the porch, frowning. He has short brown hair and a closely trimmed beard and wears khaki pants, boots, a black T-shirt, and a holstered pistol on his right hip.

"You intend to stay long?" he asks Deacon.

"As long as it takes to get things figured out," she says.

He shrugs. "You get thirty minutes, that's all."

CHAPTER 67

INSIDE, THE HOUSE is a mix of military equipment (weapons, from pistols to automatic rifles mounted on walls; eight small screens on a kitchen counter show various video feeds from around the property) and the cute and mundane (Barbie dolls and Legos scattered across the wooden floor).

Bastinelli points us to chairs at a large dining table, and when Deacon and I sit down, he comes over with muffins and a carafe of coffee.

I say, "Good to see you, Gary. Even under the circumstances."

"Nice of you to say, John. Sorry about Billie."

"Thanks."

"How's Willow doing?"

I say, "Scaring me every day with how tough and smart she is." I look around the house. "Kyra? And the kids, Joe and Vicky?"

He picks up a mug of coffee. "Sent them away to the proverbial undisclosed location. Figured things might get dicey here in the next few days."

Deacon says, "Nice to get caught up on family affairs and all that shit, but let's get to the topic at hand, shall we?"

Gary says, "Who wants to start?"

"I will," I say. "Recently, Alex Cross and I were assigned to an interagency task force looking into the recent bombings and terrorist attacks. Before the second meeting, Alex and I were ambushed outside of DC Metro Police headquarters by professionals. He was seriously wounded and is in the ICU at George Washington University Hospital. Since then, there have been two more attempts to shoot me."

Gary says, "Nice to be popular."

"Safer to be a wallflower," I say, and I spend the next five minutes telling him and Deacon about the task force, my meet-up with Mel, and my interactions with the Army CID. I wrap it up with our Zoom session, the deaths of Ruiz and Mel, and the creepy farewell from Harry Maynard.

That gets Bastinelli's attention. "Were you friends with this guy Maynard?"

"No—we did some training modules together, that's all. Seemed like a good guy at the time. When I figured out who he was, I passed his name and background along to an FBI friend of mine who's on the task force. Maynard is the first real lead we've gotten."

Deacon is quiet. I say, "Elizabeth? Could you run down Maynard's name as well?"

"Doubtful," she says. "You know the Agency isn't supposed to operate in the U.S."

It isn't supposed *to. Major loophole indeed,* I think. I say, "Elizabeth, give us a recap of our mission back in Afghanistan and what happened afterward."

She says, "You two and the others provided overwatch for me as we passed over the border from Tajikistan to Afghanistan. I had three parts to my mission. One, drop off classified ground observation platforms on various trailheads and roads. Overhead satellites and drones do a ninety percent effective job, but we needed to get that number to one hundred percent. Two, meet up with new members of the National Resistance Front, give them financial support for their fight against the new Taliban government."

Bastinelli shakes his head. "In other words, drop off canvas sacks full of Benjamins."

"If it works, it works," she says.

"Sure," he says. "Paying other folks to bleed and die on our behalf—"

I interrupt them. "What was the third part?"

She puts her hands around the coffee mug. "To meet up with a prominent tribal leader in that region of Afghanistan and exchange some…information."

"Did that meet happen?"

"No, he didn't show up," she says. "Even though he'd shown up for five previous meetings, and on time, which is a remarkable achievement in that part of the world."

"Other than that, anything out of the ordinary?"

She shakes her head.

"Just before we left," I say, "I remember you having a heated conversation with an army general in our briefing tent in Tajikistan. You remember that?"

"No," she says.

"You remember the general's name?" I ask.

"John, if I don't remember the meeting, why would I remember his name?"

"Just asking," I say, thinking, *Just verifying, because I remember you talking to that general, and from the looks on your faces, the two of you weren't discussing next year's Super Bowl.* To Bastinelli I say, "Your turn. Anything come to mind?"

He says, "First night we were in-country, I had watch. Cold as hell. And there was a row of flashes in the west…then I heard the rumbling. Did a time count. It was about five miles out."

I know what he's talking about. Sound travels at roughly a thousand feet per second.

"Why didn't you say anything about that when we got moving again?" Deacon asks.

A shrug. "It was five miles out and not in the direction we were going. Didn't seem relevant. But it looked big, like one of the old B-52 Arc Light missions."

"Before Ruiz was killed, he mentioned a bombing," I say. "A couple of locals told him that a village some distance from where we were located had been flattened from one end to another."

"By us?" Bastinelli asks.

Deacon says, "No. I had no information that anything like that was in the works. If a village was attacked, it wasn't by our military."

Bastinelli catches my eye and we exchange a look: *Sure, the CIA can always be trusted. Always.*

He coughs.

Right. As if.

CHAPTER 68

I SAY, "IF the village wasn't struck by our military, who did it?"

With ease, Deacon says, "There are a variety of possibilities. Maybe a false-flag op run by the Russians or the Chinese or an extensive attack by the Taliban with captured air assets once belonging to us on a village they considered rebellious. But you, John, what do you have?"

"There was an aid camp we came across, remember?" I ask. "At the junction of two trails. Three tents, a small generator, and a beat-up white Humvee with red crescents painted on the roof and the hood. We were already late to the next rendezvous point, but I wanted to check them out, make sure there were no Taliban fighters there."

Bastinelli says, "What did you find?"

"Under a fly tent, there were about ten or so locals. Older men, women, children. Lots of bloody wounds, soaked-through bandages. One doctor and one nurse working frantically to help them." I feel the guilt returning—I knew I should have stayed and assisted, but I couldn't. The mission first, always.

"When I was sure the place was secure," I say, "I started moving to catch up with you. But the doctor—he saw me, said something, grabbed my arm, and spat in my face."

"What did he say?" Bastinelli asks.

"It was French," I say. "I didn't understand it."

Deacon looks to me. "Do you remember any of it?"

I close my eyes, thinking back to that moment, knowing we were there illegally, that we were always on the brink of being ambushed, and remembering the doctor with the scraggly beard, red-rimmed eyes, blood on his surgeon's clothes...

I open my eyes. "It sounded like *'Voo lav fate...say vota fote.'*"

Bastinelli says nothing, but I can sense something in Deacon's look. "Elizabeth?" I say.

She says, "Could it have been *'Vous l'avez fait. C'est votre faute'*?"

I didn't know Deacon spoke French. "Yeah, that sounds about right. What does it mean?"

She reaches for her coffee. "'You did it,'" she says. "'It's your fault.'"

I'm about to ask her again what she knows about that village being destroyed when from the other side of the kitchen comes a low-toned *bong-bong-bong.*

Bastinelli gets up from his chair, takes a look at the small TV screens showing exterior views, and flips a switch. The alarm shuts off.

"Visitors," he says.

CHAPTER

69

MAYNARD IS JUST outside Arlington, Virginia, in a small motel room near I-66; interstate traffic passes at a constant low roar. The place is starting to get on his nerves. There are cigarette burns on the walls and the carpet, and the air smells of grease and Lysol. And then there's the clacking keyboard sound coming from the room's other occupant.

The obese man—Willard—is a former fellow contract employee from the National Security Agency, and Maynard owns him, lock, stock, and barrel. Many years ago, due to a slip on Willard's part—when his little man was definitely doing the thinking for the big man—he used the NSA's incredibly powerful and classified computer system to access certain video files on the dark web.

Willard spent only two minutes and ten seconds on that site, but Maynard, his supervisor back then, knew it was enough. An agreement was reached, and Willard's violation was covered by a postdated work authorization.

"But don't think you've gotten away with it," Maynard told him. "Your ass is mine for the foreseeable future. One word of pushback, and your search history and the resulting video will be sent off to the FBI's Crimes Against Children task force. And what you saw and downloaded guarantees a life sentence, which in your case might mean a year or two before some guys in your new home shank you to death."

Now Willard is staring at two large screens fed by banks of servers on the floor beside his fat legs. Even with his fat fingers, he works the keyboard quickly.

"All right," Willard says in a soft voice. "Give me what you've got."

Maynard passes over a thumb drive. Willard takes the drive, and Maynard is repulsed by the touch of Willard's fingers.

"How long to decipher?" he asks.

Willard shrugs. "Depends on how encrypted the voice sample is. On the quality of your recording. Whether the NSA's software can find the back door to let us in."

"Get to it," Maynard says. "I don't have all day."

"Yeah, I figured."

The thumb drive is nearly invisible in Willard's fingers, but he inserts it into a port at the side of the nearest terminal, puts a pair of earphones over his head, and starts working, murmuring to himself.

On the left screen, there are jagged lines in green that repeat and repeat, and Maynard knows Willard is listening to the original recorded message from the Boss.

"Okay," Willard whispers. "Let's try this."

On the right screen, rows upon rows of green numbers and letters flash by on the black background in one long rolling display. Every few seconds, Willard slaps the space bar, the scrolling of the numbers and letters stop, and he peers at the screen like he's the first man to look at the Rosetta stone.

More work, more keyboard pounding, and then Willard leans back in the chair and scratches his plump neck. After a moment, he snaps forward, works the keyboard again. The jagged lines on the other side appear, and there's a second display right below it. Willard tears off the earphones, turns as best he can, and says, "Got it."

Maynard steps closer. "Show me."

Willard grins. His teeth are damn near tan. "You mean, let you listen."

Maynard clenches his hands. "Just do it."

Sensing the anger, Willard says, "Okay, here we go. This is a bit of the sample you gave me." He presses a key, and from the speakers comes the familiar electronic voice of the Boss: "We've an emerging situation, and I want you to take care of it. Personally."

"And now," Willard announces triumphantly. "This is what the real voice sounds like."

He presses a button, and Maynard listens to a human voice saying, "We've an emerging situation, and I want you to take care of it. Personally."

Maynard says, "This is it? The real deal?"

"Yep," Willard says, still grinning. "One hundred percent guaranteed. How does it feel, working for a woman?"

CHAPTER 70

DEACON AND I crowd around Bastinelli at his kitchen counter as he looks at eight small screens showing feeds from security cameras. Two of them point at dirt roads where armed men climb out of three black Chevrolet Suburbans.

About a dozen of them in black jumpsuits, boots, and ballistic helmets head into the woods surrounding Bastinelli's compound. Three remain back at the parked Suburbans, radio handsets in their gloved hands.

Bastinelli whistles. "Man, when you guys take a stick to a hornet's nest, you don't just hit it—you knock it on the ground and use it as a fucking soccer ball."

I say, "They started it."

Bastinelli says, "Yeah, well, I'm gonna finish it. Excuse me."

He exits the kitchen and I look at Deacon, who's staring at the screens showing armed men coming our way. We're isolated, outnumbered, and probably outgunned, but Deacon has a blank expression on her face.

Like she was expecting this raid.

I follow Bastinelli down a short hall to a living room filled with furniture and books but no TV. He opens up a closet with a large safe that locks with a keypad instead of the usual dial. His explanation as he punches in the numbers: "When bad guys are coming up at you, you don't want to worry about your fingers shaking."

There's a soft click. He tugs at the handle, and I blink at the sight of the small armory: handguns, shotguns, long rifles, and, tucked in one corner, a huge rifle I recognize as a .50-caliber Barrett M82, a semiautomatic rifle that fires the world's largest cartridge. One round can penetrate a car's engine block with ease.

Bastinelli throws on a bullet-resistant vest. He says, "I see you spotted my little friend."

"Impressive," I say.

"It tends to stop people in their tracks and make them rethink their career choices."

Deacon joins us. "What are you planning to do?"

He tightens the Velcro straps. "Well, like a good homeowner, I'm going to protect the old homestead. My entire property is posted with no trespassing signs."

I say, "We didn't spot any signs on our way in."

He takes two steps down the hallway, stops beneath a square ceiling panel, and reaches for a dangling cord. "What, you want me to advertise that there's a house deep in the woods? Nope, there's lots of them and they're visible, but not from the road." Bastinelli pulls on the rope, and a folded ladder descends from the ceiling. I peer up, and lights have flicked on, revealing a ladder rising about fifty feet to a metal grid floor.

"You like my tower of terror? I go up there and I can last a long time. I've got fields of fire cleared, I've got pyrotechnic surprises scattered through the woods, and the only weapon I can't withstand is an anti-tank missile."

Deacon says, "You mean you're going to shoot them first?"

He goes back to the safe, puts the slinged Barrett over one shoulder, picks up two metal boxes of ammunition. "Yep."

"You'll go to prison."

He shakes his head. "The property is posted. The men are armed. I fear for my life. This is the Live Free or Die state; no jury here will convict me. But we're wasting time."

I say, "Come with us, Gary."

He heads to the ladder. "Nope."

Deacon says, "We need you."

He stops at the bottom of the ladder. "Feeling's not mutual, sorry. I enlisted right after 9/11, when the entire nation was united, filled with determination to strike back against the attackers and settle accounts. Well, thanks to the politicians, the uniformed bureaucrats in the Pentagon, and the talking heads on cable, that unity was pissed away. I don't even recognize this country anymore. I once pledged to defend the Constitution and the nation. Now, it's just my close friends and family I'll defend."

Deacon says, "But—"

"Go," he says. "Drive around the rear of the property. There's a kids' swing set there. Use it as your marker, line up straight in front of it. Go right through the trees and keep going due south until you hit a dirt road. I'll be up in my tower, providing cover."

No time to argue. "Elizabeth, we've got to go."

"But—"

Bastinelli starts climbing the ladder. "Whatever happens, I got your backs here. But you're on your own once you leave the area. And good luck figuring out what in hell is going on out there, either in the States or in the 'Stan."

Up he goes and I give credit to Deacon—she doesn't argue. She turns and we move quickly to the front door to leave before the bad guys get here.

CHAPTER

71

IN THE MOTEL room, Maynard tells Willard, the NSA contractor, "Run it again."

"Got it."

Once more the voice comes through the speakers, strong and firm and definitely a woman's.

"That voice sounds familiar," Maynard says.

"Yeah, to me too."

"Can you send a copy of the cleaned-up sound file to my thumb drive?"

Willard says, "Certainly."

There's a quick motion of his fingers, then the *click-click* of a mouse, and Willard pulls out the thumb drive and hands it over to Maynard. This time, Maynard makes sure that his fingers don't touch Willard's. He slips the thumb drive into his shirt pocket.

Damn, the voice does sound familiar, and he's still surprised that the Boss is a woman. Nothing wrong with that, but it's good to know. Over the years, whenever he came across fellow travelers who claimed that women weren't tough enough to make the hard decisions, he'd shut them up by saying three names: Meir, Gandhi, Thatcher.

Willard swivels in his seat. "We need to talk."

Maynard is surprised. "We do? About what?"

His chubby face flushes. "This…situation we have. It's over. I don't want you bothering me anymore."

Maynard says, "What, you found God all of a sudden? You've stopped visiting the dark web and sharing all those nasty files?"

The man's face reddens even more. "What I do or don't do is none of your business. But it's over. Today's the last time you contact me to do your dirty work."

Maynard thinks that this pervert complaining about Maynard's dirty work is the height of irony, but he doesn't have time to discuss it; he needs to get going and leave this foul room. "There's always an *or else* tacked on the end of such a statement," Maynard says. "Let's hear it."

Willard gently caresses his keyboard. "Over the years, I've kept track of all your illegal information requests, with dates and details. We come to an agreement right here and now that you'll never, ever bother me again, or those files get released. The *New York Times,* CNN, ranking members of the House and Senate Intelligence Committees, maybe even your mother, living comfortably at the Villages in Florida—in one week, I'll make the info dump."

Maynard knows he's never discussed personal information with this creature, but he's managed to find out where Mom lives. "In one week, you say?"

Willard nods. "Seven days."

Maynard says, "That sounds like a fair arrangement. I mean, I know I've pressed you over the years, sometimes under difficult circumstances, to go dumpster-diving on the internet for me. Tell you what—I agree."

Willard says, "For real?"

"Sure," Maynard says. "Let's shake on it."

Willard gets up from his chair and Maynard slips his hand into his right jacket pocket, removes a Filipino butterfly knife, gives it a quick rotation, and, when the blade is secured, stabs Willard twice in the chest. Willard gasps and falls back in his chair.

Maynard wipes the blade clean on Willard's shirt, and as Willard gasps, he says, "You might've tried to do the info dump tomorrow, and I couldn't let that happen. But in a week?" He flips the knife back to its carrying position, puts it in his jacket pocket.

"In a week, no one will care," he says. He leaves as Willard bleeds out in the chair.

CHAPTER

72

I CLIMB INTO the driver's seat of the Tahoe and push the ignition switch, and about two seconds later Deacon gets into the passenger's seat.

She says, "I don't remember saying you could drive."

"Blame the patriarchy," I say, buckling up. I put the Tahoe in reverse. "You drove us here, and it seems fair I drive us out. Fasten your seat belt, Elizabeth, we're going to hit some bumps."

I shift the Tahoe into drive, circle the building, and spot the swing set. I keep driving until the visual display on the Tahoe's dashboard reads SOUTH/180 DEGREES. Then I drive right into the woods.

When we're in the saplings and brush, I again admire Bastinelli's foresight to pack gravel and dirt into an invisible road. Invisible, but not smooth. There are bumps and sways, and Deacon says, "You know what you're doing?"

"Relax," I say, keeping my grip tight on the steering wheel, which is shaking hard. "We're going downhill, and gravity's doing most of the work."

While Deacon is telling me what I can do with the theory

of gravity, I spot two armed men to our left, moving up toward Bastinelli's compound. "Duck!" I yell.

Deacon quickly lowers herself as a round snaps through the rear liftgate window. I push the accelerator down harder. Standard operating procedure to evade a shooter is to weave, but if I get off this hard-packed gravel road, I might get us bogged down in the soft forest floor.

The Tahoe bucks and rises as we burst through the woods and onto a dirt road. I turn left and the car skids, and dust is tossed up, but I get the Tahoe straightened out and hit the accelerator again.

"Any idea where we're going?" Deacon asks.

"Right now, out of the kill zone," I say, speeding up as much as I dare on this narrow road.

I turn a corner, and there's a Chevrolet Suburban nearly blocking our way, but its front hood is emitting steam, two of its tires are flat, the windows are shattered, and the Suburban's body is pockmarked with what I'm sure are .50-caliber rounds. Lying on the dirt next to it is an armed man; what's left of his head is dangling over a drainage ditch.

I slip by the shot-up Suburban and keep driving. Deacon has her nine-millimeter pistol in her lap. I think that's a good idea, and I tug my coat aside to have easy access to my Glock.

In the rearview mirror, I see a blur, and there's a heavy thump as another black Chevrolet Suburban rams our tail. Deacon and I bounce forward against the seat belts, and the Suburban rears back and starts accelerating again.

Up ahead, the dirt road widens into an area big enough for a snowplow to turn around, and I glance up at the rearview mirror and see the Suburban racing up on our tail again. I swerve over to the wide part of the road, hit the emergency brake, and downshift into low.

With a cloud of dust, the Suburban races past us, and I release the emergency brake, shift into drive, and go hard and fast to catch up to the SUV. When the Tahoe's front wheels are aligned with the Suburban's rear wheels, a guy with a pistol leans out of the passenger side. I swerve to the left, into the right rear bumper of the Suburban, and accelerate as the Suburban's rear wheels lose traction. This is what's called a PIT maneuver, and nine times out of ten, it will cause the other vehicle to spin out and lose control.

Which it does, spectacularly. We speed past, and in the rearview mirror I see the Suburban flip over at least twice before coming to a stop, ejecting the man who was trying to shoot us in the process.

He ends up roughly hugging a pine tree.

We turn a sharp corner. Two men step out into the middle of the road, aiming assault rifles right at us, and again I say, "Duck," and Deacon says, "What the hell?"

I'm planning to slide down in my seat, punch the accelerator, and hope for the best, but it turns out that's not necessary. Even with the windows closed, I hear two booming cracks coming from up the hill behind us, and both men crumple to the ground. They're wearing full body armor, but a .50-caliber round from a Barrett rifle can punch through that like an icepick through tissue paper.

Thankfully, there's enough room to drive between, not over, the two bodies, and I say, "Damn, you've got to admit that's some fine shooting Gary gave us."

"Agreed," she says.

I keep driving. The dirt road is straight and empty. "Nice to have friends, don't you think?"

Deacon's hand is tight on her pistol. "I wouldn't know," she says.

CHAPTER

73

GENERAL WAYNE GRISSOM is concluding another unsatisfactory meeting with the task force, and most of the time was spent on a discussion of all the shootings and bombings that took place during the president's address to the nation last night.

"Look," he finally snaps, "we all know what happened during the president's talk. The terrorists were sending a message that they can strike anywhere and at any time. Besides spreading terror, it was a taunt. Agent Mahoney, what's the latest from the FBI?"

Like everyone else at this meeting—which this time is held in a conference room deep in the Department of Labor building—he looks tired and jumpy.

He says, "We've arrested one person involved in the shooting of a Black Lives Matter meeting in Chicago and two people who were part of the attack on a white separatist group in Idaho. Our initial interviews were... puzzling."

"Puzzling how?" Grissom asks.

"Before they shut up and demanded counsel, they gave us similar information on their funding source and who supplied them with weapons and explosives," Mahoney says.

Doris Landsdale from Homeland Security says, "You have a name? An organization?"

Mahoney says, "No, but they used the same phrasing. A number of months ago, they were approached via encrypted e-mail and text messages by someone claiming to be a supporter of their cause. Each group took advantage of the offer."

The people in the crowded and warm conference room are silent.

"Don't you get it?" Mahoney asks. "You have two radically different armed groups, one going after a Black organization in Chicago, the other going against white supremacists in Idaho. Yet both groups have the same story of how they went from street protests to armed attacks—support and weapons from someone claiming to be a fellow traveler."

Grissom says, "The purpose of terror is terror. That's what concerns me. There's no single thread, no political position, that pulls these attacks together. What does the NSA say?"

There are several minutes of technical discussion concerning data analyses of captured cell phones from the attackers in Chicago and Iowa and the NSA's attempts to see if any increase in cell tower use can be traced back to suspicious data packs.

Grissom says, "You've got nothing solid, then. Nothing we can use to track the terrorists down or prevent another attack."

"No, sir," replies the air force colonel representing the NSA.

Sitting next to Grissom is Helen Taft, the president's chief of staff. "Helen," he says, "I'd like to meet with the president later. Can you arrange that?"

"I'll see what I can do," she says dismissively.

Grissom nearly explodes. *The most serious domestic threat this nation has faced in decades, and all you've got to say is "I'll see what I can do"?* Even his assistant, Colonel Carla Kendricks, looks stunned at Taft's response.

He keeps his cool and takes one last glance around the conference table, eager to get out of here and back to the Pentagon. "Ladies and gentlemen, I know we're all frustrated with these attacks, with the lack of progress in our investigations, and with the knowledge that a larger and more destructive attack is imminent." He takes a breath. "But please, keep focused, keep fresh. While I don't know all of you personally, I do know that you've arrived in your current positions because of hard work, determination, the desire to serve this nation, and a lot of sacrifice. Some of you have sacrificed time with your family and the opportunity to have larger salaries in the private sector, and others have pressed on in the face of even harder sacrifices."

All eyes are now on him, and he feels his throat tighten. "Including myself." He pauses. "As I'm sure most of you know, I lost my son, Nathan, five years ago in an IED attack in Afghanistan. Yet I've pressed on, and I'm asking you to continue on with me in this effort. This nation is worth saving. And we will do that, no matter what it takes—"

Secretary Landsdale interrupts. "With all due respect, General, what have our efforts accomplished? We supposedly have the largest and most capable foreign and domestic intelligence services in the world, and all we've come up with are ghosts, hints, and the ever-popular chatter. Do we have any real idea of what's going on?"

Grissom snaps, "What the hell do you want, Doris? An organization tree with every terrorist's phone number and e-mail? That's TV and Hollywood bullshit, and unfortunately, this is reality—gritty, confusing, and, in the end, exceptionally dangerous. Anybody else?"

Silence.

Grissom stands up. "Fine. We'll put out a communication later today with the next meeting's time and location."

Everyone else gets up too, and to the chief of staff's well-groomed back, Grissom calls out, "Helen! Can I get a moment, please?"

Taft either doesn't hear him or ignores him; she quickly exits the conference room.

Accompanied by Secretary Doris Landsdale, the two of them deep in conversation.

Colonel Kendricks is next to him. "I don't like what I'm seeing," she says.

Grissom says, "Neither do I."

CHAPTER

74

ABOUT TEN MINUTES after our friend on the hill gunned down the two armed men approaching us on the dirt road, Deacon and I are on a narrow paved lane that laughably calls itself State Highway 19.

I'm driving a few miles over the speed limit when I see flashing blue lights ahead. I slow down some.

Elizabeth Deacon sees them too. "Police vehicles," she says. "You intend to stop?"

Two New Hampshire State Police cruisers roar past us.

"No," I say.

About ten seconds later, more blue lights appear. They're on light poles, secured to the bumpers of tan-colored army Humvees. They go by quickly as well.

Deacon turns to watch them pass and says, "Active-duty army or National Guard responding with local police? Never happens, not ever, unless there's been some sort of emergency declaration."

"Maybe there has been and we just don't know it. I could turn around and follow the Humvees, ask the drivers when they stop."

Deacon shifts in the seat. "John, stop trying to lighten up the mood. It's not working."

"Says you," I say.

Much later, in a far corner booth at a McDonald's on the Massachusetts Turnpike, I'm having coffee with Deacon, who has an odd habit of tearing the brown paper napkins into long strips. She's got a pile of the strips in front of her.

The place is busy with travelers stopping for food, coffee, and bathroom breaks, and there are three flat-screen TVs hanging from the ceiling, broadcasting the troubled news of the world.

"It's been at least four hours," I say. "We've been monitoring the radio news stations in New Hampshire and Massachusetts, and there hasn't been one report of a gun battle breaking out in Healy, New Hampshire."

She nods and picks up another napkin.

I go on. "We both saw state police cruisers and army Humvees responding to the scene. What does that tell you?"

Deacon focuses on the paper napkin. "You tell me."

"What—is this an exam, Professor Deacon?"

She doesn't answer. *Rip, rip, rip.*

"It means that we're up against opponents, either foreign or domestic, who have great resources and focus," I say. "And they've been proving what Mel told me: These terror attacks, from snipers to bombings, are connected to what we saw in Afghanistan. And our skilled and determined opponents have eliminated all the witnesses to that except you and me." I reach over, grab her napkin strips, crumple them up, and toss them to the side of the table. "Got your attention now?" I ask.

Deacon says, "I've been paying attention. I can multitask. And for what it's worth, I agree with your analysis."

"Good," I say. "Hope you agree with what I'm about to say next. We've been spinning our wheels, going around and around, trying to figure things out here. All that's gotten us is a few scraps of information and some dead companions. We need to go back to the 'Stan, get to the root of everything."

She gives me a hard stare. "I hate to mention the obvious, John, but there aren't many Western flights going to Kabul nowadays."

I shake my head. "Don't want to go to Kabul. We need to get back to that base in Tajikistan, find our way across the border, and recon the place. Locate the village that was bombed. Talk to any witnesses that might still be living. If that bombing and our presence there is the source of our troubles, that's where we've got to go."

She reaches for another napkin, stops, pulls her hand back. "Fine. How do we get there?"

I pick up my coffee. "Why, through you, of course. The mighty CIA. You've recovered Russian subs, overthrown governments from Guatemala to Iran, smuggled people across various borders, and accomplished plenty of other things that have never been brought to light. Getting the two of us to Tajikistan with arms and communications should be a piece of cake."

"I'm only a consultant."

I sip my coffee. "So get consulting and get us over there. As soon as you can."

"You in a hurry to get to a third-world country?" she asks.

I point to a TV showing a CNN report of a car bombing in Seattle. There's smoke billowing up, and firefighters, surrounded by heavily armed police officers, are hosing down the burning vehicles.

"No," I say. "I'm in a hurry to get over there and do our job. If we wait much longer, we'll be forced to stay there as refugees, because there won't be a United States to come back to."

CHAPTER

75

BREE STONE WAKES up and instinctively reaches over to touch Alex before it all comes back to her—her Alex, her man, is still in the ICU. She rolls over and checks the time. It's 2:10 a.m.

What woke her up?

A creak of a floorboard, and she sees a tall shape silhouetted in the bedroom doorway. Before she can react, her stepson Damon says, "Bree?"

She sits up. "What is it? Did the hospital call? Is something wrong with your dad?"

He steps in and she sees he's carrying something. A pump-action twelve-gauge shotgun. In most homes in DC, seeing one's college-age stepson carrying a weapon would be frightening. Not here, not now. Because of the lives they live, she and Alex have made sure all the children respect firearms, and they've taught the oldest, Damon, how to use them.

"No, Bree, nothing like that, but there's somebody out there. I don't like it."

"Okay, stay right here."

She gets out of bed, pulls on a robe, and slides her iPhone into one of the robe's pockets. She opens the upper drawer to the nightstand and a little light comes on, illuminating the interior, which holds a small gun case with a pressure switch in the center. She pushes her thumb down and the scanner recognizes her thumbprint; the lid swings up to reveal a Ruger .357 revolver. She picks up the loaded weapon and goes to Damon. Quietly, she says, "What's going on?"

He motions for her to follow him into the dark living room. When her eyes adjust, she sees that her stepson is wearing a T-shirt and shorts. His hands are still firmly holding the shotgun.

"I was hungry, came down to the kitchen, and I was going to open the refrigerator door, but I stopped. I don't know why, but I got this feeling I didn't want to open the door and light everything up."

"I see," she says as she slowly walks into the kitchen. "What then?"

"I went to the porch door. Kept the lights off. Saw someone across the street, just standing there, looking at the house. Then he walked off. A couple of minutes later, he came back to the sidewalk. Then he ducked into the Sanchezes' backyard and headed this way."

Bree looks out into the street. There's the familiar sight of streetlights and sounds of traffic and a siren wailing out there somewhere.

"The car is gone," she says. Two operatives from her security firm had been parked in a dark blue GMC sedan up the street.

"Yeah, Bree, I saw that too. Didn't like it. That's when I got the shotgun and went to wake you up."

She waits, thinks, revolver heavy in her hand.

"Should we call the cops?" her stepson asks.

A slight noise comes from the kitchen.

She touches Damon's shoulder, and the two of them go through the dining room into the kitchen.

Another bit of noise.

Damon touches Bree and points to the door that opens onto their backyard. In the dim glow of a light above the stove, Bree sees the knob rotate left, stop, then rotate right.

"Bree?" Damon whispers.

She points to the doorway to the dining room, puts her mouth up to his ear, and whispers, "Get over there, take cover. Aim at the center of the door. I shoot first, you shoot second, then you go upstairs and call the cops."

He nods, steps back. Bree moves forward, kneels down behind the small round kitchen table, and pulls two chairs over to give her some cover.

The doorknob turns one more time.

Then nothing.

She's holding the revolver in the approved two-handed grip, and she takes a deep breath, lets it out, waits. Whoever's on the other side of that door looking to break into *her* home and cause *her* family harm, well, he's in for one big friggin' surprise.

The sound of her phone ringing in her robe pocket makes her jump and nearly drop the Ruger. It rings again and she digs it out and decides to answer it so at least there'll be an earwitness to whatever happens next. She whispers, "Yes?"

A strong and familiar voice on the other end of the call nearly makes her sob in relief.

"Hey, Bree, it's John," he says. "You and Alex change the locks again?"

CHAPTER

76

I'M SITTING AT the small table in Bree's kitchen drinking coffee and eating scrambled eggs and toast. "I hope I didn't wake up anyone besides you and Damon," I say.

Bree pours more coffee into my cup. "Well, Nana Mama and Jannie are at the hospital, keeping a vigil in the waiting room."

I glance at my watch. "Nana Mama? For real? I mean..."

Bree smiles, shakes her head. "I lost that fight a couple of days ago, John."

"How's Alex?"

Her smile widens. "They took him off the vent this afternoon; he's breathing on his own now. They moved him out of the ICU and..." Bree's eyes well up. She can't go on.

I squeeze her hand. "What happened to the fake nurse who tried to kill him? Is she talking yet?"

Bree says, "She died in surgery, they said. But I don't believe it."

Damon comes into the room. "Bree, the two guys from the Bluestone Group are back. You want me to talk to them, find out why they left?"

I see Bree's eyes harden and I feel sorry for those two guys, whoever they are.

"No," she snaps. "I'll take care of them later."

Damon squeezes my shoulder. "Good to see you, Uncle John. Willow is sleeping upstairs, sharing Ali's room. I can wake her up and bring her down."

Oh my. To hold my girl, hug her, kiss her, and talk to her…

And then what?

She'll be so excited about her daddy coming home, but I'll have to break her heart because I'm leaving again in a few minutes.

"No," I say, voice tight. "Let her sleep. I can't stay long."

Bree says, "John, what's going on?"

I look around the kitchen, make a point of touching my ears and my eyes. Bree says, "My people sweep this house twice a day, and they have active detection systems in place for countersurveillance. It's okay for us to talk."

"Good," I say, and I give her a rundown of what I've been up to: the firefights at the motel and the fishing cabin in North Carolina and the events at Gary Bastinelli's compound. "Bottom line," I say, "is that whatever happened back in Afghanistan is key to the terror attacks. Forces have eliminated almost everyone who went into Afghanistan two years ago."

Damon is sitting quietly in one of the kitchen chairs, face somber. I feel a stab of guilt and responsibility. What kind of nation will he be left with if we can't stop these terror attacks and the ultimate attack coming soon?

"Now what?" Bree asks.

"Simple," I say. "We're going back to the scene of the crime, find out what we can."

Damon says, "How, Uncle John?"

"I'm leaving that up to Elizabeth," I say. "In two hours we're meeting up again. In the meantime, Bree, I need two favors."

"Absolutely," she says.

"Don't be so quick to say yes," I say. "The first one is the hardest. You need to move everyone from here to another location. Someplace only you'll know, someplace that can easily be protected. Even I don't want to know where it is. I'm afraid things are going to get a lot worse before they get better. If they get better."

Bree slowly nods. "I don't like it, but I understand. Your other favor?"

I take a pen out, scribble a date on a torn-off piece of napkin, slide it over to her. "This," I say. "On this date, an army general was present at a classified airbase in Tajikistan. At the time the base was called Zulu Field."

"You need a rundown?" she asks.

"Full and complete, as soon as you can." I scoop up a last forkful of scrambled eggs.

"It's that important?" she asks.

I remember the general talking sharply to Elizabeth Deacon back there in Tajikistan and Elizabeth later claiming she didn't remember him or the argument.

"End-of-the-world-as-we-know-it important," I say.

CHAPTER 77

THIRTY MINUTES LATER, I'm still in DC but a world apart from the rough-and-tumble neighborhood of Bree and Alex Cross. My transportation is yet another vehicle borrowed from a shopping mall in Massachusetts, a transaction I'm not going to mention to my host. I'm in the book-lined living room of a brick home owned by FBI agent Ned Mahoney, and we're both sitting in comfortable chairs with glasses of Courvoisier VSOP in our hands. I'm sure that ten-year-old John Sampson, shivering and trying to survive in an abandoned and unheated house, would never have believed he could end up being friends with a man who lives like this.

Our drinks at this hour seem ridiculously over the top, but considering what's happened in the past few days, what the hell.

Mahoney, in a dark blue bathrobe, his muscular, hairy lower legs exposed, says, "Your Harry Maynard doesn't exist anymore."

"I beg to differ, Ned," I say. "I personally saw the son of a bitch."

"I'm sure," he says. "But once he left his work in Treasury, he dropped off the grid. I did a deep search and found three friends of his over the years—army, FBI, Homeland Security—

who did the same thing. No further records, no change of address. Swept clean."

"Takes some weight to do that," I say, warming the cognac tumbler in my hands. "What is the task force saying now? Foreign? Domestic? Some mix of both?"

"Mostly they're saying, 'We don't rightly know, let's have another meeting in twelve hours.'" His scowl deepens. "There's a disease out there that goes deeper than anyone can imagine. You didn't hear it from me, but there's a purge going on in the Texas Rangers—they're firing officers who were conducting unauthorized cross-border raids into Mexico. And our field office in Phoenix is practically empty. Officially, agents have been redeployed to address the current crisis. Unofficially, they've been redeployed to a secure area at Luke Air Force Base, while their loyalty is being examined."

He shakes his head, takes a sip of the cognac, and says, "You sure as hell have had your hands full the past few days. How are things with Metro Police?"

"At this point, I don't know," I say. "There are bigger games afoot, and if it means me losing my career and pension trying to get this thing solved, I don't care."

"Brave and bold talk, John."

"Just talk right now."

Ned says, "You're off to Afghanistan, then. You and Elizabeth Deacon."

"Only solution for this magician's misdirection we're caught up in," I say. "The bombings, the snipings, the killings in the United States, are getting our attention, but the real mystery is in the 'Stan."

"You need any help?"

"Elizabeth is handling transport and supplies," I say. "In one hour, I'll be picked up at a certain corner. But there is something I need. I want to know about Elizabeth Deacon—her background, where she's been, and, most of all, if she can be trusted."

Ned looks to me.

I say, "In exchange, whatever we learn over there, I'll feed it straight to you. God knows we're running out of time."

He runs a thick thumb around the edge of the glass. "The Company doesn't like it when we poke into its personnel matters."

"She says she's a consultant now."

His eyebrows lift at that. "A consultant? You know what that means, right?"

I nod, take another bracing sip. "CIA consultants do the Agency's dirty work off the books. If things go wrong or they get captured, the Agency denies knowing anything about them."

"Can I offer you some words of advice?"

"Sure," I say.

"If you're with her, make sure things go right, and for God's sake, don't get captured."

CHAPTER 78

IT'S NEARING DAWN as I make my way into George Washington University Hospital. It's not even close to visiting hours, but I need to be here, and a pleasant smile and a detective's badge from the Metro Police can open doors and elevators.

I go upstairs to the fourth floor and after checking in at the nurses' station, I make my way to room 409. I'm pleased to see two DC Metro Police officers sitting in chairs flanking the door, both of them wide awake and visibly armed.

After I show them my shield, the near one says, "Detective Sampson?"

"Yes?"

"Er, word is, well…I thought you were suspended," he says, a touch of embarrassment in his voice.

I put my shield away. "That's the official story. I'm still working. Can't say anything more than that."

The other officer says, "That makes sense. Hold on, I'll need to let you in. There's two Bluestone Group guys in there and they can be jumpy."

He gets up, knocks twice on the door, and says, "Officer Slayton coming in."

I hear murmured conversation, and Slayton comes out and says, "You're clear."

"Thanks."

Two unsmiling men are sitting in chairs looking at me. They have on jeans and tight black T-shirts and their hair is cut high and tight; they're instantly recognizable as ex-military.

We exchange nods and I walk over to Alex.

There are the usual IVs stuck in his arms, electronic leads running out to monitors, and a urine drainage tube running from underneath the blankets to a bag hanging from the bed. I go up to him. His face is slack, like he's sleeping away a hard night out with friends; there's stubble on his cheeks and chin. It's good to see him breathe on his own, no ventilator tube in sight.

I gently take his right hand in mine; it's cool and dry. I lean over, kiss his forehead. "Love you, brother," I say, squeezing his hand. "Really wish you were out here with me. I'm fighting some complicated stuff and it's scaring the shit out of me."

His breathing is slow and measured. Despite all that's happened to him and to the country, I feel a lightness in my chest at seeing his improvement. I squeeze his hand again. "Gotta run," I say.

I turn away and there's a cough.

I whirl around.

His eyes are open.

"Alex?" I ask.

His eyes focus and a slight smile appears. "Big John," he whispers. "Good to see…"

I go back to his side, hold his hand again; my eyes tear up. "Yeah, well, you better hurry up and get better and get the hell out of here. You won't believe the bills that are piling up." I add a stupid joke. "City insurance can only pay so much, Alex, so get your ass to healing and moving."

He closes his eyes, still smiling, and whispers, "John…the random attacks…I looked into it…not random…how it started. It's not random…" His voice trails off.

He's asleep again.

The detective in me wants to shake him awake, find out what the hell he's talking about.

But his friend won't do that. His friend will let him sleep and heal.

I kiss his forehead again. Walk to the door. As I leave, one of the men on his security detail says, "Whatever you're doing, body-bag those sons of bitches for him, will you?"

"On it," I say.

CHAPTER

79

OUTSIDE THE MAIN entrance to the Smithsonian's National Air and Space Museum on 600 Independence Avenue SW, Sergeant Louise Tempe of the DC Metro Police is watching the group of demonstrators grow larger, and her concern is growing right along with it. The sidewalks outside the entrance are packed with people, many carrying signs. It seems like a mix of the usual nutcases and cranks.

NO MANDATES

EXPOSE THE MOON HOAX

SUPPORT THE NO-EVOLUTION REVOLUTION

Tempe is in charge of this fourteen-officer detail, and truth be told, she's scared out of her wits. Twice she's radioed dispatch asking for more backup, and each time, she was told briskly that there were no more officers to be had. She'd wanted to go out here in full riot gear, with visored helmets and protective shields, but her captain shook her head and said, "No, the chief is worried about the optics. He doesn't want photos showing the force being militarized."

Well, damn, she thinks, *when things go south, there'll be plenty of photos showing this tiny force being trampled.*

The shouting is getting louder. She has ten officers standing back to back in formation, tactical batons in their hands, trying to prevent fighting from breaking out.

She and three others are at the main entrance to the museum, and thankfully, the directors and security managers have emptied the place of tourists, shuttling them out of side entrances, and locked all the doors.

One of her officers, Bailey, steps up to her and says, "Sarge, this is getting out of hand. Can you make another call to dispatch?"

Before she can answer, there are two heavy thumps, the sound beating at her ears and chest, and she thinks, *Concussion grenades.*

The crowds swirl and shout, scream and yell, and there's another concussion grenade—thank God it's not carrying shrapnel—and she sees what's happening: the grenade explosions are pushing the crowds, like panicked cattle, to the museum's entrance.

Straight at her.

She stumbles, falls, gets up, is pressed against the stone wall of the building. With her baton, Tempe tries to push back the shouting, yelling, red-faced demonstrators, but it's like trying to stop an ocean wave with a canoe paddle.

She sees four people in black jumpsuits and black balaclavas pulled over their heads make their way to the locked doors, and there's quick movement of their hands, and then—*bang-bang-bang-bang.*

Door charges, Tempe thinks, and the doors are shattered and the crowds roar in approval and move in like a tsunami. Tempe is swept inside; the baton and her uniform cap are pulled away, and hands are tugging at her utility belt, but she keeps a firm grasp on her holstered pistol.

More chants break out, loud and echoing in the main lobby:

"Screw science!"

"No mandates!"

"Moon hoax, moon hoax, moon hoax!"

Tempe is knocked to the floor, and she watches in horror as the crowds go after the displays of humanity's many achievements in air and space with hammers and crowbars, smashing them off their stands. She tries to get up but is knocked down again, and this time she hits her head hard. Two men are pounding the Apollo 11 capsule with sledgehammers and yelling, "Hoax, hoax, hoax!"

Her last thought before she slips into unconsciousness is *What has happened to us?*

Part Four

CHAPTER 80

I STEP OUT of the air force aircraft back in Tajikistan, a place I never thought I'd be again in my life. The station looks even smaller and grimmer than before. Just off the runway, several horses are hitched to a long line of rope near three old, battered Humvees, and a large tent is flapping in the breeze. Two tan-colored shipping containers have been converted into sleeping and working quarters, and a garage-size building is topped with antennas and satellite dishes.

A black and oddly shaped air force jet maneuvers its needle-shaped nose around this end of the runway; light gray U.S. Air Force roundels are displayed on the fuselage, and a gray American flag silhouette is on the tail. Sunlight gleams off the forward windows, and the pilot revs the two huge boxy engines. The aircraft speeds down the runway, takes off, and starts climbing, and in seconds it disappears into the light blue Tajikistan sky just above the Pamir Mountains that dominate the horizon in this part of the world.

A few seconds pass.

Boom-boom.

I say to Deacon, "I read in the *Post* last year that the U.S. Air Force received four test supersonic transport aircraft. And you managed to get one of them to bring us here. Impressive."

"Yes, I did," she says, shouldering her rucksack. She starts walking to the main tent.

"That's one hell of a consulting job," I say.

"Sure was," she says. "Just be glad you're not footing the bill."

We're both dressed in traditional local clothing: leather boots, tan trousers, sheepskin-lined coats, and loose brown turbans on our heads. We're both carrying rucksacks with water bottles, pistols, grenades, and American M4 rifles. A few years ago, if you wanted to blend in here, you carried an AK-47, Russian- or Chinese-made, no difference. But due to an unfortunate chain of events, the Taliban, now in power, had tons of American vehicles, ammunition, weapons, mortars, artillery, and other military goodies.

Deacon goes to the tent and opens a large flap, and the two of us step in onto a wooden plank floor. Topo maps and whiteboards hang from the canvas walls. About a dozen men—all stocky with long hair and beards, wearing a mix of camo and local clothing—look up. Some are sitting around long tables cleaning weapons, others are in front of keyboards, and three are sitting and drinking coffee, legs stretched toward the kerosene heater set in the tent's center.

An American flag dangles overhead, and a handwritten sign reads: *We the unwilling, led by the unqualified to kill the unfortunate, die for the ungrateful.*

The nearest man looks at Deacon and says, "Liz."

"Bobby," she replies. "Can we talk outside?"

"Love to," he says. He gets up, pistol holstered at his side.

The other men ignore us as Deacon and I follow him out.

A few yards away from the tent, Bobby digs into a pocket and pulls out a crumpled pack of Marlboros and a cigarette lighter. He lights one and laughs. "Even on this side of the world, health and safety rules still exist. Can't smoke inside." He takes a defiant puff and says,

"I didn't know you were coming until that brand-spanking-new SST was about ten minutes out. What are you up to, Liz?"

"Nothing much, Bobby," she says. "My friend and I are planning a little cross-border excursion. Shouldn't take more than two days, tops."

"You two going alone?"

"A local will be our guide."

Bobby glances around the small compound. "Looks like your guide hasn't arrived yet."

"He's supposed to show up this afternoon."

He nods. "Which means at dawn, if you're lucky. You trust this guy?"

"We've used him before."

"What if he screws with you?"

"Then I don't pay him," Deacon says. "And I'll kill him."

Bobby smiles. "In that order?"

"Whichever works best," she says.

He looks me up and down and says, "No offense, but I don't see how a woman and her tall Black companion are going to fit in with the locals."

I say, "As her tall Black companion, I'm telling you not to worry your pretty little head about it. We're just here to do a job, in and out."

"Yeah," he says. "You don't plan to stir things up, do you?"

"Not if we can help it," I say.

"Do your best not to," he says. "This tiny outpost of America is on its own. Tajikistan pretends we're not here, so if you piss off the local Taliban and they decide to come over the border and wipe out this little nest of heretics, there's not much we can do. We've got no military units in theater, and the closest air support is about six hours out. Remember that, okay?"

"Remembered," Deacon says.

He takes a deep drag on the Marlboro, drops it on the ground, crushes it with his boot, and, with well-trained ease, picks up the butt and strips it.

Bobby says, "Remember this too: You get into trouble over there, we can't help you. We're not the cavalry, and we don't pretend to be. The minute you're in the 'Stan, Liz, you and your tall friend are on your own. Got that?"

I say, "Thanks for the words of encouragement."

Bobby turns and walks back to the tent. Over his shoulder, he says, "Glad you took it that way."

CHAPTER

81

THE SUN IS starting to set when a man appears in the south, slowly walking our way. First-time visitors to the 'Stan and other nearby countries always mention how slowly the locals move, not knowing that they are on their own time and that men of sixty, seventy, or eighty years of age can keep up a steady pace that leaves twenty-year-old American soldiers panting for breath.

He gets closer and I recognize him as Bibi Ahmadi, a local guide and fixer we used during our last visit. He's heavily bearded, and he has bright shiny eyes that hide mistrust behind the promise of lots of laughs.

He's wearing clothing similar to ours, and he carries a small rucksack and an AK-47 over his shoulder. When he reaches us, he bows to Elizabeth and puts a hand to his chest. "Madam Deacon," he says. He turns to me.

"Sampson," I say.

"I remember you," he says. "You are so tall. And so black."

"And you're so late."

Bibi looks at Deacon. "No time for tea?"

She shakes her head. “No, not until we cross the border. I want to cover some ground while there’s still a little light.”

Bibi purses his lips and says, “There’s the matter of compensation. I am still owed money by you. The debt must be settled.”

Deacon looks at our guide and interpreter with cold eyes. “I always settle my debts before I leave. I don’t owe you a thing.”

A slight shrug. “Ah, but there is the matter of your other comrades with the Agency. I provided them with many services—at the risk of my life, I might add—and they left without paying me.”

Deacon says, “Not my problem.”

“It is your problem, because you are with the Agency and their debt is your debt. Fifty thousand dollars in American one-hundred-dollar bills.”

Deacon says, “Not on your life.”

Another slight shrug. “Then here I will stay.”

Deacon and Bibi go back and forth for a while, point, counter-point. The setting sun is sinking below the Pamir Mountains.

Time to get things moving.

“Hey, Bibi,” I say, interrupting their negotiations. “Here’s what I can do. How about half what the Agency owes you now and the other half when we come back—how does that sound?”

He grins, his teeth worn and brown. Deacon says, “Wait, wait—” Bibi wanders over to me and says, “Yes, most agreeable. Thank you.”

I move my hand to my holster, pull out my Glock, slap his face, and grab the back of his head. I bring up my pistol and shove it into his mouth.

His eyes widen. I say in a calm and clear voice, “In case you haven’t noticed, Bibi, we’re in kind of a hurry. We don’t have time to dick around. We’re not planning to spend any more time haggling with you like we’re at the Pul-e Khishti Bazaar in Kabul. Here’s my proposal. In the chamber of this pistol is a nine-millimeter round, street value in the United States of about twenty-three cents. In your current situation, would you recognize this bullet’s value as satisfying half of your debt?" A slow nod from him. "Glad to hear it. But I'm a suspicious sort, so when I take my pistol away, you're going to make a pledge that you will safely escort us to the village we're looking for and that you'll safely escort us back. Can I get a nod, Bibi?"

He nods again, but his dark brown eyes are expressionless. I slowly remove my pistol, wipe the muzzle end on his jacket, and say, "You're up, Bibi."

Bibi coughs and says, "My solemn pledge, Miss Deacon and Mr. Sampson, I will safely escort you to the village you seek, and I will safely bring you back."

"Outstanding," I say.

I can't tell what Deacon is thinking, but she says, "Enough talking. Let's move."

I slowly return my pistol to its holster. "Thanks, Bibi, and just so we're speaking the same language, if at any point I think you're threatening us, leading us astray, or directing us to a Taliban ambush, I'll blow your fucking head off. Clear?"

Bibi turns and starts walking south toward the Afghan border, and I guess I'm going to have to make do with that nonanswer answer.

CHAPTER 82

THE MOON RISES in the east over the Pamir Mountains toward the light of thousands of stars, and we have good visibility as we follow the rocky trail south. I spot the far-off headlights of vehicles traveling on unmarked dirt roads and hear a burst of automatic-weapon fire somewhere in the west.

Deacon says, "Who's fighting whom?"

Bibi says, "Allah only knows. Perhaps a cousin against a cousin. Or a Taliban unit chasing a National Resistance Front patrol. Or some village having a celebration. This district is controlled by Gul Hazara. He was with the Ministry of Defense in the old Kabul government. We see him, we'll get all the answers we need."

The trail disappears into a muddy creek, and we slosh across as quietly as we can, and on the other side, Bibi says triumphantly, "That was the Panj River, my friends. We are now officially in Afghanistan."

I think, *You might be here officially, but we're not.*

He says, "Time for tea, perhaps?"

I say, "Up ahead there, where those boulders are. It'll give us some cover. Elizabeth?"

She checks her watch. "All right, as long as it's a quick Afghan tea, not an hours-long British tea."

The break for tea deep in a tumble of rocks is indeed quick. Our position hidden, Bibi lights a small gas stove, then prepares tea and slices of flatbread spread with cold greasy mutton. I'm not choosy about what I eat, since I still have vivid childhood memories of dumpster-diving for tossed-out food. Once the stove cools and our eyes readjust to the darkness, Bibi puts the stove back in his rucksack.

Deacon checks her watch again. "It looks like we'll get to the bombed village sometime after dawn. That square with you, Bibi?"

"Yes, it does, Miss Deacon."

"Then let's get moving."

I'm thousands of miles away from home, away from electric lights, warm rooms, flush toilets, and my friends and my Willow. But it's amazing how my body slips back into what was once routine, humping gear and a weapon along a barely lit and barely there trail, all my senses on alert, looking and smelling and, most of all, listening.

For voices.

For a rock falling on a rock.

For metal striking metal.

Light begins to appear in the rocky east, and I hear it: Bells. Little bells.

We cross a slight rise, and a village comes into view: stone corrals holding sheep and goats, a collection of one-story brick and rock buildings. Smoke is rising up, men are moving about, and little barefoot boys kick a soccer ball so dirty, its white hexagons have blended into the black pentagons.

Two armed men watch us approach with calm, curious, nonthreatening expressions.

"Elizabeth," I say.

"I know," she says.

"This can't be the right village. This village is still alive," I say. "None of the buildings even have a cracked wall."

In a sharp voice, Deacon says, "Bibi! Where the hell did you bring us?"

But Bibi doesn't answer. He starts running away.

I stand there, stunned, but Deacon brings up her M4, puts her finger in the trigger guard—

A man running away.

I slap at her weapon, and it jerks to the left. Deacon lowers the M4.

"You about to shoot a guy in the back for running away?" I say.

Deacon's face is calm. "Maybe it was going to be a warning shot."

"Was that your plan?"

She swings the M4 over her right shoulder.

"Guess we'll never know," she says.

CHAPTER 83

THREE FLAGPOLES RISE from a small grassy park in front of the entrance to Union Station in Washington, DC. FBI agent Ned Mahoney shoulders his way through the police lines, holding his shield up, taking in the situation. Police and National Guard officers are holding back the news media and the crowds of onlookers streaming in from nearby streets.

Ned nods to DC Metro Police captain Susan Jones, who is in charge of the scene. She's wearing a bullet-resistant vest over her uniform, and Ned wishes now he'd brought his own vest, which is still secure back in his government-issue black Impala, along with a spare.

Ned says, "Word I've got is that there's a suicide bomber in there."

"That's right," she replies, eyes flickering around the line of police officers and National Guardsmen, evaluating their positions and placements. "Happened entirely by accident about thirty minutes ago, during the morning rush. Some clown from Bethesda who works in the Agriculture Department came through, bumped into her—"

"A woman?" Ned interrupts. "For real? That's damn rare."

In a glum voice, Susan says, "Yeah, that's what all the training says, right? Anyway, a guy bumps into her, dumps his Starbucks Venti Caramel Apple Frappuccino or whatever on her coat, apologizes, and tries to mop up the mess. Her coat opens up, and there it is, a vest with ball bearings and wires, and he shits himself and starts screaming."

"It didn't go off?"

"Nope," the captain says. "Right now, the concourse is empty except for a couple of my guys with shields, and we're waiting for the hostage negotiator to show up. At the moment, the would-be suicide bomber is standing under the barrel-vaulted arches, sobbing."

"Any demands?"

"Not a one," she says.

Ned looks over at the crowds, tries to remember the last time he had a good night's sleep or a good scrap of information that might help him find out just what in hell's been going on during the last few months. "I'm going in," he says. "Let your people know so they don't freak when a new face shows up."

"Ned," the captain says, "there's no way I'm letting you in there. Wait for the hostage negotiator to get here."

"Not enough time, and you know it, Susan," he says. "And there's also not enough time to do the turf dance. This is a terrorist incident and it belongs to me. I'm going in."

"If she pulls the trigger, you and everyone in there will get a bellyful of steel ball bearings."

Ned says, "So if she pulls the trigger, I better duck, right?"

Susan swears, starts undoing the Velcro straps of her bullet-resistant vest. "All right, take this," she says, then yells to one of the officers, "You! Give this man your shield."

Ned puts on the police captain's bullet-resistant vest and takes the heavy Plexiglas shield, POLICE centered on a black strip across the middle of it, from an officer.

Susan says, “Good luck, if that means anything.”

“I’ll take it,” Ned says.

In the main hall of Union Station, his footsteps clatter loudly in the nearly empty space littered with dropped newspapers, briefcases, purses, and spilled coffee. A disheveled-looking woman is standing in the center of the large hall; pretty arched columns swoop overhead, and hexagon-shaped lights glow softly. One of the five DC police officers taking cover behind ticket counters loudly whispers something unintelligible into the silence, but Ned ignores him.

He slowly walks toward the woman, his empty left hand raised, holding the riot shield in his right hand. “Ma’am,” Ned says, “I’d like to help you, honest. What’s your name? Where are you from?”

She’s a well-dressed, well-made-up blond woman in her mid- to late fifties wearing black slacks and a light yellow down jacket. The jacket is open, revealing a vest with wired and tubular charges and clear plastic bags filled with small metal ball bearings.

She looks like she’s been crying.

“Ma’am,” Ned says, “can I help?”

In a frustrated voice, she says, “It didn’t work, it didn’t work!”

She moves her arm, and Ned freezes, seeing the triggering device in her right hand. “Hey, ma’am, drop what you’re holding,” Ned calls out. “Please!”

Her thumb presses down. “It still doesn’t work!”

Ned yells louder, “Lady, drop it!”

Another press of the thumb. “It was supposed to work!”

“Ma’am, please—”

When she presses down a third time, it works.

CHAPTER 84

IT'S NIGHT AGAIN when Deacon and I take shelter in another village, this one called Ab Doi. After Bibi ran off, we stayed just long enough to find out from a young boy who knew a smattering of English that the place's name was Numay and that it had never been attacked, not ever. When Deacon asked if he knew of a nearby village destroyed two years ago, he shook his head, left, and came back with two unopened plastic bottles of water.

I told Deacon we should travel west because that's where Bastinelli had seen the explosions, and surprisingly enough, she agreed. Now we're huddled up in a small, smelly stone building that might once have been used to store manure. This village is as unscathed as the first, and thanks to the Afghan custom of *pashtunwali,* we are fed, given shelter, and treated as guests.

Well, it's not much of a shelter, with most of the roof gone, but at least the walls are cutting the wind. Deacon and I have crawled into our respective sleeping bags and we're huddling together to stay warm. The stars overhead are very bright indeed.

I doze off but wake up a few minutes later. Deacon is shivering hard next to me. "Elizabeth?" I say.

"Yeah. Who else did you think would be here?"

"Hold on." I unzip my bag and, with the light from a headlamp, manage to get her bag zipped to mine so we're sharing one covering. I pull a dusty carpet over us and say, "Roll over."

She does, and I cuddle her from behind, rubbing her arms, pressing my body against hers. "Shhh," I say. "Just hold on. We'll get you warmed right up."

"I sure as hell hope so," she whispers back.

We wait. My feet and lower legs are dangling out in the open. I'm sure my breath is on the back of her neck, but she doesn't complain. She whispers, "First time we've had a break since we got together back in Vermont."

"Sounds about right."

She pauses, then says, "You married, John?"

"I was once. To Billie. We have a daughter, Willow. Billie died a while back."

"God, I'm sorry I asked," she says.

"No, it's all right," I say. "It's good to say her name, to remember her. I don't mind talking about her, and Willow is like having a version of Billie still in my life." Out there somewhere, a baby cries. "You? Married?"

She says, "Once. Divorced. No kids."

"Why the divorce?" I ask.

"Our schedules and work life never meshed," she says in the near darkness. "Pretty soon we were like roommates, just two people sharing a house and not much else, and eventually I figured I could save money by leaving him and getting a smaller place."

The spasms of her shivering slow down and stop, but I keep on holding her tight, and her hair tickles my nose, and I move and she moves and now we're kissing.

That sweetness goes on and seems to warm us both up, but then I say, "Elizabeth, we should stop this."

"Why?" she asks, her voice amused. "Too dedicated to the mission?"

"No," I say. "I want to put this on pause and then pick up where we left off in a few days. In a place with clean water, clean sheets, electricity, and room service."

She kisses me one more time. "Detective Sampson, you got yourself a deal."

When the cold rays of sunshine start coming through the open roof, we both get up, arrange our gear, and step outside. We don't talk about last night, but with all that's been going on this past week, it's an unspoiled sweet memory I want to cherish.

Outside, about a dozen villagers have gathered, and my hand goes to my holstered Glock.

I don't like crowds.

An older man emerges from a small building; he's wearing tan cotton slacks, heavy boots, and a white collarless shirt with a sheepskin vest. His long beard is white and neatly trimmed, and what I can see of his hair is also white. That he's unarmed is unusual in this part of the world, and the men in the crowd—no women, of course—watch him with respect and affection.

He comes closer, smiles at Deacon, then looks at me.

I take a wild guess.

I say, "Nice to make your acquaintance, Gul Hazara."

CHAPTER 85

FBI AGENT NED MAHONEY opens his eyes; his ears are ringing. He sits up, sees the Plexiglas shield shattered on the tile floor.

His left foot is warm.

He glances down, sees his pants legs have been shredded, and there's blood just above his left ankle.

Cops and EMTs are racing in, and there's the smell of smoke and gunpowder, and despite his ringing ears, he hears someone yell, "She's alive! No shit, she's still alive!"

Ned struggles to stand. When he puts weight on his injured foot, he has to bite his lip to keep from crying out. It hurts like hell and he knows it's only going to get worse, but there's no time to waste. He limps toward the crumpled figure on the floor as the EMTs arrive. A cop says, "Looks like her vest didn't fully go off, but man, she took a hit."

Ned pushes through the growing knot of EMTs and cops. The woman is flat on her back, her abdomen torn and bloody, her slacks and coat torn to shreds. Her eyes are open and so is her mouth, and Ned kneels down next to her. The woman's face is going gray.

Ned yells, "Who sent you here? Who are you? Why are you here?"

Her eyes are unfocused and he shakes her shoulder. An EMT says, "Jesus, man, leave her be," but he ignores him and yells again, "Who sent you here?"

The woman finally looks at Ned and smiles, blood coming out of her mouth.

"America did..."

Her eyes close.

Twenty minutes later, his lower shin wrapped with a temporary bandage, Ned is in the front seat of a DC Metro Police cruiser with its engine running. Behind the wheel is Captain Susan Jones, the woman who earlier donated her bullet-resistant vest to him. She looks both exhausted and angry when she says to Ned, "You're one lucky bastard."

"Lucky, yes," Ned answers, trying to ignore the red-hot throbbing of his left shin. "As to the noun you used, I'm honestly not. I can show you the proof when this is over."

She says, "*If* this is ever over, you mean." Susan sighs. "Yeah, let's talk about luck. We were lucky that crazy bitch was discovered before she could try to set off that suicide vest. And lucky again that it malfunctioned and wounded only a few bystanders. Including one bystander that shouldn't have been there, meaning you. How are you feeling?"

"Outstanding," Ned says. "Uh-oh, we got visitors. Winny is here."

Standing by a flagpole and talking to two police sergeants is a tall and determined-looking Black woman in a black wool coat. Three male aides in fine suits are standing near her.

Susan says, "The Honorable Winifred Crocker, mayor of Washington, DC? How come you're on a first-name basis with her?"

Ned says, "We were in the same FBI Academy class, and both of us were at the Boston field office before she entered DC politics. Fair warning, it looks like she's on her way over."

"Then let's get to work," Jones says. "Before she starts knocking on my door."

In her left hand she holds the blood-smeared Ohio driver's license of Lucille Palmer, the now-deceased suicide bomber. In her right hand is her cell phone, and she punches in the phone number for Walter Palmer, Lucille's husband.

Ned watches. How many times has he had to do this, call and break the news of a loved one's death to some father or mother, husband or wife, shattering them and bringing down an avalanche of grief?

The phone rings and rings and rings. *Answer, damn it, answer,* he thinks.

Mayor Crocker is quickly walking over to the cruiser.

"Hello?" comes a male voice from Susan's phone.

"Good morning," Susan says in a brisk professional voice. "Is Walter Palmer there?"

"Speaking," he says.

"This is Captain Susan Jones of the DC Metro Police. Mr. Palmer, is your wife Lucille Palmer?"

"Yes, yes, she is. What's this about?"

"I'm afraid—"

Walter interrupts. "Wait, what? DC? The District of Columbia? My wife isn't in DC."

"Where is she, then?"

His voice rises. "Orlando! In Florida! At a Mary Kay convention."

Susan glances at Ned, and Ned nods. He's got a lot on his plate. He has to tell John what he found out about Elizabeth Deacon, prep for the next status meeting, and send a team of FBI agents to the home of Walter and his late wife to look for clues as to why a middle-class suburban mom would come to the District and strap on a suicide vest.

Oh, yeah, and he has to get his left shin looked at before it bleeds through the bandages.

The Metro Police captain takes a breath. "Mr. Palmer, I'm afraid I have some very bad news for you."

CHAPTER

86

BREAKFAST IS RELATIVELY luxurious because we're in the home of the local tribal leader, Gul Hazara. We gather in one big room with plenty of soft carpets under our feet, and there are large platters of flatbread, cottage cheese, tomatoes, cucumbers, boiled eggs, sweet biscuits, and lots of tea.

Some of the tribesmen in the crowded room are staring at my skin, others are staring at Elizabeth, and a couple look from one of us to the other like spectators at a tennis match.

At one point, Gul excuses himself from this room, and in a quiet voice, Deacon asks, "How did you know that was Gul Hazara?"

"You should know my methods, Watson," I say, eating a piece of flatbread with some kind of jam spread on it. "Our traitorous guide Bibi said Gul Hazara controlled this area, and when I first saw him, he was surrounded by guards and followers. Mostly, though, it was because he recognized you on sight. I figured he had to be the local leader you mentioned earlier, the one who didn't show up for that meeting."

"Good call," she replies, sipping a cup of tea.

I say, "Who is this guy, then, that you'd risk your ass to sneak into Afghanistan at least five times to meet with him?"

There's the briefest of pauses, and I know her intelligence-officer mind is working hard, deciding how much to reveal to me.

"We're hoping that two or three years down the road, when the Taliban are defeated, Gul Hazara will be the new president of Afghanistan."

I say, "Defeated? For the second time? Man, you Company folks do love to dream."

She doesn't answer. Gul Hazara comes back in, squats down, and speaks rapidly in Tajik. All the guests get up and slowly walk out, most of them giving us one more look before departing.

He folds his hands in his lap and says, "Well, Miss Elizabeth, Mr. John. What brings you here?"

Deacon says, "Thank you for your hospitality, your graciousness, and this marvelous meal. We are in your debt."

He says, "It is hard sometimes to keep track of those debts owed to you."

Deacon reaches into her rucksack and pulls out a small black zippered bag. She places it on the carpet and says, "You know I always settle my debts, Gul Hazara."

He doesn't take the bag, but a hint of a smile appears on his bearded face. "So you do. And what other debt do you intend to incur today?"

"There is a village nearby that was bombed and destroyed two years ago," she says. "My comrade and I need to visit it."

Within seconds, Gul Hazara transforms from confident leader to a shrinking man clutching at worry beads. "Why?"

"We need to see it so we can learn who did it. And perhaps why."

He shakes his head. "It's dangerous for you two to be here, you know. You, an armed woman, and your friend, a very tall African-looking man. If you value your life, you should return to the border immediately." He puts a hand on his chest. "I will provide safe escort."

I say, "With all due respect, sir, we need to get there."

"Again I ask: Why?"

I say, "There are disturbances and bloodshed in our country, and we have been told that what happened in that village is somehow connected to those events."

Silence in the room.

Deacon asks, "Were you here when it happened?"

He looks down for a moment. "Yes. The village, it was called Mir Kas. One night, the bombs and rockets came. Most of us have experienced some form of attack or bombing from the air. A few explosions, a few buildings destroyed, some killed or wounded, and then it's over. But not poor Mir Kas."

He's starting to reveal things, and Deacon does not press him, just lets him tell his story.

"For long hours, the village was bombed from one end to the other. Machine-gun fire from the air cut down everyone who tried to run. Everyone—the old, the infirm, the children. A few managed to escape, and we helped them, and then they kept running, as if they and their village were cursed."

I say, "We'd still like to see it."

"There's nothing there but bones and rubble."

"That doesn't matter," Deacon says. "We believe it's connected to the terrorist attacks in our nation."

He sighs. "I have heard that. A few who were once in power in Kabul and who still have friends and contacts in your capital say that what happened to Mir Kas was the start of something in the United States."

"What's the connection?" I ask.

"Oh," he says as if he's surprised we don't know. "The attacks were made by those who are killing people in your country now in preparation for...I'm sorry, I can't remember the correct word.

A French word, I believe. When a government is overthrown by violent means."

I say, "A coup?"

He clasps his hands together. "Ah, a coup. Quite right."

Damn, damn, damn. I can feel Deacon get tense at that dangerous and heavy word. *Coup.* I say, "Do you have any information about who's behind the coup? What group or country or organization?"

A sad shake of his head. "I wish I could help you, Miss Elizabeth, Mr. John. But I have no other information to give to you."

Deacon says, "We need to get to that village. Now."

He gets up and we do the same. "I will give you directions. It's only an hour's walk from here. But you will go alone. I can't give you any of my men to escort you."

I say, "You were ready to give us escorts to get back to the border, but not to the village. What's the difference?"

He speaks like an old teacher lecturing an ignorant student. "The bones and broken stones of that village are haunted. No one will approach it."

CHAPTER

87

ACCORDING TO GUL HAZARA, once we climb this one last bit of rocky trail, we will be on the outskirts of whatever's left of Mir Kas. There are stone-covered hills, mountains, low shrubs, and stunted trees, and the cold wind is buffeting us. We stop to catch our breath and pass a water bottle back and forth, and then, in the middle of a rocky no-man's-land, a chime sounds in my rucksack.

"What the hell?" I say.

Deacon says, "Sounds like someone's trying to call you, John."

"Stop joking."

"Who's joking?" she says. "It sure as hell isn't my rucksack that's making a noise. Get it out and quiet it before half the district hears it."

I shrug off my M4 and rucksack and dig in a side pocket, not quite believing it, but yes, it's my burner cell phone, chiming with a text.

Breathing hard from the altitude, I bring up the screen. A garbled message appears:

> Ran records check best I could on E. Deacxxx. Smart, ruthless, divorced . . . herself is first, Agency s@#ond, country third . . . 8*&^ . . . .

Can she be trusted? Well . . . it seems ##@@

Be safe get home ASAP ti09876 . . .

#674mpw9,,,,

We need to know what you know . . .

Ned

I want to reply but the little icon says No Service.

Then how in hell did this message get through? I look around but see nothing that wasn't there before. How did I get this message?

I put the phone back in my rucksack. Could be weird atmospherics or the magnetic field of the Earth shifting, or maybe the signal piggybacked off some drone or high-flying aircraft.

Almost anything's possible in this land.

Deacon says, "What was the call?"

I say, "Wrong number. Let's saddle up and get moving."

Our hike continues, slow and painful. I take point and Deacon is right behind me, so close I can hear her panting and smell her skin. I think of our little moment last night, and I think of Ned Mahoney's scrambled message and how the most important part didn't make it through.

Can she be trusted? Well . . . it seems ##@@

Not very helpful.

I reach the top of the rise, look at what's in front of me. Deacon comes up and stops next to me, breathing hard.

"Good God," she whispers.

"Sorry," I say. "Looks like God was somewhere else that day."

CHAPTER

AS FAST AS he can, Bibi Ahmadi moves along the trail leading to what is left of Mir Kas. Five of his cousins are trotting behind him, all of them heavily armed, and Bibi carries hate and a desire for revenge in his heart.

No man who has humiliated him will live, and especially not a man who humiliated him in front of a woman!

His plan is simple: They will find and ambush the pair of Americans, kill the male, and take their time with the woman.

And with the woman, he will be first, and his cousins can fight over who gets to be next.

He turns, his vest and pants legs flapping in the wind, and says, "Hurry, hurry, there's no time to waste!"

Bibi's cousin Azeez calls, "But the village is haunted—full of ghosts."

"And we will add two more before the day is out, but only if you move faster than a mule, fool!"

CHAPTER

89

AGAIN, DEACON SAYS, "Good God," as the two of us look at a field of rubble.

I've seen damaged and ruined villages before, both here and in Iraq, but nothing like this.

Nothing.

Deacon says, "Can you believe this?"

There's a slight depression before us filled with broken bricks and stone, no piece larger than a coffee table. Burned and charred timbers and more broken stone as far as the eye can see.

"No," I say.

The only color comes from green and black banners, some with writing on them, posted on poles shoved into the tortured ground.

Funeral flags, marking the final resting places of the deceased.

I say, "This wasn't just an attack. It was a slaughter. It looks like the village was bombed, then bombed again, and then bombed one more time to flatten everything. The air force has a joke about using so much ordnance on a target that in the end, the only thing pilots can do is make the rubble bounce. Two years ago, Elizabeth, the rubble here must have been dancing."

"I want to take a closer look," she says.

"Not too close," I say. "There might be unexploded munitions still among the rubble."

She nods and I take lead again, stepping carefully. The wind rises, and I hear the flapping of the funeral flags in the distance. I look down and see scraps of cloth, bits of metal and bones.

Lots of bones.

Deacon swears and says, "Who did this, John?"

"Like that French doctor I ran into at the aid station said two years back—we did."

"What, a rogue military mission?"

I say, "You heard Gul. This is part of something that's going to happen back in the States. A coup. A goddamn coup. Maybe rogue, maybe planned, who the hell knows."

On the ground is something that looks like a dark brown brick wrapped in clear plastic, about the size of one of our MREs. I crush it with my boot.

Deacon says, "What is it?"

"Brick of opium," I say. "Worth about a hundred bucks here, maybe ten thousand over in the States."

Deacon is quiet as I take my time destroying the opium brick completely with my boot, and it strikes me: Was it opium from here that was converted to the heroin that poisoned my parents? Was this the place where it all started? This barren place—is this where it began for my long-dead father and long-absent mother back in the States? And what weird or strange quirk of fate or kismet brought me here?

"Well? What next?" Deacon asks.

"Let's wait another five or ten minutes, then head out."

She says nothing, but I can sense her disappointment. Still, what did she hope to find here? A sole survivor living in the rubble, ready to reveal all and solve our crisis thousands of miles away?

We both walk carefully through the rubble, and I see more scraps of cloth, a leather sandal, and broken pottery.

What was it like here that night when the bombs and rockets fell over and over again? I imagine the explosions, the screams, the roar of buildings collapsing, and then the brief moment when the explosions stopped and the few survivors tried to race to the safety of the nearby hills, only to be cut down by the harsh chatter of machine-gun fire.

And for what?

Something catches my eye—a piece of green plastic.

I am about to say something but keep my mouth shut. I take a knee, pretend to retie my left boot, and gingerly pick up the piece of plastic. It's a bit of a circuit board, about the size of a playing card, lots of circuitry and—

A serial number. Nice and clear and whole: ANZ-10-8907688 P Q.

I stare at it, turn it over and over again in my gloved hand.

Then I slip it in a thigh pocket of my BDUs and stand up.

Deacon is about five yards away. "Everything okay?" she asks.

"Sure is," I say.

Then rapid gunfire breaks out, the rounds snapping over our heads and ricocheting off the rubble.

Together, we start running.

CHAPTER

90

GENERAL WAYNE GRISSOM is back at the White House for another briefing with the president. Well, technically, he's underneath the White House, nearly two hundred feet down in one of the most recently built bomb shelters.

He's been here twice before, but only on training modules, and he feels sick knowing this is the first time he's entering the place officially.

Grissom is in a room adjoining the president's temporary office, sitting on an uncomfortable couch, briefcase at his feet, hat in his lap, clear disposable gloves on his hands. The walls are concrete and painted a sickly green color, and two Secret Service agents in full battle gear are staring at him.

Earlier, Grissom went through the humiliation of having every part of his body searched. Then his temperature was taken, his blood drawn—to make sure he wasn't carrying any communicable pathogens—and he and his briefcase were x-rayed.

"Sorry," a Secret Service technician had said. "New procedures."

He held up his hands. "And the gloves?"

The technician seemed almost ashamed. "Sorry. Always a possibility there's poison under your fingernails. We have to account for that."

Sure, Grissom thinks. Always new procedures to protect POTUS. Like this shelter, built a few years back to protect the president in case a Russian Borei-class submarine off the coast of Maryland suddenly lobs an SS-NX-30 into DC, giving the White House maybe five minutes' warning before nuclear destruction.

Now the shelter is protecting the president not from a foreign adversary but apparently from some of his very own people.

The heavy steel door of the president's quarters opens. A female Secret Service agent in a black pantsuit comes out and says, "The president will see you now."

"Thank you," Grissom says. He gets up and takes the few strides into the large room.

Unlike the Oval Office two hundred feet up, this place is well lit, though the fluorescent lights overhead give the place a sickly pallor. The president is sitting behind a reproduction of the Resolute Desk, and there are two flat-screen televisions set into the concrete wall, one showing a forest and the other showing a lake.

Grissom thinks, *If those screens are supposed to brighten up the place, they're utterly failing.*

President Lucas Kent looks about ten years older than he did when Grissom met with him on the Oval Office patio. He's dressed casually in blue jeans and a checkered flannel shirt.

Kent doesn't get up, and Grissom doesn't make the effort to shake his hand. He takes a seat in front of the desk. The room is the same sickly green as the waiting area, and even though the place is carpeted, there's a chill in the air.

"Well?" the president says.

"Sir, we've come to an impasse, I'm sorry to say."

The president says nothing for a moment, then starts talking quietly. "I've felt something for the past several days," he says, his voice hoarse. "The news media hasn't picked up on it yet, but most members of Congress are gone, out taking tours or visiting their home districts. The vice president is at Mount Weather, and even most of the cabinet secretaries are out in the countryside." He wipes his face with a trembling hand. "The First Lady and the girls...they're in California, at the western White House."

"That does sound prudent," Grissom says, not liking the thought of the president of the United States riding out this storm of violence alone in a deep bunker. Too many dreary historical parallels.

The president finally acknowledges his presence. "Yes, it is prudent, just like this administration. But the latest I've heard from the CIA and the NSA is that the attack is coming in one or two days. And it will probably involve a nuclear device or some other weapon of mass destruction." The president stops speaking. There is utter silence in this underground office. Then: "I'm sorry, General. You were saying? Something about an impasse?"

Grissom says, "That's correct, sir. We are at an impasse. It's doubtful that, after months of investigation, we will be able to come up with the sources of these terrorist attacks and halt them before the major attack that's expected."

"What do you suggest, then, General?"

Grissom opens his briefcase, pulls out a red-bordered file folder, and removes from it a single sheet of paper with his seal on it. He passes it over the faux Resolute Desk.

"Martial law, sir," Grissom says. "It's time you declare it. You have no other choice."

CHAPTER 91

IT'S STANDARD MILITARY doctrine that when ambushed, you fight forward toward the ambushers, spoiling their aim and killing those whom you can kill.

But our situation is anything but standard here; we're alone, with no reinforcements and no air assets over the horizon. Making a stand amid the rubble might work for a while, but soon we'll be outflanked, within the attackers' grenade range, or otherwise overwhelmed.

I think through all of this in about a second, then push Deacon and say, "Peel, now! You first!"

Deacon runs, keeping her head down and zigzagging, while I drop and take cover among broken stone and rubble, sending off three-round bursts at our ambushers. I do a quick scan and see maybe five or six attackers in motion, and Deacon yells, "Covering fire!"

She starts firing and it's my turn to move, peeling away from my position and doing what Deacon did, head down, zigzagging, making my six-foot-nine-inch frame as small a target as possible.

I race behind Deacon as she continues her shooting, and when

I get about thirty or so yards from her, I take cover behind brush-covered boulders and yell, "Covering fire!"

I snap out three-round bursts as she hauls ass in my direction, and I see our attackers have stretched out in a skirmish line. Except for the first burst of gunfire when we were ambushed—done in the undisciplined spray-and-pray method—their shooting has been focused.

Deacon yells, "Covering fire!" and it's my turn again. I pick up the pace and keep running, and I hear a *snap* as a bullet goes over my head, way too close for comfort. Before us is the same monotonous landscape of rocks, scrub brush, and boulders, and then a small hill comes into view. I skid to a halt near Deacon and fire off another three-round burst, and the action of my M4 snaps back into the open position, meaning my thirty-round magazine is empty.

"Reloading," I call out. I insert a fresh magazine into my M4 and let the bolt snap back into position.

Deacon yells, "Why the hell are you still here? Move it!"

I fire again, and I hear the satisfying yelp of one of our attackers getting hit. I scan, look for more targets, and say, "Move where? They're going to outlast or outflank us eventually, Elizabeth. We can't run forever."

She fires again. "You got a better idea?"

I tap her shoulder, point to the nearby hill. "Yeah. I go up there, set up overwatch, and keep them busy while you get away."

She mutters an obscene phrase and says, "Get away where?"

"To your Agency friends across the border," I say. I dig into the side pocket of my pants and pull out the circuit board I recovered from the cracked bricks and rubble. I press it into her hand. "This," I say. "There's a serial number on it. Get it analyzed, find out who in hell had this ordnance and why it was used here. Walk back the cat, find out what you can. We don't have much time left. Gul told us about a coup. Maybe he's exaggerating, maybe he's not. The U.S. is not Bolivia...yet."

"John—"

I see movement, fire off another three-round burst, then give her a hard stare. "Can I trust you, Elizabeth? Trust that you'll follow this up and do the right thing for the country, not just for you and the Agency?"

She looks like she's going to spit at me. Then she looks at the circuit board.

Secures it in a pocket.

"You sure as hell can," she says.

"Outstanding."

We both put another set of three-round bursts down. I say, "That's evidence, and it's got to get back to the States. You're it. I'll hold 'em off as long as I can."

"John—"

"Damn it, you silly bitch, go! Every second you delay, they gain ground on us. Move!"

She nods, opens a magazine pouch, removes two thirty-round magazines, and hands them over. Then she gives me a quick and hard kiss on the lips. "It'll take time for transport to get to the base," she says. "I'll be waiting for you."

"Thanks," I say. "Haul ass."

Deacon hauls ass, and I resume firing.

CHAPTER 92

THE PRESIDENT LOOKS at the document, frowns, and pokes a finger at it like it's a raw piece of chicken presented to him as lunch.

"Martial law?" he asks.

Grissom says, "Yes, sir. I'm afraid so. We are at the limit of the powers accorded to us by the Constitution. We have to take the next step, as distasteful as it is, to protect you and the nation."

The president says, "And what does that entail, martial law?"

"It's all in that letter, sir. You should consult with the attorney general as soon as you can and make the announcement. It means the suspension of habeas corpus, the arrest and detainment of individuals the FBI and CIA know have connections to various terrorist and extremist groups, travel restrictions, and government oversight of the news media."

"Oversight?" the president says. "You mean censorship?"

Grissom says, "No, sir. Oversight. It's the news media's job to report the news. That won't be affected. But when you have certain cable networks and their respective talking heads spreading lies, rumors, and absolute bitterness in order to drive up their ratings, that's not news anymore. It's inciting hate, inciting violence, poisoning civil discourse."

"And what about the National Guard?"

"Activated across the nation to support regular army troops, assist law enforcement in making arrests, and provide security for vital infrastructure."

The president stares at the memo, his eyes welling up with tears. "I can't do this, General Grissom. I can't declare martial law and go down in history as a U.S. president who became a dictator."

Grissom has been expecting this response. "With all due respect, Mr. President, nearly a hundred years ago, another president faced incredible challenges as well. He met these challenges by sometimes skirting the law and issuing executive orders. He even illegally sent more than one hundred thousand loyal Americans of Japanese descent to internment camps, where nearly two thousand eventually met their death."

Grissom reaches into his trouser pocket, pulls out a handful of change, removes a dime, and slides it across the desk. "But was this president demonized? Impeached? Hated from generation to generation? No, he remains one of our most admired presidents."

The president shakes his head again. "I can't do it. I won't do it. I swore an oath to defend the Constitution, and I won't violate that oath."

"Mr. President, one of your predecessors, Abraham Lincoln, once said that the Constitution is not a death pact. He did what he had to do to save the Union." Grissom reaches across, taps the letter. "You need to do the same."

The president stares at the sheet of paper, then abruptly pushes it back across the desk. "Take it," he says. "I won't do it."

"Sir, you—"

"That's all, General Grissom," he says. "You are dismissed."

Grissom works his jaw and puts the letter back into his briefcase, picks up his hat, and says, "With your permission, sir, I'd like to dispatch a company of soldiers from the Third U.S. Infantry Regiment at Fort Myers to the White House grounds as an added layer of protection. They can be here within hours."

"No," the president says. "This is the people's house. Not a fortress."

Grissom sourly thinks, *Well, I offered.* "Very well, sir," he says, wondering if he's talking to a dead man. "The best of luck to you, sir."

The president doesn't answer, just stares at his clear desk.

Grissom walks to the door, desperate to get fresh air.

CHAPTER 93

WITH DEACON GONE, I'm under no illusion that I can win this battle. My little fighting force has lost half its effectiveness, and the enemy—the Taliban, angry tribal members, or farmers who think we stole their goats—is still advancing.

But I'm not giving up. I'm buying time for Deacon to get back to the CIA outpost just over the border, and I plan to join her as soon as I can.

I start to clamber up the small, rocky hill to get a better view of the battlefield below and behind me. I stop halfway, break out a small pair of binoculars, scan the terrain. I see at least six attackers moving toward me slowly and deliberately, taking cover as they approach, and I fire off four three-round bursts to slow them down, then resume my climb upward.

Minutes later, I'm at the top.

My lungs are burning, my legs are aching, and my rucksack seems fifty pounds heavier. The top of the hill is nearly flat, a square stretch about the size of two tennis courts, with dirt and more rocks, boulders, and crevasses.

I drop my rucksack, take aim down below. I see three fighters moving closer to the hill.

I fire until my bolt snaps open and quickly reload, and then I hear the snap of a bullet going over my head and ricocheting off a near rock.

A bullet coming from the opposite direction.

Damn it!

I scurry to the other side, and sure enough, I see the bastards have outflanked me. Two are coming up at me from that side.

Two more bursts from me to slow them down.

I really hope Deacon is running like hell.

What now?

I move and duck; two more rounds slap my way. My attackers have split into three groups, and they're all advancing on me at the same time. I can hold them off for a while, but eventually they'll get close enough to pour on the fire and overwhelm me.

I go back to the top of my little command.

I think, *Keep running, Elizabeth, keep running safely with that evidence.*

I peer again, see movement, fire off another three-round burst. The action to my M4 snaps open and locks. Reloading time.

I drop the empty magazine and slap another one in, noting I have just four more left. I move across the soft bare dirt in the center of this little hilltop, frantically trying to come up with a plan, knowing I owe it to Willow and Alex and the Cross family and everybody else to get out of here alive.

Alive.

I drop my rucksack, get to work.

Billie, I pray again, *one more time, that's all I ask.*

CHAPTER

94

ELIZABETH DEACON COLLAPSES, breathing hard, legs trembling, thirsty as hell. She pulls out her water bottle, takes a long swallow, puts the cap back on, rolls over among the rocks, and looks at the distance she's covered.

She grabs her binoculars and looks at the small hill where John is making his stand. She hears the distant echoes of gunfire and sees two figures leapfrogging up the side of the hill.

"John," she whispers. "Kill them. Kill them all."

She has a sudden urge to run back and hit John's attackers from the rear, but she shakes it off. She has to get back to Tajikistan. Has to.

She blinks tears from her eyes, whispers, "Good luck." The attackers are getting close to the top, and it seems like John's run out of ammunition.

"Oh, damn it to hell," she says; she puts the binoculars in her rucksack, gets up, and starts running, not looking back.

CHAPTER

95

ONLY A YARD or so left before getting to the top of this accursed hill, but Bibi Ahmadi is feeling the taste of triumph. They have chased this tall Black man like an escaped goat, and now he's trapped on top of this hill. No place to go. Bibi's cousin Fateh is lying dead back there, a bullet through his forehead, but Bibi envies the warrior. He is now in paradise, enjoying the rewards from Allah.

Bibi stops, takes a deep breath. His own reward will be his in just a few moments. Kill the Black man, then chase after his companion whore.

He takes cover behind two cracked boulders at the top of the hill. He yells out, "Hey, Sampson. Black man! Surrender! You are trapped!"

One by one, his cousins also shout, announcing their advances.

"Bibi, I'm here."

"Tell us when, Bibi!"

"Ready, cousin!"

Bibi looks around, offers a quick prayer to Allah, and yells, "Now!"

He moves around the two cracked boulders, AK-47 held out in

front of him, and sees his cousins emerge from the other side of the rocky hilltop.

No Sampson.

Bibi looks around wildly. Where did he go?

"Bibi," his cousin Azeez says, looking as puzzled as the other three. "Where is he?"

"Look over there," Bibi says, "see if he's hiding in one of these cracks."

"But he's so tall, how could he do that?"

Bibi says, "Look, curse you, look!"

Azeez moves about the rocks and boulders. There's a large bumpy patch of dirt in the center, and Azeez cries out, "Look! Here! He must have run away, but see what he's left."

Bibi makes quick time to where his cousin is standing and pointing.

Balanced against a rock is the Black man's M4, and on the ground next to it is his rucksack. But no Sampson.

How could he have slipped by?

Impossible.

Azeez moves to the rucksack and says, "I saw it first, it belongs to me!"

Bibi sees his cousin kneel down and grab the rucksack, and too late, Bibi yells, "No!"

CHAPTER 96

I WAIT, TWISTED in an uncomfortable position, breathing through my nose.

The voices are getting closer.

I tense up; every nerve ending seems to vibrate with anticipation.

The voices are louder now, and even though I can't understand their language, I can tell they're confused, surprised, amazed.

Good.

I'm waiting for another noise.

It comes hard and quick.

Boom!

I uncurl myself from the hidey-hole I had hurriedly dug underneath an overhanging slab of rock, toss off the ground tarp that was about the same color as the surrounding soft dirt; dirt and small rocks slide off the tarp.

I pull out my pistol, and in three long paces I get to where I left my M4, rucksack, and an army-issue M67 fragmentation grenade, pin pulled and placed under the heavy rucksack.

There's a haze of smoke and the smell of burned gunpowder and blood, and my attackers are spread out, a bloody mess. I do a quick count in the mess of legs, arms, and torsos: there are five heads.

My rucksack is gone, my M4 is in pieces, but it's a fair exchange.

I still have water, the hand-drawn map, a compass, my pistol, a spare grenade, and three magazines of nine-millimeter ammunition on my MOLLE harness.

That's all I need for the next several hours.

From the pile of shattered bodies, I hear, "You... you..."

I go over.

It's what's left of Bibi. One eye is gone, and there's blood all over him. It looks like he was shielded by one of his fighters when the grenade went off.

He stares up at me with anger and hate, and I say, "Yep, it's me."

I shoot him in the middle of his forehead.

CHAPTER 97

ELIZABETH DEACON FORDS the Panj River and enters Tajikistan. She's tired but feels a burst of energy, knowing she's almost there, almost back to the CIA base, and from there she can get home.

She turns around and looks back into Afghanistan, wondering how John Sampson is doing. Is he still alive, and if he's alive, how far behind her is he?

Could he have made it?

She doesn't know.

Waste of time to worry about it, though. Too many other things to think about.

In her rucksack is a sat phone she can use to reach her contact in the air force, who'll provide quick transport back to DC.

But there's one more thing she has to do.

Deacon pulls out the broken circuit board Sampson gave her a few hours ago. She stares at it, then gently places it on a rock near the slow-moving and shallow river.

She looks around, finds another rock, and pounds on the circuit board until it's in pieces, and she makes sure all of the broken pieces are swept into the moving water.

CHAPTER 98

IT'S LESS THAN an hour since I crossed back into Tajikistan, and based on the map Gul gave me, I'm close to the airstrip and the small CIA installation.

I scramble up a rocky rise, and at the top, as I catch my breath, I see two beautiful sights.

First, the tents and buildings of the CIA outpost.

And second, a U.S. Air Force SST jet, either the one that brought us here or its twin.

I start running down the hill and think, *Where first?*

The bird, I decide. *Let's get on the jet and worry about everything else later.* Aloud I say, "Bless you, Liz, you kept your word."

I trot across the cracked runway to a set of metal stairs going up to the smooth fuselage, right behind the cockpit. A senior airman wearing camos and holding an M4 says, "You Sampson?"

"I am," I say, almost out of breath.

"Come on in," he says, waving a gloved hand. "We need to get moving."

I duck into the aircraft and look down the two rows of red webbing seating and the flat bulkhead where gear can be secured.

It's empty.

"Where's Deacon?"

"Who?" the senior airman asks.

"Elizabeth Deacon," I say. "She was with me earlier. She should be here."

He shakes his head. "Sorry, order we got was to pick up one passenger, and one passenger only. John Sampson. And that's you, right?"

"Shit," I say, and I add, "Give me a minute. I need to check something out."

The air force NCO glances at his watch. "You got your sixty seconds, pal, but not a second more."

I duck my head, go back to the airstrip, run over to the big tent, and tug open the flap. It looks like the interior of the tent is stuck in time, because I see the same number of guys doing the same things they were doing before: drinking coffee, cleaning weapons, checking the screens on their terminals.

I say to the near guy, "Bobby, where the hell is she?"

He says, "Deacon? She's been gone for about two hours."

I don't know what to say. She left without me. "She leave a message?"

He laughs. "Liz? Would she ever leave a message, leave behind evidence of anything?"

I hear the engines of the SST transport start to whine. Bobby nods in the direction of the tent flaps. "You better get going, Sampson. Your flight back to the promised land is about to leave."

I don't argue; I push through the flaps, run back to the aircraft. Dust and gravel are being kicked up, and I go up the collapsible steps and clamber inside. The senior airman says, "Ten seconds to spare. Good timing!"

He pulls the steps in, swings the cabin door closed, and fastens it tight, and I sit back on the red webbing, feeling exhausted, hungry, and thirsty, but most of all…

Feeling betrayed.

I remember Ned Mahoney saying, *Don't trust anyone.*

I made a mistake.

I trusted Elizabeth Deacon, a CIA consultant.

The NCO yells over at me, and I fasten my seat belt. The aircraft speeds down the runway and climbs into the Tajikistan air.

I won't make that mistake again.

Part Five

CHAPTER 99

SUPERVISING SPECIAL AGENT Ned Mahoney is in his office, yawning, trying to concentrate on the various memos and reports scattered across his desk. Right now he's focusing on three recent reports.

First up is a dispatch from field offices in Oklahoma City and St. Louis. Agents from both offices are concerned that their SACs—special agents in charge—have gone rogue; they're conducting investigations on their own, keeping everything close to the vest, not bringing anyone else in on the work.

Ned thinks, *Is this the real deal or just some disgruntled agents using the current crisis to strike out against their bosses?*

The second memo is from the Bureau's Counterintelligence Division, which—among its many duties—keeps track of foreign diplomats on American soil. This report is troubling as hell—it says that, quietly and unofficially, the Russian and Chinese embassies in Washington have sent most of their staff home.

Meaning?

Maybe that they know the District is going to be attacked in a few days, and they want as few of their people as possible in the target area.

Question: Are they doing this out of caution, having eavesdropped on domestic law enforcement agencies, or because they've either planned it or helped support it?

He puts that message aside, resists an urge to rub at the throbbing in his left leg just above his ankle, where two pieces of shattered ball bearings tore up skin and muscle.

Ned grabs the third report, this one from the field office in Cincinnati. Agents had immediately raced to the home of the late Lucille Palmer, whose newly widowed husband, Walter, was in shock. He agreed to give the FBI agents full access to his home and his wife's possessions. The only interesting fact they discovered was that Lucille had belonged to a local book club whose five other members, both male and female, had disappeared after the news came out about the Union Station bombing. Leads are currently being developed on the background and whereabouts of—

Loud voices are coming from outside his office.

Getting louder.

Ned's suspicions and paranoia have grown over the summer, and he gingerly slips out his Bureau-issue Glock 19 nine-millimeter pistol as the door opens up. It's Barry Leonard, his aide, looking flustered. "Excuse me, sir, I told her you were busy, but—"

Barry's elbowed aside by Her Honor the mayor of the District of Columbia Winifred Crocker, and Ned returns the pistol to its place. "It's all right, Barry, I'll see her," Ned says. "Hold my calls, all right?"

"Yes, sir."

The mayor strides into his office, dumps her large black leather purse and long tan coat on one of the two chairs in front of his desk, and sits down in the other, hands clasped tightly.

"Winny," he says, standing up to shake her hand. "I want—"

"Forget it," she says. "Right now, I don't care about the time we've spent together or the bonds we have. Right now you're the FBI, and you sure as hell don't have permission to call me by my first name. Got it?"

Ned sits back down. "Got it, Madam Mayor."

"Good," she says, her eyes burning right into him. "I want to know right now what the hell is going to happen here in my city."

"Madam Mayor, with all due respect, I think you should be talking with Chief— "

"That fool?" she interrupts. "He wants just two things—his photo on the front page of the *Post* and to run against me next year. All I get from him is the crap he gets from his folks who attend a law enforcement meeting twice a day." She unclasps her hands, leans forward. "Ever since the sniper attacks and bombings started here in DC, I've been like a mushroom with the chief—kept in the dark and fed bullshit. That ends now, Agent Mahoney."

He feels her anger and frustration roll over him like a huge heat lamp. He says, "All right. It ends now. Ask away."

She seems taken aback. "That's it? 'Ask away'? No sweet words about going through channels or shit like that?"

"Ask away, Madam Mayor," he repeats.

The mayor still seems surprised. "All right, well, this is a nice change of pace. We've always been treated like some goddamn poor relation here. We're at the end of the line for federal aid, have no real representation in Congress—we're mostly ignored. So tell me this, Ned: Who's behind all these attacks?"

"We don't know."

"Oh, don't give me that," she says. "You've got to have some sort of lead, some intelligence."

"I wish we did," he says. "We've managed to make some arrests, crack some domestic terrorist cells, but there's nothing connecting them together. We have right-wing militia groups. We have people associated with Antifa and with Black Lives Matter. We have rabid environmentalists, anarchists, Marxists, and yesterday, we had a suburban mom from Ohio who wore a suicide vest and tried to murder scores of commuters at Union Station."

"I know, I know," she says. "I was there. But you can't find a connection?"

"None at all," he says. "My agency, the CIA, the NSA, and pretty much every law enforcement outfit in the nation are able to track these people up to a point, and then it stops. No incriminating phone calls, texts, or e-mails. What we do know is that beginning nearly a year ago, all of these groups got a sudden infusion of cash and intelligence."

"A supporter with lots of money and influence," she says.

"That's right," Ned says. "But whoever is providing those funds is doing it from various sites on the dark web that use cryptocurrency. We try to trace those sites, but they pop up for a day or two, then disappear."

They're both quiet for a moment.

"So that's it, then," she says.

"I'm afraid it is."

She seems to steel herself. "I've heard rumors that you have intelligence indicating that one final, spectacular attack is going to happen soon. Do you know when?"

The answer to that question is one of the most closely guarded secrets in government, but Ned doesn't hesitate.

"Tomorrow," he says. "Or maybe the day after. No later than that."

She nods crisply. "All right. Any idea what's coming our way?"

"Something big," Ned says. "Perhaps bioterrorism, a gas attack, maybe a dirty bomb or something bigger. But it's coming."

The mayor lowers her head for a moment, composing herself, and when she looks up, Ned says, "Just so you know, there's been an unofficial evacuation of key people from the government and Congress. Nothing public, but there's been a steady outflow of people either visiting their home states or taking a couple of sick days."

"Why are you telling me this?" she asks, voice hard as stone.

"Because you could do the same, Madam Mayor. No shame in it."

Her next words are almost spat out. "The hell there isn't. I'm not running away, not for one damn second. Nobody's running me out of my city. Are you leaving?"

"No," Ned says. "My work is here."

"Good," she says, gathering up her coat and purse. "Same for me. And if you need anything, anything at all from me or in DC, call me and you've got it. No questions asked."

"Thank you, Madam Mayor."

A slight smile. "You're welcome, Ned. You take care of yourself, okay?"

She heads to the door and Ned says, "You too, Winny."

CHAPTER

100

VALERIE PENNY LIVES in a lovely retirement community in Silver Spring, Maryland, just off Route 29 but not so close that she hears traffic at night. She's a retired Department of Labor accountant, and thanks to her late husband's careful investments, she lives a very comfortable life on Sunset Shore Drive.

The other day, Valerie saw two dark blue SUVs roll up to the Balantics' house. She doesn't know much about the Balantics except that they both served in the navy—*Ugh, imagine having to wear a uniform every day*—and after working for defense contractors, they retired here.

The Balantics' visitors were a large Black family: An older woman, a woman in her forties or thereabouts, and four children, ranging in age from maybe first grade to their late teens. Not a problem, of course, but still…having all these kids abruptly arrive in her quiet neighborhood was certain to stir up concern among the older residents.

For the better part of a day, she watches the large family through a pair of binoculars she uses for field trips with the local Audubon

Society chapter, and when she recognizes the younger woman's face—not the one who looked like she was seventy or something—she is startled.

The next day, while volunteering at a Silver Spring food bank, putting boxes of instant macaroni and cheese up on a crowded shelf, she says to her friend Becky Zimmer, "You won't believe who's living next door to me."

"Who?" Becky asks.

"Bree Stone," Valerie says. "Remember her? A few years back, she was a big deal with the police department in the District, then there was some sort of scandal and she left. She's married to Alex Cross."

"Oh, yes," Becky says, putting up cans of Dinty Moore beef stew. "That investigator and psychologist, the one who wrote those books. Wasn't he almost killed the other day, got shot?"

Valerie says, "Yes, I know, how horrible. Too many guns and nuts in this country, if you ask me. Anyway, she's moved in with the Balantics, and it looks like she's brought her entire family with her, from the grandma to the littlest. Six in total."

"Six!"

Valerie nods.

"But why move someplace like your neighborhood?'

Valerie carefully places another box of macaroni and cheese on the shelf. "I bet with Alex recovering, they're low on money. It's expensive to take care of all those kids. And I bet the Balantics are letting them live there rent-free."

Her friend says, "Isn't that nice."

The next day, Becky Zimmer is having lunch with three of her closest friends at the Capital Grille in Chevy Chase. She waits for a pause in the conversation—which covers topics ranging from the latest doctor's visits to ungrateful grandchildren to husbands who still leave the toilet seat up—and says, "You'll never guess who's moved in next door to my friend Valerie Penny."

After a chorus of "Who? Don't hold back! Tell us!" Becky says, "Bree Stone and the whole Cross family, that's who. She's married to Alex Cross, that doctor and detective who's written all those books. Can you believe that?"

Her three friends most definitely can't believe that, and they discuss the puzzling news as their lunch is served: four Cobb salads with sliced tenderloin.

Hector Ramirez doesn't consider himself a spy; he thinks of himself as an information courier. For the past year and a half, he's worked for a number of folks who want to know about the gossip and bits of news he picks up from the diners he serves. Military personnel, government employees, and executives from certain corporations in and around the Beltway have all been at his tables.

His latest request is for anything involving Brianna Stone, Alex Cross, or John Sampson. It's to be passed along via a call to a number in the burner phone he uses only for his part-time work.

When his shift is over—it was a rough day, with one tray dropped and two orders screwed up—he calls the supplied phone number from his burner and says, "This is Hector Ramirez. I have information on the location of Brianna Stone."

"Go," says a male voice.

He says, "She and her family are living in the household of the Balantics in a gated retirement community in Silver Spring."

"Good," the man says. "How much were you promised for this information?"

He's tempted to lie but doesn't. The man's tone frightens him. Hector says, "Five hundred dollars."

"You'll get one thousand," the man says.

Hector disconnects the call, smiles. What a great day this is turning out to be.

* * *

Two hours after Hector Ramirez's phone call, a dark blue GMC van bearing the logo of Lorenzo's Deli and Catering rolls slowly down Sunset Shore Drive, and the armed man sitting in the passenger seat says, "Okay, got it. That white Colonial."

The driver, a former Homeland Security investigator, says, "The place has got good forest coverage at the rear yard, a few nearby oaks. Good staging point."

"Yeah," the other man says. "I mean, how hard could it be to snatch a seven-year-old girl?"

They drive past the target house. In the rear of the van are other operators for the task at hand. The driver says, "It is a snatch job, right? Not an elimination?"

"Well," the other man says, "at least for the first day."

CHAPTER 101

EVEN AT SUPERSONIC speeds, it's a long damn trip back to the States. I drink bottled water and eat some energy bars and doze, and when I'm awake, all I think about is Elizabeth Deacon.

Ned Mahoney said, *Don't trust anyone.*

But Elizabeth and I were both on the battlefield, and I slipped up.

When we're about a half an hour out of Joint Base Andrews in Maryland, my burner cell phone comes to life. I log in to my regular phone account, and there's a continuous beeping noise as e-mails, texts, and updates flow into my cell.

I give the list a quick, disheartened scroll, thinking of what I'm going to do when we finally land.

Lots of messages from the DC Metro Police, and those I'll ignore.

Four messages from Ned Mahoney, all with the same subject line: CHECK IN PLEASE.

I'm about to call Ned when I see there's a message from yesterday from Bree Stone. Its subject line is YOUR TAJIKISTAN GENERAL.

The note says:

Took some digging but the officer you saw on that Tajikistan airfield two years ago is General Gerrold Mason. He retired shortly after you spotted him. His CV is attached in another document, but it looks like a typical officer who went up the career ladder, entering the army via West Point. Rose in the ranks with service in the Eighty-Second Airborne Division in Kuwait, Iraq, and Afghanistan.

You'll see he went to various schools along the way, including the NATO Defense College, the School of Advanced Military Studies at Fort Leavenworth, and the Center for Strategic and International Studies.

Also wrote a number of papers for proceedings concerning the future of military warfare with an emphasis on drone weapons and other over-the-horizon combat systems.

He's currently a VP of operational development at Global Security Services, based in Arlington.

But here's the kicker: Check out this link to the Stars and Stripes newspaper.

I do just that and see a news brief announcing General Mason's retirement, and sure enough, the guy in the photo is the officer I saw arguing vigorously with Elizabeth Deacon at that CIA airfield.

I go back to Bree's note.

Did you see the date in the story, John? It looks like Mason had a retirement ceremony on the same day you saw him overseas.

Guess he was already playing in the spook world at the time.

I look up from the screen. More questions, more puzzles.

I go back to Bree's message.

Hope this helps. Call us as soon as you can. Willow misses her dad. Alex is recovering. He's in and out of consciousness, but he keeps saying, "It's not random, it's not random," whatever that means.

Love, Bree

And there's a second kicker, much harder than the first one, in the postscript.

P.S. As to Mason's marital status, he's divorced but used to be married to Elizabeth Deacon, a CIA officer now working as a consultant.

CHAPTER

102

IT'S PAST MIDNIGHT and Bree Stone is sitting at a large round oak table in the luxurious dining room that belongs to her Bluestone Group associates Frank and Lori Balantic. They're navy veterans who now work in her company's counterintelligence section, and both are away tonight, visiting a sick nephew.

In the house with her are her stepdaughter, Jannie, and John's daughter, Willow. Her stepsons, Ali and Damon, are spending the night with their father at George Washington University Hospital, where he's improving by the hour, thank God. Nana Mama, who can't sleep, is in the large kitchen, working on a dinner to freeze for later.

Bree smiles as she hears Nana Mama muttering in the supposedly well-equipped Balantic kitchen: "Why the hell do you have to hang up these pots and pans so damn high?" and "What kind of kitchen doesn't have cayenne?" and "Bread crumbs. Is that so hard to keep on hand?"

Bree continues working on her company-issue laptop, trying to catch up by reading the minutes taken at the meetings she's missed over the past week.

She senses Jannie standing next to her, and Jannie says, "Bree."

Bree holds up a finger. "Give me a sec." *Where in hell is that last set of minutes? Is it in the trash folder?*

"Bree."

Her colleagues have been very sympathetic and understanding ever since Alex was shot, but still, she needs to show everyone that she's keeping on top of matters and—

Jannie raises her voice. "Bree, please!"

Bree looks over, says, "What's going on?"

When Jannie speaks again, Bree hears the fear in her voice.

"I've got to show you something right now," Jannie says.

In the living room, Jannie points out the large bay window and says, "There's a van parked at the end of the cul-de-sac, under that streetlight. It's been there for at least fifteen minutes. I checked it out a few minutes ago with Mrs. Balantic's old spyglass, the gift she got when she retired from the navy."

Bree picks up the heavy and ungainly spyglass. It trembles in her hand, and when she looks through the window, the view isn't that sharp. It's a typical GMC van belonging to a catering company.

Bree lowers the spyglass. "Some caterers. Maybe they're prepping for an early event."

Jannie shakes her head. "The van says Lorenzo's Deli and Catering."

"So?"

"That catering company belongs to Lorenzo DeMarco. I go to school with his niece Stacy. She told me he had to close his business a few months ago because he has high blood pressure and his wife told him enough was enough. There's no more Lorenzo's Deli and Catering." Jannie points to the van again. "That's a fake."

CHAPTER

103

ABOUT FORTY-FIVE MINUTES after the late-night landing at Joint Base Andrews and after I steal yet another car, I'm back at the Cross house.

With the new spare key to the back door I secured from Bree during my last visit—which seems ages ago—I let myself into the kitchen and quietly close the door behind me. I pause for a few sweet seconds, taking in the familiar smells of this blessed place, recalling all the fun times here with Alex and his family, the wonderful meals from Nana Mama, the shrieks and yells from his children, my own Willow lovingly being part of the action, part of this family.

I feel like standing here forever. But God, I can't.

When my eyes have adjusted to the dim light of the kitchen appliances, I gingerly make my way through the first-floor rooms and up the stairs.

It's darker up here, so I keep a hand on the wall as I walk to Alex's office. The door is open and I go in, then stand still.

Is it here, what he's been talking about? What Alex talked about just before he got shot, what he whispered to me before I flew off to Afghanistan, and what he's been saying to Bree?

It's not random.

I gently close the door behind me.

I fumble a bit as I draw the shades to two of the office's windows, and with a small penlight cupped in my large hand, I sit at Alex's wide and cluttered desk, feeling like an intruder. There are bookshelves, filing cabinets, piles of folders.

How can I be here, in his office, in his chair, pretending to be one-fifth the man he is when it comes to figuring out puzzles and seeing details with his cold and smart logic?

"Patterns," I whisper. "Get your ass to work, John."

I carefully go through the papers and notepads on his desk, seeing the information we received during that very first briefing, the list of the terrorist attacks beginning April 15 in Columbus, Georgia, scribbled in Alex's handwriting. There are check marks next to a few, probably meaning Alex had done confirming research on those cases.

At the bottom is a circled handwritten notation: *Pros are the source!*

True. But whose pros? Foreign? Domestic? Combination of both?

Not random, he had said. *Not random.*

But nothing in the papers on his desk suggests who the source was or why it wasn't random.

I think back to the day Alex was shot. He was carrying his briefcase when he was cut down. Was the evidence in there? And where is that briefcase now? In the evidence room at police headquarters or stolen by one of those taking part in these terrorist attacks?

I know how Alex works. He'd have a nice, prepared report, but that nice work would be based on lots of earlier work and drafts and—

I move my big left foot. Hit a wastebasket. Bend over and pull it out from underneath the desk. It's filled with scribbled notes, printouts of Google maps, arrows and numbers and lines connecting names.

I spread out on his desk the three most important crumpled sheets of paper.

There it is.

There it is.

CHAPTER

104

TO JANNIE, BREE calmly says, "You've got your cell on you?"

"Yes, Bree," she says, voice slightly quavering.

"Then dial 911 and tell the police a home invasion is under way at this address. Don't explain, just speak clearly and slowly, then hang up."

Bree walks deliberately out of the living room to the bottom of the grand stairs. She calls, "Willow? Can you hear me, Willow?"

She waits a minute or two and hears the quick *trot-trot-trot* of the girl's seven-year-old feet on the upstairs floor. A pajamaed Willow appears at the top of the stairs. "Yes, Auntie Bree?"

Bree says, "We're going to play a little game. I want you to go into the bedroom you're using, close and lock the door, then go in the bathroom and hide in the bathtub. Okay?"

Willow looks confused. "What kind of game is this, Auntie Bree?"

"Willow!" Bree snaps. "Just do it. Now."

Willow looks hurt, but she leaves, and Bree turns around and sees Jannie.

"Bree, I can't dial out," Jannie says. "I keep getting a busy signal. I can't get through."

Bree goes to her purse and pulls out her own iPhone. Yes, Jannie is right.

Beep-beep-beep.

Shit, Bree thinks, and she feels a deep thud of guilt at her own stupidity hit her chest. She could have had a car outside with Bluestone Group personnel in it, but this neighborhood being what it is, it would have meant a stream of calls to the local police about a suspicious-looking parked car. So she had turned down that offer, as well as Bluestone's offer to have men inside the house. The Balantics were gracious hosts, but the place was full enough with the Cross family stuffed inside.

Bree walks into the kitchen. Nana Mama is standing in front of the stove stirring something in a large black cast-iron pot. Bree goes up to her, turns off the stove.

Nana Mama turns, surprised. She's holding a wooden spoon in her hand. "Bree?"

"There's trouble out there," she says. "Men are coming to attack us."

"How many?"

"Don't know," she says. "We've tried calling the police but our calls are being blocked. Jannie, turn off all the lights," she says to her stepdaughter. "Make sure the doors are locked. Then you and Nana Mama go upstairs to the main bathroom, lock the doors, and crawl into the bathtub." She goes back to her purse, removes her nine-millimeter Glock. She has two spare magazines.

Bree looks at her laptop. She suddenly sits down.

She checks her connection to the Bluestone Group's corporate cloud. The heavy-duty high-tech laptop from the Bluestone Group isn't being jammed. She still has internet access.

Make a Skype call to the local police? Or send an e-mail?

And how long before someone can get here?

Someone squeezes her shoulder. It's Nana Mama, holding a large and shiny knife in her hand. "Jannie's gone upstairs, child," she says, her voice strong. "But I'm not leaving your side."

"Nana Mama, please."

The hand on her shoulder squeezes harder. "Bree, I went through things you can't even imagine when Jim Crow ruled the land. I'm staying. We'll get through this together. What are you going to do?"

Bree's fingers start flying across the keyboard. "Work smarter, not harder," she says.

Nana Mama smiles. "Make it faster, too, if there's bad men out there."

CHAPTER 105

I STUFF THE folded sheets of evidence in my jacket pocket and slowly walk out of Alex's home. It's so empty and quiet.

It's not right. This home should be filled with laughter, arguments, voices from the TV, smells coming from the kitchen, Nana Mama's firm voice cutting through everything.

It's not right.

Time to make it right.

I go out of the house and lock the door behind me, then cross the small yard to the sidewalk. It's either late at night or early in the morning. Even with the streetlights and headlights of passing cars, I still feel like I'm in utter darkness.

I walk to my stolen car. What now?

I'll go to the only person I trust at the moment, Ned Mahoney of the FBI. I'll tell him what I've found, and things will start moving.

If it isn't too late.

God, Billie, please don't let us be too late.

A dark blue Mercedes-Benz comes to a sudden halt next to me. I turn.

The passenger door pops open.

The driver is leaning over the fine leather seats pointing a pistol at me.

"Get in, John," Elizabeth Deacon says. "We don't have much time."

CHAPTER 106

THE MAN LEADING the squad is moving slowly and confidently in the woods behind the target house. The four of them have come to the edge of the woods where the finely manicured lawn begins, and he looks at the rear of the house, taking it all in. Usually ops like this require lots of planning and prep, but Maynard told him earlier that there was no time.

"Just snatch the girl and let me know when she's secured," Maynard said. "Then we'll tell John Sampson we have the little brat and if he wants to see her again, he'll go sit on a park bench in Lafayette Square for twenty-four hours and do absolutely nothing. No phone calls, no messages, no visits. Then he'll get her back."

"Alive?"

Maynard said, "Don't go putting words in my mouth. Get the job done."

Seems like a pretty straightforward task. The house is two stories high and has a small deck with sliding doors. At the rear there are three windows on the ground floor and four on the second.

Strange. No lights are on, even though there were a few lights on just a couple of minutes ago when they drove by.

Have the targets left?

The other three operators are lined up by the trees, preparing.

He starts to lower his night-vision goggles when it all goes wrong all at once.

Willow doesn't like being in the tub, doesn't like being alone, doesn't like Aunt Bree snapping at her, and she misses her dad. She gets out of the tub, unlocks the door, and goes into the bedroom. The only nice part about this whole thing is that she has this room to herself and doesn't have to share it with her cousin Ali, who stays up late playing with his iPhone and giggling and farting like a boy.

She hears Aunt Bree and Nana Mama talking seriously downstairs, and they sound scared.

If they're scared, then so is she.

A shadow comes across the window.

The squad leader hears the chiming, the music, the voices, and he realizes that all the cell phones in this little squad are announcing incoming calls, even though their phones were powered off an hour ago!

What the hell?

He pulls his cell out of his back pocket to see what in the world is going on. He has an incoming text:

Dear trespassers:

You four are currently being targeted by infrared lasers centered on your foreheads. Due to their unique frequency shifting, the lasers will remain invisible no matter what gear you possess.

Sounds high-tech, but if you think I'm bluffing, recall how all four of your cell phones were activated remotely.

You have fifteen seconds to reverse course and depart. If you don't, your brains and fragments of your skulls will be scattered all over this backyard. Restore our communications and go.

He waits, heart racing, and then he lifts his right arm and makes the retreat motion, and the four of them go back into the woods.

Bree looks at her laptop screen with deep satisfaction at how she successfully negotiated with the Bluestone Group operations center. After some serious give-and-take, they released a classified stealth drone that had been doing contract work for Homeland Security.

The drone easily located the four gunmen moving through the woods, and through additional help from her employer's operations center, she managed to trigger their four cell phones and pass on her text message.

She watches the four men retreat, the drone keeping pace with them, their thermal images visible through the trees and foliage.

The part about special infrared spotting lasers is so much bullshit, but it seems to be working. *Well done,* she thinks, a thought she carries for only a few seconds.

"Bree?" Jannie's voice is trembling. "Willow is gone."

CHAPTER 107

I STARE AT Elizabeth Deacon, frozen with shock. She waves her pistol at me.

"In," she says. "Now. We've got to get going."

A lot of thoughts are racing through my mind, but now is the time for action, not for standing speechless on a sidewalk. And I won't waste time asking her how she found me.

Finding people is her job.

I open the door wider, get in, and as I sit down and shut the door, I slip out my Glock. I turn and press it against her abdomen. "If you remember your training, Liz, this is what's called a Mexican standoff," I say. "Not particularly PC, but it is what it is."

"I guess so," she says, still pointing her pistol at me. "What now?"

"You put yours away, and I'll do the same."

"Why should I go first?" she says, pistol not moving.

"Because you started it," I say.

We stare at each other, then she lowers her pistol to her side.

I lower mine too.

She puts the Mercedes in drive, and we get on the road.

We travel in silence for a few minutes. I decide to work my way through my list of questions and start with "You left me behind in Tajikistan. Why?"

Deacon says, "No, I didn't."

"You weren't at the base when I got there."

"That's right," she says. "But there was still transportation waiting for you."

"But you weren't there," I say. "What was the rush?"

She turns right onto Virginia Avenue. The horizon to the east begins to turn gray as a new day approaches.

Deacon says, "I had to make a decision. I had to get back to the States as fast as I could, and no offense, John, but half a dozen attackers were gunning for you. The odds weren't in your favor. At least I made sure you had a ride back if you survived." She accelerates as we approach an on-ramp to I-695 West. "You could say thanks, you know."

"Maybe later," I say. "What now?"

"Now?" she asks. "Now we're off to meet a traitor."

CHAPTER 108

BREE GETS UP from her laptop and goes up the stairs; Jannie and Nana Mama follow.

"Willow!" Bree calls. "Are you hiding up here?" She walks into Willow's room, and Jannie and Nana Mama go down the hall to check the other bedrooms. Bree sees Willow's toys, knapsack, and stuffed animals, but no Willow. She enters the bathroom.

Empty.

"Willow! This isn't funny!"

Nana Mama and Jannie return. "We checked all the rooms and the closets. She's not there," Jannie says, her eyes red.

Bree gets on her knees, looks under the bed. Nothing.

She stands up, feels a draft.

From the window.

The window is partially open. "We must have missed another operator," she says, thinking, *Damn it, you were so focused on those four gunmen by the trees that you overlooked the rest of the scene.* "Jannie, if the phones are working, dial 911 and report a kidnapping."

Nana Mama still has the knife in her hand. "Let's go outside,

Bree. They might not have gotten far. That little girl will be putting up one hell of a fight."

Bree runs down the stairs, taking them two at a time. She doesn't want to shatter Nana Mama's illusions, but she knows that it doesn't matter to kidnappers how young or strong their victim is. They know how to snatch a person and go.

But still...

With her pistol in her hand, she tears through the living room and the spacious kitchen. She stops at the door leading to the rear yard. There's a row of light switches, and she palms them on all at once, and the yard lights up like it's high noon.

Bree opens the door with one hand, the other one holding her Glock. In her fear and desperation, she thinks of only one thing: *John, oh, John, you trusted me with your daughter and I screwed up. Big-time. The bad guys got her and I don't know what to do next.*

She steps outside. Nana Mama follows her and yells, "Willow! Are you out here, girl?"

Bree bites her tongue, wanting to tell Nana Mama to stop wasting her breath, then hears someone saying...something. *What the hell?*

"A pie. I'm a pie."

Jannie comes out, carrying a flashlight. "I've called the cops. They're on their way."

"Listen," Bree says. "I think I heard something."

The voice comes again: "A pie."

Nana Mama says, "Up that tree. Jannie, shine that light up the tree."

Bree tilts her head and follows the flashlight beam as it goes higher and higher. It stops at a large branch that brushes the house.

Lighting up seven-year-old Willow Sampson.

The girl calls out again, her voice frightened, and now Bree understands what she's saying: "I'm up high. I'm up high!"

Bree nearly sobs with relief. "You sure are, hon, you sure are! Hold on, we'll come up and get you."

CHAPTER 109

THE ALARM ON his clock radio is set for six a.m., but as usual, Maynard gets up a couple of minutes beforehand. A habit he picked up in the NYPD and a habit that's saved his life at least twice when he got up before armed operators broke into his place to kill him.

He dresses and emerges from the guest bedroom of this house they've been using for the past two weeks as an operational base. He smells coffee and meets up with Willis, a sweet-looking woman who was with the Army Rangers before she joined the CIA's Directorate of Operations and applied her killing talents overseas.

She's dressed as a U.S. Park Police officer, and she hands over a coffee mug that says WORLD'S BEST GRANDPA and walks out the open sliding glass door to the rear deck.

Maynard follows her and takes a sip of the coffee, and she says, "Gorgeous morning."

It is a gorgeous morning. This Virginia estate that's owned by a mortgage company has a large rear lawn, where mist is shrouding a grove of trees. Maynard sees movement, and then three deer cross the distant yard.

Not a bad start to the day, even though he's now seen the text messages informing him that the mission to snatch John Sampson's girl didn't succeed last night. Which is fine, he thinks, because on a battlefield you never get a 100 percent success rate. You just strive to do so all the time.

"Certainly is," Maynard says, but he's distracted, thinking that at this moment, scores of vehicles—Amazon delivery vans, UPS and FedEx trucks, unmarked white vans—are on the move, closing in on the District of Columbia, ready to use this beautiful day to make history.

"You know your history?" Willis asks.

"Of course," Maynard says.

She says, "Remember what Ben Franklin said when the Constitutional Convention was winding down in Philadelphia?"

"Sure," Maynard says. "A woman came up to him and said, 'Well, Doctor, what have we got, a republic or a monarchy?' "

Willis finishes the quote. " 'A republic, if you can keep it,' Franklin told her. What do you think the good doctor would have said about what's going to happen today?"

Maynard sips his coffee. "Probably 'Nothing lasts forever.' "

CHAPTER

110

DEACON DRIVES EXPERTLY through the busy lanes of traffic on I-695. I keep my pistol in my lap, still not trusting her.

"Do you have that circuit board with the serial number I gave you?" I ask.

Deacon makes an abrupt lane change; horns blare behind us.

"Elizabeth? Do you still have it?"

"No," she says.

"Where is it? At Langley, being analyzed and traced?"

"No," she says, going even faster.

"Where is it, then?" I ask, losing my patience with her.

She gives me a glance. "It's back in Afghanistan. In pieces."

I stare at her in disbelief.

"I destroyed it, John."

CHAPTER 111

BREE HOLDS HER breath as Jannie climbs down the oak tree with Willow's arms around her neck. Nana Mama is standing next to Bree and she realizes they have been holding each other's hands in fear.

She's never been prouder of her stepdaughter than she is right now, watching her bring young Willow down from high up in the oak tree in the early morning light. Bree had wanted to find a ladder somewhere in this big house and attached garage, but Jannie said, "Bree, there's no time. Willow might slip and fall while we're looking for it."

Bree holds her breath as Jannie gets closer, closer. Jannie slides down so her hands are grasping the lowest limb and says, "Okay, Willow, hang on tight, we're gonna make a little drop. Keep your eyes closed."

Willow's eyes are indeed closed. Jannie drops to the ground, Willow yelps, Bree and Nana Mama rush over, and there are hugs, kisses, and loving words. Bree kneels down and holds Willow by her thin shoulders.

"Girl, what were you doing so high up in that tree?" Bree asks.

Willow is both crying and laughing. "Daddy... Daddy always told me that if there were bad men, I should... I should climb up high. Daddy said I should go up high because... because the bad guys don't look up most times."

With awe in her voice, Bree says, "You mean you opened up that bedroom window and crawled out onto that tree limb?"

Willow sniffles and rubs her nose on her pajama sleeve. "Did I do right, Aunt Bree?"

Bree hugs Willow so hard, she's afraid she might bruise her. "Yes, Willow, you did right. Your daddy would be so proud of you."

Willow presses her face against Bree's shoulder. "I want my daddy! I don't want to be scared anymore. I want to go home!"

Bree strokes her hair. "Me too, sweetie. Me too."

CHAPTER

112

AFTER HEARING DEACON say she destroyed that vital piece of evidence back in Afghanistan, I almost bring my pistol up and jam it into her abdomen again.

Instead, I take a deep breath. "Elizabeth, why in the hell did you do that?"

The traffic up ahead starts to slow, and Deacon curses and hits the brakes. She turns to me, angry. "What did you think, that I was going to go back to the States with that in my possession? Get swept and interrogated once I landed, have to explain why I had that piece of circuit board with that serial number in my belongings and announce where I found it?"

"Who in hell was going to sweep you?"

The traffic ahead starts moving.

We don't.

She says, "Why do you think I'm just a consultant, John?"

A horn behind us blares. She whispers an obscenity and resumes driving, weaving through the traffic.

I recognize the way she's driving. She's trying to avoid any tails that might be back there. I say, "So you can do your work without being accountable."

"Partially true," she says. "Being a consultant means never having to say you're sorry. Which means I have a long, long leash to go where I have to go and ask the right questions. Problem is, certain people are watching me. This sickness and rot out there that's causing all these attacks—don't think the Company is immune. I couldn't risk coming back with that kind of physical evidence."

"These people watching you," I say, "does that include your ex-husband, General Gerrold Mason?"

That gets her attention, and she looks at me long enough that there's another honk of horns as she almost sideswipes a UPS delivery truck.

I go on. "Currently a vice president of operational development at Global Security Services, correct? A worldwide defense organization that specializes in industrial security and espionage and high-tech military systems, including—"

I stop.

She looks at me. Nods.

She slows the car as the traffic backs up again.

I continue: "Including unmanned aerial vehicles and combat drones that can dominate a battlefield and destroy anything in their path. The serial number on that circuit board..."

"I left the board behind in the 'Stan, John, but I memorized the serial number."

"And it matched a weapons system belonging to your ex-husband's company."

Elizabeth nods. "Of course it did. Why do you think I picked you up?"

"For muscle?"

"Among other things," she says. "We're off for a visit to his office in Crystal City, and if this goddamn traffic lightens up, we should get there before everything here in DC goes to shit."

CHAPTER 113

GENERAL WAYNE GRISSOM is in his spartan office at the Pentagon, today dressed in plain BDUs, waiting. The office is large with couches, bookcases, and photos of past JCS chairmen, but there's not much in the way of personal possessions or souvenirs. In years past, climbing up the slippery ladder of command, he often saw officers who plastered the walls of their offices with *Look at me!* plaques, trophies, and photos.

Not him—not now, not ever. It seems too silly, too presumptuous.

There's an untouched cup of coffee on his clean desk, brought in earlier by his assistant, Colonel Kendricks.

He folds his hands in his lap, looks at his one personal photo. Of his son and his wife. Nathan and Janice at West Point on the day their son graduated, both smiling widely, arms around each other's shoulders. Beautiful blond Janice, handsome and lean Nathan.

A familiar ache starts in his chest.

Their golden boy, Nathan, who was going places, who never gave up, never stopped, and who was blown to pieces by an IED on an unnamed dirt road outside a forgotten village in Afghanistan.

His loving wife, Janice, who put up with his late hours, his tours, the many moves over his career, and who, on the one-year anniversary of Nathan's death, when Grissom was at NATO headquarters in Brussels, drank a fifth of vodka, swallowed a fistful of Percocet, went to bed, and never woke up.

He hears loud voices in his outer office, and his phone starts ringing, and he thinks, *Is it coming? Is it now?*

Grissom slides open the right-hand desk drawer, revealing an army-issue SIG Sauer M17.

CHAPTER

114

DEACON CONTINUES HER fast driving, weaving back and forth, constantly looking in the rearview and side-view mirrors.

I say, "So two years back, in Tajikistan, what were you saying to dear hubby?"

"He wasn't my dear hubby then," she says. "He was my soon-to-be-divorced hubby, and I was telling him that he shouldn't be working at Global Security Services. Even though they sponsored programming on NPR, they had the blood of innocents on their hands."

"What did he say?"

"He said, 'Lizzie, we all have blood on our hands. The only difference is that now I'll be making ten times as much working for Global Security Services and I won't have to wear this goddamn uniform.' God, I hated when he called me Lizzie."

I say, "Any idea why that village was destroyed by his company?"

"That, my friend, is what we're going to find out," she says as we cross over the Francis Case Memorial Bridge, which spans the Washington Channel. To the right I can barely make out the Jefferson Memorial.

Deacon says, “My turn for questions.”

“Go for it,” I say.

“Why were you in Alex Cross’s house?”

“Looking for evidence on who’s behind the shootings and bombings,” I say. “Before Alex was shot in front of police headquarters in DC, he told me that he had found something out about the randomness of the attacks.”

“Which was?”

“That they weren’t random,” I say. “He was going to tell me more, but then the shooting happened. And that’s why I was in his office. I found his notes. Now I know what he meant. The first attacks weren’t random. They were planned. And when the planners knew they weren’t going to get caught, they spread out the attacks’ techniques and locations.”

“Go on,” she says.

“The first one,” I say. “Sniper attack in downtown Columbus, Georgia. Six killed, fourteen wounded. Last April.”

“I remember.”

“Columbus is a short drive from Fort Benning. Where the U.S. Army sniper school is located. The second attack was also a sniper, in DC. Fourteen dead, thirty wounded. Within easy driving range of Marine Base Quantico, where the Marines’ sniper school is located.”

“Could just be coincidence,” she says.

I say, “The notes I found in Alex’s office go on. St. Louis, Missouri, and Kansas City, Missouri. Both car bombs in the downtown sections, both caused deaths, horrific injuries, and property damage. Elizabeth, both cities are within easy reach of Fort Leonard in Missouri.”

Deacon keeps quiet.

“That’s where army combat engineers are trained. Among other skills, they learn the ins and outs of all types of explosives.”

We’ve finished crossing the Potomac River, and now we’re in Virginia.

"Are you saying the army's behind all of this?"

"No," I say. "The next attack after the ones in Missouri was the dirty bomb that fizzled out. Birmingham, Alabama."

"That near an army base?"

Traffic is coming to a crawl as we leave I-395 and merge onto Route 1, which will bring us to Crystal City and the answers we're so desperately seeking.

I say, "No, Elizabeth. It's near FEMA's Center for Domestic Preparedness in Anniston, Alabama. It's part of Homeland Security's weapons of mass destruction training center. And Alex dug deeper. The sniper and explosives schools...they all have students that come from Homeland Security."

CHAPTER 115

AT THE COMMAND post for the U.S. Secret Service's Uniformed Division—which protects the buildings and grounds of the White House—Captain Jennifer Webster is grimly going through the schedule sheets for next week, knowing she's going to have to ask her overworked officers to put in overtime yet again.

As she looks at the schedule on her computer screen, she remembers that a few years ago, the Secret Service ranked last in job satisfaction among federal law enforcement agencies.

Well, she thinks, *it sure as hell hasn't improved since then.* Budget cuts, outdated equipment, poor leadership, and inadequate staffing make this a miserable place to work, despite the supposed glamour. If anything, the staffing has gotten worse. The GAO is currently conducting an audit of just how understaffed the Uniformed Division is and how much of the surveillance and protective equipment here is in serious need of replacing. Hell, nothing much has changed since she was a rookie officer and a guy had climbed the fence and actually entered the White House before he was brought down.

That time, it was a nut with a knife. Next time, it could be someone with canisters of nerve gas.

There's a quiet knock on her open door and she looks up and nods. Lieutenant Jimmy Scopes comes in, looking concerned. "What's up, Jimmy?" she asks, leaning back in her chair and stretching, for, like so many others, she's working a double today.

"Zone two and zone three alarms are offline again," he says. "That means we don't have—"

"Yeah, yeah, Jimmy, I know. We don't have the defense in depth that's required around the West Wing."

"More bad news," he says. "Protocol is to call in extra staff to beef up coverage, but people are dodging phone calls and texts. You can't really blame them."

"No, you can't," she says, tired of it all, rubbing the back of her neck. "Okay, shift around as best you can, and let's just hope that the *Post* and the *Times* don't find out about it."

He offers her a warm smile. "When my uncle was serving in the Secret Service, he said the worst day of his career was when Secret Service was pulled from Treasury and given to Homeland Security. Things were never the same after that."

The captain goes back to her computer. "Preach it, brother."

"I do," he says, turning to leave. "But nobody listens. Or cares."

CHAPTER

116

THE DOOR TO General Wayne Grissom's office flies open and a female captain he doesn't know bursts into the room. His assistant, Colonel Kendricks, is right behind her, and her usually placid face is twisted in anger.

"Sir, I'm sorry, but she pushed past me and—"

Grissom holds up a hand. "All right, Colonel. All right, Captain, what's going on?"

The captain is slim with short black hair and a bad complexion; she's wearing black-rimmed glasses and holding a sheaf of papers. She swallows hard and says, "General Grissom, I'm sorry, but I had to see you. It's an emergency."

"And you are?" he asks, voice cold.

"Captain Hillary Cardinal," she says. "Defense Intelligence Agency, sir."

His voice is sharp when he says, "And you violated good order and discipline and jumped over your chain of command to come here?"

"It's important, General," she says, stepping closer to his desk. "I drove over here as fast as I could from Joint Base Anacostia-Bolling. I mean, it's only about a fifteen-minute drive, but I was afraid I might get pulled over for speeding, because I was really speeding, but once I finished our analysis, I—"

"Our?" he says.

She nods, takes a chair without being invited to. "Yes. I've got a cousin who works for the CIA and another one at the NSA, and last month, we were in Tessie's hot tub, me and Paula, having some wine, and we started talking about the terrorist attacks and..."

A hot tub, he thinks. *A damn hot tub.* "Go on."

She smiles, taps a finger on the papers she brought. The nail has been chewed down to the quick. "We were all working on finding the sourcing and funding for the attacks, and we realized that each of us just had a part of the problem. We should have gone to our respective supervisors, but we didn't think there was enough time. Plus, the bureaucracy and paperwork and the permissions...well, we, um, sort of took it into our own hands. Sir."

Grissom says, "And what did you find out?"

Another nod. "We realized the scope of our work, our individual investigations, was too narrow. All we knew was that the various groups were getting support, funding, and orders via pop-up sites on the dark web. The information was being transmitted on data packets using various VPNs, and the traces were gone before we could find them."

"But you did find something."

"Yes, sir, we did," she says. "That's what we meant by expanding the scope of our investigation. Instead of just relying on our own intelligence agencies, we took it a step further."

He feels a sense of horror at what he's hearing. "You brought in foreign intelligence services?"

"Not exactly, sir," she says. "We knew that the Chinese, the Russians, the British, the Israelis, they all had to be doing similar investigations. We sent in a highly sophisticated phishing program called Pitbull—it's called Pitbull because once this program snaps up the intelligence you're looking for, it won't let it go. We got bits of intelligence from those overseas agencies, then compared and contrasted it to what each of our agencies—the CIA, the NSA, and the DIA—had found, and we cracked it. We know where all of it—the funding and the operational orders to the groups and individuals to commence their attacks—comes from."

Grissom is speechless for a moment. "Then give it up, Captain Cardinal. Please."

Her face flushes. "At first we didn't believe it, but it checked out. You see, sir, one thing that Congress doesn't know is that each cabinet department has its own discretionary funds to spend at the request of that department's secretary. Some departments have more funds than others, although all of this is kept quiet and close to the vest. But once we started going down the trail, it was reasonably easy to nail it down."

"Captain Cardinal, what did you find out? Now, if you please."

"Oh, yes, General, so sorry," she says, licking her chapped lips. She takes a breath, taps the papers once again.

"It's the Department of Homeland Security," she says. "We've been doing it to ourselves these past months."

CHAPTER

117

SYLVESTER IS DRIVING the bright red two-axle Mack integrated tow truck—big enough to haul a tractor-trailer and its load without breaking a sweat—northeast on I-395. As he approaches Washington, DC, traffic slows down, and he sees flashing lights.

His passenger, Casey, says, "Problem?"

Sylvester downshifts; the truck sighs and grumbles. "I don't think so," he says.

"Good. I don't have to tell you we're on a tight schedule."

"We'll be all right."

"Better be," Casey says. "Maynard is depending on us."

Sylvester just shakes his head, slows down more, then comes to a halt. He's been on the road with a quiet Casey for the past three hours. Between them is a folded copy of that day's *USA Today,* a McDonald's bag still holding two Egg McMuffin sandwiches, and a couple of other important items. There's a fender bender up ahead involving a white Volvo and a dark blue Range Rover, and a Virginia State Police cruiser is pulled behind the two vehicles. A trooper is coming their way, holding up his hand.

Casey says, "Looks like the poh-lice."

Sylvester says, "I got it, don't worry."

"You'd better."

The trooper makes a rolling motion; Sylvester lowers his window. The trooper pulls himself up, looks in, and says, "Jesus, this is one big rig you got. When I was in college, I used to work for a repo company, and that truck was a Matchbox car compared to this."

"I'm sure," Sylvester says.

The trooper peers at the back of the rig and says, "Lots of chains you got there."

"We like to be prepared, sir."

The trooper shakes his head. "Sorry, I'm going to need to write you up. Those chains should be properly secured, and from what I can see, they're not."

Sylvester sighs. The traffic ahead is moving. Time is really starting to get tight. He smiles. "I understand, sir," he says, and he slides his hand underneath the copy of *USA Today*, picks up his Ruger .357 revolver, and shoots the trooper in the face.

The trooper grunts, falls back in a cloudy mist of blood and bone. Sylvester puts the truck in drive and manages to get past the scene before other drivers notice what happened.

Next to him, Casey rubs his left ear and says, "You know what?"

"What?" Sylvester asks, picking up speed. Probably some motorist back there saw their license plate, but it doesn't matter. By the time word gets out about the shooting, they'll be at 1600 Pennsylvania Avenue backing this tow truck over the sidewalk with guys waiting nearby to secure the truck's chains to the fence.

"Traffic's still a bitch," Casey says. "Think we'll keep to the schedule?"

Sylvester says, "You got your checkpoint pass?"

Casey pats the leather dispatch case between them. "Right here, along with yours."

"Then don't worry."

After they travel a few miles, Casey says, "When I was a senior in high school, my history class went to DC for a White House tour. I was home sick that day. Always regretted missing it."

Sylvester says, "Today your high-school dream comes true."

CHAPTER

118

IN EARLY AUGUST 1957, Leo Hoegh, head of the Federal Civil Defense Administration, expressed his concerns to President Dwight Eisenhower regarding the previous month's four-day national civil defense drill, Operation Alert.

This drill simulated an attack on the United States by the Soviet Union, and one key aspect of the exercise was the evacuation of the president from the White House by helicopter. However, in a classified after-action report, the feasibility of using a helicopter to evacuate the president was questioned, since helicopters assigned to the White House might not be able to complete their mission due to sabotage, bad weather, or engine malfunction.

So a secret working group consisting of the Secret Service, the U.S. Army, and the District of Columbia Metropolitan Police came up with a classified plan to remove the president from the White House by vehicle. This plan—named Operation Wrangler, a reference to the president's fondness for novels about the American West—called for the Metro Police to block key intersections in the District of Columbia and allow only official vehicles to enter and leave the

White House grounds. The drivers of these civilian and military vehicles were to carry a pass allowing them to go through police blockades. Operation Wrangler would be activated by a phone call from the head of the Federal Civil Defense Administration—or his or her designee—to the DC Metro Police chief. An exchange of code phrases would set the plan in motion.

Operation Wrangler was tested only twice, both times via tabletop exercises, but it remained in effect over the years as the Federal Civil Defense Administration became the Office of Civil and Defense Mobilization, then the Office of Civil Defense; eventually, the division's responsibilities were taken over by the Federal Emergency Management Agency, which, in March 2003, became part of the Department of Homeland Security.

CHAPTER

119

I'VE BEEN IN more tight situations than I can recall, but I'm sure I'll never forget this one. As we get closer to the headquarters of Global Security Services, Deacon drives like a woman possessed, passing cars slowing in traffic, blowing through red lights, and, once, driving partway up a sidewalk.

I hold on to the dashboard and say, "Remember that promise to you I made back in Afghanistan?"

More horns blaring, more brakes screeching. "Which one?"

"The one about a date in a place with clean water, clean sheets, electricity, and room service?" I reflexively close my eyes for a second. "Hard to keep that promise if I get killed."

She screeches the blue Mercedes sedan through an exit leading to 234th Street South and says, "Calm down, John. I was at the top of my defensive-driving courses at the Farm."

"Maybe so, but..."

Deacon slows the Mercedes to the thirty-five-mile-an-hour speed limit and says, "Closer to the target, there're more surveillance cameras and observation platforms. Lots of contractors and government agencies—they see a speeding car approaching, they'll kick up their security."

She turns left onto a tree-lined avenue called Defensive Way. Clustered around the oval-shaped and carefully planned parking areas are several cookie-cutter office buildings, all about fifteen or twenty stories high.

Deacon parks us in a space marked VISITOR in front of a building that has a large sign on its perfect lawn that reads GLOBAL SECURITY SERVICES. It's written in blue and white script that's bisected by a swooping red line.

I get out and look around. Deacon says, "What, thinking you've been here before?"

"Not hardly," I say. "Back when I was a rookie on the Metro Police, they had a program where you rotated from precinct to precinct. I was patrolling with some old vet along K Street and he pointed to all the shiny office buildings and said, 'Man, there's more criminals per square inch up there than in any other place in DC, and we're out here busting brothers for dime bags.'"

Deacon says, "If you move along, you'll be coming face to face with a real criminal, someone worse than anyone on K Street."

"Looking forward to it," I say.

We go through a wide entrance of double glass doors, each bearing the GSS logo. Up ahead is a curved desk-like counter with three women sitting behind it, all wearing headsets and talking to visitors. Deacon goes to the oldest woman in the trio and says, "Cassie, you still playing video games on company time?"

Cassie grins. "I won't tell. What brings you here today, girl?"

Deacon puts her hands on the counter, leans over. "I need to see my asshole ex-hubby, but I don't want him to know I'm here yet. Can you give my friend and me a temporary pass?"

Cassie's grin slips away. "Shit, Liz, you tossed him out on his ass two years ago. Why in hell do you need to see him now?"

"Because I just found out the shithead was concealing assets during the divorce proceedings, and my large friend here"—she shrugs in my direction—"is about to serve his flabby white ass the paperwork for another hearing."

Cassie shakes her head, starts typing. "The more I hang out with my dog, Cooper, the less I like men." She prints out two square VISITOR stickers with a bar code and the ever-present company logo. Deacon and I put them on and move through the bustling lobby to a bank of four elevators. Security officers in light blue shirts and dark blue trousers are at various checkpoints, and we go to the one that says VISITORS ONLY.

A bored guard uses a hand scanner on our badges and passes us through. We enter an empty elevator, and Deacon pushes the button for the tenth floor.

"Nice to know you still have friends in high places," I say.

She looks at the flickering lights. "Friends, contacts, acquaintances—they all count when you need them."

A sudden chime breaks through the silence. My burner phone. I pull it out, and the words of Bree's text hit me hard: John, where are you? We need you. Willow needs you. Please contact us ASAP. It's been too long.

I put the phone away. "Everything all right?" Deacon asks.

In a tight voice I say, "No, everything is not all right. Stay focused."

CHAPTER 120

WHEN THE ELEVATOR stops, Deacon leads the way to a reception area, smaller than the lobby, then to a closed wooden door with GERROLD MASON on it in shiny brass letters, and a woman gets up from a desk and calls, "Ma'am, sir, you can't go—"

We don't hear the rest because Deacon opens the door and we step in.

The office is large, luxurious, with two leather couches facing each other across a coffee table with copies of today's newspapers—*New York Times, Washington Post, Wall Street Journal*—next to a spread of magazines ranging from *Fortune* to *Aviation Week and Space Technology* to *Defense Weekly*.

There are bookshelves on which sit models of aircraft and drones—I wonder which model represents the one that destroyed Mir Kas—and on the walls are photos and paintings. Retired army general Gerrold Mason is sitting behind his desk in a fine gray suit that probably cost twice as much as my SUV's monthly gasoline bill. He's just as I remember him from Tajikistan except his face is fleshier.

He smiles and starts tapping on his keyboard, his eyes on the computer screen. "Good to see you, Lizzie," he says.

"You were always a lousy liar, Gerry."

We get closer to his desk and I say, "Stop typing. Now."

He smiles more and continues typing. "If I don't, what are you going to do, shoot me?"

I take out my Glock and point it at him.

He keeps his hands on the keyboard; his eyes stay on the screen. "Lizzie, you're not going to have me shot, are you? After all we've been through?"

With a sigh she says, "No, I'm not, Gerry. You're right. I'll tell him not to do it." She pauses for the briefest of moments. "But he won't listen. Get your fucking hands off the keyboard."

Mason does just that and finally looks up from the screen. "What the hell is going on here?"

She smiles, motions to me, and we both sit in the deep brown leather chairs in front of his wide and large desk.

"That, my former dear," she says, "is what you're going to tell us."

CHAPTER 121

ONE OF THE CLOSEST hotels to the White House is the famed Hay-Adams, located at 1 Lafayette Square. From the balcony of his sixth-floor suite, Maynard has a clear and unobstructed view of the White House. This is the second time he's stepped out onto the balcony to look down at the White House with a pair of 7x50 binoculars; he's also carrying the latest edition of *Field Guide to the Birds of North America* for the benefit of the watchers out there.

His phone rings, and the familiar computer-disguised voice says one word: "Proceed."

And he responds with one word: "Acknowledged."

He wonders for a moment if he'll ever find out her true identity.

He leaves the balcony and goes back into the suite, thinking about the scores of watchers at the White House and the surrounding buildings who don't know that they themselves are being watched and who also don't know that at the appointed hour, their observation posts will be destroyed by pre-planted C-4 charges or they will get .50-caliber rounds through their heads.

In his suite, he listens in satisfaction to the sound of keyboards, the static-filled transmissions, and the low voices of his upper team, ready for this day of days. He looks them over. They're dressed in the uniforms of various services—U.S. Park Police, the Uniformed Division of the Secret Service, the DC Metro Police.

One thing the movies and TV never get right is what it's like being in the middle of an ops center. The actors on-screen are always yelling, shouting, cursing, running around in a frenzy. Which is all bullshit. The people on a good team like this one keep their heads down and mouths shut as they look over the continuing deployment of—

"Sir? You need to see this."

Maynard goes to the workstation belonging to a woman—is her name Taunton?—who worked for the Capitol Police for thirty years before being forced to retire over a bogus charge concerning the alleged assault of a tourist.

She taps her large screen. "Message just came in via one of your older e-mail addresses."

He looks at it:

MAYNARD, I'M IN MY OFFICE WITH MY BITCH CIA EX-WIFE AND JOHN SAMPSON. THEY KNOW THINGS. GET HERE QUICK. I'LL STALL AS BEST I CAN. MASON.

He says, "Shit!" He glances around the room, then yells, "Smith, Lopez, McCoole, grab your go bags! You're with me! Now!"

Maynard ducks into his office, grabs his own go bag, steps out, and says to Maria Tucker, a former Marine gunnery sergeant, "Maria, you're in charge until I get back."

She doesn't even look up from her workstation. "Understood, sir," she says.

He and his three men, all of them carrying black duffel bags in their hands, go and wait for the elevator to arrive. When its doors open, two older women take their time walking out. One of them says, "You boys look like you're headed to the gym."

Maynard says, "Yeah, we're heading for one hell of a workout." They enter the elevator, and McCoole punches the button for the lobby.

CHAPTER

122

I'M SITTING ACROSS from Deacon's former husband, and he's smiling as he says, "You can put that pistol away."

"I can but I won't," I tell him. "Hands where I can see them. Flat on your desk."

Mason smirks but does as he's told. "What, you think I have a panic button to press? Or, even better, that I'm one of those James Bond villains with a gun tube under my desk, ready to shoot you in the balls?"

Deacon says, "Wouldn't work, Gerry. They're brass. Now, we have evidence that two years ago, a Kestrel unmanned drone that was under development at Global Security Services destroyed the village of Mir Kas."

"Mir what?" he asks.

"Mir Kas," she says. "In Afghanistan."

"And what kind of evidence do you have?"

Deacon recites the circuit board's serial number, then says, "How's that for evidence?

Mason is smiling like he's at a poker table in Las Vegas holding four aces. "Sounds like it's a combination code for a safe, maybe the one where you keep your warmth and sexuality."

"No, it's the serial number of a computer routing board built by Texas Instruments and installed in one of your company's Kestrel drones. It was part of an airborne unit that destroyed the village and machine-gunned everyone who tried to escape."

He says, "That's just your supposition, Lizzie. Thought you learned more at Langley."

"What I have learned," she snaps, "is that almost everyone who was on the cross-border mission I led is now dead. The only exceptions are one veteran on the run and Detective Sampson. I've also learned that what happened in Mir Kas is directly linked to the terrorist attacks that started last April. Gerry, what's the connection?"

He's still smiling the smile of someone who's holding all the cards, but I'm not looking at his face as he says, "Lizzie, honest, I have no idea what you're talking about. Maybe most of the people in your squad are dead because of your poor leadership skills. Again, I don't know anything about the Kestrel drone or that village that may or may not have been destroyed."

My pistol is still pointed right at his head. I say, "Elizabeth, he's lying."

She says, "I know that, but how do you know that?"

"Years of detective work," I say. "Your former spouse may think he's being cool as ice, but he's exhibiting all the tells that indicate he's lying. He won't look directly at you or me. His hands are fidgeting. If you were to touch them, they'd be moist."

"Ugh," she says. "Don't even suggest that."

"Plus he's stalling, Elizabeth. I'm sure he blasted out an e-mail telling his coconspirators to come rescue him. We don't have much time." I'm waiting for Deacon to give me a suggestion, a tip, something that will help me get around her ex-husband's obstinacy, but what she says next surprises me so much, I wonder if she's suddenly lost her mind.

Deacon stands and says, "All right, Gerry. Guess you're not going to talk to us. John? Holster your weapon. We're leaving."

I say, "Elizabeth—"

Her voice is cold. "Now. We're wasting time. Holster and leave."

She heads to the door. Confused, I follow her. As we walk out, I hear Mason laughing.

CHAPTER 123

WE LEAVE MASON'S office, and Deacon gives the door a good slam, then she holds my wrist and says, "Give me a minute, John."

"Better make it a quick minute," I say. "I'm sure help is on the way for him."

"I know," she says. "Which means we're going back in to do what has to be done. Are you with me?"

"One hundred percent," I say. "But we've got to break him fast, Elizabeth."

She says, "I know. That's why we're not in there with him, so we can talk."

"Tell me how we do it, then," I say. "If we had the time, we could drag him to the nearest men's room, tie him up, and start waterboarding him. But we don't have time."

The staffers out in the small lobby are looking at us, but no one seems to be on the phone.

She says, "Break his fingers?"

"He's ex-military," I say. "He might just grit his way through that, knowing he's going to be rescued. Wound him? Cut him?"

She runs a hand through her hair, shakes her head. "He can be a tough fat bastard when he wants to be. I don't know if pain or the threat of pain will do it."

So pain is off the table. Fear?

"Elizabeth, you've read *Nineteen Eighty-Four*, right?"

"Stupid question. Yes."

"What's waiting for your husband in room one-oh-one?"

At first she doesn't seem to understand, but then her eyes widen and she smiles. "That's a good one, John. Can we do it?"

"No other choice," I say. "What's waiting for him?"

She tells me and I grunt with surprise. "Really?"

"Really," she says. "No doubt about it."

"All right, let's do this thing."

I open the door and we go back in. Mason is on the phone; he looks surprised and says, "I'm going to put you on hold for a sec. Got two visitors here I need to get rid of."

Behind me Deacon closes the office door, tosses the dead bolt, drags over one of the fancy leather chairs, and jams it underneath the doorknob.

Mason laughs. "You think that's going to hold off security?"

Deacon walks to him, smiling, the look of a hawk descending on an oblivious field mouse. "You got that wrong, Gerry. We're not locking out any security guards. We're locking you in with us."

I step closer to Mason's desk, take out my Glock, and tighten my finger on the trigger.

CHAPTER 124

CAPTAIN CARDINAL FROM the Defense Intelligence Agency is pointing to numbers and lines on a series of papers, and Grissom half listens, admiring her poise and dedication. Coming in like this, bypassing the chain of command and practically ambushing him in his office, is a career-killer.

But Captain Cardinal is smart, and she knows that what she has is too vital to go through the usual channels. Grissom thinks, *Damn, this girl is skinny as a rail, but she knows her stuff and she's as tough as titanium.*

"Captain?" he asks, interrupting the flow of tech-speak.

"Yes, sir?"

He gestures to the papers spread out on his desk. "This is incredible work. Well done."

Her face colors like she's a teen girl being complimented on her hair and makeup just before leaving for the senior prom.

He says, "You said you worked with your cousins, one in the CIA, the other in the NSA, to come up with this intel."

"That's right, sir," she says. "Tessie and Paula."

"Are they both going to their superiors with this same account?"

Captain Cardinal shakes her head. "No, sir. We decided that I should be the one making the case because...well, sir, you have a reputation for getting things done, sir. If Tessie and Paula tried to alert their supervisors, it would just be delayed by bureaucracy. You know how it is, sir—an assistant section leader needs to sign off on it and kick it over to the section leader, then he or she needs to sign off on it, and that's the way it goes all the way up the line." Cardinal takes a deep breath. "We didn't feel we had enough time. We deciphered enough phrases to indicate the final attack will take place today. At noon, sir."

Grissom smiles and says to the smart young lady, "Captain Cardinal, you've done tremendous work, and no worries, you won't get into trouble for your unorthodox methods or for seeing me without going through channels."

Cardinal smiles back. "Thank you, sir."

Still smiling, Grissom reaches into the open desk drawer, removes his pistol, and shoots Captain Cardinal in the forehead.

CHAPTER 125

WITH LOPEZ AT the wheel, the dark blue Chevrolet Suburban with flashing red and blue lights in its grille speeds into the parking lot of Global Security Services. The well-equipped Suburban got the four men here from the Hay-Adams hotel in reasonably good time, and now they're close to the building.

The glass lobby doors open, and Maynard sees two figures emerge. "Shit, there they are!"

Damn it all to hell, he didn't tell Lopez to stop, but that's exactly what the moron does; he hits the brakes and squeals to a halt practically on the sidewalk near the front entrance. And assuming they've arrived, the two men in the back, Smith and McCoole, open their respective doors, and Maynard thinks, *Lopez, when this is done, you're a dead man.*

But he doesn't hesitate; he unzips his black duffel bag and pulls out his compact M4 automatic rifle.

CHAPTER

126

DEACON AND I run down the emergency stairs after leaving Gerrold Mason's office, avoiding the elevators in case some smart security officer freezes all of them until the police arrive.

Breathing hard, I say to Deacon as I open the stairway door, "No running. Running will call attention to us. A nice casual stroll."

"How are your arms and shoulders doing?"

They're throbbing painfully, but I ignore it. "Manageable. Your ex-husband went through parachute schools and advanced training, and he's still afraid of heights?"

Deacon sticks close to me as we walk across the lobby. She's carrying her ex-husband's laptop under her arm, and I have four thumb drives in my pants pocket. God, I want to talk everything through with Deacon, talk about what we've discovered, what's going to happen in less than two hours, but we don't have time for conversation.

"How hard was it," she asks, "holding him out the window?"

I say, "Once I got a good grip on his pants and shirt collar, not that bad. And thanks for helping by grabbing my belt. Truth is, it wasn't the weight that bothered me. It was the smell when his bladder and bowels let loose. That was the worst. I doubt he's recovered enough yet to make another phone call."

"Seeing him sobbing in the corner made me smile, John. I'm sorry," she says. "But he kept on calling me Lizzie. He knows how much I hate that."

We exit the lobby through the glass doors, and to our left, nearly on the sidewalk, is a dark blue Chevy Suburban, red and blue lights flashing, its doors opening, and I yell, *"Gun,"* grab my pistol, and start shooting.

CHAPTER 127

THE DOOR TO Grissom's office snaps open, and Colonel Kendricks looks in and sees the sprawled body of Captain Cardinal on the floor, the bright red blood from her shattered head soaking into the carpet.

Kendricks says not a word; she just enters, closes the door behind her, and locks it. "Are you all right, sir?" she asks.

"Yes, yes, I am," he says, putting the pistol on his desk.

She steps closer, and he says, "Sorry to say, Captain Cardinal found herself in the position of the DIA officer who knew too much. Colonel, you've worked at both the NSA and the DIA. Do you recognize her?"

The colonel leans over the body. "Sorry, sir, she's unrecognizable. How much did she know?"

"Enough so I had to do that," he says. He's sad at the death of such a promising young soldier, but he's also satisfied that he's done his duty, no matter how bitter it was. He says, "What can we do with her body?"

Colonel Kendricks raises her head and smiles reassuringly. "There are two CID officers in Quantico who owe me favors, sir. We could say it was a suicide, and by the time the investigation got under way…well, you know."

He does know, and he's also known for quite a while that Colonel Kendricks is desperately in love with him and will do anything for him, although not once has he responded to her quiet and sometimes not-so-quiet overtures. For one thing, it's against regulations to have a relationship with a subordinate, and for another, even though it's been a long time, he's still keeping a flame alive for his dead wife, Janice.

Also, during the past two years, he has been working nearly every day and night to get to this point. He has become a warrior monk, dedicated to his mission and nothing else.

The colonel reaches over, takes a pen from his desk, and gingerly pulls his pistol toward her by the trigger guard. She picks it up with a piece of tissue and puts the pistol into the dead captain's right hand.

She stands up and says, "Are we all set in other areas, sir? Any more phone calls you need me to place on your behalf?"

"No," he says. "You've done your work well. It's now out of our hands."

She nods. "After the captain's body is removed, sir, I can put the orders in to get your carpet replaced."

Grissom shakes his head. "Take your time."

"Sir?"

He looks again at the captain's body. "When I leave later today, I don't plan to return to this office. Or the Pentagon."

CHAPTER

128

AFTER YOU'VE WORKED on the street for years, your gut and instincts become your best friends. You see a guy walking down a bad section of DC, his Washington Capitals jacket sagging on one side, you know he's carrying a piece. You see a young girl on a park bench, teary-eyed and looking around, you know she's in trouble. And you see a beat-up car with its engine running double-parked in front of a bodega, you know the driver didn't stroll in there to grab a Pepsi.

When the Suburban's doors flew open, I saw a gun barrel, and that was all I needed to see to start shooting.

In a normal world, shooting like this would be dangerous, reckless, but Deacon and I left the normal world in the rearview mirror a long time ago.

Deacon jumps right in and shoots too, keeping the laptop under her arm, and we quickly take cover behind the concrete flower planters in front of the building. People nearby are running away as Deacon and I keep steady fire on the Suburban.

There are three men firing back, using automatic rifles, and rounds are chipping away at the concrete. The men are good, quite good, but not perfect. Two are taking cover behind the bulk of the Suburban, but a third one is crouching behind the open driver's-side door.

Revealing his feet and lower legs.

I shoot him there, and he cries out and collapses. I say, "Elizabeth, the fob to the Mercedes, now!"

For once, she doesn't argue or question, just tosses me the fob. I catch it with one hand. "Keep up the covering fire, and I'll be back with the Mercedes. And don't drop the laptop!"

She fires until the action snaps back, indicating the magazine is empty, then quickly reloads and says, "Just get the goddamn car, John. Move!"

I fire twice and Deacon snaps off rounds again, and I take a deep breath, start running across the empty parking lot toward the dark blue Mercedes. The distance is maybe ten or twenty yards, but it looks and feels like ten miles.

Rounds whistle over my head, and I duck—with my height, that doesn't matter much—and zig and zag as best as I can, then throw myself onto the pavement between the Mercedes and a white Lexus. I crawl to the driver's side, the shooting still going on, and into my mind pops a random fact from an FBI study: A gunfight between cops and bad guys usually lasts only seven seconds.

It feels like this one has been going on for seven minutes by the time I open the door and crawl in.

The German engine starts right up and I try to keep my head down as I race the Mercedes toward the concrete planters and Deacon. I catch a glimpse of her as I brake to a halt; I toggle the driver's door open, lean out, and fire off six more rounds as Deacon climbs into the passenger seat, laptop under her arm. She flattens herself on the seat, and even before she closes the door, I'm driving us the hell out of there.

CHAPTER 129

LOPEZ IS ROLLING on the ground, grabbing at his shattered and shredded lower legs; Smith's body is slumped against the rear bumper. McCoole is doing his best, firing with his right hand, his left arm hanging useless and bleeding at his side, but his shots are going wide.

Maynard knows he has just seconds left when he sees a dark blue Mercedes roar to the building entrance and come to a squealing halt, and he fires two rounds from his M4 as Mason's CIA ex-wife throws herself into the car. He ejects the magazine, puts in a fresh one, snaps the action shut, and as the Mercedes pulls away, he steps out from behind the shot-up Suburban and coolly advances, firing off three-round bursts.

It looks like Sampson manages to steer with one hand and fire back through the open driver's window with the other, but his aim sucks. Maynard's aim is just fine. He shatters the rear windshield and fires into the trunk—these specialized M4 rounds can go through the trunk, the rear seats, and front seats. The taillights shatter, and the left rear tire collapses. A couple of muzzle flashes erupt from the front seat. He shoots right back.

The Mercedes swerves and—*Damn, look at that*—rolls to a stop.

No more muzzle flashes. Nothing moves.

Sampson's bloodied arm comes out of the car window; he's holding a pistol. He tries to raise the pistol but instead it drops to the ground.

Very nice. Maynard keeps moving forward, wanting to strip them of whatever they got from Mason's office and put kill shots into both their fucking heads.

CHAPTER

130

WE'RE A FEW yards out of the parking lot when the rear windshield blows out, and I grab Elizabeth's shoulder, yell, "Down, down, down!"

More rounds strike the car and I shoot back, knowing it's practically useless. Instead of listening to me, Deacon is kneeling on the car seat returning fire, then she's knocked back.

"Elizabeth?" I say. "Elizabeth?"

Her legs are folded underneath her, her torso and head resting on the front seat. The top of her head is a bloody mess. On the dashboard is a spray of blood, bone fragments, and hair.

I grow very, very cold.

"Damn," I whisper.

I smear her blood on my arm, put my arm out the driver's-side window, drop my pistol, and flatten myself down on the front seat.

"Elizabeth?" I say again. I look at the center console's information screen and toggle through until I get the rear camera's view of what's coming my way.

CHAPTER 131

MAYNARD ADVANCES QUICKLY and purposefully, knowing that in a few seconds, cops from every department within fifty miles will be roaring in. He's focused on snapping kill shots into Sampson and Deacon, grabbing what they've stolen, and getting back to the hotel where he belongs, away from this goddamn high-noon shootout in Crystal City—

The Mercedes lurches backward, picking up speed, picking up speed, and Maynard lifts his M4, thinking he'll put a bullet in the driver's head, splatter his brains, and the Mercedes will swerve and miss him, and he'll be alive to do what he's been chosen to do, which is—

He's still lifting his M4 and thinking all this through when he's struck hard by the car's rear bumper.

There's no pain at first, just the odd sensation of flying through the air.

CHAPTER

132

THERE'S A SICKENING thud as I blast into Maynard, and he's lifted up and hurled to the rear; he hits the pavement hard and flops away.

I swerve around him as I continue to back up, then I brake, shift into drive, and head right for Maynard's limp form.

Crunch.

I reverse and run over him again.

Crunch.

I shift into drive and aim for his head, and there's a *crunch-pop* as I do the job. I glance up at the rearview mirror, see the bloody tangled mess back there, and head for the parking lot's exit. The steering feels sluggish and I'm sure we've lost a tire, but I'm also sure this top-of-the-line Mercedes has those new safety tires that can be used even when they're flat.

And then I try one more time.

"Elizabeth?"

CHAPTER

133

MARIA TUCKER, FORMER Marine gunnery sergeant, stays in the suite in the Hay-Adams hotel after the operators have gone to their preassigned positions, which they did sometime after Maynard disappeared with his three armed men.

She's here with two communications techs—Styles, a woman, and Flynn, a young guy in a wheelchair. They're keeping in touch with the units, and they'll inform her of any developments.

Tucker sips at a cup of coffee, barely sees the White House down there, just a hundred or so yards away it seems. She could step out on the balcony, but Maynard's done that a couple of times, and she doesn't want to add to the viewing log kept by the Secret Service observers out there in the last hours of their lives. Plus, ever since her unhappy departure from the Marine Corps, she's kept a pistol strapped to her side, and she doesn't want any watcher out there seeing an armed woman on this balcony.

The suite is quiet, just the tapping of the keyboards and the low murmurs of three flat-screen televisions tuned to CNN, MSNBC, and Fox, respectively. She checks her watch. Everything kicks off in two hours.

She's about to refresh her coffee when Styles says, "We've got a problem here, ma'am."

Tucker goes to the woman's workstation and looks at her screen, which is displaying wiggly lines like you'd see on a medical device.

Styles says, "It looks like Maynard and his crew are in trouble. Their med monitors—they show McCoole and Lopez are injured. Blood pressure's down, respiration and heart rate are elevated. I've tried calling them but there's no answer."

"What about Maynard and Smith?"

"They're not answering either."

Tucker says, "I don't give a shit about their phones, I mean their med monitors."

"Either their monitors have been disabled or they're dead, ma'am."

Tucker nods, goes to the coffee machine, tops off her cup, then turns to look at her communications techs. Styles's family farm was seized by the State of Montana years back, and Flynn was injured by a Massachusetts State Police trooper five years ago and he's still waiting for a settlement. Tucker notes the looks on their faces and gives them both a smile. The three of them are all in the same boat. In her case, she filed a sexual harassment complaint about a captain in her unit, but the complaint got broomed and her career was ruined.

They are part of an assembly of the betrayed and overlooked.

"We stick to the plan," she says. "It's bigger than all of us."

CHAPTER 134

AGENT NED MAHONEY IS exhausted; his mind is racing, and he feels like he's on a roller coaster that's shuddering on its rails and is about to fly into space. But he's here, just outside his two-story brick home in Georgetown, away from his busy office, his Impala parked on the street in front of his house.

He glances at his iPhone, sees the text message from Sampson, the only message that could have gotten him here today:

NED—AT YOUR HOUSE. HAVE EVIDENCE AND MORE. GET HERE ASAP. COME ALONE. I'LL KILL WHOEVER ELSE SHOWS UP.

Mahoney walks up the flagstone path, past the carefully maintained shrubbery, notices something on the dark gray stones.

Blood.

He squats down, touches one spot. Still sticky. Fresh.

He goes to the side door, which leads into the kitchen. More blood on the steps.

He takes out his Glock 19 pistol and gently pushes on the door.

It swings open.

The kitchen is empty, but there's more blood on the white tile floor.

"John?" he calls out, holding his pistol in both hands.

"In the den," John says, sounding tired and stressed. "You alone?"

"Yes."

"Good," John says. "Fair warning, I'm pretty jumpy, so I don't want to see any weapons, all right? You're a good friend, Ned, but I just want to see you and empty hands."

Ned holsters his pistol. "I understand, John."

Mahoney traces the familiar steps toward his den, but nothing seems right; it feels like his home has tilted on its foundation, making everything askew. He walks into his den, his favorite place here at home, and he knows it'll never, ever be the same.

John Sampson is sitting in one of the two comfortable leather chairs, one hand holding his pistol, which is resting in his lap. His clothes are worn and soiled. His eyes are puffy and haunted, and there's gray-black stubble on his gaunt face. On the couch is a woman Ned believes is Elizabeth Deacon. She's stretched out with her shoes off and her feet on a pile of pillows. Her breathing is slow and rasping. Most of her head is covered by gauze bandages. Her eyes are closed.

John says, "Have a seat."

Mahoney sits and says, "What happened?"

"She was shot in the head while doing her job," John says.

"John, she needs to be in a hospital!"

He shakes his head. "Sure. Which one? And will she be safe? Alex was in a hospital and he was almost murdered." He barks out a sharp laugh. "Don't trust anyone, right? That's what you told me."

Mahoney says, "I did. And the Bureau has on-call medical staff for situations like this. Vital and discreet. Can I text them?"

John says, "No. Maybe in a few minutes. Too much is at stake now."

"You said evidence, John," Mahoney says. "What is it?"

On the coffee table between them is an open laptop. John slowly rotates it so Mahoney can see the screen.

John reaches around it, pushes a key.

"Here it is," he says, voice exhausted.

CHAPTER

135

NED BRIEFLY LOOKS at John's face as the video begins. It shows General Wayne Grissom sitting in front of two flags, the American flag and the standard of the Joint Chiefs of Staff. From John's dark expression, Ned is sure he's seen this video several times before.

Grissom is sitting behind a polished desk in what looks like the Oval Office, and he's wearing his formal army blue service uniform, complete with an impressive display of medals and ribbons.

His voice through the speakers is strong and confident:

"My fellow Americans, I am General Wayne Grissom, chairman of the Joint Chiefs of Staff of the United States and the country's senior military official, tasked to defend this nation and its people against all enemies, foreign and domestic.

"From the time I entered Norwich University and continuing through decades of service, my oath of office has been my constant North Star, a dedication that has never changed, never wavered.

"Until now.

"My fellow Americans, we all know, deep in the marrow of our bones, that our great nation has gone astray these past decades.

Wars are entered but never won, resulting in billions of dollars lost, thousands dead, and thousands more wounded for life. Giant corporations pay little or nothing in taxes. Big-city politicians are elected and reelected on promises they never keep; bridges collapse, the streets become unsafe, and students leave school almost as ignorant as when they arrived.

"Our great nation and its Congress are in an unbreakable gridlock, with no chance of improvement on the horizon.

"Since April, a series of terrorist attacks have tormented our great country. Hundreds are dead, thousands are injured, and the trust and bonds that hold us together as a people are fraying and will soon break.

"And how has our system of laws and agencies responded to these attacks?

"We all know that answer.

"With failure."

CHAPTER

136

I SEE NED'S eyes narrow and his face darken as he sinks deeper into the chair, staring at the screen with a hard intensity. I know what he's feeling—his first reaction is that this must be some sort of horrible elaborate joke.

The highly professional recorded video continues.

"In reviewing the status of our great nation, as the lead military officer responsible for its safety, I saw that I had two options. I could maintain the status quo, see more deaths, more failures, or I could take a controversial path to save this nation and stop the killing.

"I have chosen the latter path. Forces under my command today repulsed a last-minute terrorist attack on the president and the White House and have taken control of the building and its grounds.

"As of this moment, the actions and the authority of the executive branch, Congress, and the Supreme Court have been temporarily suspended. Your trusted military will take command until this national crisis subsides. President Kent is safe in an undisclosed location, and I will confer with him through the days ahead.

"I have taken this action reluctantly, but I know it is necessary to save this country and its blessed people..."

On the screen Grissom pauses, coughs, and says, "Shit, sorry to screw that up. Should we start from the beginning?"

A woman off camera says, "Not a problem, sir, we'll pick it up from here and edit it in."

"Good," Grissom says on the screen. "Let's—"

Enough. I stop the video. "Nice mock-up of the Oval Office, don't you think?" I ask.

Ned says, "That son of a bitch. That...John, where did you get this laptop?"

I say, "From Elizabeth Deacon's ex-husband, retired general Gerrold Mason. He's now a vice president at Global Security Services, an arms dealer and manufacturer of a number of black ops over-the-horizon and drone systems."

"But that video, how did it get on—"

"On his laptop?" I say, looking over at the breathing but still unconscious Elizabeth Deacon, knowing I should call in medical help but also knowing I have just minutes to get Ned up to speed. "A few years ago, Mason was assigned by Grissom to the region between Tajikistan and Afghanistan, the area where that village was destroyed two years ago. Destroyed to keep a secret: That Mason and others were assisting cross-country opium smuggling from that location. They made millions of dollars, but they didn't keep that money for themselves. It was sent to the United States, meant to be used to raise all kinds of hell, and it ended up in a classified account at Homeland Security."

Mahoney says, "Homeland Security is behind all of this?"

I say, "That's what Elizabeth and I thought and what Alex initially thought. But there are records on the laptop that show the money went to Homeland Security but left within days, assisted by a colonel within the U.S. Army's Financial Management Command who was on temporary assignment to Homeland

Security. Those millions of dollars wound up under Grissom's control."

Mahoney's eyes widen. "The funds were used to finance the terror groups. But why?"

I say, "It was simple yet brutal, Ned. Grissom and his trusted people—working with cutouts and various sites on the dark web that would pop up and disappear—gave strategic and financial support to every domestic group that had a grudge against this nation or government. Grissom wanted chaos, death, destruction, and, ultimately, national mistrust, clearing the way for him to take control."

"John..."

I push on. "After seizing control, he's going to use his new powers to arrest and crush every one of those terrorists. Which will be a cakewalk, since he knows who and where they are and how to take them out."

Ned seems to be thinking through what I just said.

I say, "And you know what? A solid majority of the American people will rally around him for finally ending the terrorist threat. Everything else will be minor. Most Americans want to be able to go to work and send their children to school without having to worry about anyone being blown up by a car bomb."

"How do you know that, John?"

"Mason told me."

"Are you sure he was telling the truth?"

I say, "I shot out the window of his tenth-floor office and dangled him out of it. After he shit and pissed himself, yeah, he showed me the documents on his laptop and thumb drives. He was telling the truth, Ned."

"My God..."

I say, "Ned, at noon today, General Grissom is going to the White House to overthrow the government of the United States. What do we do?"

CHAPTER 137

IN A PRIVATE conference room adjacent to his office, General Wayne Grissom reviews the orders that will be issued later today after his recorded message is broadcast to the nation and the world.

There's a soft knock on the door, and Colonel Kendricks comes in. She, too, is dressed in army BDUs, and she has a pistol holstered to her belt.

He says, "Yes?"

"The body's been removed. CID is beginning its investigation, and they took your pistol to fire a test cartridge to compare it with the empty cartridge case on your office floor. It'll be a match, of course."

"Of course," Grissom says. He won't say it to Kendricks, but he has a throbbing headache right behind his eyes. "But it won't make any difference, will it."

"No, sir."

"Any change in the status of the other chiefs?"

"No, sir," she says. "General Bouchard of the air force is still in Tokyo, Admiral Barnes is in Singapore, General Signorello is at NSA Naples, and General Krantz is at Cape Canaveral."

"Good," he says, looking again at the pile of orders on the desk; they just need his signature to be official. "I'll only have to deal with their deputies once we're at the White House, which will be a plus. But we have a full day ahead of us, Colonel."

Colonel Kendricks slowly takes a seat without asking for permission. He lets this breach of military etiquette slide. "Are you all right, Kendricks?"

She smiles. "Last-minute jitters, I guess. Like your first step off an aircraft on your first parachute jump. You hope everything in the chute works, that the jumpmaster dropped you over the right zone, that you won't land in a power line and get zapped or be impaled by a tall pine."

Grissom says, "Kendricks, we've planned this for more than two years. We've run tabletop drills and field tests, and every eventuality has been addressed."

"Still..."

He goes on, voice confident. "The people are tired, frustrated, angry. They don't trust the president, Congress, or the media. The nation is divided, crumbling, and we're steps away from armed insurrection by various different populations. There's only one organization that consistently remains popular among the American people year after year, and you and I belong to it."

"I know," she says. "Their support is what I'm counting on."

Grissom says, "And the people are used to the military coming in to provide assistance. After a hurricane, who's there? The navy or the army. Rioters burn a city down? The National Guard is there, providing security and food. Who helps control the borders, who interdicts drug dealers, who seizes criminals overseas? We do. Believe me, Colonel, the people are aching for strong leadership, and we're going to give it to them."

Grissom knows the love and admiration his aide has for him, and his headache fades.

She now seems at ease.

"Thank you for the pep talk, sir."

"Not a problem," he says.

Kendricks gets up and heads to the door. "Your ride to the White House will be ready in an hour, sir."

CHAPTER

138

I SAY, "A BIT more evidence to make your day, Ned," and I scatter four thumb drives taken from Mason's office across the coffee table like I'm playing some horrific game of dice.

"Plans for military and intelligence operatives to conduct media monitoring across all network and cable news channels as well as social media accounts," I say. "Establishment of preventive detention centers, where certain celebrities and media influencers will be sent."

"Arrested, you mean?"

"No, they're too smart for that," I say. "Preventive detention for their own safety, of course. There are other lists of members of the news media who will be placed in preventive detention or who will have military escorts at work. Oh, and lists of those to be arrested."

Ned's voice is strained. "How many?"

"Thousands, not including the terror cells. That's an entirely different file, people from nearly every state in the union and organizations from right-wing militias to Black Lives Matter–type groups to environmentalists."

"Who else will be arrested?"

"Too many to point out, Ned," I say. "But I'm on the list, and so is Alex Cross, and so are members of his family."

Ned shakes his head. "It's like a nightmare. Impossible to believe."

I say, "Well, believe this, Ned. Most of the FBI's management is on that list. Including you."

CHAPTER

139

SYLVESTER IS MANEUVERING the two-axle Mack integrated tow truck along the crowded streets of the District of Columbia as his passenger, Casey, calls out directions from a handwritten sheet of paper. Crude, but sheets of paper can't be hacked or traced.

"Okay," Casey says. "Turn left at the next light."

Sylvester says, "If this traffic doesn't clear up in ten minutes, we're not going to meet our deadline."

"I told you we should have left an hour earlier."

"And get to the target an hour ahead of time, drive around in circles, and get asked by the Metro Police or Secret Service why we're hanging out near the White House?"

"We could have parked somewhere."

"And get ticketed or rousted?"

The light turns red. Sylvester stops, swears.

Casey says, "In the next couple of minutes, we're gonna need a miracle."

CHAPTER

140

CASEY'S MIRACLE OCCURS fifty-eight seconds later.

It starts with a phone call from a U.S. Army colonel at the Pentagon to the chief of the DC Metro Police on his office's private line.

In a crisp and clear voice, the colonel says, "Chief, please retrieve a hard copy of your external operational plan manual. Let me know when you have it in hand."

The chief nearly chokes on his late-morning latte and spends a few frantic moments looking for the thin volume, which he finds stuck between two old budget binders on an upper shelf in his office. He tugs out the dusty book, recalling the first time he read it and how it had chilled him. It contains the Metro Police's procedures for responding to a variety of apocalyptic events, from a chemical attack to nuclear war.

"I... I've got it, Colonel."

"Open it to page nineteen."

He flips through the old pages. "Got it."

"You are to institute Operation Wrangler immediately," the

colonel says. “Your code word to activate Operation Wrangler is *Omaha.* Does that match?”

“Yes, yes, it does,” the chief says.

“Good,” the colonel says. “Proceed as ordered.”

“Wait, wait,” the chief says. “Can you tell me what’s going on?”

The colonel says, “No,” and hangs up.

The chief quickly makes two phone calls. The first is to tell the head of dispatch to get orders for Operation Wrangler transmitted to his on-duty officers.

The second is to tell his wife, Tracy, to take the girls out of school and get the hell out of DC.

CHAPTER

141

NED SAYS, "WHAT about the Secret Service?"

"What about them?" John says. "Ned, they're tasked with physically protecting the president, *not* the office of the presidency. They'll keep President Kent safe, but they can't protect his authority and powers."

"But Congress—"

John touches another thumb drive. "The leaders of both houses and their deputies will be detained as well."

"Well, before they start making arrests at the Hoover Building, I can—"

"Ned, you know who's not on the list? The director of the FBI."

Ned feels like he's been punched in the throat.

John looks up at the wall clock in the den. "You're friends with the mayor, right?"

"Yes, I am. That's no secret."

"You're going to call her."

"What, use the Metro Police to defend the White House?"

"No, something else," John says. He turns and looks at the wounded, unconscious Deacon. "I'll tell you, but we have to make another call first."

Ned says, "For her?"

"Yes, and quick," John says. "We have a new enemy—time."

CHAPTER 142

GENERAL WAYNE GRISSOM walks out of a rarely used side entrance to the Pentagon and over to his personal armored black Tahoe, idling at the curb. In front of the Tahoe are two white Pentagon Police cruisers, and behind the Tahoe are two black Chevrolet Suburbans carrying members of the Pentagon's protective service.

Colonel Kendricks opens the rear door for the general, and he nods in appreciation and climbs in, his briefcase in his steady right hand. She comes around to the other side and says, "Don't forget your seat belt, sir."

He fastens the seat belt in silence, looks over at one of the world's largest office buildings, and remembers with a half smile a joke one of his predecessors had allegedly made during a newspaper interview: "How many people work at the Pentagon?" he was asked. "About half" came the wry answer.

Well, he thinks, *that's still pretty true.* Over the years, though, he's quietly located those who do work and who will work in the nation's interests to follow his orders today.

Simple to do, really. All generals and colonels have staffers and NCOs underneath them who, for the most part, do the real work. They make the phone calls, prepare and write orders and memorandums, and present papers to be signed. So it's easy to block information from getting to a superior officer or issue orders in that officer's name.

Happens all the time.

His little procession exits the Pentagon's parking lot and heads toward the on-ramp that will bring them to I-395. To his left is the massive parking lot for the building, and to the right is a fence and a steep sloping grassy hill leading to the adjacent highways.

Traffic slows as they approach I-395, and he checks his watch, a gift from Janice when he received his first star.

"We've got only twenty-nine minutes," he says to Colonel Kendricks.

Her smile is full of love and confidence. "No worries, sir. Soon enough, the way will be clear."

CHAPTER 143

AFTER MAKING THE two necessary phone calls—one lasting under a minute, the other lasting much longer—Ned Mahoney says, "Time to move, John."

John says, "Give me a second."

"You got it," Ned says. "I'll start my car. You come out when you're ready."

John kneels down by the couch, takes Elizabeth's hand, and stares at her bandaged head.

Ned goes through the large kitchen and out the side entrance. He hears a heavy knocking on the front door and sees two DC Metro Police officers standing there.

He turns to go back into the house but it's too late—he's been spotted.

"Agent Mahoney," one cop calls out. "We see you there. We need to talk to you. Now."

CHAPTER

144

BACK IN THE day, Sylvester had been an army specialist driving heavy fuel trucks to and from Baghdad. Your butt was always tense then because you were waiting for an IED to tear through you and turn you into a crispy critter, but driving the truck today is worse, much worse, he thinks.

They're heading down Pennsylvania Avenue and traffic is stop-and-go as they merge onto Washington Circle.

He looks at the dashboard clock. Twenty-five minutes left to get into position, and he doubts they will make it.

His passenger, Casey, says, "What's bugging you?"

"What the fuck do you think?" he asks. "We're not going to get to the rendezvous point in time. And that'll throw the whole schedule off."

Casey says, "Told you we should have left earlier."

"Go to hell."

Casey laughs. "Man, say a prayer. You gotta believe."

"In what?"

"In miracles."

Sylvester is about to tell Casey where he can shove his miracles when he hears the distant howl of sirens.

The sirens grow louder, and in his rearview and side-view mirrors he sees a line of DC Metro Police cruisers coming their way, with a cruiser peeling off at each intersection, blocking traffic.

Casey says, "Okay, maybe not a miracle from God, but how about one from the DC police?"

Sylvester checks the clock once more. The tight feeling across his chest eases.

"I'll take it," he says.

CHAPTER 145

NED MAHONEY SLOWLY opens the door and nods to the two police officers, both heavyset fellows who look like they've been on the force for twenty years and never advanced up the ranks but don't really mind.

"Guys," he asks. "What's up? I need to get back to the Hoover Building as soon as possible. Can't this wait?"

The one on the left shakes his head. "No, sir. A while ago we received a BOLO for a dark blue Mercedes sedan with Virginia license plates involved in a mass shooting over at Crystal City."

He stops talking, and his partner picks up the story. "Thing is, we just located that Mercedes, parked down the street. One flat tire, rear window blown out, bullet holes in the rear and trunk, and fresh blood on the upholstery."

Ned says, "That's awful, but I didn't hear or see anything that can help."

"Are you certain?" the cop on the left says. "Are you certain you can't help us?"

Too late, Ned realizes he's stepped into a trap, and he keeps his mouth shut as the same cop says, "Well, that's odd to hear, Agent Mahoney, because there's a trail of blood going from that shot-up Mercedes through your side gate and right up to your side steps. See?" The cop taps a black shoe near a smear of blood.

Ned says, "Officers, really, I don't have time and I need to—"

"Sir." The man's voice is cold and no longer so polite. "We're going to need you to turn around and place your hands behind your back."

"That's not necessary," he says, wondering what they would say if he told them he had less than half an hour to stop a coup d'état.

"Sir, move," the other cop says, "or we'll have to secure you by force."

Ned says, "Please, this can all be explained."

The first cop steps back, removes a yellow pistol-shaped weapon from his utility belt, and says, "You have ten seconds to submit, sir, or you will be tasered."

CHAPTER 146

AS HIS ASSISTANT promised, the traffic does clear and soon they're making good time on I-395, approaching the Potomac River and the Fourteenth Street Bridge. Earlier, Grissom had told his staff that he didn't want any sirens for his trip to the White House, just an escort, which he would need only in the unlikely event that something went wrong.

Everything is to be done right.

To Kendricks he says, "You know where I was born and raised?"

She's focused on her iPhone but instantly answers, "Massachusetts."

"That's right," he says. "A town just outside of Boston. My parents were active in politics back when the average voter could make a difference. This was before the lobbyists, focus groups, and pollsters came along and took it all away from the people." He folds his arms, looks down at the slow-moving Potomac River, then up at the barely visible Jefferson Memorial.

What is that Jefferson quote? That's right: "The tree of liberty must be refreshed from time to time with the blood of patriots and tyrants."

Grissom thinks, *Not bad, Long Tom, not bad.*

Aloud he says, "There was an election for governor when I was a kid, a Democratic primary between a liberal candidate and a conservative candidate back when the Democrats actually had conservatives. To everyone's surprise, the conservative candidate won. And later, one of his campaign consultants said the key to victory was taking all of the hate groups and stirring them into one pot."

The way ahead is still clear.

"That's what we've done," he says, "and I make no apologies for it. Eventually they were going to tear this nation apart. I just took them under my wing, and in twenty-four hours, I'm going to crush them all."

Kendricks doesn't answer.

"Something wrong?" he asks.

"No, sir," she says. "Everything's on schedule. The president is still in the underground bunker and all three power sources to the elevators are offline. Communications were cut just as the president was in the middle of a phone call."

"Do we know who he was talking to?" Grissom asks.

"The DC mayor," Kendricks says.

"Oh, that's fine," he says. "Glad he wasn't talking to anyone important."

CHAPTER

147

I SLIP OUT of Ned Mahoney's house, carefully move across the fine lawn, and take cover behind the bushes and shrubbery so I can get a clear view of the two DC Metro Police who are trying to arrest him.

From that position, I call out, "You two, freeze, or I'll blow your damn heads off!"

There are three surprised folks in front of me, Ned and the two cops, and I move a bit more so they're square in my sights. I say, "Gents, I've got a nine-millimeter pistol pointed at you, and you're both wearing ballistic vests, but I'm a goddamn good shot. If you move or try to come at me with a weapon, I'm going to drop you both. But I don't intend to harm you. Do I have your attention?"

I hear a strained but murmured "Yeah" from each one, and I say, "Each of you, with your left hand, take your service weapon by the muzzle and drop it to the ground. Your Taser as well."

They both comply, and the one on the right says, "Big John, is that you?"

"Doesn't matter," I say.

"It's Gus Tinnamen from the Second District. I did backup for you and Alex Cross two years back. You remember?"

He starts to turn and I say, "Gus, when I say don't move, I mean don't friggin' move."

"I just want to talk," he pleads. "Can't we work this out?"

"No," I say. "And I don't want you to move, 'cause if I shoot you, I don't want to see your face. Now. With one hand, unbuckle and drop your utility belts. Good. Now put your hands behind your heads, fingers intertwined, drop to your knees, and cross your ankles."

As they move, the other cop says, "You won't get away with this."

"I just need to get away with this for a couple of hours."

When they're on their knees, I go forward, kick away their weapons, strip their utility belts of their handcuffs—two each, perfect—and in less than a minute, their hands and ankles are cuffed and I've gently laid them on the ground. Eventually they'll be discovered by neighbors or the FBI medical team that's coming, but by then, we'll be long gone.

"Sorry, guys," I say. "If this works out, I'll buy you both beers, apologize, and tell you why I did this."

Gus says nothing. The other cop says, "You can take that beer and shove it up your ass."

I don't answer. Ned joins me, briefcase in one hand, key fob in the other.

"Ready?" he asks.

"Someone coming here for Elizabeth?"

"Less than ten minutes, John."

"Okay," I say. "Thanks—one less thing to worry about."

We race to his black Impala, and I'm thinking, *Yeah, but there's still a boatload of things to worry about out there.*

I check my watch.

Twenty-three minutes left.

CHAPTER

148

THEY ARE TWO blocks away from their target point at the White House, and Sylvester downshifts and slows the big tow truck as four armed DC Metro Police officers step out from behind their parked cruisers and wave them down.

"All right," he says to Casey. "Dig out the IDs. We'll see if they work."

"And if they don't work?"

Sylvester says, "We proceed. Mission is always first."

Casey goes through a leather pouch. "Boy, such big brass ones you have."

"Screw you," he says, bringing the truck to a halt. "Give me my ID."

Casey passes over the large embossed plastic card, and Sylvester lowers the window on his side. Casey does the same, and a cop clambers up and looks inside the truck's cabin.

Even before he and his companion ask, Sylvester and Casey pass over their forged government-issue identification cards. The cop's nervous-looking face is sweating, and he almost drops the oversize card.

Even Sylvester thinks the gold-threaded and embossed ID cards look pretty intimidating. Underneath Sylvester's name, photo, signature, and thumbprint is this:

> UNDER ORDER OF THE PRESIDENT OF THE UNITED STATES, THIS INDIVIDUAL AUTHORIZED TO PASS THROUGH ALL LOCAL, REGIONAL, AND NATIONAL CHECKPOINTS. ALSO AUTHORIZED TO TAKE COMMAND OF LOCAL LAW ENFORCEMENT AND USE ALL CIVILIAN AND LAW ENFORCEMENT RESOURCES AS NECESSARY.

The cop passes the card over. "Okay, go through. Any idea what the hell is going on?"

Sylvester shrugs. "I'm just following orders like everybody else."

His companion gives Casey's pass back and says, "Any chance this is some sort of drill?"

Sylvester revs up the diesel engine. "What, you think the biggest traffic jam ever to hit DC is going to be a drill?"

The cop nods. "Then…I mean, what are you here for? You and your truck?"

Sylvester shifts the truck into first. "When you have collapsed buildings and lots of destroyed cars, that's the best way to move debris, right?"

The cop nods and jumps off the side of the truck, and Sylvester rolls up his window and starts driving toward the trees surrounding the White House grounds.

Casey says, "Jesus, did you see how pale that cop's face was? I thought he was going to pass out."

Another shift of the gear. "Oh, the kid was all right," Sylvester says. "He was scared, but he knew one important thing."

"What's that?" Casey asks.

"To follow orders."

CHAPTER 149

GRISSOM CHECKS HIS WATCH.

Well, we're at least five minutes ahead of schedule. Always good to have some slack in your timeline.

Kendricks says, "Look at that, sir. Just as planned. The Metro Police are holding traffic back, and there's a single checkpoint coming up."

"You have our IDs?"

"Absolutely, sir," she says, removing two identification cards from her leather briefcase. The driver and security officer up front have similar cards, as do the officers in the vehicles behind them and the Pentagon Police up ahead.

He takes the card and says, "Amazing that an old contingency plan is still useful."

"All a matter of timing, sir," Kendricks says.

Grissom rubs the smooth plastic, eyes his photo. He looks...composed? At peace? Ready to do what's necessary?

"My son, Nathan, and his unit were due to be rotated out in two days," he says, voice soft. "Can you believe that? Just forty-eight hours later, he'd have been at Bagram Air Base, ready to come home. Instead, what was left of him was put in a metal box and sent home to Dover. And for what? A sacrifice he and thousands of others paid for with their blood and that this nation spent billions on—and for what? Nothing. Absolutely nothing. I'll make sure that kind of soul-killing mistake never happens again."

"I know you will, sir," she says. "Beginning today."

He rubs the card again. "Timing."

Up ahead there are blue and white wooden sawhorses marking a DC Metro Police checkpoint. The Tahoe starts to slow.

"Sir?" she says.

"You know who Alexandre Dumas is, don't you?"

"Yes, sir," she says. "The French author who wrote *The Three Musketeers.*"

"That he did," he says. "But he also wrote *The Count of Monte Cristo.*"

The little convoy comes to a halt.

His identification card is in his lap. He looks down, and for a strange moment, the person in the photo seems to be his son, Nathan.

Grissom says, "In that important novel, Dumas wrote: 'The difference between treason and patriotism is only a matter of dates.' As this day progresses, let's keep that in mind, Colonel."

"Absolutely, sir," she replies.

CHAPTER

150

AS NED RACES to the White House through the crowded streets of DC, lights and siren on, I send a quick text to Bree Stone:

SITUATION IS EXTREMELY DANGEROUS. MAKE SURE EVERYONE IN THE FAMILY IS OFF THE STREETS.

Ned says, "Okay, John, we've got a police roadblock up ahead at I Street. And we've got about fifteen minutes before we hit noon. Should we blast through it?"

"No," I say. "Let's try something else."

"Like what?" Ned asks.

"I'll come up with something, don't worry about it," I say, rapidly texting. "Hold on, almost done here."

IF SOMETHING HAPPENS, TELL WILLOW I LOVE HER VERY, VERY MUCH AND NEVER STOPPED THINKING OF HER. PLEASE, YOU AND ALEX RAISE HER AS YOUR OWN.

I send off the text as the Impala comes to a halt in front of the two DC Metro Police cruisers and six heavily armed MPD cops.

I say, "They're jumpy. Let's move slow and let me take lead."

"You got it," Ned says.

I step out and so does Ned. I hear car horns, sirens, and the voices of people clustered on the sidewalk, looking around and pointing. A helicopter from one of the local TV stations roars low overhead, and a DC Metro Police lieutenant comes forward and says, "Gentlemen, I need to see your identification."

I think, *Oh, shit,* because it's Lieutenant Matt Caine, who's hated me pretty much from the first day I was on the force. He's fleshy and overweight, and his face is always red, like he's perpetually angry. I know from others that he thought the force started going downhill the day they let women and minorities join.

He says, "Actually, I see only one gentleman. Hey, Detective, what are you doing here? Word is that your fat ass has been suspended."

I say, "Matt, we're trying to pass through."

"No can do," he says. "Orders, you know? Oh, right, fuck, you don't know. You and your buddy Alex follow your own orders. Sorry. Not gonna work this time."

Ned shows his identification. "Lieutenant, I'm Agent Ned Mahoney, FBI."

"Good for you, Agent Mahoney," Caine says. "We're pretty frigging busy here in case you didn't notice."

"I know and I appreciate that, Lieutenant," Ned says, "but it's vital that we pass through your checkpoint."

Caine says, "I need another form of identification, not the one you're showing me."

I'm feeling hemmed in, trapped in the kind of bad dream when you're running from danger through sticky taffy. Out of all the supervisors in the Metro Police, I have to deal with this one.

What to do? Plead, beg, threaten?

Ned's voice is calm and steady when he says, "I know the ID you're looking for. Oversize, gold-threaded, and embossed, with my photo, signature, and thumbprint, and orders underneath that I have the authorization of the president to go anywhere and seize anything I need for the good of the nation. Right?"

A reluctant nod from Caine. "Right. And where's yours?"

"Stuck in a filing cabinet somewhere. I really don't know, Lieutenant," Ned says. "Some clerk is busy right now trying to find it. But you see I know what kind of ID is required for us to pass through. This response is called Operation Wrangler, correct?"

"Agent Mahoney, I—"

Ned steps closer—trying to build a face-to-face bond, I think—and says, "Lieutenant, this response package was developed when Ike was president. More than seventy years ago! It's to be used in only the most extreme emergencies, and I need to get to the White House right now. ID or no ID. That's how desperate the situation is."

I sense Caine is wavering. Ned says, "I take full responsibility. It's all on me."

Caine looks at me, then back at Ned.

I want to check to see how much time is left but I don't dare move.

"Why the hell is John Sampson with you?"

Ned laughs. "The asshole said he could pass us through any police lines in less than thirty seconds. Guess I was wrong to trust him, huh?"

Caine laughs in response, steps back, and waves to two officers to move the blue and white sawhorses out of the way. "You guess right, Agent Mahoney, and I'll hold you to what you just said about taking responsibility. And I got witnesses to back me up."

"Thanks, Lieutenant, and if it goes wrong, I'll cheerfully toss John Sampson under the nearest bus," Ned says.

He goes back to his Impala, red and blue lights still flashing in the grille and windshield. I get in and as we pass through the checkpoint, he says, "Sorry for calling you an asshole, John."

Now I check my watch.

Just seven minutes left.

"It worked," I say. "That's all that matters."

CHAPTER 151

IN A HIGHLY restricted and obscure dusty subbasement of the White House, Eliza DeVos, deputy head of the Secret Service presidential detail, impatiently waits for two burly White House maintenance men to undo the last bolt from a thick manhole-cover-type lid and drag it away. The floor is brick, and the solitary light overhead is flickering off and on.

Trent Woodson, head of the protective detail, says to the two workers, "Safety harnesses and belts, as soon as you can. At least a half a dozen."

The workers exit through a small door leading to a smooth concrete corridor. Eliza uses her flashlight to check out the shelves crowded with cardboard boxes, some with scribbled dates going back to 1967.

Trent uses his own flashlight to peer down the opening. His light illuminates the top rung of a ladder and fades out into the depths.

"How deep?" he asks.

"Six stories," Eliza answers. "That's about seventy feet."

"Jesus," he says, leaning over more. "That's one long climb."

"Yeah, and it'd be worse if a Russian nuke hit DC and collapsed the White House over our heads. This is plan D or E for getting POTUS out of the White House in case of nuclear strike."

"Any more communications from POTUS?"

"Not for at least twenty minutes," she says. "All of the secure comms are offline, phone lines are disabled, and cell phones won't work with all this steel and concrete overhead."

The head of the protective detail says, "One way or another, we're going to get POTUS out of there."

"Why?" she asks. "He's safe, he's secure, and we don't know what the hell is going on up top."

He says, "Procedure and policy. The White House is secure but it might be breached at any moment. We get him out and on Marine One and then to Air Force One."

"What if he falls climbing up? He could get killed if the harness broke."

"Not open for discussion, DeVos," he says, voice sharp. "We're exfiling POTUS soonest."

Eliza nods in agreement. She leans over and says, "Hold on, I think I see someone down there flashing a light."

"Really?" Woodson says. "Where?"

"At the bottom, at your six o'clock."

Woodson leans over to take a look, and with both hands, Eliza gives him a sharp shove. He tumbles down instantly and she hears a yell and then a series of thuds as he hits the ladder on the way down. He lands on the metal and concrete at the bottom with a sharp cry.

She steps back, straightens up, dusts off her hands.

For the past few years, she's wanted to head the president's protective detail, and now the job is hers.

CHAPTER

152

FOR BRIEF SECONDS, Sylvester and Casey and their huge Mack tow truck are almost two minutes ahead of schedule. They're closing in on Seventeenth Street NW and the White House when Sylvester says, "Damn, damn, damn."

Ahead of them is a black and yellow Diamond Cab crushed between a Lexus and a Camry, steam rising up from the cab's crumpled hood.

All three vehicles are blocking the road.

Lots of folks are standing on the sidewalks, coming out from the office buildings on both sides of the wide street.

Casey says, "Well, this sucks."

A woman in black yoga pants and a gray sweatshirt holding a bloody handkerchief to her head runs at them. She calls, "Can you help? The taxi driver and his two passengers are trapped, they can't get out. A mother and a little girl. Can you tow the vehicles so the EMTs can get to the injured?"

Sylvester says, "Lady, I don't see any ambulances around."

"They're coming, honest," she says. "And I'm a nurse. I can give them first aid before the EMTs get here."

Next to him Casey murmurs, "Time..."

"I'll take care of it," Sylvester says.

The woman says, "Oh, bless you."

Casey says something but Sylvester ignores him; he puts the Mack into reverse, backs up on Pennsylvania Avenue NW, then puts the big truck in drive and pushes down the accelerator.

Sylvester says, "Hold on to your shorts."

"Oh, man," Casey says.

Sylvester stares straight at the mess of three vehicles, gauging where the weak point is, and he shifts again and the truck picks up speed. Sylvester barely sees the shocked faces of the folks standing by when the truck strikes hard.

The vehicles blow apart and there's screaming and yelling, and Sylvester thinks he sees the black fencing of the White House come into view.

Casey says, "Man, when you say you'll take care of it, you take care of it."

CHAPTER

153

AT THE INTERSECTION of Seventeenth Street NW and Constitution Avenue—the southern end of the Ellipse and the South Lawn of the White House—Ned Mahoney swerves his government-issue Impala to a stop. He and I get out.

Part of the plan. Send out a false alarm to get people out of the area of the White House.

As we trot up Seventeenth Street, people are running away from the area, just like they did on 9/11 when rumors spread that a hijacked airliner was coming to strike the White House.

There's a row of vendor trucks selling everything from hot take-out food to ice cream, all of them abandoned. The keys to the third truck are still in the ignition. Ned starts it up, drives it back to the Impala, and parks it directly in front of the sedan. The two vehicles effectively block the entire intersection.

He gets out, takes the keys, and tosses them down a sewer grate.

I ask, "How in hell did you know the details of that special ID?"

Ned leans into the driver's side of the Impala and pops open the trunk. "Three years ago, I was reviewing DC emergency planning that had the agency's involvement. That one just stuck in my mind."

The streets are distressingly empty of vehicles, though blocks away in each direction I can see the flashing lights of police cruisers.

"Feel like we're the only survivors in a zombie movie," I say, going with Ned to the trunk of his car. He pulls out two ballistic vests with FBI in bright yellow letters. We help each other put them on, and he says, "Time?"

"Ten till noon," I say.

"All right," he says, coming out with an M4 automatic rifle and a twelve-gauge Remington pump-action shotgun. "Got a plan, John?"

Without asking, I take the M4. "Their plan is for General Grissom to get to the White House and take control. You and I are going to stop him. Simple, huh?"

"Simple as it gets," he says, racking a shotgun shell into the chamber.

I say, "Why this intersection?"

He grabs a pair of binoculars, looks south down Seventeenth Street. No vehicles moving. Ned says, "This is the quickest way to get to the main White House gate from the Pentagon. He's a general. He won't do anything different." Ned lowers the binoculars. "I think."

I check the M4 for ammo, go to the trunk, see a belt with two pouches for thirty-round magazines. Not a lot of firepower to save the nation, but it'll have to do. I take the belt and say, "If they won't stop, fire at the tires. That'll slow them down. But I have a feeling they'll stop."

"Why's that?" Ned asks.

"Because even if Grissom is planning a coup, he still has to have drivers and bodyguards with him. Working stiffs. And they'll pause when they see our little roadblock and won't attack us with guns blazing."

Way down Seventeenth Street, flashing blue and red lights appear.

"I hope," I add.

CHAPTER

154

NED LIFTS UP the binoculars again and says, "Hope's not a plan, John. We've got a small convoy coming our way. Looks like two police cruisers, three big SUVs. Maybe Tahoes or Suburbans."

I work the bolt to the M4, and now there's a round in the chamber. "Time?" I ask.

"About eight minutes to noon."

I say, "From everything I've learned from Mason's laptop and the thumb drives, the assault kicks off at noon, with Grissom at the White House making a speech to the world. We're not going to let that happen."

Ned says, "Agreed."

I'm standing behind the open trunk. I close the lid so my view isn't obstructed. I say, "Ned, set up at the front of the car. You've got the engine to protect you."

Ned frowns but moves over. "What's going to protect you, John?"

I remove the full magazines from the ammo pouches, put them on the closed trunk lid for easy access. "Why, the full resources of the FBI, that's what."

He takes the shotgun, reaches into his coat pocket, stacks up some twelve-gauge shells in the gap between the windshield and hood.

The vehicles are coming closer. The two police cruisers are now driving side by side. A Tahoe is in the center, followed by a pair of Suburbans.

My hands are cold and my mouth is dry, but other than that, I feel good.

I say, "Time?"

"Since you last asked? One minute later."

"Okay."

They come closer, and I say, "If they speed up like they're going to ram us, you aim for the tires, I'll aim for the drivers."

"Got it."

I can hear the engines of the approaching vehicles. Hard to believe that in one of them is the general who started this wave of terror and who's using that false flag operation to overthrow the government of the United States of America.

The lights keep flashing.

The convoy keeps approaching.

I clear my throat. "Ned?"

"Yeah?"

"It's been an honor and a privilege working with you and having you as a friend."

No answer for a second. Then Ned says, "Jesus, a moment like this, you want to get me choked up and teary-eyed?"

I laugh. "Sorry."

"Okay."

I say, "They're almost here."

CHAPTER 155

INSIDE THE TAHOE, Grissom looks up from his papers and says, "What the hell is going on?"

"We're slowing, sir," Kendricks says.

"I know that," Grissom snaps. "Find out why and fix it. We don't have time to screw around."

"Yes, sir," she says, and she opens the door and gets out after the Tahoe comes to a stop.

Grissom looks at his watch, irritated. About five minutes before noon. They're two blocks away from the White House and this happens? Unacceptable.

He takes a deep breath. It'll be all right. He's been driven up this route scores of times, and he's positive this time will go as smoothly as the rest.

There's no doubt—

Kendricks opens the door. "I'm sorry, sir, there's a roadblock up ahead."

"A roadblock? From the Metro Police? This isn't one of their roadblock positions. There has to be a mistake."

Kendricks says, “Sir, it’s not a Metro Police unit.”

“Then who the hell is up there?”

“Two men. One says he’s an FBI agent and the other says he’s a police detective. They’re blocking the road with an Impala and a vendor’s truck. And they’re…adamant that we can’t proceed.”

“Well, just drive past them.”

“They’re armed,” she says.

Grissom puts his papers down. “Then I’ll handle it myself, damn it. We don’t have time for this shit.”

CHAPTER

156

I BREATHE EASIER now that the two police cars from the Pentagon's police force have come to a halt.

That means the shooting is delayed, at least for now.

The doors to the two cruisers swing open, and four Pentagon Police officers scramble out. One of them, a heavyset man, steps so close that I can see the color of his eyes—blue—and says, "I'm Captain Roy Jemison, Pentagon Police."

"Nice to meet you, even under these circumstances," I say. "I'm John Sampson, Metro Police detective, and my companion here is Ned Mahoney, FBI."

He looks at us both. "You've got to move your vehicle and let us through."

I say, "Why?"

That seems to startle him. "Because we're escorting General Wayne Grissom to the White House and it's vital that he gets there in the next few minutes. Step back, move the vehicle."

"Or?" Ned asks from the other side of the Impala.

"We'll be forced to take action."

I smile wide even though I'm not in a humorous mood. "Captain Jemison? You and your fellow officers, you need to return to your vehicles and get out of here. You're Pentagon Police. You have no jurisdiction here. Go back across the Potomac where you belong."

The captain steps forward. "This is a national emergency! General Grissom needs to be at the White House now!" His hand moves to his holster.

I raise my voice and say, "What national emergency? Do you know why he's going to the White House? He's declaring martial law and seizing control of the government. Captain, you've sworn an oath to the Constitution. The general you're escorting is about to shove the Constitution into a shredder. You okay with that?"

Jemison says, "That all sounds like conspiracy bullshit. I don't care what you say. Move your vehicle. Now."

I say, "Captain, again, you and your officers have no jurisdiction here. I'm a member of the District police and Mr. Mahoney is with the FBI, which has complete jurisdiction throughout this location. In other words, everything you see—streets, sidewalks, parks—belongs to us. Not you."

I'm looking at the captain's face, then at the confused and concerned faces of his fellow officers, and I say, "Get the hell out while you can."

"I have my orders."

"Yeah, we do too. You're not passing through."

Jemison says, "You don't move, it's going to be escalated."

"Escalated by you," I say. "Anyone in front of us reaches for a weapon, shooting is going to start. You've got us, four versus two, but you're out in the open and we're behind a barrier, the finest steel from Chevrolet. We've got a shotgun and an M4. It won't end pretty."

Jemison looks toward his officers for support and I see his hand move again to his holster, and I lift up my M4—

"Halt this, right now!" comes a loud male voice. "Stand down, all of you!"

And like something from an action movie, General Wayne Grissom, accompanied by another military officer and four men wearing black fatigues and body armor and carrying M4s like mine, start coming right at us like they own the joint.

Ned whispers, "So far, so good. What now?"

"The same as before," I say. "Grissom doesn't get past."

CHAPTER

157

AMONG THE MANY talents a general officer needs is the ability to negotiate, whether with illiterate tribal leaders or an ignorant Congress or an even stupider SecDef, and General Wayne Grissom has this ability. He immediately takes in the scene and checks his watch.

Three minutes to go.

All right, he thinks, *getting past these two should be easy, and if we lose a minute or two, it won't make that much of a difference.* He's still getting to the White House and taking control.

The four Pentagon Police officers move to the side, and Colonel Kendricks keeps pace with him, as do the four heavily armed Pentagon Force Protection Agency members who are shadowing him.

He steps ahead of the four Pentagon officers, puts his hands on his hips, and says, "Well? What seems to be the problem?"

The Black man on the right, the one with an M4, says, "General, the problem seems to be treason. Which is why you're not going forward and you're not getting to the White House."

Once in Iraq, a Humvee driving in front of Grissom hit a land mine, and the shock and overpressure that struck his head and gut back then is nothing compared to what he feels now.

How does he know?

He looks closely and recognizes the man, a DC police detective who had attended some of the principals' meetings when the president was so desperate to defeat the terrorist attacks. Sampson—John Sampson, that's who he is.

Grissom shakes it off. "Detective, you've obviously gotten some disinformation sent your way. May I ask who your companion is? And who's in charge?"

The other man says, "Ned Mahoney, FBI. Neither of us is in charge. Believe it or not, we're having interagency cooperation here."

"That's nice, but you can't stop me," Grissom says. "Move, right now."

Sampson says, "So far, we are stopping you. Noon is kickoff time, right? You're going to stand here and wait while noon slips by. Ned and I have a funny idea about the Constitution. We feel once you've sworn an oath to it, it's your duty to defend it. Guess you've forgotten that, General Grissom."

Colonel Kendricks speaks up. "You two, you don't have the right to hold the general anywhere! He's got to get to the White House. The country needs him."

Sampson shakes his head, says, "If the nation really needs him, there'll be a Draft Grissom movement at the next political convention. In the meantime, you're an officer in the U.S. Army. Which is under civilian control. Not the other way around."

Kendricks says, "You fools, this man has sacrificed everything for this country—blood, sweat, tears. He can't—"

Grissom gently takes hold of Kendricks's right wrist. "That's enough, Colonel." He lets go of her arm, nods to the two men.

"We seem to have reached an impasse," Grissom says. "No matter. We'll reverse course and find another route."

Grissom thinks, *And fast, because all the other pieces are falling into place at this very moment.*

CHAPTER

158

AFTER THE GENERAL says he intends to move, I say, "Ned, you're up."

Ned says, "I'm sorry, General, we can't allow you to leave."

Grissom stops in midturn. "What?"

Ned says, "I'm sorry to say this, sir, but no, you can't leave."

The general's expression twists as he reacts to a word he's not used to hearing: *No.*

"The hell I can't," he says. "There's nothing on earth that's going to keep me here."

Ned says, "Well, U.S. code title eighteen is going to do its very best, sir. General Grissom, you're under arrest for violating eighteen U.S. code section 1956, laundering of monetary instruments; eighteen U.S. code section 2381, treason; and eighteen U.S. code section 2384, seditious conspiracy. And that's just the beginning. Sir, I ask you to remove your protective force as I place you into custody."

Ned steps away from the Impala, one hand holding the pump-action shotgun, the other a dangling pair of handcuffs, and I know what's going through the minds of Grissom and his entourage: *This isn't part of the plan!*

Good.

I keep my position but I wonder how long Ned can stand like this, exposed and vulnerable. Grissom says in a steel-hard voice, "Agent Mahoney, this is intolerable. There are decisions to be made and forces on the move that are way, way above your job title."

He turns to the four well-armed members of his security force and makes a motion, and they slide back to the protection of the parked Chevrolet Suburbans. The four Pentagon officers, seeing what's going on, move back to the cover of their cruisers. The female army colonel stays with him.

"Ned," I say.

But Ned walks out, one firm step at a time. Grissom says, "Not one step closer, Agent Mahoney." Grissom looks at his watch, frowns.

We're screwing up his schedule, I think. *Outstanding.*

The general says, "You have five seconds to remove yourself and your vehicle from this position. At the end of that time, if you two haven't moved, I will tell my protective force that I am in fear for my life, and they will respond appropriately. Do you understand?"

I have the M4 in my hands. I aim and stare right back.

"Five," Grissom begins.

Behind me, I hear the *thump-thump-thump* of explosives. I don't turn around.

"Four," Grissom says.

I say, "Ned, you're a brave soul, but please come back here."

Ned says, "Not a chance. I'm arresting the general."

"Three."

Ned keeps on walking to Grissom, and in my peripheral vision, I see people lining up on the sidewalk, curious to see what the hell is going on. I want to tell them to back off, but no, if this slides into violence, I want witnesses to tell their children what happened this day.

"Two."

Ned says, "General Grissom, I'm placing you under arrest. You have the right to remain silent. Anything you say can and will be used against you in a court of law. You have the right to an attorney."

Grissom's security force and the Pentagon Police raise their weapons. I aim straight at Grissom's forehead, and as soon as he gets to one and orders his men to open fire, I plan to drill a round right into the middle of that smug, traitorous face.

I think, *Bree, I sure hope you got that last text.*

I see Grissom's lips beginning to form the last number. My finger slides onto the trigger, and from behind me comes the loud rumble of diesel engines.

I keep staring at Grissom, and the shocked look on the general's face makes it all worthwhile.

Even Ned has stopped walking. He quickly turns and looks behind me with relief.

CHAPTER

159

WHEN HE SEES two desert-tan army Humvees coming to a halt behind the parked Impala and the vendor truck, Grissom thinks, *This isn't part of the plan. They're not supposed to be deployed until this evening to enforce the curfew.*

The doors open, and eight National Guardsmen are walking his way, seven of them armed with M4s, the eighth one an officer leading them. He's a slim Black man, uniform crisp and clean, wearing body armor, a utility belt, a holstered pistol, and a soft utility cap. As the man passes the Impala and steps closer, Grissom spots his colonel insignia and his last name, TOUSSANT.

The colonel salutes and Grissom salutes back. The man says, "General, I'm Colonel Lionel Toussant, Two Hundred Seventy-Sixth Military Police Company, Three Hundred Seventy-Second Military Police Battalion, District of Columbia, Army National Guard."

Grissom smiles, shakes the man's hand. "Colonel Toussant, General Wayne Grissom."

With a grin in return, Toussant says, "I know who you are, sir."

"Good," Grissom says. "Glad to see you here. Colonel, I need you to place those two men over by the Impala under arrest, get that car out of the way, and then—"

Colonel Toussant's smile disappears. "I'm sorry, sir, those aren't my orders."

Two more Humvees hauling trailers come to a stop. Other National Guardsmen go to the trailers, undo the canvas coverings, and start removing large coils of barbed wire and wooden sawhorses. They quickly set up the sawhorses, and the rolls of barbed wire are undone and pulled apart.

"Colonel," Grissom says, voice strained, "what are your orders?"

The colonel says, "My orders are to secure the streets and grounds around the White House. No vehicle and no persons are allowed into the area under our control."

Grissom says, "I'm countermanding those orders right now. I want this street cleared and access provided to my party and me."

Toussant says, "I'm sorry, sir, I can't do it. I have my orders."

Grissom says sharply, "And I'm overriding those orders. Do it now, Colonel Toussant!"

The colonel shakes his head. "With all due respect, General Grissom, you're not in my chain of command. I'm sure you'll recall, General, that we are the only National Guard unit that reports directly to the president. He is our commander in chief, and he has activated us and ordered us to place the White House under a cordon sanitaire."

Grissom clenches his fists. "It's my understanding that the president can no longer communicate with the outside."

"We're working on that, sir," the colonel says. "But before he lost those communications, he talked to our mayor, and she requested the National Guard's activation to protect the White House against a possible insurrection."

Grissom stares in anger at the cocky and confident colonel standing in front of him. This colonel reminds him of those rules-based

JAG officers back in Afghanistan. When his artillery units received a target designation, the lawyers from JAG had to verify the target to ensure no civilian or collateral damage occurred. A normal fire mission that should have taken only three minutes could stretch out for half an hour before JAG and other higher-ups signed off on it.

Hell of a way to run a fire mission, run an army, run an operation to save this nation.

More Humvees pull up and discharge National Guard soldiers. In his mind's eye, Grissom can see similar detachments going to other intersections around the White House and occupying Lafayette Park and the Ellipse.

"General," Colonel Kendricks whispers to him, "what are we going to do?"

He's starting to taste the bitterness of defeat in his mouth, and he sees Colonel Toussant and the FBI man deep in conversation. One of the Guardsmen is holding the FBI man's shotgun, and Colonel Toussant nods and takes three steps to Grissom and his aide.

"General," Toussant says. "Again, my apologies, but FBI supervising special agent Ned Mahoney has informed me that he intends to place you under arrest. That is not in my jurisdiction, so I'm going to allow him to proceed while my unit deploys."

The FBI agent is close enough that Grissom can see the light reflecting off the bright handcuffs, and for the first time in a very long while, he is at a loss for words.

But someone else is not.

His wrist is seized by Colonel Kendricks, and she yells, "Everybody freeze, right now!"

In her other hand is her nine-millimeter pistol.

CHAPTER

160

SYLVESTER IS CONCERNED because when he reaches the White House grounds, his two contacts—a man and a woman, both dressed in Park Service uniforms—are not at their preplanned locations by a certain lamppost.

Either they're late or they're not coming.

Casey says, "Where in hell are Frick and Frack?"

"I don't know," Sylvester says, "but that's not going to stop us. Might slow us down, but we're still doing the job."

Casey says, "That's the spirit. Let's do it."

There's no traffic on Pennsylvania Avenue, so Sylvester easily maneuvers the large tow truck, glancing with a practiced eye into the side-view mirrors to execute a turn.

He shifts into reverse and is about to gently press the accelerator when two men wearing helmets and army fatigues step up on the running boards, one on each side.

The one next to Sylvester raps the window with a closed fist, and Casey says, "Don't do it, don't do it," but Sylvester lowers the window. The guy in fatigues says, "What the hell do you think you're doing?"

"My job," Sylvester replies. He sees other soldiers gathering along the sidewalk.

"What the fuck kind of job is that?"

Sylvester starts to speak, but the soldier interrupts him. "Look, bud, I don't see any disabled trucks or cars in the area. Turn around and get the hell out."

"Not happening," Sylvester says. "I've got a job to do."

The soldier says, "Yeah, and I got a job to do too. Nobody is allowed on this street—nobody. And you ain't somebody, so get the hell out. Now."

Sylvester glances over at Casey, who slightly shakes his head no.

The soldier adds, "Just to show you how fucking serious this is, we're authorized to use deadly force. That get your attention? Now move!"

Again Sylvester looks at Casey, and in a low quiet voice, Casey says, "Screw 'em. They're weekend soldiers. They won't dare shoot. Come on, back 'er up."

"You sure?"

"Christ, I'm sure," Casey says. "They're just play soldiers. They won't shoot."

Sylvester is filled with confidence; he nods and puts the heavy truck in reverse.

Less than ten seconds later, Sylvester is lying on the seat, broken glass on his face and chest, feeling his wounds bleed out. His last thought is that he shouldn't have listened to Casey.

CHAPTER 161

WITH THE ARRIVAL of the DC National Guard units, I feel the tight band around my chest loosen. The desperate phone call Ned made from his house to the DC mayor is paying off. I lower my M4, then put it on the trunk of Ned's Impala. More people and one TV camera crew are on the crowded sidewalks watching this drama unfold.

And what a drama it is. The National Guard colonel is standing with Ned, and Ned is carrying a set of handcuffs. Grissom's Pentagon Police and security service have backed off and lowered their weapons, and things seem under control.

Except for the angry colonel standing next to General Grissom, pistol in her right hand.

Nobody is moving.

The scene is frozen.

I walk around the trunk of the Impala and head toward General Grissom and the colonel standing next to him. Her pistol is now pointing straight at me.

Not the first time in my life this has happened.

Then I'm stunned when I hear someone call out from the growing line of National Guard members, "You go, Big John! We got your back!"

I don't turn. I keep slowly advancing, but despite what I'm facing—an angry army officer aiming her pistol at me—I'm incredibly calm and peaceful. A friend of mine is back there in the National Guard force, and most of them there, defending their city, their White House, and their president, are the most overlooked workers in and around DC. They're engineers, clerks, beauticians, hotel staff, sanitation workers, IT professionals, and people of so many other professions, now one unit, one force, the District of Columbia National Guard.

Nicknamed the Capital Guardians, for obvious reasons.

I step closer, hands up, and say, "Good afternoon, Colonel Kendricks. Hell of a situation we've got here, eh?"

The pistol doesn't waver. "You're Sampson, right? Detective with the DC Metro Police?"

"That's right, Colonel. Good memory."

Voice sharp, she says, "You and your FBI friend had no right to stop General Grissom from performing his mission. No right!"

I take two more steps, empty hands held up, face friendly. "You may be correct, Colonel, but that's up to others to decide. In the meantime, what's your first name? You can call me John if you'd like."

She shakes her head. Grissom says, "Colonel, you are to—"

"General, please," she says. "I know what I'm doing." Her eyes narrow. "And I know what the detective wants. He wants my first name to establish some sort of rapport with me, get me to trust his intentions. To hell with that."

I say, "Pretty smart, Colonel, but I'll tell you my intentions straight up, name or no name. It's to dial down this situation, relax things so no one gets hurt."

"And how do you plan to do that?"

"Well, maybe you can put your pistol down, reduce the chance of an accidental shooting. That'd be a nice start."

She laughs. "And what do I get in return? I'll tell you—I get arrested, right? But armed like this, I still hold a wild card."

Colonel Toussant and Ned are standing still, watching.

I say, "All right, I'll concede that. You hold a wild card. What do you plan to do with it?"

"Get you all to back away, move the vehicles, and allow General Grissom to get to the White House."

I shake my head slowly, sorrowfully. "No, Colonel, that's not going to happen. The current situation won't allow that."

"It has to happen. He has to get to the White House," she says. "General Grissom has sacrificed so much for this nation, has bled for this nation, has lost his family for this nation. The country needs him like they needed Washington, Grant, and Eisenhower. His time has come."

Another sad shake of my head. I take a few more steps. "Colonel, you're smart, you're experienced, you know that General Grissom is not going to the White House. It's just not gonna happen."

Wearily, Grissom says, "Kendricks, it's over. Put your weapon on the ground."

Kendricks's face reddens. "I do that, sir, and what happens? I'll be arrested, and so will you. Am I correct?" she asks me.

I nod. In hostage negotiations, you never lie. "That's right, Colonel," I say. "You'll both be arrested. I don't see any way out of that."

"Fine," she says, her voice even angrier. "Then this man, General Wayne Grissom, this dedicated and tough and patriotic general—his life, his career, his years of service—he'll be destroyed, won't he? He'll be the subject of hate, scorn, humor. His face will be on the front page of every newspaper, every cable show, every internet site, and he'll be portrayed as a traitor, this century's Benedict Arnold. His decades of proud service will be reduced to the cliché of a madman. And then will come the trial, months and months of daily humiliation, followed by a life sentence at Leavenworth. That's what's ahead for this great man, isn't it?"

I'm trying to come up with a reasonable response when Kendricks answers her own question.

"I'm sorry, General, I can't allow this to happen to you," she says, bringing up her pistol. She places it against his right temple and shoots him once in the head.

There are shouts, moans, and gasps, then a series of gunshots erupt from behind me, and Colonel Kendricks collapses next to her beloved general, both of them probably dead before they struck the pavement.

CHAPTER

162

MARIA TUCKER, PISTOL still holstered at her waist, steps onto the suite's balcony at the Hay-Adams hotel, thinking, *It's gone to shit,* as she brings up her binoculars to survey the scene around the White House.

At noon, the charges secretly hidden at the Secret Service observation posts went off on schedule, and she even heard the muffled *chuff-chuff-chuff* of sound-suppressed sniper rifles taking down other Secret Service agents out there.

Excellent.

But as seconds and minutes ticked away…nothing! Where was the huge tow truck to tear down the fences? Where were the fake delivery vehicles from UPS and FedEx and Amazon that were to roll in and discharge scores of armed men and women? Where were the helicopters going over the supposedly closed White House airspace to fast-drop operators onto the undefended White House roof?

Where is everybody?

She walks back into the suite, remembering her grandfather who was seriously burned in 1980 when the attempt to rescue

American hostages in Iran ended in a flaming disaster in the middle of a desert.

As a child, she'd wondered how Grandpa felt that night.

Now she knows.

To Styles and Flynn, both in front of their terminals, she says, "Updates?"

Flynn says not a word, but Styles says, "Some disjointed and scrambled messages, ma'am. It looks like the assault is failing. Our people are being scooped up and arrested."

Flynn says, "What now?"

Maria says, "Follow your orders. Wipe all hard drives, thumb drives, anything and everything that's electronically recorded. I'll gather up any paperwork and take care of it."

The next few minutes pass with the techs punching keyboards as Maria feeds sheets of paper into a top-of-the-line GSA shredder, which not only shreds the notes and paperwork but also flash-burns the shredded bits into ashes and soaks them in acid.

When the three of them are finished, there's the constant sound of sirens outside, along with the thrumming of helicopter blades.

Maria goes to Styles and Flynn. "All done?"

"Yes, ma'am," Styles says.

"All wrapped up," Flynn says. "Time for us to slip out?"

Maria shakes her head. "Not right now," she says. "I've got orders as well."

She takes out her pistol, and Flynn says, "Please, God, no!" and Maria shoots each of them twice, then retrieves the empty casings from the carpeted floor and grabs her go bag.

She goes out to the hallway, closes the door behind her, heads to the nearest elevator bank, and punches the button to bring an elevator car to her floor.

Didn't work, did it, she thinks. There's a *ding* as the door slides open, and Maria whispers, "Maybe next time."

CHAPTER

163

IT'S NEARLY NOON and the scene is loud, chaotic, with laughter interspersed with sweet insults and a few curses, but this is turning into one of the happiest days of my life—and of the Cross family's life—and I won't complain for one second.

We are in a small procession, Alex Cross leading the way in his wheelchair. I have the privilege, having earlier shoved aside Ali, Damon, and Jannie, of pushing him along as he finally leaves George Washington University Hospital.

Bree is on Alex's right, tightly holding his hand, and Nana Mama is on his left, doing the same. Jannie is holding a bundle of strings belonging to a squadron of balloons, all of which wish Alex good health, and Damon and Ali are both carrying plastic bags containing greeting cards, gifts, and Alex's discharge papers.

There's laughter and joking. Nana Mama is running down a week's worth of planned meals—"'Cause I know they do their best, but their food ain't fit for anyone, healthy or healing"—and Ali babbles about going on a camping trip once his dad gets better, and Damon occasionally pats his father on the shoulder. Jannie just smiles with tears running down her cheeks.

And grabbing my left leg, making it hard to keep up with folks and maintain a steady pace, is my little Willow, happy to have Daddy home again.

Me too, I think, *me too.*

Alex turns and looks up at me, smiling. He's freshly bathed and shaved, and he's wearing khaki slacks and a dark blue polo shirt from home, but they are baggy around his shrunken frame.

Nana Mama has her work cut out for her, putting meat back on those tired bones.

A male nurse who's accompanying us shoos away visitors and patients in front of us, and we're out of the large lobby and into the fresh air of a late Washington, DC, morning, and it's a beautiful day.

We're on a curved driveway leading from the hospital lobby to I Street, right near the Foggy Bottom farmers' market, and through the cars and the pedestrians, many of whom are people from the university, we can see scores of vendors and farmers working under tents and large umbrellas.

The nurse who's with us bends down to Alex and says, "All right, Dr. Cross, I know you hate to hear this, but it's hospital rules—you have to stay in your wheelchair until the vehicle taking you home is right in front of you. When that happens, you'll require assistance moving from the chair to the car. Got that? Any questions?"

"Not a single one," Alex says, his voice soft but strong.

The nurse leaves and I look around, waiting for the two Chevrolet Suburbans from the Bluestone Group to take this brood home. I still have my service weapon on my hip.

Just in case.

I lock the wheels of the wheelchair and go around and take a knee by Alex. I give him a hard look and say, "How are you doing?"

His bright smile is a relief. "Achy and shaky, but I'm ready to go home."

He frees his right hand from Bree's and holds it out, and I give it a good squeeze. I'm thrilled at how strong his return squeeze is. Alex says, "I owe you a lot, John, for keeping my family safe."

"You'd do the same for me," I say as Willow comes up behind me and wraps her small arms around my thick neck.

"And the nation owes you a lot too. You and Ned Mahoney. And Elizabeth Deacon. How's she doing?"

I nod in the direction of the hospital. "Still in a coma, but she's stable. The next few days will make the difference, the docs say."

"Sounds like a good woman."

"She is. I plan to come back here later today for a long visit."

"Good," he says, still smiling, but I note something in his eyes. I say, "Give it up, Alex. What are you thinking about?"

His voice is somber. "I'm thinking about getting back to work."

Thank God Bree didn't hear that—she's talking to Jannie—because I'm sure that sentence would have resulted in a slap upside Alex's head, no matter his condition.

"What work?" I ask. "Alex, Ned and the FBI and others are going twenty-four/seven, rolling up those terrorist networks. The president went on the air yesterday to announce that the threat of future terrorist attacks is now over. Tomorrow, General Wayne Grissom is going to be buried with full military honors at Arlington National Cemetery after being shot by gunmen during his mission to personally protect the president."

Alex smiles. "How long do you think that cover story will last?"

"Long enough for me to stay in the DC Metro Police and go out on full pension without embarrassing questions being asked of me in front of Congress."

"You can't fire a hero, right?"

I say, "That's right. But let's get back to what you just said. What do you mean, getting back to work?"

Ali calls out, "They're here!"

I see two Suburbans approach, and their license plates match the letters and numbers I memorized earlier; the SUVs belong to Bree's employer.

Alex shifts in the wheelchair and says, "Colonel Carla Kendricks."

"Grissom's aide, shot down right after she killed him."

"But who killed her?" Alex asks. "And why so quickly?"

"Somebody from the National Guard unit standing nearby," I reply. "That's what I've been told. After Kendricks fired the shot, somebody returned fire instinctively. The National Guard is conducting its own investigation."

He nods. "I'm sure. But was she killed because she posed a threat, or was there a modern-day Jack Ruby among the National Guard, someone who killed her so she couldn't talk, couldn't be a witness? That needs to be checked out. We're going to do that, John."

I shake my head and straighten up, my arm around Willow, who is leaning into me. "Damn it, sugar, can't you take at least one day off?"

He grins. "Okay. I promise. I'll take off the rest of today. Meet me at the house tomorrow, eight a.m."

"Nine," I say. "You need your rest. And I've got to drop Willow off at school."

The Suburbans stop in front of us, the doors swing open, and Bree calls out to the security operators from Bluestone. "Tim and Carlos, come over here and get Alex inside."

Then something amazing happens.

Alex grabs the armrests of the wheelchair, hauls himself up with a grunt, and starts walking under his own power to the nearer Suburban.

The sight makes my eyes water.

There's nobody on this earth who can keep my Alex down.

Nana Mama calls out, "You silly man, you're supposed to follow the rules! Stay in that chair!"

We're all looking at him as he keeps walking to the Suburban. He grabs the frame of the open door and turns, smiling.

"I'm Alex Cross," he says. "I make my own rules."

ACKNOWLEDGMENTS

James Patterson and Brendan DuBois would like to thank the following for their assistance on *Cross Down:* Dr. Babak Sarani, director of Trauma and Acute Care Surgery and co-medical director of Critical Care at the George Washington University Hospital; Air Force Lt. Col. Robert Carver, spokesman for the Joint Task Force for the District of Columbia; Michael Davidson, former officer, Central Intelligence Agency; Vito Maggiolo, public information officer for DC Fire and EMS Department; and Edie Hicks, retired critical care RN and EMS-Paramedic.

ABOUT THE AUTHORS

James Patterson is one of the best-known and biggest-selling writers of all time. His books have sold in excess of 400 million copies worldwide. He is the author of some of the most popular series of the past two decades – the Alex Cross, Women's Murder Club, Detective Michael Bennett and Private novels – and he has written many other number one bestsellers including stand-alone thrillers and non-fiction.

James is passionate about encouraging children to read. Inspired by his own son who was a reluctant reader, he also writes a range of books for young readers including the Middle School, Dog Diaries, Treasure Hunters and Max Einstein series. James has donated millions in grants to independent bookshops and has been the most borrowed adult author in UK libraries for the past thirteen years in a row. He lives in Florida with his family.

Brendan DuBois is the award-winning author of twenty-seven novels and more than two hundred short stories, garnering him three Shamus Awards from the Private Eye Writers of America as well as the Edward D. Hoch Memorial Golden Derringer for Lifetime Achievement from the Short Mystery Fiction Society. He is also a *Jeopardy!* champion.

Discover the next exciting instalment
in the Alex Cross series . . .

CROSS Out

PUBLISHING OCTOBER 2023

Read for an exclusive extract . . .

CHAPTER

South Camp Springs, Maryland

ON THAT MID-NOVEMBER MONDAY morning, after nearly three years of careful planning, the forty-eight-year-old man donned latex gloves and scanned the rental-car agreement one last time.

His eyes paused on the flowing signature *Marion Davis* before he stuffed the agreement into an aluminum clipboard storage box, the kind construction estimators use. He set it on plastic sheeting on the credenza in a dingy motel room not far from Joint Base Andrews.

Davis had been there the past three days; he'd told the young woman at the front desk that he was holing up to finish his first movie script. His claim seemed to impress her enough that she agreed to keep housekeeping away, which was good, because how could he have explained the thin plastic sheeting covering every bit of furniture and taped over the floors and walls? Or, even harder to explain, the four large plastic storage bins he'd bought at Walmart and filled with bleach, hydrogen peroxide, and distilled water?

The acrid chemical scent irritated Davis's eyes and nose, but he didn't dare open the windows for ventilation. Instead, he'd kept the air conditioner going nonstop and wore goggles and a KN95 mask. He left the room only in the dead of night, when it was safe to ferry supplies. Now Davis crouched by the closest storage bin, reached with gloved hands into the chemical solution, and pulled out a long belt of .50-caliber bullets bought two years before on the blackest of black markets, this one at a remote ranch in northern Colorado.

He knew from training and experience that a soldier could adjust his aim at a moving target by using this ammunition belt. Every fourth cartridge fired a tracer round that glowed hot orange as it sped through the air.

However, the tracers also revealed the position of the shooter. Davis left in the first four tracer rounds but removed the remaining ones and replaced them with live rounds from a second bleached ammunition belt.

When he was done, he sank the first belt back in the chemicals and went into the bathroom. There, Davis stripped off his clothes and put them in a plastic garbage bag that he closed and sealed with duct tape.

Next, he stepped into the shower stall—all but the drain covered in plastic sheeting—turned on the hot water, picked up a razor, and shaved every inch of skin he could reach, from his already shaved head to the insteps of his feet.

He poured two cups of bleach down the drain when he was finished shaving, turned off the water, and retrieved a large tube of Airassi hair remover. Davis used a sponge on a long handle to smear the stuff on the skin he'd just shaved and all over his back. His eyebrows, eyelids, and ear canals were also dabbed. The cream burned, especially on his testicles, but he waited nearly fifteen minutes before rinsing it off. It was worth the pain to ensure that no FBI crime scene tech would find his hair anywhere.

Davis stepped out of the shower, stood and waited for his body to dry, then applied copious amounts of CeraVe moisturizer, again head to toe, to keep flecks of his skin from shedding. Only then did he step into a white disposable hazmat suit. He pulled the hood over his head and zipped it to his neck.

With the goggles and respirator on, Davis lugged the storage bins into the bathroom and drained them, leaving the various components of his weapon and custom tripod in them. He used two blow-dryers to remove the rest of the moisture and lubricated the parts with oil and graphite.

When he was satisfied, Davis put lids on the bins, tore down the plastic sheeting, gathered everything he had used in the past seventy-two hours, and stuffed it all into four lawn-and-leaf bags. These he sealed with duct tape and put next to the motel room's door.

He pushed back the curtains and saw the rear of the tan utility van. No one else was in the parking lot. But why would anyone be? It was a weekday morning. The kids who lived at the motel were all in school, and their mothers were working or sleeping it off.

Davis opened another bag, retrieved a new Baltimore Ravens hoodie, and put it on over the hazmat suit. A new brown cover-all with the logo of the National Park Service went on next. He finished with a pair of glasses with heavy black frames and clear lenses. He added a respirator to cover his face, checked his look, then tugged the mask down around his neck.

All of this had taken several hours. Davis had a great deal of confidence in his preparation, but his heart still raced when he finally opened the motel room door. He quickly moved the storage bins and bulging plastic bags into the rear of the van, near a mountain bike and two blue fifty-five-gallon drums, one strapped to each wall. A laptop computer, purchased the year before from a pawnshop in Kentucky, went in the front seat.

Davis left the key to the spotless room on a chair by the door and drove out of the parking lot a few minutes after two p.m. He felt fully in control of his fate and pleased about the impact he was about to have.

Davis allowed himself a smile, thinking: *Isn't that the way you want to be when you're about to commit mass murder for a righteous cause?*

CHAPTER 2

FOR THE NEXT THREE hours, Davis drove around greater Washington, DC, tossing the trash bags in separate dumpsters. When he was done with that, he went to Thrifton Hill Park, off Interstate 66 in Woodmont, Virginia.

He kept the vehicle running and the air-conditioning blasting when he got out with two magnetic signs reading GROUND CREW below the emblem of the National Park Service system. They were exact replicas of ones he had seen and photographed on a trip to the Shenandoah Valley earlier in the year.

Davis stuck them on the sides of his van, climbed into the rear between the fifty-five-gallon drums, and began assembling a relic left over from Vietnam War days, a Browning M2 .50-caliber machine gun. He'd bought it at the same remote Colorado ranch where he'd bought the bullets.

When he was done putting the Browning together, he fitted a thermal scope on it, then screwed the tripod panhead into the front stock of the machine gun. He bolted the three legs of the tripod to a rotating steel plate mounted on the van's floor and checked the thin hydraulic connection to the tripod's neck.

Earlier, he had screwed a solid steel cylinder, four inches long and a quarter of an inch in diameter, into the rear bottom of the machine gun's stock. That stout nub fit into the receiver of a hydraulic unit that was smaller than a card deck and mounted on a track between two strips of steel that curved from one side of the van to the other. The tracks were screwed tightly into the floor.

The machine gun now stood on its own, fully controlled, barrel cocked slightly upward, the muzzle less than an inch from where the two back doors met.

To finish, Davis attached a small pneumatic vise around the trigger and connected it and the other hydraulic lines and pumps to a palm-size digital control. Davis used the laptop to activate the thermal sight, connected by Bluetooth to the computer, and was soon looking at the scope's reticle and the rear door of the van.

He triggered one of the hydraulic lines and saw the barrel rise as the tripod's neck lifted and extended.

He gave another order. The rear of the gun swept smoothly left and right; he tested the trigger vise and heard the firing pin click. Satisfied, Davis retrieved the ammunition belt and fed it into the receiver, making sure to lay the belt out so it would not bunch or bind and jam the weapon.

Dusk gathered as he put the van in gear and headed east on I-66, then picked up the southbound George Washington Memorial Parkway. Davis turned on his headlights as he passed beneath the Fourteenth Street Bridge and took the exit to Gravelly Point Park, hard by the Potomac River.

He pulled into the nearly empty parking lot and found the stall he wanted. As darkness descended, the last visitors got in their cars and left. Davis called up a public link on the laptop.

Air traffic controllers began chattering to pilots.

Just then a roaring sound came from behind the van. From the north, a United Airlines jet crossed above the Fourteenth Street Bridge, Gravelly Point Park, Davis's van, and a backwater of the Potomac and touched down at Ronald Reagan National Airport.

Davis thrilled at the vibration the passing jet's engines sent through the van and his body. It had been less than two hundred feet above him! He knew this because he had been to the park multiple times over the past three years, purposely going months between visits to study landing patterns and approaches until he felt as if he could put a jet down on that runway himself.

The air traffic control chatter directed the next three planes to approach the airport at the same specific speeds and angles of descent. The wind, they said, was due south, barely eight knots, which made for smooth landings.

The next plane and the one after that came in on the same vectors. Davis fed this information into the laptop just before a police cruiser turned into the parking lot.

He'd anticipated a visit. A cruiser showed up every evening to make sure the parking lot was empty and gated off from vehicles. Davis leaned over and retrieved a sprayer from the floor of the passenger side. He tugged his respirator up so it covered the lower part of his face and got out with a headlamp on his head. The cruiser pulled up. The window rolled down.

"Late night?" the female officer asked.

"On overtime, Officer," Davis said, lowering the mask a little. "They want this place sprayed with insecticide when no one is around."

"You're lucky it's fairly warm and not raining."

"I was kind of wishing for rain so I could go home and see my kids," he said. He unzipped his coverall enough to show the Ravens logo on his hoodie. "Watch the game."

"That's right, Baltimore's playing tonight. You have the key to the gate?"

Davis nodded. "I'll shut and lock it when I leave."

"Thanks," the officer said. She rolled up the window and pulled away.

Davis made a show of leaving the parking lot and trudging down the bike path. The cruiser's taillights disappeared. After a bicyclist passed him heading north, he buttonhooked back to the van, got in, and set the chemical sprayer on the floor. He listened to the next plane land on the same vectors and trajectories and checked to make sure his cell phone was connected to the laptop. Then he sent the computer a command from the phone. Behind him, he heard the gun swivel and adjust for elevation and windage based on the information he'd gleaned from the air traffic controllers.

"Delta nine-four-four, you are clear for landing," a female controller on the laptop connection said. "American eight-three-nine, begin your approach."

"Roger that, National," both pilots said.

Davis got out fast, went around the back of the van, and opened the rear doors. Careful not to bump the barrel of the gun, he eased out the mountain bike, got on it, and pedaled away. By the time the Delta flight landed, Davis was out along the Potomac, listening to the air traffic controllers over his phone and earbuds.

He caught sight of the American jet's landing lights far upriver and stopped the bike south of the Fourteenth Street Bridge. He could barely see the van back in the parking lot.

It didn't matter, and neither did the men, women, and children on the plane. Davis thumbed the screen of his phone to see the feed from the scope.

American 839, arriving from Palm Beach International, was above and behind him over the bridge. The heat signature of the jet was just showing on the gun sight's thermal feed.

Davis activated the firing program and waited for the mayhem to commence.

Also By James Patterson

ALEX CROSS NOVELS

Along Came a Spider • Kiss the Girls • Jack and Jill • Cat and Mouse • Pop Goes the Weasel • Roses are Red • Violets are Blue • Four Blind Mice • The Big Bad Wolf • London Bridges • Mary, Mary • Cross • Double Cross • Cross Country • Alex Cross's Trial (*with Richard DiLallo*) • I, Alex Cross • Cross Fire • Kill Alex Cross • Merry Christmas, Alex Cross • Alex Cross, Run • Cross My Heart • Hope to Die • Cross Justice • Cross the Line • The People vs. Alex Cross • Target: Alex Cross • Criss Cross • Deadly Cross • Fear No Evil • Triple Cross

THE WOMEN'S MURDER CLUB SERIES

1st to Die (*with Andrew Gross*) • 2nd Chance (*with Andrew Gross*) • 3rd Degree (*with Andrew Gross*) • 4th of July (*with Maxine Paetro*) • The 5th Horseman (*with Maxine Paetro*) • The 6th Target (*with Maxine Paetro*) • 7th Heaven (*with Maxine Paetro*) • 8th Confession (*with Maxine Paetro*) • 9th Judgement (*with Maxine Paetro*) • 10th Anniversary (*with Maxine Paetro*) • 11th Hour (*with Maxine Paetro*) • 12th of Never (*with Maxine Paetro*) • Unlucky 13 (*with Maxine Paetro*) • 14th Deadly Sin (*with Maxine Paetro*) • 15th Affair (*with Maxine Paetro*) • 16th Seduction (*with Maxine Paetro*) • 17th Suspect (*with Maxine Paetro*) • 18th Abduction (*with Maxine Paetro*) • 19th Christmas (*with Maxine Paetro*) • 20th Victim (*with Maxine Paetro*) • 21st Birthday (*with Maxine Paetro*) • 22 Seconds (*with Maxine Paetro*) • 23rd Midnight (*with Maxine Paetro*)

DETECTIVE MICHAEL BENNETT SERIES

Step on a Crack (*with Michael Ledwidge*) • Run for Your Life (*with Michael Ledwidge*) • Worst Case (*with Michael Ledwidge*) • Tick Tock (*with Michael Ledwidge*) • I, Michael Bennett (*with Michael Ledwidge*) • Gone (*with Michael Ledwidge*) • Burn (*with Michael Ledwidge*) • Alert (*with Michael Ledwidge*) • Bullseye (*with Michael Ledwidge*) • Haunted (*with James O. Born*) • Ambush (*with James O. Born*) • Blindside (*with James O. Born*) • The Russian (*with James O. Born*) • Shattered (*with James O. Born*)

PRIVATE NOVELS

Private (*with Maxine Paetro*) • Private London (*with Mark Pearson*) • Private Games (*with Mark Sullivan*) • Private: No. 1 Suspect (*with Maxine Paetro*) • Private Berlin (*with Mark Sullivan*) • Private Down Under (*with Michael White*) • Private L.A. (*with Mark Sullivan*) • Private India (*with Ashwin Sanghi*) • Private Vegas (*with Maxine Paetro*) • Private Sydney (*with Kathryn Fox*) • Private Paris (*with Mark Sullivan*) • The Games (*with Mark Sullivan*) • Private Delhi (*with Ashwin Sanghi*) • Private Princess (*with Rees Jones*) • Private Moscow (*with Adam Hamdy*) • Private Rogue (*with Adam Hamdy*) • Private Beijing (*with Adam Hamdy*)

NYPD RED SERIES

NYPD Red (*with Marshall Karp*) • NYPD Red 2 (*with Marshall Karp*) • NYPD Red 3 (*with Marshall Karp*) • NYPD Red 4 (*with Marshall Karp*) • NYPD Red 5 (*with Marshall Karp*) • NYPD Red 6 (*with Marshall Karp*)

DETECTIVE HARRIET BLUE SERIES

Never Never (*with Candice Fox*) • Fifty Fifty (*with Candice Fox*) • Liar Liar (*with Candice Fox*) • Hush Hush (*with Candice Fox*)

INSTINCT SERIES

Instinct (*with Howard Roughan, previously published as* Murder Games) • Killer Instinct (*with Howard Roughan*) • Steal (*with Howard Roughan*)

THE BLACK BOOK SERIES

The Black Book (*with David Ellis*) • The Red Book (*with David Ellis*) • Escape (*with David Ellis*)

STAND-ALONE THRILLERS

The Thomas Berryman Number • Hide and Seek • Black Market • The Midnight Club • Sail (*with Howard Roughan*) • Swimsuit (*with Maxine Paetro*) • Don't Blink (*with Howard Roughan*) • Postcard Killers (*with Liza Marklund*) • Toys (*with Neil McMahon*) • Now You See Her (*with Michael Ledwidge*) • Kill Me If You Can (*with Marshall Karp*) • Guilty Wives (*with David Ellis*) • Zoo (*with Michael Ledwidge*) • Second Honeymoon (*with Howard Roughan*) • Mistress (*with David Ellis*) • Invisible (*with David*

Ellis) • Truth or Die (*with Howard Roughan*) • Murder House (*with David Ellis*) • The Store (*with Richard DiLallo*) • Texas Ranger (*with Andrew Bourelle*) • The President is Missing (*with Bill Clinton*) • Revenge (*with Andrew Holmes*) • Juror No. 3 (*with Nancy Allen*) • The First Lady (*with Brendan DuBois*) • The Chef (*with Max DiLallo*) • Out of Sight (*with Brendan DuBois*) • Unsolved (*with David Ellis*) • The Inn (*with Candice Fox*) • Lost (*with James O. Born*) • Texas Outlaw (*with Andrew Bourelle*) • The Summer House (*with Brendan DuBois*) • 1st Case (*with Chris Tebbetts*) • Cajun Justice (*with Tucker Axum*)• The Midwife Murders (*with Richard DiLallo*) • The Coast-to-Coast Murders (*with J.D. Barker*) • Three Women Disappear (*with Shan Serafin*) • The President's Daughter (*with Bill Clinton*) • The Shadow (*with Brian Sitts*) • The Noise (*with J.D. Barker*) • 2 Sisters Detective Agency (*with Candice Fox*) • Jailhouse Lawyer (*with Nancy Allen*) • The Horsewoman (*with Mike Lupica*) • Run Rose Run (*with Dolly Parton*) • Death of the Black Widow (*with J.D. Barker*) • The Ninth Month (*with Richard DiLallo*) • The Girl in the Castle (*with Emily Raymond*) • Blowback (*with Brendan DuBois*) • The Twelve Topsy-Turvy, Very Messy Days of Christmas (*with Tad Safran*) • The Perfect Assassin (*with Brian Sitts*) • House of Wolves (*with Mike Lupica*) • Countdown (*with Brendan DuBois*)

NON-FICTION

Torn Apart (*with Hal and Cory Friedman*) • The Murder of King Tut (*with Martin Dugard*) • All-American Murder (*with Alex Abramovich and Mike Harvkey*) • The Kennedy Curse (*with Cynthia Fagen*) • The Last Days of John Lennon (*with Casey Sherman and Dave Wedge*) • Walk in My Combat Boots (*with Matt Eversmann and Chris Mooney*) • ER Nurses (*with Matt Eversmann*) • James Patterson by James Patterson: The Stories of My Life • Diana, William and Harry (*with Chris Mooney*) • American Cops (*with Matt Eversmann*)

MURDER IS FOREVER TRUE CRIME

Murder, Interrupted (*with Alex Abramovich and Christopher Charles*) • Home Sweet Murder (*with Andrew Bourelle and Scott Slaven*) • Murder Beyond the Grave (*with Andrew Bourelle and Christopher Charles*) • Murder Thy Neighbour (*with Andrew Bourelle and Max DiLallo*) • Murder of Innocence (*with Max DiLallo and Andrew Bourelle*) • Till Murder Do Us Part (*with Andrew Bourelle and Max DiLallo*)

COLLECTIONS

Triple Threat (*with Max DiLallo and Andrew Bourelle*) • Kill or Be Killed (*with Maxine Paetro, Rees Jones, Shan Serafin and Emily Raymond*) • The Moores are Missing (*with Loren D. Estleman, Sam Hawken and Ed Chatterton*) • The Family Lawyer (*with Robert Rotstein, Christopher Charles and Rachel Howzell Hall*) • Murder in Paradise (*with Doug Allyn, Connor Hyde and Duane Swierczynski*) • The House Next Door (*with Susan DiLallo, Max DiLallo and Brendan DuBois*) • 13-Minute Murder (*with Shan Serafin, Christopher Farnsworth and Scott Slaven*) • The River Murders (*with James O. Born*) • The Palm Beach Murders (*with James O. Born, Duane Swierczynski and Tim Arnold*) • Paris Detective • 3 Days to Live

For more information about James Patterson's novels, visit www.penguin.co.uk.